By the same author

Empire
Wounds of Honour
Arrows of Fury
Fortress of Spears
The Leopard Sword
The Wolf's Gold
The Eagle's Vengeance
The Emperor's Knives
Thunder of the Gods
Altar of Blood
The Scorpion's Strike
River of Gold
Vengeance

The Centurions
Betrayal
Onslaught
Retribution

Storm of War

Empire: Volume Thirteen

Anthony Riches

HODDER

First published in Great Britain in 2023 by Hodder & Stoughton
An Hachette UK company

This paperback edition published in 2023

1

Copyright © Anthony Riches 2023

A CIP catalogue record for this title is available from the British Library

Paperback ISBN 978 1 399 70144 0
ebook ISBN 978 1 399 70145 7

Typeset in Plantin Light by Manipal Technologies Limited

Printed and bound in Great Britain by Clays Ltd, Elcograf S.p.A.

Hodder & Stoughton policy is to use papers that are natural, renewable
and recyclable products and made from wood grown in sustainable forests.
The logging and manufacturing processes are expected to conform to the
environmental regulations of the country of origin.

Hodder & Stoughton Ltd
Carmelite House
50 Victoria Embankment
London EC4Y 0DZ

www.hodder.co.uk

For Helen

ACKNOWLEDGEMENTS

This story has been no easier (or harder) to write than any of the previous eleven – let's not talk about *Wounds of Honour*'s twelve-year gestation – the usual combination of competition for brain time with a busy day job, the uneven pace of writing given the author's infamous 'making stuff up as I go along' method and, well, just life.

Which means that the first thanks due must go to my long-standing (suffering?) editor Carolyn Caughey, and the team behind her, who accept delivery delays with outward stoicism and the long practice of dealing with an author who manages projects for a living with all the disruption that can bring to the creative process. I sometimes imagine scenes of angst at yet another delay as akin to an H.M. Bateman 'The Man Who . . .' cartoon (they're very funny, take a look) – with gnashing of teeth at the news that 'he's late *again*!!', but in reality I expect it's more like a wry raise of the eyebrow in the relevant Zoom call and 'yes, of *course* he's late again.' Either way, to all in the Hodder production process, thanks for coping with the delays!

And whatever the reaction behind the scenes, Carolyn is always kind in accommodating the author's delays – I suspect it's a skill imbued in the editorial profession very early – and her encouragements are pitched perfectly to inspire the right degree of need to get on with it that (eventually) results in the familia getting their stuff in a pile and sorting out the latest bad person. So thank you Carolyn, your tact and patience are as ever appreciated.

I have two agents now, Robin Wade having given life to the series and taken it as far as Book Twelve, and Sara O'Keefe having picked it up along with my other writing efforts (try *Nemesis* and *Target Zero* for size if you like a fast-paced modern thriller), so thanks go to both of these most excellent industry professionals for their parts in getting us into the second half of this long story.

And lastly (and mostly) I am as ever indebted to my wife Helen for her usual encouragement to get up at 0600 and write the next thousand words before starting the day job, and for acting as a sounding board and provider of common sense.

So, thanks everyone, I know the writer's life is supposed to be a lonely one but I've never felt any such thing in all the years that we've been collaborating to give life to the people that live in my head and on these pages. I couldn't do it without you.

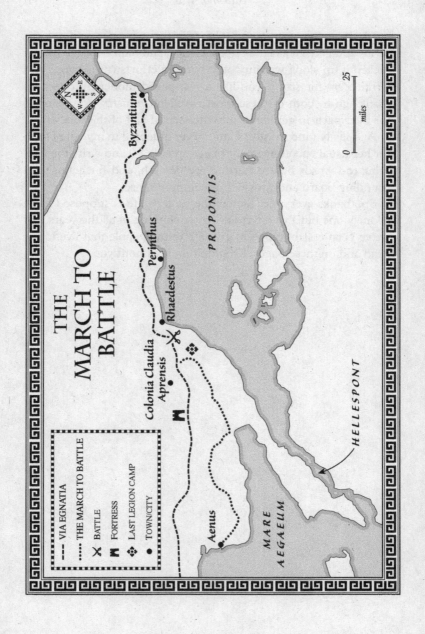

THE
MARCH TO
BATTLE

N

miles
0   25

Byzantium

PROPONTIS

Perinthus

Rhaedestus

Colonia Claudia
Aprensis

HELLESPONT

Aenus

MARE
AEGAEUM

--- VIA EGNATIA
····· THE MARCH TO BATTLE
✗ BATTLE
Ϻ FORTRESS
❖ LAST LEGION CAMP
● TOWN/CITY

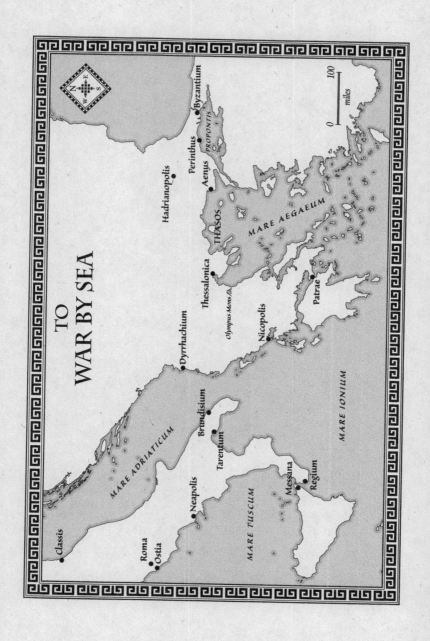

TO
WAR BY SEA

Classis

Roma
Ostia

MARE TUSCUM

Neapolis

Tarentum

Brundisium

Messana

Regium

MARE ADRIATICUM

Dyrrhachium

Nicopolis

MARE IONIUM

Olympus Mons A.

Thessalonica

Hadrianopolis

Aenus

Perinthus

Byzantium

PROPONTIS

THASOS

MARE AEGAEUM

Patrae

0   100
miles

Prologue

'Are your officers all here, First Spear Felix?'

The legion's senior centurion nodded in reply, lifting his wooden tablet into the meagre light provided by a dozen flickering oil lamps as proof. Outside night had fallen, the hours since the end of the day's march having been spent digging out a marching camp for the legions of their new emperor's army.

'All centurions are mustered and present, Legatus.'

His superior nodded, the gesture curt to the degree of being supercilious, an unspoken statement of the underlying belief that to a man of his exalted senatorial rank there could never be any answer other than in the positive.

'Just as well. The slightest hint of disrespect would go down like a beaker of vinegar with this emperor. He is a great man, and magnanimous, under the right circumstances, but show him even a *hint* of anything other than total devotion and—'

'Gentlemen! The emperor!'

The chief lictor was standing in the tent's doorway, his ceremonial bundle of rods and an axe held more like a weapon than a badge of office, and both men snapped to attention. The forty centurions packed in behind them in the legion's temporary principia, the hard men who led the legion's centuries, followed their example an instant later. The air inside the command tent was rank, none of them having seen the inside of a bathhouse since they had left Carnuntum for the long march south to Rome twenty days before, although all present had long since stopped noticing the long-familiar stomach-turning soil, sweat and faeces stench of an army on campaign.

The soldiers of the imperial bodyguard preceded their master in absolute silence, followed a moment later by the emperor himself, his eyes scanning the tent's poorly lit interior with the brisk mien of a man who was, former senator or not, first and foremost a soldier. Behind him came the three men who were entrusted with making his march on Rome a success. Felix looked at each one in turn, remembering their names from the secret message he had received from Rome days before.

First into the tent behind the emperor was Marcus Rossius Vitulus, a military supply expert with the title *praepositus annonae*, chief of supply, responsible for the scouring of the country through which Severus's legions were marching for enough food to keep thousands of soldiers fed. His role made him the most important man in the new emperor's world, even if only for the time required for the army's march on Rome. And a target for Felix's blade.

The message from the capital, a chatty letter written in tiny, cramped characters in an oversized message tablet, had purported to come from his family in Rome. Felix had met and settled down with a woman of the city during his time operating out of the Camp of the Foreigners, the notorious home of the frumentarii, the small but highly proficient body of spies and murderers whose operations were carried out under the disguise of managing the empire's grain supply. Albeit written in her style, and with every sign of being from her hand, it had immediately sounded an alarm bell to a man well used to the ways of the throne's clandestine operations.

The next man to enter was Lucius Valerius Valerianus, a Pannonian with extensive military experience who had been chosen to command the emperor's cavalry. Diligent scouting of the road ahead was essential if an attack by the usurper emperor's army, no matter how improbable, was to be avoided. Another man Felix was instructed to murder.

The hidden order in the message, revealed by means of a routine frumentarii code of removing all but every tenth character, had been stark and simple. *Kill Severus. Kill his key men. Vitulus, Valerianus, Laetus.* The pay-off having been, as he had feared from the moment he decoded the first two words, a simple threat. *We have your family.*

Julius Laetus was last into the tent, a man as close to Severus as anyone, legionary legatus and hard-eyed fanatic in the new emperor's cause. The perfect commander for the army's advance guard, ready to throw his men at an enemy to allow the remainder of the army's legions time to deploy for battle. Professing to be ready to die for his emperor, he was clearly in reality more than ready to sacrifice thousands of his own men in the cause of his own career.

The death of any of these men would be a blow to the emperor, although Felix knew that it would be unlikely to save his wife and sons. If they weren't already dead, of course. A single assassin would have no chance of surviving even he succeeded in his role, and Felix was no innocent when it came to understanding how the shadowy figures behind the throne went about their assignments. Or how much pleasure they managed to take in the process.

'Officers of the Eleventh Claudia!'

The emperor had waved his bodyguard aside and walked forward into the tent, opening his arms wide in a symbolic gesture of embrace. Even though the legion's first spear had known all too well what Severus's approach to his soldiers would be, he found it hard not to be impressed by the man. He shot a glance at his legatus, standing beside him, to find the senator apparently dazzled by the great man's presence as he formally greeted his master.

'Imperator! The Eleventh Legion Claudia, named loyal and faithful by the divine Claudius, stands ready to serve with you and to stand to the last man!'

Severus smiled at his legion commander, although his raised eyebrow was perhaps an indication of a slight disagreement with the sentiment.

'To the last man? We shall have to hope that it does not come to that, shall we not?' He clapped a hand to the other man's shoulder to dispel any hint of disfavour. 'It will be our enemies who will be doing the standing to the last man, if they even choose to fight, that much is obvious! My former colleague Niger commands ten legions, but they are men of the east and therefore not *men* in the conventional sense of the word!'

A ripple of laughter greeted his words. Even if the assembled officers of the legion would have laughed at their emperor's joke in any case, it was widely accepted that the legions of the eastern empire had long since surrendered to the softer ways of living that overcame the most virile of warriors, given enough time.

'And in the west, *his* former colleague Albinus commands a pitiful three legions, all of which have been based in Britannia for so long that they have become miserable Brits themselves!'

Another ripple of amusement greeted his opinion on his other challenger for the throne.

'While in Rome . . .' Severus paused for dramatic effect. 'In Rome, as we all know, there is nothing more valiant standing between our swords and the false emperor Didius Julianus than the praetorians. And we all know what they're good for! A knife in the back, and nothing with any more dignity to it! They are murderers, men who slaughtered an honourable emperor in my predecessor Helvius Pertinax! And they are thieves, who compounded their insult to Rome itself by selling the throne to that poor deluded fool that calls himself the master of the world!'

He looked about himself with an expression of disgust at such treacherous vulgarity.

'Officers of the Eleventh Claudia, loyal and faithful, I cannot allow such ignominy to go unpunished! It is not for vanity that I have taken the formal title Imperator Caesar Lucius Septimius Severus *Pertinax* Augustus, but as an expression of my rage at a decent man's murder! My esteemed colleague was trying his best to bring order to the empire, even if it is doubtful that he could have succeeded without the support of an army like this one!'

Severus allowed that point to sink in before continuing. Every man present knew that his possession of every army group based along the twin river borders of the Rhenus and Danubius, sixteen legions in total, made him the most powerful contender for the throne. More than that, Felix knew all too well that Severus had been scheming for years towards the day when he had been declared emperor. Using his influence with the previous praetorian prefect to be appointed as governor of Pannonia Superior, he had managed to gain the loyalty of every army commander along the frontier defined by the two mighty rivers. And so carefully had he prepared the ground that when news of Pertinax's assassination had reached his headquarters in Carnuntum his traditionally reluctant acceptance of the purple, bowing to his legions' well-rehearsed insistence, had been little more than a formalisation of what had already been decided.

'We are like charioteers with the strongest horses, my brothers in arms! We are so obviously going to be the first men to reach Rome that Niger will not even try to beat us to it, but will rather sit on his false throne in Antioch among his debauched legions, and dream of an imperium he will never live to enjoy! While Albinus in Britannia has agreed to my proposal to share imperium, leaving me free to first deal with the usurper Julianus and then march to unseat the eastern pretender!'

The unspoken corollary to which, Felix guessed, was that once Niger and the eastern legions had been subdued, Severus would turn his attention to Britannia, with all pretence of sharing the empire abandoned. He stood to attention while Severus spoke, knowing that if he was going to follow the message's instruction there would never be a better moment to strike. Or any other opportunity. Once Severus had finished speaking, accepted the cheers and plaudits of the legion's fiercely loyal officers, drunk a swift cup of wine in toast in their honour and then left the tent, all chance of taking his life would be lost. And if anyone recognised a fleeting chance to make the kill, it was the former grain officer Marcus Aquilius Felix.

Felix was, by his own rueful assessment of a life given to the dark arts of spying and assassination, a peerless master of political murder, experienced to the tune of a dozen and more killings of members of the senatorial and equestrian classes. All had been men who had earned the lethal attentions of the frumentarii by what they had said, or done, or had failed to say or do. He was without conscience or remorse, having endured a childhood made harsh by his father's death in the German wars twenty-five years before. And he was superbly skilled, having fought in Parthia as a centurion in one of the so-called debauched eastern legions, under the command of a hawk-faced legatus by the name of Scaurus, before being selected by the then imperial chamberlain Cleander to help with the throne's dirty work. All of which had made him an expert in the theory and practice of assassination. And even if he was, as he himself recognised readily enough in moments of intro-spection, a few years past his physical prime, fierce determination and the advantage of surprise could give even an ageing swords-man a sharp edge in the first few seconds of any fight.

As Severus spoke, expounding, as was usual and expected, on the Eleventh Claudia's proud history and battle record, Felix sized up his bodyguard. The chief lictor, a former first spear himself, was a big man. Imposing even, but soft. Gone to seed, with good living and too much wine. A decade before, when he'd been in his pomp, a muscular athlete carrying a legion standard, he would have been a serious obstacle. Now Aquilius didn't think he'd even have to break stride to deal with the man as he attacked through the emperor's bodyguard. A swift knife blade in the throat would be too fast for a man whose reflexes were long gone.

The bodyguard themselves though would be a different matter, four soldiers arrayed in a loose half-circle around the man who had promised to make them the new praetorians once his backside was on the throne. Severus was going to make them wealthy, the dives miles they had longed to be as they had put a purple cloak about his shoulders and chanted the words, 'rich soldier, rich sol-dier', as much to reassure themselves as to make sure the new emperor remembered who to thank when the time came. They looked combat ready, and worse, they were alert, knowing all too well that the men facing them were all equally capable of deadly violence. And no matter how he thought through his attack, he could see no way to get through them without taking so much damage that he wouldn't be able to finish the job. No way to get through them at all, truth be told. He might kill one of them, two at the most, but the only likely eventual result was his death on the survivors' spears.

Severus was winding up his speech. The legion's centuries-long loyalty and valiant contribution to half a dozen victories had been extolled in the warmest of terms. And its less than stellar moments over that time quietly ignored. The speed with which they had rallied to the new emperor's cause had been praised, and the expected promise that they were eager to hear had been made, an assurance that they would not be forgotten when the time came to divide out the spoils of victory over the pretender Julianus, a statement that had earned the gathered officers' evident satisfaction. The emperor turned to his left, the cue for his wine to be presented by one of his freedmen who had been waiting just outside the tent, doubtless with his own escort to make sure the wine remained untainted. A toast to the legion's long life, a swift tip of the cup and swallow, and the great man would be on his way to the next legion's encampment to repeat the whole dreary but essential rigmarole.

Seeing his last chance about to disappear, Felix acted. Without warning he drew his sword, the three-foot-long weapon gleaming in the light of the lamps that had been lit to illuminate the tent's further recesses, its blade scraping over its scabbard's iron throat with an urgent, menacing hiss. As the bodyguards started to react, turning to face him and levelling their spear points, he went down on one knee and raised the weapon in front of him in both hands, one under the hilt, one cupping the blade, and bowed his head.

'*Hold!*'

Severus's command stayed the spear thrusts that his guards were shaping to deliver to the first spear's defenceless head and neck. Felix heard the note of terror and outrage in his legatus's voice as he reacted to the sudden development.

'First Spear Felix, what the fuck do you think you're—'

The emperor overrode him with effortless ease.

'Let us see what possible reason your senior centurion could have to air his iron, shall we? Even if he is offering it to me in the manner of an act of self-sacrifice. Well, Centurion?'

'My name is Marcus Aquilius Felix, Imperator, and I am a former frumentarius!' Felix looked up over the sword's blade, watching the emperor's face as realisation dawned upon him. 'My position here was not earned by long service with the legion, but as a reward for services rendered to the throne!'

Severus nodded.

'I know the sort of services the inhabitants of the castra peregrina perform on behalf of the empire. Who was your master? Cleander?'

'Cleander, and then Eclectus, Imperator. Those were the chamberlains I served under. I was rewarded with this position last autumn.'

Making the point that his departure from Rome had been relatively recent, and that his knowledge of the Palatine Hill and its imperial secretariat were still fresh. That he could be a man of value to a new regime.

'I see. And this . . . ?'

The emperor waved a hand at the proffered sword.

'Imperator, I received a message from Rome some days ago. I was instructed to take your life, and end your threat to the rule of the usurper Julianus. My family will die if I do not succeed.' So far, all true. Now, Felix knew, he was about to gamble his ability to tell a convincing lie against Severus's ability to spot a falsehood. 'But I knew that I could not take such an action against the only man I believe can provide the empire with the firm leadership it needs.'

The alternative interpretation being that he would never have succeeded in anything more than getting himself killed. As he suspected was all too clear to the man with the power of life and death over him.

'I see. And on what do you base this belief in my unique abilities, First Spear, given that you do not know me?'

Time to drop in the biggest lie of all.

'As a frumentarius, Imperator, I was privy to much knowledge that the average man would neither perceive nor understand. And instructions for our missions would sometimes be imparted to us in the chamberlain's office, to allow him to use the large map of the empire painted on his wall to illustrate our tasks, those few of us who undertook the most sensitive of jobs for the emperor.'

Severus nodded slowly, and the soldier knew that his bait was close to being taken.

'And I will never forget the occasion on which Eclectus stated an opinion of the men most likely to step forward, were his master Commodus to meet with an earlier death than everyone in the empire prayed.'

The deceit was carefully calculated. On the one hand, no such opinion had ever been stated within his hearing. On the other, there was no one left alive to challenge the lie.

'And that opinion was?'

The lie was almost sold. Time to drive the nail home.

'He believed that Senator Pertinax was actively planning to take the throne, with strong support from his fellow city fathers who, he believed, hated Commodus with a passion.' Unsurprisingly, since the previous emperor had persecuted the senate constantly and cruelly. 'And while he believed Pertinax to be a better candidate than most of the alternatives in Rome, he stated a belief that there was one man far better suited serving on the northern frontier. A man with a hard mind for hard times, and the ability to think what would usually be unthinkable, who had been sent to command an army as a contingency in case of such an assassination, to provide him with the means of taking power and restoring order to the empire. He named that man to me. The name, Imperator, was yours.'

Severus looked down at him for a moment, then laughed softly.

'I find your story hard to credit, Centurion. For one thing I was never a close friend of Eclectus, and for another I owed my position in Pannonia to Laetus, the praetorian prefect. A man now executed by Julianus, curse him. But I find the telling of it to be expertly judged, and perfectly delivered. Sheathe your sword and accompany me as I make my way to speak with my other legions.'

Felix stood, returning his gladius to the scabbard at his waist.

'I am yours to command, Imperator!'

Severus smiled thinly.

'Indeed you are. I have it in mind to make you an imperial beneficiarius, and have you oversee the operations of the imperial treasury with regard to the gathering of tax from the senatorial class. After all, a man with the sort of skill with a falsehood you have displayed today will be perfect for the unearthing of gold needed to pay my legions from men who will be reluctant in the extreme. I expect that you will spot their lies a mile off, and that your severity of appearance and reputation will scare the gold out of many of them without your even having to resort to threats. While your willingness to make and if need be deliver on the sort of threats required will soon enough become common knowledge and cow the rest into submission. In the meantime you can provide the message you received from Rome to my secretariat. Once we have the city in our grasp I'll have the writing compared with that of the men who clustered around the usurper, and find out exactly who it was that issued you with the order to murder an emperor.'

Felix knew that he should keep his mouth shut and simply ride his incredible good fortune, but he was unable to not ask the question he knew was on every man's mind.

'And when you have that man, Imperator?'

Severus looked at him with a faint smile for a moment, and the centurion got a momentary impression of the man behind the hard-faced exterior. Something reptilian lurked behind the emperor's eyes, remorseless and unforgiving.

'When I have that man, First Spear? I'll have him taken to the interrogation chambers deep beneath the palace. He will be blinded, to emphasise the helplessness of his position, and then I will speak with him, and outline his options.'

The emperor's voice rose a little as he warmed to the subject.

'I will tell him that he can either tell me all about the orders that Didius Julianus issued for my murder, to go on record and inspire the outrage of the people, and that we can elicit that information from him in a relatively calm and reasoned way, or I'll have it tortured out of him piece by piece. And I do literally mean by pieces. And when he's told his story, whether willingly or not, I'll have him executed in the forum as a public warning to any potential conspirators. The senate needs to be brought to heel after the madness of the last few months, and I can think of no better way than having his confession read out in front of the doors of the curia, and then the man who sought my death put to death within earshot of their benches. Does that answer your question, Centurion?'

Felix nodded.

'Yes, Imperator.'

Severus turned to address the gathered officers, knowing that his words would spread across his legions by swift word of mouth.

'Good. When we take Rome, gentlemen, there will be those among the ruling class who will be discontented not to have their man on the throne. They will be unhappy that a senator from North Africa should have had the temerity to seize the empire, when more august and pliable men might have suited them better. I am all too well aware of those among my colleagues who were arrayed behind Pertinax, the poor fool, and who planned to use him as a means of unlocking the treasury to be plundered. They are a pack of dogs, and like any such collection of animals, the only way to control them is through fear. And so I'll leave the man who planned my murder's guts steaming on the ground outside their debating chamber as a salutary lesson for them. Rome has a new ruler. And the lesson will be that they can either follow my rule or perish in the same way!'

I

'In the name of all the gods, how much longer do we have to endure this? This tub should have been named Poseidon's shit bucket for all the progress we're making!'

Marcus Valerius Aquila looked up the length of the merchant ship *Diana's Arrow*, adjusting his stance with newfound ease as the big vessel pitched down into the trough of a wave. He watched with sympathy as his comrade Arminius belched up a mouthful of watery vomit, spitting it wearily over the wooden railing that was all that was preventing his exhausted body from pitching into the rain-lashed sea. The sky was a sullen grey, merging seamlessly with the horizon to give the impression of an infinite void around the pitching and wallowing merchant vessel. Raising his voice to close to a shout in order to be heard over the wind's howl, he answered the question with a shake of his head.

'Who knows? I asked the master the same question an hour or so ago, and all he had to say was that if he tried to turn to either side of our current course the force of the storm would probably capsize us! Apparently this is what sailors call an overtaking sea, with the waves rolling up from behind, and if we do anything other than run before them they'll turn us over in an instant!'

The German cupped his hands to gather rainwater, rubbing it into his beard in an attempt to remove the bile that had inevitably caught in the hairs. Once a slave owned by the head of their familia, he had been freed years before, and while he had always carried himself with the swagger of a born warrior, his one-time arrogance had become, with the passage of the years, something more akin to pride in their company, and disdain of everyone not so fortunate.

'So yesterday he said we could avoid the storm by running north, and now he's telling us that he's put us in a position where if we try to get out from under it we're all fish food? Prick!'

'Thank your gods you're not cooped up below with the rest of the familia, eh?'

Arminius nodded with a shudder, possibly from being soaked through with rain and spray, possibly from the memory of the conditions in the ship's cramped hold. It was the stink of vomit and the constant sound of retching that had driven him up on deck, and Marcus had accompanied him in order to make sure he didn't do anything that might get him washed over the side to his death.

'Does anyone know how far we can run before we run out of sea and find ourselves on the rocks?'

Marcus shook his head again.

'The crew have lost all sense of where they are. Nobody's willing to go up the mast to try to get a better view, and I can't say I'd want to risk being catapulted into the sea to drown either. All we can do is wait to see where we end up.'

A bulky figure climbed out of the hold and re-secured the tar-stiffened canvas cover that was keeping the rain and spray from cascading into the ship. He staggered across the heaving deck and joined them at the rail, his bushy beard running with the rain that was whipping into them in sheets of stringing drops. Dubnus, Marcus's oldest friend, the one-time commander of a century of axe-wielding pioneers a few of whom still accompanied him, had a grey-green pallor and the look of a man close to vomiting.

'I decided that at least up here the air's fresh! It's the children I feel sorry for, cooped up down there and not allowed to come up on deck for fear of them being washed away! That and having to listen to Ptolemy and that British monster endlessly debating the meaning of life, or whatever it was the chirping little sparrow decided to plague us with today once he'd had his morning wank over a bust of some dead Greek or other!'

He looked up at the ship's navarchus, who was more hanging onto the ship's tiller for his own safety than actually steering the vessel.

'I bet that arsehole's wishing he'd not been so greedy, eh? All this for the sake of a cargo of wine!' The other two turned to look at the captain, and, as if guessing what they were discussing, he pointedly looked out over the sea to the ship's left side until they turned back to the rail. 'If we'd just crossed the straits from Brundisium to Dyrrachium like we were supposed to we'd have been safely tucked up in harbour on the Ionium Sea by the time this storm made its unexpected appearance. But he had to go chasing a payday, didn't he?'

'To be fair, it's probably only the weight of all those amphorae that's stopping us from being flipped over by the sea and the wind!'

Dubnus laughed loud enough to be heard over the storm's buffeting tumult.

'Only you, Marcus! Only *you* could find a way to excuse that greedy seagoing bastard for putting us all in danger! If he'd not seen a few thousand in quick profit and made the decision to ignore what we were paying him for, which was a nice quick voyage from Rome to Antioch, then we could have been halfway there by now . . .'

He stopped talking and renewed his scrutiny of the ship's master. After a moment the other two men followed his gaze, and found the navarchus apparently staring straight at them. It took another moment for them to realise that he was in fact looking at something in the distance, a few points off their course to the left.

'What's he seen?'

Before they could speculate, the master bellowed an order that brought the crew out onto the pitching deck. He gestured to a point just fine of the ship's only sail, the triangular supparum at the vessel's bow, which had been left rigged to provide him with enough speed to ensure that he could still steer a course of sorts. A line of marginally darker grey where the horizon should have been hinted at the presence of land, something in its apparently featureless and barely visible presence apparently recognisable to him from long experience. He shouted one word, which had evident meaning for his crew.

'Classis!'

They turned to stare where he was pointing, and more than one of the younger men nodded agreement. The navarchus pointed to the ship's side, where the three friends were hanging onto the rail.

'Perhaps five miles! But we have to turn now! Get to the left side and be ready!'

Recognising the urgency in their captain's voice, the crew, a dozen strong, hurried to line the rail in preparation for whatever it was he had planned.

'You got mates down below, best you get them up here!'

Arminius turned to the seaman next to him at the rail, recognising the urgency in his tone as he shouted over the wind's incessant howl.

'Why?'

The weather-beaten sailor replied without taking his eyes off the horizon where the captain had pointed.

'That's Classis, over there! A keen eye can pick out the watchtowers, just about! You barbarians understand enough Latin to know what that means, the word classis? Fleet? A lot of ships?'

The German shot him a venomous look that told the sailor he was lucky the big Briton was hanging onto the rail for his very life, and the other man continued hurriedly.

'It's the main naval harbour in the Adriaticus and the port for Ravenna, and the only safe mooring we'll ever see before this storm drives us straight onto the rocks to the north! We have to head for the harbour right quick, because we're all dead if we don't!'

'But the chief of all you nautical bastards said we'd sink if we tried to turn!'

The sailor turned to grin at Dubnus.

'That's the way of the sea, friend! Most of the time she's a gentle wife to a ship, but every now and then she turns nasty and hits you with a saucepan so hard you might not get over it! And you have to ride the punches, right? I'd rather drown from trying to reach safety than just letting this poor old cow be driven onto shore! And the more men we can put on this side before he starts the turn, the more likely we are to live long enough to see another day!'

Marcus nodded at Dubnus.

'Best fetch the men up! The women are going have their work cut out keeping the children calm.'

The male members of their party staggered up from the hold, blinking in the grey light and making their way across the pitching deck to join the group gathered on the vessel's left side. Twenty or so strong, they were a mixture of hulking and heavily bearded warriors, born to batter their way into an enemy's battle line with their axes, by contrast with the sinewy Syrian archers who made up their number, accompanied by the remaining members of the familia of which Marcus was the effective second-in-command.

Watching the hatchway knowingly as the last of them came up on deck, he saw a pair of heads bob up in the warrior's wake, and left the rail to make a carefully timed crossing of the deck and squat down by the opening, holding on to the wooden frame.

'You two know you're not allowed up here.'

The admonishment was spoken in a light tone, Marcus having no desire to upset either of the two children, one of them a thin-faced boy of nine and his friend eighteen months younger, but already clearly destined to be the more heavily built of the two. The older boy replied, looking past him at the men gathered by the ship's rail.

'It's horrible down there, Father. We just wanted to get some fresh air and have a look.'

The Roman nodded, understanding the impact of such a confined space on the two boys, who in better weather had been allowed on deck under the close supervision of a pair of soldiers.

'I know, Appius, and you and Felix will be allowed up when the storm has passed, but for the time being you must stay below with Annia.'

His son nodded equably, happily having lost all trace of the reserve with Marcus that had resulted from their being kept apart in his infancy, his father having been absent on military missions across the empire and so having to leave him in the care of Annia, the wife of a fellow centurion. Felix, on the other hand, had his customary impatience written across his features, a hint of petulance in his voice when he replied.

'I don't want to go back down there!'

Marcus considered using the threat of his mother's annoyance to disarm the child's frustration, then decided that this would hardly be fair on the woman who had volunteered to raise as her own a boy who, whether Marcus liked it or not, was largely his own responsibility. The fact that every time he saw Felix he was reminded of the rape of his wife by the emperor Commodus, a repeated assault that had resulted in her bearing the boy and dying in childbirth, was, he had long since realised, unimportant. As long as the boy's origin remained a closely guarded secret, known to only a handful of people to avoid attracting the interest of the wrong ones, little else mattered other than that he be given the chance to grow up as a normal person, and afforded the love of those around him.

'I know, Felix, but your mother and father would never forgive me if you were to be washed away by a wave and eaten by a whale, would they? What if the whale choked on you?'

The boy grinned back at him, his petulance disarmed by the joke. 'No!'

'Well there you are.' He ruffled his son's hair, not wanting to leave him out of the praise for obeying his instruction. 'You two go down below and I'll buy you both a honey cake when we make shore, how's that?'

Fixing the hatch cover back in place, he went back to the rail just in time to hear the rotund former standard-bearer Morban, an infamous terroriser of his companions' purses when the opportunity to gamble presented itself, addressing the bedraggled group with a predatory grin.

'Anyone want to take odds on us making it? I'm offering four—'

The Briton flinched back as Dubnus took a firm grip of his tunic.

'No one's taking your bet, Morban, you donkey, because for us to profit from your odds we'd all have to be floating in the bloody sea!'

The veteran shrugged before replying.

'What about a sestertius on who's the next man to lose his biscuits then? I'll offer a denarius for a correct guess?'

The older and shorter of the two laggard soldiers standing beside him stopped complaining about his lost dice profits and tapped Morban on the shoulder with the hand that wasn't clinging to the rail for dear life.

'Four for one? I'll have some of that! That prick Bahir is looking as green as an apple!'

The archer in question shot him a dirty look but was clearly fighting the urge to vomit, his expression betraying his quandary.

Morban took the proffered coin and made it disappear with his customary polish.

'A bet on Bahir! Any other takers?'

He shot a knowing glance at the other soldier, but the taller man shook his head and continued staring out over the water, one of the few in the party who seemed untroubled by the ship's wallowing. Dubnus turned away in disgust at the veteran standard-bearer's customary opportunism, and Morban was just about to renew his attempts to drum up some business when he was interrupted by a shout from the ship's master.

'*All hands!*' They looked up at the navarchus, who was pointing to the left side of the ship. '*Prepare for the turn!*'

The seamen pressed in behind the soldiers, pushing them against the rail so firmly that Marcus wondered if the sturdy wood might break and deposit them all into the sea below. Satisfied that as much weight as could be pushed to the ship's side as possible was in place, the captain heaved at the tiller connected to his steering oars, pushing the ship into a slow turn to the left. As it began to cross the overtaking sea a succession of waves broke over the vessel, showering the men thronging the rail with salt water that stung their eyes and soaked what little of them wasn't already saturated with rainwater. The ship heeled over to the right with an alarming ease despite the extra weight of crew and passengers, rolling back to the left as they sailed into the trough of each wave only to repeat the sickening lurch back over to its right side with every successive swell.

'Zeus's cock and balls, but this will be the death of us!'

Dubnus's imprecations fell on deaf ears, the soldiers now for the most part helplessly returning the dried fish and biscuit they had been given at their last meal to the sea, as the ship wallowed in long, slow oscillations. Those men who were unable to get to the rail through the crush were left with no choice but to vomit on the deck, and the legs of the men closest to them, one such violent outpouring putting a swift and mutually disgusted end to a heated argument between Morban and the shorter of the two soldiers over whether the latter's candidate had been the first to vomit.

A heavy bank of almost horizontal rain slammed into the ship, its gusts threatening to push the vessel back onto its doomed course for the rocky shore to the north of the port, the stinging rain forcing them to duck their heads.

Arminius looked over at Scaurus, his former master and the head of their familia, who had covered his head with the hood of his heavy, water-sodden woollen paenula and raised both hands before his face, his lips moving in silent entreaty.

'Are you praying, Tribune?'

The patrician officer spoke without looking up, all too aware that every man around them was listening intently.

'When a man has been admitted to the inner mysteries of the Lightbringer, Arminius, he comes to understand the ways that the gods work the clay we provide! I am praying to Mithras to guide us through to safer waters, so that we may do his bidding once again! And if he deems us, his servants, to have showed him enough devotion over the years, perhaps he will answer my prayers!'

Dubnus belched loudly, visibly fighting back the urge to vomit, then grinned weakly and reached over to tap Morban on the shoulder.

'The tribune says he's praying to Mithras to spare those of us who have shown devotion to Our Father over the years, and not just when they've got an unfeasible wager to win! I'd say you're fucked all ends up!'

'All in order, Centurion?'

The officer in question sprang to attention, snapping off a smart salute and standing ramrod straight as he replied to his superior's question. Behind him a chain of bedraggled soldiers was passing grain bags out of the hold of a moored freighter, across the ship's wooden deck and down its gangplank onto the quayside, where a line of carts waited to carry them away to the legions' camp outside the fleet harbour's walls. The rain was falling steadily, blown into curtains of water by the wind's gusts, and both men were grateful for the luxury of their thick woollen cloaks, waterproofed to some degree by the wool's natural grease, whereas the soldiers were simply getting soaked.

'All in order, Tribune!'

'Good. How long to finish unloading?'

'Another hour or so. *He's* not happy though.'

The ship's master was leaning over the rail of his vessel's raised stern castle with a look of disgust on his face. Seeing the tribune looking at him, he turned and ostentatiously spat over the rail. The senior officer just smiled back, knowing how much more irritated the navarchus would be not to get a show of annoyance from him.

'Nor would I be. He'll get a promissory note for the grain, which will doubtless be paid out in the fullness of time with currency that's been clipped, or melted down and recast with even more base metal than before. So, is that—'

He stopped talking as another ship nosed into the harbour from out of the rain's shimmering, gloomy curtains, and both men watched as it wallowed towards the stone quay and came alongside.

The crew were clearly spent, but even in their state of exhaustion they lined the rail to look out at the harbour, their faces falling as they took in the scene of a fellow merchant being unloaded by soldiers. The tribune strolled down the quayside, stopping when he was close enough to the vessel to speak to the ship's navarchus without having to shout.

'What's your cargo?'

The weary captain looked at the deck for a moment and shook his head before answering.

'Wine. A thousand amphorae of wine.'

The tribune smiled in the face of his obvious disgust.

'Excellent! Your wine will be gratefully purchased by the emperor Septimius Severus's army of liberation!'

He looked up at the men lining the rail. They were all still wearing their hooded cloaks and, as the senior officer took in their clothing, he nodded with a calculating expression.

'You men have a military look to you!'

A grizzled, burly man with grey shot through what could be seen of his beard replied, his eyes hidden by the hood of his paenula. His tone was respectful enough, but without the note of obsequiousness the officer had come to expect from civilians.

'We're *ex*-military, Tribune. We served in an auxiliary cohort and recently left imperial service. Our vessel has been blown off course in its journey to Antioch!'

The senior officer nodded, pursing his lips in thought. Something about the other man's voice was nagging at him, although he was unable to pinpoint why.

'Such a simultaneous release from service is not unusual, I suppose. Where were you recruited?'

'Britannia, Tribune.'

'I thought I recognised your accent. Although it's strange that men of Britannia would be heading east, and not north to their homelands, when the east has come under the control of a usurper. Not that it matters, or changes your fate!'

The men lining the rail stared down at him uncomprehendingly.

'Have you not heard? By decree of Imperator Caesar Lucius Septimius Severus Pertinax Augustus, all men with military experience are conscripted to the imperial legions! You will join us on our march to Rome, where we will unseat the pretender Didius Julianus and place the one true emperor on the throne that was stolen by the praetorians and sold to the highest bidder. I therefore hereby command you to come down onto the quay and accompany me to my legion's camp, where you will swear the sacramentum and receive your equipment. I'm sure you'll soon enough regain your previous vigour, and be the men you were only weeks ago!'

They looked down at him in silence for a moment before a voice that was at once instantly familiar to the tribune rasped out, 'I suppose we'd better do as Gaius Vibius Varus says, hadn't we?'

The speaker parted the men at the rail to stare down at the startled young officer with a quizzical expression. His face was thin, with a weak chin, but his grey eyes were piercing in the power of their stare.

'The last I heard of you, young man, your father had packed you off to soldier on the Danubius, to prevent you from being stupid enough to accompany us on any more of our jaunts around the empire at Cleander's command.'

The tribune put his hands on his hips and shook his head in wonderment.

'Gods below! Gaius Rutilius Scaurus! And here was I thinking I'd never see any of you or your familia again. The last I heard was that you'd been sent off to a glorious but unlamented death fighting the empire of Kush, in the far south of Aegyptus! Including you, First Spear Julius, if that's you glowering at me from beneath your cloak?'

The burly greybeard swept the hood of his paenula back, grinning down at him with hard eyes.

'It is! And the reports of our deaths were premature. And since you're the one in the fine uniform you can buy us all a cup of wine and a bowl of something warm, if your legions haven't already done their usual and stripped the town of everything that's eatable, drinkable and fuckable?'

'The emperor Pertinax was killed on the twenty-eighth of March, I believe?'

Scaurus nodded at Varus, who was still looking slightly astonished at being reunited with the men with whom he had risked his life in Parthia and Germania.

'We were there when he was murdered.'

He took a sip of wine before continuing. They had carried an amphora away from the ship with them as a small recompense for their aborted journey east. Not that it had been any sort of gift. Dubnus had passed it up out of the hold after telling the navarchus in the most direct fashion possible that the loss of the wine, along with the forced refund of the cost of their passage and the sailor's freshly broken nose, were the direct consequence of his ill-considered decision to accept the cargo and sail north up the Italian east coast to deliver it, rather than stick to the direct route to Antioch he'd been paid for. The taverna owner had been only too happy to accept the amphora for a favourable price, in return for sheltering Scaurus's familia in the firelit warmth of his back room while Varus briefed his old friends as to what they were about to walk into.

'The praetorians slaughtered him, and the chamberlain, and we fought our way out of the palace grounds by the narrowest of margins. You will recall that Pertinax was both my uncle and my benefactor, and you will understand that I have sworn to have my revenge on the men who killed him.'

Varus pursed his lips sympathetically.

'My sympathies for your loss. We received news of his unfortunate death three days after it happened. A fast rider sent by Severus's allies in Rome rode in with a dispatch for the governor, and messengers were away along the river to both east and west before his horse had stopped sweating.'

Varus looked around the faces of the three men gathered around the tavern table. The rest of the familia had been ushered into a private room behind the serving counter, and only Scaurus, Marcus and Julius had remained in the deserted restaurant. No man in the town was likely to come out into the streets without having a dire necessity while the legions' centurions were on the prowl for new recruits, willing or not.

'It helped that Severus . . . or should I say "*Imperator*", as we're obviously not allowed to use his name now that he's taken the purple . . .' Varus looked around reflexively to check whether anyone had heard him before continuing, '. . . was prepared for the news. Even so, the speed with which we were swearing allegiance and listening to the soldiers shouting "dives miles" at each other as they dreamed of their reward for making him emperor was nothing short of impressively fast.'

'He was ready to move?'

Varus nodded. Known to them from their previous campaigns both in the east and on the northern frontier, he knew that he could trust them completely with his opinion.

'Like a sprinter on his toes and ready to run. Of course he put on the usual show of repugnans, allowing himself to be dragged protesting to the throne they set up for him, but everything I've heard makes it clear he'd been preparing for that moment for a good while. The rumours coming out of Rome regarding all the plotting against Pertinax were pretty much continuous, and it seems he had already sought the support of his fellow provincial governors in Germania and Dacia, in preparation for when the moment of decision presented itself. The best part of ten legions were on the march along the Rhenus and Danubius within days, and once they were all in we left Carnuntum to come south like an invading army. He's not taking any risks that Didius Julianus will manage to field some sort of army, even if all that poor fool has to depend on is the guard, some marines from the fleet at Misenum and a few circus elephants.'

'You're advancing in campaign formation then?'

Varus answered Marcus's question with a taut nod.

'Cavalry out in front to scour the countryside for supplies, then a full legion-strength advance guard marching in battle order with their packs and cooking gear following on carts, and every man in the army with his boots nailed, his sword sharpened and at least one spear ready for action. Severus and his generals mean business.'

'Whereas Julianus has very little by way of an answer.'

The younger man smiled wryly.

'The intelligence updates from our men in the city make for amusing reading. It seems that the praetorians are too pampered to dig fortifications and are spending the gold that Julianus paid them for the throne on labourers to do it for them. The marines from the fleet can't stand in a straight line, much less perform combat manoeuvres. And the elephants he's drafted in only know how to leave massive piles of their dung around the city. That and throw off their drivers if any attempt is made to fit them with fighting towers. It will take a miracle for them to prevent us from walking into the city more or less unopposed.'

'And we're going to have to go with you, aren't we?'

Scaurus's words were more statement than question, and Varus nodded apologetically.

'If I'd known who you were before I told you that you were expected to serve it might have been possible to quietly forget all about you. But I know my centurions will be curious as to what becomes of you. Add to that the fact that there are guards on every gate of the fleet encampment and it's clear that there's no way for you to leave without being arrested.'

The tribune shrugged, already resigned to this new twist of fate.

'We understand. But there's not much chance that we'll be able to simply renew the sacramentum and disappear into your legion. Is there?'

'No.' Varus matched his former mentor's direct stare. 'So you'll have to trust me when I say that we're going to have to do the opposite of trying to keep your presence here a secret.'

'So, who do we have here?'

The confidence with which Varus answered the army's senior legatus's question impressed upon Marcus and Scaurus just how much he had grown into full manhood in the six years since they had last seen him.

'Legatus Augusti, I found these men on a ship that struggled into port an hour ago, and when I recognised them I realised that they needed to be brought before the emperor at once!'

He had escorted them into the imperial army's headquarters, walking them through the imperial bodyguard and the inner circle of men who surrounded and jealously guarded Severus without any sign that he was daunted by their increasingly lofty rank. Having gained access to the cluster of tents that housed the imperial party, still under the close guard of a centurion and a tent party of his men, he had taken them straight to Julius Laetus, the emperor's right-hand man and the leader of his vanguard legion when the army was on the march.

The hard-faced general took a moment to look the newcomers up and down, his expression primarily one of disinterest. All three men were still soaked, and dripping water onto the ground from their saturated clothing.

'You intrigue me, Tribune. Just what is it about these two drowned rats that you believe merits even a moment of the Imperator's precious time? He's burdened with the tribulations of running an empire while he strives to unseat the usurper Julianus, and you want him to bandy words with . . . well, who exactly do we have here?'

Scaurus inclined his head in a respectful bow.

'I am Gaius Rutilius Scaurus, Legatus Augusti. The murdered emperor Helvius Pertinax was my sponsor in life, and under his rule I served as a praetorian tribune. I was present when he was murdered by the praetorians, and I watched from the street outside their fortress while they auctioned off the throne to the highest bidder. If you want a first-hand witness to the depths of ignominy to which they have fallen, I am that man.'

Laetus stared at him for a moment, his eyes narrowing.

'Scaurus? I seem to recall that a man of that name was lauded in the city a few years ago for his exploits in the east. A victorious campaign against the Parthians, I think it was. Was that you?'

'Yes, Legatus Augusti. I had the honour to command the Third Legion Gallica in a campaign to retake and hold the fortress town of Nisibis.'

Varus nodded.

'And I served in that campaign as a tribune under Rutilius Scaurus. It was my first experience of war, and I could not have hoped for a more effective tutor.'

Laetus pursed his lips thoughtfully.

'You achieved a victory over the Parthians with a single legion that was celebrated in Rome for a month. The emperor painted his face red and enjoyed the full panoply of an imperial triumph on the back of what sounded, from the written accounts, like masterful generalship. And then you disappeared without any further mention, just at the point when your reputation in Rome would have seen you set for life. Why was that, Rutilius Scaurus? You can stop using my formal title, by the way.'

Scaurus bowed slightly at the obvious compliment.

'I and my familia were known to the imperial chamberlain, Cleander. And not held in especially high regard, other than for our abilities to undertake what he considered to be hopeless tasks. He sent us to Germania on our return from the east, to kidnap the daughter of a tribal leader. Then he had us deal with the bandit leader Maternus in Gallia Lugdunensis—'

'That was you as well?' Laetus wore a look of genuine interest, and it wasn't hard for Marcus to guess the source of his sudden close attention. 'The plaudits for Maternus's defeat went to the man who is now pretender to the throne in the east, Pescennius Niger. Indeed Niger made great play of his victory over a bandit whose deserter army had run amok and unchallenged for the best part of two years, while Gallia Lugdunensis was under Severus's governorship, and was in consequence rewarded with the governorship of Syria, which he has used as his power base to challenge the true emperor.'

Scaurus shrugged. 'The legatus augusti was—'

'We refer to him as the "eastern pretender", Rutilius Scaurus. And in the emperor's presence you would do well to do the same.'

Scaurus inclined his head in acceptance of the point, and Laetus continued.

'Put bluntly, he was late to the party. My Britons had already broken Maternus's army by the time he reached the battlefield with his legion. He was, of course, happy enough to claim the credit for our victory, just as was the case in Dacia some years before, except that on that occasion he had to share the glory with his colleague Clodius Albinus.'

Laetus grinned, an ugly, gleeful expression.

'Excellent! Both of the emperor's competitors damned by the same unimpeachable testimony, for use when the time is right. This news will serve to tighten our grip on the throne further still!'

If Scaurus noted the use of the word 'our', rather than a reference to the emperor, he was more than intelligent enough not to show any sign of it.

'I will be happy to provide written testimony to it.'

The legatus waved a hand, clearly having taken commitment to the imperial cause of which he was a staunch champion for granted.

'And after putting paid to Maternus, what then?'

Scaurus smiled lopsidedly.

'We were sent to Aegyptus, with orders to deal with a frontier skirmish that was in reality an invasion from the south by the empire of Kush. And, by a combination of careful strategy and outrageous fortune, we managed to restore the equilibrium of Rome's relationship with its neighbour, for the time being at least.'

He looked at Laetus for a moment, weighing up just how honest to be with a man he barely knew.

'After which I made the decision to remove myself and my familia from Cleander's control. It was obvious that he would continue to use us for his dirty work until our luck ran out. We knew how he had come to power, and that knowledge was clearly too much of a risk for him.'

Laetus stared at the two men for a moment, obviously calculating.

'Cleander was executed by Commodus three years ago, having been unmasked as entertaining designs on his master's throne. Which means that if you went into hiding to avoid being used as the tool of a would-be usurper, you were in truth expressing your loyalty to the throne. But I wonder what hold was it that he had over you that made you serve him for as long as you did?'

His attention switched to Marcus, perhaps sensing that the answer to the question he had just posed lay with the younger man.

'Who is your companion? If Vibius Varus deemed him important enough to bring to the emperor then presumably he has some important role to play here?'

Marcus snapped to attention, not waiting for Scaurus to answer the question.

'My name is Marcus Valerius Aquila, Legatus Augusti. I have had the honour of serving with Rutilius Scaurus for ten years, ever since my father, his brother and both their families were murdered by Cleander's predecessor Perennis. They were slaughtered for the immense fortune that was confiscated by the throne after their deaths, both men having been falsely accused of treason to make their murders seem legitimate.'

Laetus's expression changed from calculation to a narrow-eyed stare.

'Ah, *now* I see. And yes, I remember it well enough. Your father was accused of maiestas, declared a traitor, and his estates forfeited to the throne. You were the only member of your family unaccounted for, and were declared fugitive. Tell me, where was it that you ran to?'

'Britannia.' Scaurus took the story over, ignoring Marcus's warning glance. 'Where I found him serving as a centurion with an auxiliary cohort of which I had command.'

'And you chose not to do your sworn duty and surrender him to the throne?'

Laetus's face was unreadable as he asked the question, and his tone level, making it impossible to know what his opinion was. Scaurus shrugged.

'I did. Because I knew from recent experience in Rome that Perennis was acting for his own benefit rather than that of the emperor. We discovered later that he was operating a gang of hired killers whose speciality was carrying out such imperial murder warrants and then delivering a good portion of the victim's fortunes to him personally, rather than to the treasury. They also took advantage of their power over their victims to abuse the women and children of the families they destroyed in a manner that earned them the deaths we delivered, when the time was right.'

The legatus sat back, his face still betraying no hint of any reaction.

'So, to summarise, you, Rutilius Scaurus, are perhaps the empire's most successful field commander of the last ten years, even if other men have usually managed to claim the credit for your successes. And you have undertaken these successful campaigns with the support of an imperial fugitive whose discovery within your familia at any point in Commodus's reign would probably have seen you executed. You have lived a life of deception and almost fatal risk for so long that I suspect you have become inured to both. And just when it looked as if you might have found a way to get out from under the throne's apparent desire to use you to the point of destruction, you have instead been blown ashore in the one place in the entire empire you would probably most have preferred to avoid. A fair summary?'

Scaurus nodded impassively.

'Impressively so. I firmly believed when we left Rome that we would be able to sail away into the east, and avoid becoming part of a civil war to rival that which was won by Vespasian a century ago. And now, as you say, we are at best prime candidates for recruitment to the emperor's cause, and at worst candidates for immediate execution.'

The legatus stood and walked around his desk to study Scaurus at close quarters.

'And yet you display none of the usual signs of fear, or even nervousness. You have a level gaze, there is no fidgeting or nervous tic to be seen. Even your fingernails are free from the signs of a nervous disposition. How is it that you can stand so close to death and seem not to care?'

Scaurus spoke over his shoulder to Marcus.

'Perhaps you might answer that question?'

The younger man thought for a brief moment before replying.

'The answer is a simple one, Legatus Augusti. We have fought pitched battles with British tribal war bands and Dacian tribes, skirmished with hostile German tribesmen, and faced the might of the armies of Parthia and Kush. Always at a numerical disadvantage and yet always favoured by the gods to overcome our enemies. We have hunted down bandits and deserters, and put them to the sword without compunction or mercy. A dozen times and more we have escaped death, albeit at the price of friends and comrades, until neither of us has any energy to give to fear. When death comes for me I will meet it with my sword drawn, and I will waste no energy on anticipation of that moment in the meantime. Sir.'

Laetus smiled wryly.

'So you're stoics, are you? How very well-aligned with the beliefs of our own master. Since you profess to ignore fear, let's see what he makes of you. And whether that apparent failure to care about the potential for imminent death is quite as strong once you've experienced Septimius Severus face to face.'

'To Quintus Pompeius Sosius Falco . . .'

The emperor paused for long enough that the second of his two secretaries had time to ready himself to receive dictation. Seeing the scribe signal his readiness with a swift nod, he continued at a conversational pace that very few writers could keep pace with.

'My dear Quintus, I was disappointed to hear that you had been forced to retire to your estates after the unfortunate matter of your alleged coup against Pertinax. I have no doubt that he

was exercising due caution in exiling you, and perhaps seeking
to protect you from his followers rather than to punish you, as he
assured me that—'

He stopped mid-sentence as he realised that Laetus had entered
the tent, raising a hand to forestall any attempt to speak on his
lieutenant's part before continuing.

'—as he assured me that he viewed you as innocent, but having been led astray by your brother-in-law Gaius Julius Erucius
Clarus Vibianus, when he wrote to me shortly before his murder
by the praetorians.'

'Did he really?'

Severus raised an eyebrow at Laetus's question.

'Of course he didn't. For one thing he suspected everyone,
from what I've heard, and for another he didn't ever write to me,
other than to demand I improve my province's tax revenues. What
I am doing, should you not have realised it, is greasing the wheels
of power for a smooth transition. When I make my way into the
senate I need to be greeted with rapture, as the best man to replace
that fool Didius Julianus, and to repel the usurper Niger. And to
make that happen I will have to use kind words to gratify a great
many men. We'll start with friendship purchased with compli-
ments, which is the cheapest currency available to me at this point
in time. The respect based on fear can come in the fullness of
time.'

Laetus bowed his head deferentially.

'As you say, Imperator. You are indeed by far the best man for
this calling, with the instincts and abilities to rival those of the
divine Julius himself.'

The laugh he got in reply was edged with the emperor's usual
sardonic humour.

'Careful, Julius, you're so sharp you might cut yourself. And . . . ?'

His colleague realised that it was time to get down to business.

'Imperator, we have a pair of new arrivals in camp. They staggered off a ship that had been blown off course and into the port

an hour or so ago. Apparently it was originally heading for the east, and somewhere quiet for them to hide themselves away.'

The emperor shrugged at what was, on the face of it, unimportant news.

'Julius, I am attempting to run an empire from a tent. I spend half my day dictating letters to anyone and everyone who might be able to ease our entry to Rome by having the pretender Julianus declared an enemy of the people. And the other half trying to work out how to keep this many soldiers fed while we march on Rome. Why should I care about a boat that was blown off course, or who came off it?'

Laetus grinned.

'Because, Imperator, for one thing the ship was carrying a cargo of wine. A very welcome addition to our supplies.'

Severus nodded agreement.

'I can't fault that logic. Although I think you'd have been better giving that news to the supply officers.'

'I already have. The other reason it's important is the fact that one of the two new arrivals is Gaius Rutilius Scaurus.'

The emperor frowned.

'The name rings a bell. Just not a very loud one.'

'He's an equestrian. And he was a praetorian tribune under Pertinax. Who, it seems, was his uncle.'

Severus nodded slowly.

'That's why the name sounded familiar. One of the last messages I had from the city mentioned a hard-nosed praetorian tribune who was always at the emperor's side, with an equally stone-faced man wearing two swords at his shoulder.'

'By the name of Marcus Valerius Aquila?'

'He was never named.'

'Well, the man with Scaurus fits that bill well enough. He has that deceptive air of calm about him that all the best fighters seem to grow into when they've killed enough men to know just how good they are. I have them both in the anteroom under the spears of a pair of centurions.'

'And you're certain they're not assassins sent by Didius Julianus?'
Laetus shook his head briskly.

'Completely certain, Gaius Vibius Varus vouches for them as being exactly what they are.'

'Which is what exactly?'

'Scaurus might be an equestrian, but he was once a senator's son, until his father took the blame for someone else's military disaster and fell on his sword. He's commanded a legion, on the orders of Cleander, and with some distinction. And Aquila is the son of one of the Valerius Aquila brothers. You may remember that they were murdered by command of Commodus a decade or so ago, and their estates confiscated by the state. He's been hiding in plain sight in the army all this time since his father's execution.'

'I see.' Severus stood up and stretched. 'Very well, bring them in and let's see what they're made of.'

The two men were marched in under the raised spears of their escorts, apparently untroubled by the threat at their backs. When Laetus raised his hand to stop them, both went down on one knee and lowered their heads in respect for the emperor.

'Get up, the pair of you.' Severus walked forward, eyeing them up before pointing to Scaurus. 'You're Pertinax's nephew?'

'I am, Imperator.'

'And you're not dead because . . . ?'

'Because, Imperator, he told me to run when the praetorians came to take his life.'

'And you're at peace with choosing to do as he told you, and fleeing?'

Scaurus nodded.

'Yes, Imperator. I've sworn vengeance to the Lightbringer, and I was sailing east to take my familia to safety. I fully intended to return to Rome and have my revenge on his killers once my people are no longer a concern.'

'And you have served as a praetorian tribune, during your uncle's reign. Which means you know how the guard operate. Making you perfect for what I plan for them.'

Severus turned to Marcus.

'And you're the son of Appius Valerius Aquila. A condemned and executed traitor. Are there any *good* reasons why I shouldn't deliver to you the sentence of death that Commodus ordered a decade ago?'

Marcus answered with a level return stare at the emperor.

'I could state the fact that my father was guilty of nothing more than being a rich man at a time when the throne needed wealth, Imperator. And that his only failure was not realising the threat he was under until it was too late to do anything other than send me away, to save me from his fate and preserve our line. And I could tell you that I have faced death for the empire on a dozen fields of battle, never once regretting the choice to fight and bleed for Rome. But ultimately, Imperator, you must choose to do what you believe is right for the empire, and I must follow whatever command you give.'

The emperor shook his head in amusement.

'And if I ordered you to fall on your own sword?'

The reply to his question was blunt, if quietly spoken.

'Order it, Imperator, and I will do as you command.'

Severus stared at him for a moment.

'I do believe you would.'

He walked away to the other side of the tent, then turned back to look at the two men.

'Very well, my decision is made. You, Rutilius Scaurus, will join my army with the rank of tribunus laticlavius. You were promoted to senatorial rank to command in Parthia, and you earned that rank by defeating the Parthians so cruelly, which means that it would be unbecoming of me to appoint you as anything other than a broad-stripe tribune. Who knows, you might even command a legion again someday. You will be under the command of Julius Laetus, and you will ready yourself to assist with the formation of a new praetorian guard once we have retaken Rome.'

Scaurus inclined his head.

'We will do what is ordered, and at every command we will be ready, Imperator!'

Severus nodded, evidently satisfied by the reply.

'As for you, Marcus Valerius Aquila, I am sorely tempted to have you publicly executed, simply to prove that I still respect the decisions made by Commodus in his day. Even if, as we all know very well, he was a weak-minded fool in thrall to every one of his chamberlains. But it is my calculation that doing so would not only disrespect the gods who must have watched over you these last ten years, but would deny me the service of your swords. You will serve alongside the head of your familia, with the rank of tribunus angustclavius, the narrow stripe being the most I feel appropriate given your background. If either of you makes me regret these decisions, then your execution will be both swift and ignominious. Do you both understand?'

The two men snapped to attention and barked the same words. 'Yes, Imperator!'

'Very well. You will be paid at the usual rate for your service, but since neither of you has much interest in gold, I suspect, I shall provide you with another, more motivational reward for your loyalty. When we reach the city it will be your task to find and deal with Pertinax's murderers. The one thing I will not tolerate is a regicide, and the men who killed him are to suffer appropriately. And when that's done, you can find the man who murdered Commodus and bring me his head.'

2

'So the emperor wants you to bring him the head of the man who killed Commodus? Isn't that going to put you in a bit of a cleft stick, Tribune?'

Scaurus flicked a glance at Julius, resplendent in the finery of his armour and leather boots, belt and medal harness, all retrieved from his travel chest and freshly polished by the unwilling hands of the two soldiers, Sanga and Saratos. The latter had performed the chore in silence, while Sanga had issued a constant stream of muttered complaints that the newly reinstated officer had magnanimously deigned to ignore. Having been Scaurus's senior centurion for almost a decade, a little of the tribune's subtlety had worn off on Julius over the years, and he had resisted the urge to beat the man, simply smiling at him and pointing out a spot he had missed.

Marcus, the subject of their discussion, was marching alongside him in his own newly restored splendour, and the giant Lugos, Arminius and his protégé Lupus were marching behind them wearing clean tunics and with their long hair washed, combed and plaited. Lupus, Morban's grandson and the son of a dead British soldier, had been under the German's wing for a decade, and had grown into a seasoned warrior under his tutelage.

'It's a fair question, given that the man who killed Commodus will be less than a couple of hundred paces in front of him. And with these animals in front of us hanging on Severus's every word, and ready to tear to death any man that falls foul of him. But no, I see no problem.'

Scaurus's men were marching close behind Laetus's leading legion, while the women and children were riding in a wagon

back down the supply chain with Morban and a pair of Dubnus's axemen to keep a watchful eye on them. The familia was
now formally a part of the makeshift imperial guard, a cohort-
strength force of experienced soldiers known to be fiercely loyal
to their emperor, their devotion rooted in the riches he had
promised to reward them with over and above the sum expected
by the army's legionaries for putting him on the throne. If the
ordinary soldier had been happy to chant 'dives miles', 'rich
soldier', at the prospect of a donative from their newly elevated
emperor, these grizzled veterans would in turn be even more
strongly motivated, ready to fight to the death to protect their
investment.

Julius frowned, making no effort to hide his lack of comprehen-
sion.

'But what if it becomes obvious that Commodus wasn't killed
by that idiot wrestler Narcissus? What if he comes forward and
declares himself innocent?'

Scaurus shrugged.

'It's unlikely that he'll be fool enough to try. He was happy enough
to take the money and the credit for finishing Commodus, when
the senate was still frothing with excitement at having avoided yet
another purge, and made him a hero for doing so. I see no credible
way he can prove that it wasn't him who strangled the emperor in
his bath, now that he'll be cast as a regicide rather than a patriotic
hero. I think he'll keep his head down and hope to escape Severus's
revenge.'

'I can see that, but what if someone recognises Marcus from his
time in the palace and puts two and two together? It only takes one
accusation to see us all in the shit.'

The tribune acknowledged the point with a nod, not taking his
eyes off the marching men to their front.

'Possibly, but our ever being in the palace again seems so
unlikely as to make the question moot, I'd say.'

A gruff, bass voice interrupted the discussion from behind
them.

'But doesn't it strike you as somewhat ironic that we have travelled so far only to end up back where we started?'

Dubnus, marching behind Julius, looked round at Lugos with an expression combining disbelief and disgust. The hulking Briton had only possessed the most peripheral command of dog Latin when he had thrown his lot in with the familia a decade before, but years of tuition by Ptolemy, a former member of the imperial secretariat, had both gifted him an extensive vocabulary and revealed the thinker previously concealed behind the brutal facade of his hulking seven-foot frame. Dwarfing even Dubnus, himself a warrior king among his remaining axemen, Lugos's newfound ability to express a thoughtful nature was an ever-present goad to the Briton's more robust approach to life.

'Ironic? You sound more like the Sparrow and less like a warrior with every passing day.'

Ptolemy, Lugos's tutor and the bird-like subject of the jibe, spoke up from behind him, his voice customarily peevish as with every occasion when Dubnus's verbal darts penetrated his habitual air of superiority.

'The word is rooted in the Greek, from *eironeia,* which means to feign ignorance that what was expected is different to what has actually—'

'I know what irony is, *Sparrow*! I've spent long enough listening to you and that monster quacking at each other to have absorbed that and a thousand other things I'll never get any value from learning.'

'You say that, Dubnus, but I'd swear your command of the language has improved simply by exposure to the two of them.' Arminius grinned at Marcus and winked. 'Who knows, one of these days you'll find yourself in line to replace Julius, if he ever decides to retire!'

'Him? Retire? We'll have to carry him out in a shroud.' Dubnus looked up at the cloudless sky and mopped his brow. 'I'll give you one thing though, Lugos, if we're bandying words on the subject of irony. Just when I thought I'd never again have to carry half my weight in armour across the empire here I am again, sweating my piss to the consistency of sand alongside another fifty thousand men.'

A peal of horns sounded in front of them, a repeating chorus of commands as the cornicenes whose job it was to signal basic orders repeated the call that would bring the marching legions to a halt.

'Looks like they're stopping up ahead.'

The men ahead of them were indeed being commanded to halt by braying horns and raised standards, and the command rippled down the line of march, each successive legion and cohort pulling up in turn. Soldiers who had endured the best part of a day's march in the early summer's warmth leaned on their spears and drank from their water bottles. Some men sank down on their haunches to grab a moment's rest, while others remained upright, unwilling to make the effort to get the weight of their armour and weapons back to a standing position. Dubnus shook his head at Marcus and Scaurus as he walked forward to join them, all of them watching as a runner sprinted past them, back towards the emperor's bodyguard.

'Strange, we only got back on the road no more than an hour ago, and we must still be what, fifty miles from Rome? Why stop here?'

Marcus pointed at a disturbance in the column of men in front of them.

'Here comes the answer.'

Laetus was striding back down the road between the ranks of legionaries that were parting before him to either side, their centurions bellowing commands to clear his path, Varus walking at his side. A man dressed in the uniform of a praetorian prefect was following them with his head held high under the stares of the soldiers, his bronze cuirass gleaming. The white ribbon that bound its sculpted plates around his chest was spotless, as if he had just stepped off a ceremonial parade ground. Equally pristine pteruges hung from the white subarmalis beneath the shining armour, forming a skirt of heavy linen strips decorated with finely braided gold tassels, while his belt and shoes shone with freshly applied wax.

Varus signalled with a tilt of his head for Scaurus and Marcus to follow, but, as they waited for the party to pass, Marcus realised with a start that a second praetorian officer was following the two august men. Their eyes met in a moment of mutual surprise and incomprehension, both managing to recover their equilibrium quickly enough that their momentary discomfiture went unnoticed by any of the soldiers around them. Marcus was the first to speak, falling in alongside the man he had last seen stealing away into the night after Commodus's death, keeping his voice low enough to be barely audible over the clatter of hobnails on the road's cobbles.

'Vorenus Sextus. Of all the people I didn't expect ever to see again you were probably at the top of the list.'

The praetorian tribune shot him a sideways glance as he replied equally softly.

'My surprise is the equal of your own. And I see that under this new emperor, you've advanced in rank from centurion to tribune in all but name. I presume that neither you nor your sponsor Rutilius Scaurus have anything to gain from denouncing me for the events that have led to all this?'

Marcus was unable to keep a grim smile from his face as he met the other man's questioning gaze.

'Nothing at all. And much to lose. If our new master were to discover our mutual part in his rise to power then neither of us would live to see the sun set.'

Vorenus nodded, needing no reminder of their collusion in Commodus's death.

'And how do you find yourself here, when the last time you were heard of was leaving Rome by sea?'

'How did that become public knowledge?'

Vorenus shrugged.

'You can imagine how keen the guard centurions who murdered Pertinax were to apprehend you both. For one thing, you were witnesses to the fact of exactly who struck the fatal blow, added to which they guessed that his nephew Scaurus would be eager to avenge his murder, were you able to survive his fall. The gang leader Petrus was happy enough to reveal your escape route from the city when asked, since he was safe under the new emperor's protection.'

'Having lent Julianus much of the money he needed to purchase the throne from the guard at that damned auction, I presume?'

'Exactly. What I don't understand is how you seem to have got away with it. A praetorian warship was despatched to chase you down, as soon as the means of your escape became clear and the April storms had abated. The weather must have hampered your ship's progress just as much as it prevented an earlier launch for your pursuers, so just how you escaped them must be a story worth telling.'

Marcus smiled wryly.

'They were probably safely tucked up in the harbour we'd just left when the last big storm found us wallowing about on the Adriaticus, diverted from our journey east by the ship's master's ill-judged greed to deliver a side cargo. We were blown so far north that if we hadn't managed to struggle into Classis we'd have been driven onto the northern shore.'

The praetorian stared at him for a moment, then barked out a terse laugh.

'You truly must be beloved of the gods, to enjoy so much luck! The men set to hunt you down were under orders to kill you and dispose of your bodies at sea, men, women and children alike!'

Severus was waiting for them, the runner's haste in carrying the news of the new arrival having given him enough time to have his wooden camp chair set out as an impromptu throne, upon which he was waiting. The lifeless eyes of a bust of Commodus stared from a plinth set alongside him, a reminder of his stated mission in revenging the dead emperor whose murder had unleashed the threat of civil war that was now becoming a hard truth.

The legion's senior officers had gathered, legates, their tribunes and senior centurions forming a wide circle that closed behind the praetorian as he stopped in front of the seated emperor. Only four men took places behind Severus: the supply chief Marcus Rossius Vitulus, the cavalry commander Lucius Valerius Valerianus, and Laetus, as the most influential man among the generals. And a little way behind them a veteran officer bearing the cross-crested helmet, scale armour and finely made equipment of a senior centurion lurked purposefully, his gaze locked on the prefect. Severus greeted the newcomer, a man with whom he was evidently familiar.

'Gaius Tullius Crispinus.'

The praetorian bowed deeply.

'Imperator!'

The men watching stirred, muttering comments to each other at the use of the formal title by a messenger from the man who, merited or not, sat on the throne in Rome. Prefect Crispinus continued without pause, ignoring the whispers and nodding heads of the spectators.

'Imperator, I bring you greetings from Marcus Didius Julianus! He sends you a message, and an offer—'

When was it that we last met, Tullius Crispinus?'

Severus had not raised his voice, but his interjection cut the praetorian off instantly. Stopped in mid-flow of his doubtless carefully prepared speech, Crispinus shook his head in slight bafflement.

'Imperator?'

Severus's voice was the rasp of a saw cutting away at the praetorian's confidence, and the look on the prefect's face told Marcus that he was clearly and, as Severus doubtless intended, completely thrown off his stride.

'It's a simple enough question, man. When is it that you think we last met?'

Crispinus smiled, as if recalling some pleasant memory.

'You were a guest at my wedding, Imperator.'

'Indeed I was. Your sponsor invited his most celebrated friends to celebrate your nuptials alongside your friends of the equestrian class, as a means of elevating the ceremony to a greater level of importance. He meant to set you on the way to high rank, and it appears that he succeeded in that aim.'

The prefect bowed his head.

'Thank you, Imperator. Not that I expect to remain in this role for very much longer. I will be retired, and hopefully permitted to return to my estate, while my colleague and co-prefect Titus Flavius Genialis is the man I expect to remain in post alongside whoever you nominate as the customary two prefects commanding the praetorians, if you are able to accept the emperor's proposal. The *other* emperor, I mean, with apologies to your august presence . . .'

He fell silent, blushing at the difficulty of the situation. Severus stared at him for a moment before responding.

'I deduce from this slightly garbled statement that Didius Julianus offers me a share in the throne. Does he propose a joint rule?'

The scowl with which Severus made the blunt statement did little for the messenger's equilibrium.

'He does . . . er . . . Imperator.'

'I see.' The emperor fixed him with another long stare, this time loaded with evident and almost comical disbelief. 'You've been sent here to tell me that a man who purchased the empire from *your* degenerate scum of a so-called bodyguard, and who has no more force with which to offer battle than your weak-kneed pretend soldiers, has sent you to make the offer that he will *share* the empire with a man who has sixteen legions at his back? How *very* generous of him!'

Crispinus smiled weakly at the joke, looking around uneasily at the officers encircling him and taking in the fact that none of them seemed especially amused. The emperor affected to think for a moment.

'I wonder what grounds he might think he has for any expectation that I will accept such a ludicrous idea? Can you shed any light on his thinking, Prefect? After all, you must be part of his inner circle, a member of his consilium principis?'

'I cannot say, Imperator. The emperor made the decision to send me with this offer without consulting with even his closest advisers.'

'And most of his advisers, from what I hear, have little to offer other than meaningless platitudes while they look over their shoulders and judge the right moment to make good their escape with the wealth they have managed to accumulate under his rule!' Severus barked out a laugh. 'Perhaps he has intelligence of a failure on my part of which I myself am unaware?'

He looked over his shoulder at the men behind him.

'Are we short of supplies, Rossius Vitulus? Are our soldiers going hungry?'

'No, Imperator, the supply wagons are full laden with food donated by a sympathetic populace!'

Marcus and Scaurus exchanged wry glances, having both seen the disgust and hatred of the farmers whose land had been stripped bare of anything edible by the army as it passed.

'Valerius Valerianus, is our cavalry weak, or stricken by illness?'

'No, Imperator, far from it. We have five thousand eager riders mounted on well-found and generously fed beasts. They want only for a target for their anger at any attempt to keep you from the throne!'

'And you, Julius Laetus, is your advance guard struggling with the march from the Rhenus? Do your men cower behind their shields in fear of the battle to come?'

Laetus laughed softly.

'No, Imperator. My dives miles are like hungry dogs in their eagerness to put you on the Capitoline Hill, and see you enthroned as the master of the world, if only to avail themselves of some of that gold the praetorians thought was theirs, and theirs alone!'

Severus looked up at Crispinus.

'So you see, Gaius . . . I can call you Gaius, can I not, having shared the happiest day of your life?' The praetorian nodded quickly. 'I cannot discern any good reason why your master the usurper should imagine that this laughable offer will do anything other than either amuse or, perhaps worse, enrage me? What sort of man can he take me for? A fool, incapable of seeing the huge disparity in our forces? A coward, terrified of even the smallest battle? Well?'

Crispinus was unable to stop himself taking an uneasy glance about, evidently all too aware of the hostility encircling him, and of the traditional fate of envoys whose messages failed to please under such circumstances.

'I cannot say, Imperator. I simply received my orders, to deliver this message to you, and like any good soldier I obeyed.'

The emperor nodded slowly.

'And now here you are, in the heart of your sworn enemy's army . . . you did swear an oath to the usurper, did you not? Did you never stop to consider the potential consequences of bearing so unpalatable an invitation, to surrender my current advantages and serve myself up like a prize bull being led to the cleaver?'

Crispinus slowly straightened his back, looking down at Severus with an expression combining fear and more than a hint of contempt.

'You must do, Imperator, whatever it is that you feel essential. History will judge your actions, I can only accept your will.'

And in that moment Marcus realised that he was seeing the real Septimius Severus, stripped of even the most cursory attempt to consider the implications as his fury rose to the surface, goaded by the praetorian's icy disdain.

'Centurion Felix!'

The centurion walked forward around the throne, and Crispinus, who had started at hearing his name, stared at him in evident horror. Felix looked him up and down with no more emotion than a slaughterhouse butcher considering a beast in its last moments.

'Imperator?'

'Gaius Tullius Crispinus should be returned to Rome in the most appropriate manner for a man who has chosen to carry a message that grossly insults its exalted recipient. What that method is I will leave you to decide, in the light of your experience in providing service to the throne with such difficult questions. And bearing in mind your recent experiences of the regime he represents, perhaps.'

Severus smiled at the prefect, but when he spoke again his tone was richly sardonic.

'You know Aquilius Felix, of course, don't you, Gaius? You're a senior praetorian officer, and have been for years, and for a long time he was a frumentarius. The grain officers are such a powerful tool in keeping the ruling classes in line that there's no way you won't be aware exactly what they're capable of.'

Crispinus visibly shivered, obviously aware of the frumentarii's infamous reputation as the throne's imperial enforcers. Their operations since their repurposing from a body of military grain collectors to imperial agents by Hadrian were shrouded in mystery, but were known to encompass spying on both friends and enemies and assassination of either when necessary.

'Centurion Felix was inserted into one of my legions a year or so ago, with the task of striking me down should I seek to use my legions to unseat the emperor. I believe that this is a standard precaution employed by successive emperors and their chamberlains . . .' He paused for long enough that the tension started to mount. '. . . and, of course, the prefects commanding the praetorian guard.'

'But . . . I . . .'

Severus ignored the attempted interjection.

'He received an order to kill me only two weeks ago, delivered to him secretly by a fast courier from Rome once his official dispatch had been delivered. Which means that order must have been issued by Didius Julianus, and I am very confident that such a momentous decision, to order the murder of an important senator and army commander, could only have been taken by the emperor's council. A body of which you, Gaius, are a member.'

'I argued against such a step!'

Crispinus's face was ashen with fear as he looked from Felix, standing before him with a blank, almost uninterested expression, to Severus's questioning scowl.

'And I suppose you'd like us to believe that you also counselled against the arrest of Centurion Felix's family? And their probable fate?'

The emperor's soft tone narrowed Crispinus's eyes for a moment, before he realised the implications of what he was saying. Taking a step back from the man standing before him, he shook his head in denial.

'I was no part of any of it! My promotion to prefect was solely intended to pacify the senate with the placement of a man known to one of their senior members, and as a counterweight against that of my fanatical colleague Genialis.'

Severus shook his head.

'If you didn't wish to be held to account for the crimes of your emperor's reign then you should not have accepted the role! Centurion . . . ?'

Felix, whose gaze had been locked on the emperor, turned back to look at Crispinus, his eyes as dead as those painted onto the bust of Commodus beside his chair. Crispinus, realising that he was at the mercy of a man who saw him as responsible for the imprisonment and probable death of his family, opened his mouth to protest, only to snap it shut with an agonised grunt as an enervating pain gripped his body. Looking down, he realised that the former frumentarius had drawn his pugio and plunged its foot-long blade into his groin, beneath the protection of his armour. Gripping the dagger's handle with a two-handed grip, Felix wrenched it down into the soft flesh of his victim's crotch, then twisted it free in a shower of blood. Crispinus tottered on unresponsive legs, watching in horror as blood flooded from the massive wound to pool at his feet.

'Put him out of his misery, will you, Felix? It's not as if we're sadists, to leave a man to bleed to death in such agony. And besides, we're going to need his head to send back to that fool Julianus, so you might as well take it now.'

The emperor watched in satisfaction as the centurion did as he was bidden, cutting the prefect's throat with a swift economical stroke and letting his corpse slump to the ground, then going to work with the blade to sever his neck. Once the prize had been taken, Felix holding the head by its hair with no more concern than if he were holding a bag of meat from the market, Severus looked about him at his officers and gauged their reaction to the brutal murder. His gaze alighted, as if by chance, on Scaurus, and he raised a questioning eyebrow.

'You, Tribune, what do you think of that?'

He leaned forward in the chair, watching the subject of his question intently.

'What do I think of that, Imperator?' Scaurus smiled, although to Marcus's experienced eye the expression looked a little forced. 'I'd say he was doubly deserving of the death sentence. Once for choosing to ally himself with the pretender Julianus. And once for the fact that he was a serving guard officer when his centurions disgraced themselves by selling the throne to the highest bidder. And the arrival of his severed head in Rome will serve to send both Julianus and the praetorians a powerful message.'

The emperor nodded, evidently satisfied by the answer.

'Very true. You harbour some hatred for the guard, I expect?'

'I would see every one of Pertinax's killers hanged with their own entrails, Imperator.'

The smile that spread across Severus's face was one of beatific satisfaction.

'Eloquently put, Tribune. As would I. And I know a way to let you work off at least some of that animus to your personal satisfaction.'

He shot a hard stare at Vorenus, and the praetorian tribune's body stiffened in anticipation of a similarly grisly fate.

'And you, Praetorian, can also play a part in bringing this farce of a reign to an end in an orderly manner, and without the bloodshed that might otherwise be necessary among your cohorts of thieves and murderers. I presume you'll be willing to do your duty in that respect?'

The subject of his iron gaze met the challenge with a swift salute and an instant response.

'I am at your command, Imperator!'

Severus nodded with an expression of grim satisfaction, looking at Scaurus and Vorenus in turn.

'I know you are. The two keys to gaining control of the city are the embezzlers in the senate and the thugs in the praetorian fortress. And between the two of you I expect to have both in my pocket within a day. Just don't let me down, gentlemen, I'm not a man who suffers disappointment gladly.'

'We're definitely in the right part of the city.'

Dubnus looked about him before replying to Arminius's statement.

'How can you tell?'

'Easy. There are no robbers.'

The German had insisted on accompanying his former master into the city, having had enough experience of the violence that could befall the unwary or unprepared in the city's streets after nightfall. He sheathed his pugio, having been carrying it ostentatiously on display, glinting in the moonlight and causing more than one gang of footpads to fade back into the shadows as the party traversed some of the rougher suburbs of Rome. Marcus followed his example, sliding his own blade back into the sheath concealed in the folds of his cloak and adjusting the strap of a heavy bag across his shoulders.

'There's no point trying to rob anyone that lives in these houses. They all have bodyguards, and all of the bodyguards have swords.'

Dubnus shook his head with a snort of dark amusement.

'And there was me thinking that carrying weapons was forbidden in the city.'

'It is. And if they were ever to be convicted the legal penalty is very clear. Although I wouldn't want to be the magistrate who tried to enforce it against a man with this sort of money.'

'This is the one.' Scaurus pointed at the gatehouse of a magnificent mansion.

'You're sure?' Vorenus patted the handle of his own pugio, hidden beneath his cloak. 'Five armed men unexpectedly appearing out of the night without warning might be enough to have the entire street up in arms.'

'Let's find out, shall we?'

Scaurus lifted the door's lion-headed door-knocker and rapped three times. The answering challenge was firm and authoritative, but pitched low, in the manner of a man who didn't wish to be heard beyond the door's immediate vicinity.

'Who's that knocking at this time of night?'

'Friends, with a message from outside of the city.' The code words given, Scaurus stepped back, putting a hand to his own weapon and muttering to his companions as he waited: 'That'll get the door open, but whether they'll be throwing roses or spears is yet to be seen.'

The heavy wooden door opened a crack and a shaven-headed man in his middle age stared at them suspiciously through the gap. Behind him Marcus could sense rather than see the presence of others, the scrape of hobnails on stone and the creak of weapons harnesses betraying the presence of the house's protectors.

'I am Tertius, maior domus to senator Lucius Fabius Cilo. You are expected, but not in such numbers. One alone may enter.'

'No.' Marcus stepped forward, staring into the darkness behind the doorway. 'Either we all enter, or no one does. You can either admit us or tell the senator that he has missed his one chance to align himself with the rightful power in Rome.'

'There are only five of you. What sort of power is—'

'There is an army of fifty thousand men marching on the city, and no more than two days away. This time tomorrow their watch fires will encircle the walls, but by then it will be too late for your master. He needs to pick a side and he needs to do so *now*. You either admit us or consign everyone within to an uncertain fate. The new emperor will remember who his friends are . . . and those people who have chosen not to be his friends.'

He fell silent, and the pause was long enough to have the party looking at each other as the maior domus considered Marcus's words. But at length he spoke again in a resigned tone.

'Very well, but you will have to disarm.'

Marcus looked to Scaurus, who shrugged.

'Why not? If our host has the sort of protection I'd have if I were in his place, a few daggers aren't going to be much use.'

They surrendered their pugios to four watchful and heavily armed men, the leader of whom gave Marcus's bag a suspicious look.

'Open the bag, please.'

With a shrug he did as he was asked, smiling grimly as the bodyguard recoiled at the sight and smell of the bag's contents. They were escorted through the gardens and into the house's atrium, where a lone figure was waiting for them in the middle of its magnificent splendour, a man in his late middle age with the demeanour and presentation of a patrician. Upright, and with the bearing of a man who knew and revelled in his position as a city father, he was of medium height and yet carried himself with the confidence of a bigger man. His hair was styled into tight curls and his heavy beard oiled in the fashion made popular among the city's elite by the long reign of Commodus, who had made himself into a vision of the god Hercules and whose look had been slavishly copied by the men around him.

Dressed in a pristine white toga, he had clearly prepared for any eventuality, an impression backed up by the presence of several more well-equipped bodyguards. Their physical bulk and air of competence marked them as gladiators, either moonlighting or recently retired, to judge by their apparent ages. Cilo turned and dismissed them, reassuring the suspicious maior domus with a pat on his shoulder.

'You've taken their arms, and the gate is locked behind them, so if they've come to assassinate me they'll be paying a high price for my life. Besides which, this is a discussion you'd be better not overhearing, old friend. Wait close by with the hired swords and be ready to come back if I cry out.'

He waited until the armed men had left the room, which in itself was large enough to comfortably swallow Marcus's former house on the Aventine Hill, then gestured to a table set with jugs, cups and an assortment of food.

'So, that's the ears that don't need to hear our discussion removed from any risk of their doing so. There is wine on that table, help yourselves, and bring me a cup too, so that I can demonstrate that it's just wine and nothing more sinister. If you are hungry, eat, and I will taste a morsel of whatever you choose before you if that will calm any concerns you might have.' He turned to Scaurus. 'You have a message for me from Septimius Severus?'

The younger man handed over the scroll he'd been given, and waited while Cilo read it by the light of the dozens of torches that were illuminating the atrium's cavernous and beautifully decorated space. He accepted a cup of wine from Vorenus, as did the senator, shooting the men around him an amused smile as they waited for him to drink before sipping from their own cups. He looked at Scaurus over the scroll with a calculating expression.

'Severus names you as Gaius Rutilius Scaurus. And I recall you, if only vaguely. You're an equestrian, are you not?'

'Yes, sir.'

'And I hear tell that a man by the same name stood at Pertinax's shoulder during his short and disappointing reign. A man who served as a praetorian tribune, but whose past was reputed to be littered with examples of his cunning and ruthlessness?'

'That was me.'

The older man nodded.

'Then you will know just as well as I do that the throne is either a blessing or curse. And for most men, I can assure you, it's the latter. It takes the cunning genius of an Augustus, the simple purpose of a Vespasian or the towering ego and drive of a Hadrian to make it work for both the emperor and empire. And those men who are unable to wield their power for the good of all tend not to last very long. Your uncle, may the gods give his spirit peace, was one such, I hear.'

'That's true. And yet while he was busy failing to live up to your standards of what makes a good emperor, *you* were not even in Rome.'

Cilo could not fail to hear the acerbic note in Scaurus's question.

'What are you implying?'

The younger man met his affronted stare without any sign of deference to such an august member of the city's elite.

'That the assistance of a man with as much experience of ruling the empire might have made the difference between my *uncle's* success and failure.'

'Perhaps it might.'

Scaurus took a step closer, his face white with anger.

'And yet you criticise a man for failing to achieve a herculean task that you might have helped him to grapple with. Instead of which you retired to your estate after Commodus's death, rather than staying to try to make the best of the situation!'

But rather than wilt under Scaurus's verbal attack, Cilo shook his head, his expression pitying rather than abashed.

'Fled? Of course I fled! I was a consul designate for the coming year, for one thing, which made me a prime target. I knew all too well that my brothers the honoured senators would be little better than a pack of bloodthirsty wolves, once the word of his death got out. They hated him with a passion, except for those he'd recently adlected into their number, to dilute their influence and reward those he favoured, a mix of plebs and freed slaves who were terrified that they would become victims of the senate's revenge. I knew that like the gutter scum they are, all of these gutless newcomers would fade into the shadows when the calls for revenge started, the shouting for Commodus to be dragged around the city with hooks and for those who had been close to him to be put to death!'

The men around him exchanged glances at the vitriol in his words, and the disgust he clearly felt for those not of his class.

'I knew that when it came to either formal execution and dragging with the hook or just a swift case of back-alley knife work, I was at the top of the list. And so I made sure Commodus's body was given an honourable burial in Hadrian's mausoleum, in my role as a priest of the cult of *Sodalis Hadrianalis,* and with that done I made myself scarce. And you, Rutilius Scaurus, would have done just the same, were you in my position!'

The two men stared at each other in mutual dislike for a moment.

'But now you're back. Why? What prompted you to return? Did you see a chance to lend your undoubted political skills to Didius Julianus? The potential to insert yourself into his inner circle?'

'That fool?' Cilo shook his head. 'I didn't come back to assist the man who had taken the throne, but to save the empire from him. With Pertinax dead, and his co-conspirators scattered and in hiding, I determined that I might just be able to do my duty to Rome without having my head cut off or my back used for a knife block. And so I returned to do my best to save the city from ruin. Once I was here, of course, and it was clear what an awful mess Julianus was making, and that at least one of the powerful men in the provinces would march on the city, I knew that my first duty was to make sure that Severus was successful.'

He thought for a moment before speaking again.

'Do you know how close to destruction Rome came in the year of the four emperors? A year when all but one of the contestants were grossly unsuitable to rule? Galba, too old. Otho too young, and too weak-minded. Vitellius a gluttonous narcissist. Only Vespasian, a battle-hardened general, fitted the bill, which made it a matter of the empire's very survival for him to triumph. So now just think how much worse it could be if the three strongest men in the empire actually fight it out with all the strength available to them? The war might last for years! The answer, the *only* answer, is for the most powerful of them, both in the strength of his legions and, as it happens, his force of will, to be the victor. And quickly. Severus has to be the next emperor! I have known the man for thirty years, and I can name no one any better suited to the task. He's hardly a Hadrian or a Marcus Aurelius, but he's the best man that's available to us.'

Scaurus nodded, unable to disagree with the distasteful but powerful argument.

'I see. And your proposed part in Severus's victory is what, exactly?'

'As I said, we have been more than colleagues since we both came to the city as young men. We commanded legions in Syria together, he the Fourth Scythia and me the Sixteenth Flavia. And when he was governor of Gallia Lugdunensis, I was his neighbour ruling Gallia Narbonensis. We have shared opinions over wine on many occasions, and I respect him for a hard but fair man. Which means, put simply, that I trust him and he trusts me. I have already secured his sons from the threat of kidnap and ransom, which means that I am quite likely to be invited to serve in his consilium once he rules the city. Both the trust between us and my likely future influence are well known among the senior men of the city. And so tomorrow I intend going down the hill to the forum, walking into the senate for the first time since Commodus's death, and telling the city's fathers the hard truth.'

'Which is?'

'I will tell them that the so-called "emperor" Julianus already knows that his bid to hang on to power with an offer of joint imperium has failed. A failure that will be confirmed by Severus in the grimmest manner possible, by the depositing of the messenger's head on the steps of the senate house tomorrow before dawn. That *is* what you have for me in the bag, I presume?'

Marcus nodded.

'Yes, Senator.'

'Julianus has therefore decided to propose that he will walk out to meet Severus on the road outside the city, accompanied by the senate, the vestal sisters, and the priests. His intended ruse is to demonstrate that we are all collectively responsible for Rome's well-being. He is looking to use the men and women who are at the heart of the empire's governance as shields against Severus's obvious intention to put him to death.'

'And how do you know this?'

'Severus has informers in the palace, of course. He has informers everywhere.' Cilo shrugged. 'How else could you have entered the city, known fugitives and armed to boot?'

Scaurus nodded in acceptance of the point. The party had been waved through the Viminal Gate, within eyeshot of the praetorian fortress, without either inspection or question by members of the vigiles he knew had been bribed to turn a blind eye to their entry to the city.

'I will also tell them that any one of them foolish enough to join in such a suicidal course of action will find himself dining with his ancestors all too soon. Because I don't expect Severus to show any mercy to anyone stupid enough to align themselves even that loosely with the pretender.' He shrugged. 'It's harsh, but sometimes it just takes a man with the right authority to explain the facts to colleagues whose fears he understands.'

'Which will ensure that Julianus finds himself alone and unsupported. With the choice of waiting in the palace for assassination or fleeing the city knowing that he is a hunted man.' Scaurus nodded. 'A fate he has paid handsomely to purchase.'

'Exactly. He is doomed. And whether he stays or runs, death will overtake him inside a matter of days. Quite possibly even hours.' Cilo gestured with both hands, palms up at his waist, his eyebrows raised in question. 'After all, who better than to seek him out in the palace than men who were praetorians under Pertinax? Men like yourselves?'

Scaurus looked back at him without speaking, and the senator nodded knowingly.

'And now you know why I have chosen to return to the city at this time. Not for my own purposes, but to facilitate the transfer of imperial power to the only fitting contender. A man capable of sending assassins like you into the city without Julianus having even the faintest clue that his doom is at hand. Capable assassins, unlike the feeble attempts Julianus made to procure Severus's death. I could wish that there were another Augustus waiting in the wings, but it is completely evident to me that we have no choice but to put our hope in Severus.'

He drained his cup and held it out for a refill.

'And you? You had no real business with me, did you? You're only here now as a means of sheltering your party for the night, in case those few vigiles or praetorians who still care about their duty get wind of your presence in the city. What is your purpose in coming into Rome the night before Severus's armies arrive? If you're assassins you could just as easily have entered the city tomorrow morning, and gone straight to the palace to do Severus's dirty work.'

Praetorian Tribune Vorenus stepped forward out of the group that had stood behind Scaurus, who turned and gestured to him.

'Our purpose? It is exactly the same as yours, Fabius Cilo. We're here to prepare the ground for the true emperor's triumphant arrival. As a senator you have the ability to sway your peers, and persuade them to align with Severus for the good of the empire. And as former praetorians we have much the same ability to influence our former comrades. Some of us more so than others.' He gestured to Vorenus. 'The tribune here was a praetorian officer for his entire adult life until just a few weeks ago. Which means that he has just as much sway with the guard as you do with the senate. After all, you said it yourself. Sometimes it just takes a man with the right understanding to tell the hard truth to colleagues whose fears he understands.'

'Open the gate for *who*?'

Vorenus stepped back, making himself fully visible to the duty centurion. Staring out through a one-foot-square lattice of thin metal bars, set in the praetorian fortress's massive wooden main gate, and squinting in the pre-dawn gloom, the guardsman shook his head in incomprehension. Pulling his cloak back to display his magnificently ornate chest plate, the tribune took his plumed helmet from the bag in which it had been concealed and strapped it to his head, and the officer of the guard looked at him for a moment before realising who he was addressing. His look of superiority faded, and he turned to snap out an order.

'Open the gate! Tribune of the guard recognised and safe to enter!'

Vorenus walked through the opened wicket door set in the gate, gesturing Scaurus and his companions to follow him through before it was closed and bolted behind them. To their left a tent party of nervous-looking praetorians was standing in a line with their spears held ready, while on the right the officer of the guard looked dubiously at the other members of Vorenus's party.

'You are free to go about your business, Tribune! But I do not recognise the men with you.'

Vorenus took a moment to answer, looking up at the fortress's walls with a calculating gaze. There were fewer guardsmen than usual on the walkways, and those there were looked less than crisp in their demeanour.

'It seems like we're short on guardsmen, Centurion. There have been desertions, I presume, with Severus so close to the city?' He didn't wait for an answer. 'And these men? They're a deputation from Severus himself, come to offer us a way out of this quickly closing trap. They need to speak with the prefect, so I suggest that you and your men escort us to the principia.'

The atmosphere inside the headquarters building was febrile, several centurions looking around from hushed conversations as the party entered. A tribune came out of an inner office at the officer of the watch's call and greeted Vorenus like a long-lost brother. Stepping back from their embrace, he took in the rest of the party, nodding his recognition at Scaurus.

'Vorenus Sextus! We've been wondering if we were ever going to see you again, and wondering if all we'd ever get back was your head in a bag like that poor innocent bastard Tullius! I tried to warn him he was likely to return from his mission to offer Severus a joint rule in two pieces, but he wouldn't listen to me. Too bound up with "doing his duty" to see the danger until it was too late. You've come with word from the advancing conquerer, I presume?'

He exchanged glances with the centurions standing to one side of the party, and it wasn't hard to guess what he was thinking.

'And are these his chosen representatives? If they are, is there a good reason why we shouldn't send their heads back to him, the way he sent our prefect's back to the emperor?' He looked more closely at Scaurus, his eyes lighting up in recognition. 'You? You were a tribune within these walls until a few weeks ago, when your uncle was . . .'

Scaurus took a step closer to him, close enough for blade work, one hand on the hilt of his sword, his eyes watching the praetorian intently.

'Murdered by your scum of a make-believe bodyguard? Yes, I was! Which ought to make you very, *very* careful around me if you don't want to be an early but welcome part of my revenge for his assassination by *your* men!'

He held the stare until the other man dropped his gaze.

'And as for your fanciful threat to behead us, if you think you can live up to the idea, there's no reason whatsoever why you couldn't send our heads back to the leader of the legions that already have the city in their grip. No reason other than the fact that Severus has promised me that in the event that we are mistreated in any way he'll have every officer and guardsman who can be apprehended crucified for such wanton disrespect. But let's pretend you're too brave and bloodthirsty to have any concern about Severus's revenge, despite appearances to the contrary.' He gave a subtle hand signal and Dubnus, Marcus and Arminius turned to face the other guardsmen, each one giving his sword enough of a pull to loosen the blade in its scabbard, ready to draw. 'In that case you might want to consider the fact that my men are combat veterans, while you and these other barracks flowers probably couldn't fight your way out of a brothel without the bouncers lending a hand. But feel free to prove me wrong, if you think you have it in you. Your guardsmen might find the courage to take us down, but by the time they did you would all be dead, and so miss the pleasure of witnessing our deaths!'

He locked stares with the other man, smiling without mirth as the tribune's attempted bravado melted under his gaze.

'No? Very well then, let's get down to business. I bear an offer that the emperor – the *real* emperor, that is – is willing to extend to you all for a very short time. So I suggest that you gather your fellow tribunes and senior centurions so that I can explain it to you all at one time. Those men who are still actually doing their sworn duty to Rome, that is.'

Only six of the guard's ten tribunes could be found, Scaurus and his men waiting patiently while two of them were summoned from their homes in the city, but every senior centurion had remained within the fortress, determined to see the matter of the imminent change of ruler through to the end no matter what the outcome. He walked out in front of them, waiting until the murmured comments had died down.

'It does your reputations no harm that you have chosen to stay with your commands, gentlemen! Those among your officers who have chosen to abandon their posts may well find themselves wishing dearly that they had followed your example. Septimius Severus is not forgiving when it comes to dereliction of duty, but you at least will have already accrued *some* credit with your new emperor for not fleeing the scene of the crime.'

He waited a moment to let that sink in before speaking again.

'Some of you already know me from my brief time as a prefect within your ranks. For the rest of you, my name is Gaius Rutilius Scaurus, nephew of the former emperor Helvius Pertinax. I was there when he was murdered by your centurions, and I was also present when they sold the empire to Didius Julianus, like some bauble they had found in the street. I am going to assume, as is the emperor's opinion, that you officers chose to keep your heads down, and not to challenge their venal stupidity, because you realised that nothing would be allowed to get in the way of their lust for the empire's gold. Which was an act of self-preservation that Severus does not condone, but which he is willing to overlook, under certain conditions.'

He waited for any questions, but the gathered officers simply waited to hear their fate in silence.

'At this very moment, your man Didius Julianus – your failed experiment in appointing an emperor by selling the throne to the candidate with the largest sack of gold – is speaking to the senate. He is asking them to join him, with the vestals and the priests, as he goes out to meet Severus's army in an act of supplication. He hopes to avoid death, if he is subservient enough and surrounded by the nobles and holy men and women of Rome. And the senate, I can absolutely assure you, will reject any such idea, partly because they will be led in that direction by Severus's friends, but also because, frankly, they do not wish to enrage their new emperor and risk their own deaths.

'What will happen next is open to question, but it is likely that Julianus will send word that he wishes you to mount a campaign of terror against the senate, either to intimidate them into compliance or simply for reasons of vengeance. You will of course refuse, because doing what he commands will earn you the hatred of the senate and inevitably lead to your all being condemned to death by the survivors, with the emperor's total support. *All* of you, no matter who follows such an order or refuses it.'

The most senior of the centurions shook his head dismissively.

'I think you can assume that nobody here is stupid enough to obey any command from a man in his last hours as emperor, Tribune Scaurus. But what are these conditions you mentioned earlier?'

Scaurus turned to face him, realising that he was the real source of power in the room.

'Firstly, you are to imprison and surrender the men who killed Pertinax. *All* of them. This is not negotiable. I was there when he died, so I know how many they were and I can recall their faces as clearly as if it had happened this morning. If any of them is absent I will personally make sure that every officer in his chain of command takes the missing man's place when they are executed. If any of them have taken refuge in the city, I suggest you get them back. By force if need be. Unless of course you are happy to take their places?'

The older man shrugged.

'That will not be a problem. I've been wanting to sort that little shit Tausius out for a while.'

Scaurus shook his head.

'There will be no violence done to them, not to Tausius or any other of the fools who followed him in their treason. You will deliver all of them alive, and unharmed other than for any damage they will sustain in their apprehension. They must be alive, and compos mentis, able to receive the punishment that the emperor has in mind for them. Understood?'

The senior centurion replied without blinking, clearly uncowed by Scaurus's foreboding stare.

'Understood. Just don't expect their apprehensions not to have been, shall we say, vigorous?'

Scaurus nodded.

'Second, you are to march your men out of the city tomorrow morning and parade them so that they can take the sacramentum in the presence of their new emperor. They are to wear their ceremonial uniforms, carry laurel wreaths, and they are to leave their weapons and armour here in their barracks. They may be belted, and carry their pugios, but any man carrying sword or spear, shield, armour or helmet will be assumed to be hostile.'

'You want us to parade the guard unarmed, into the heart of Severus's—' The centurion corrected himself. 'Into the heart of the emperor's army?'

'Yes. And in return for this act of unquestioning obeisance you officers will be allowed to leave quietly, with your gold unconfiscated and your dignity unsullied. And with your lives, of course. It's your choice.'

'And our men?'

Scaurus shrugged.

'I am not aware of the emperor's intentions towards them. Although I suspect you would do well to take this offer and not stay to share whatever fate it is he has in mind for them.'

He paused for any comments, but the collected officers remained silent as the gravity of their situation sank in.

'So let us be clear as to the offer that is extended to you for a very short time only. If your men follow these orders then *you* will be rewarded generously. You will all be retired with immediate effect, once you have explained the details of your duties to your successors, and none of you will be punished for the crimes you have allowed your men to commit, or suffer financially. Whereas your men, to be frank, will not be quite as fortunate. You may now have a little time in which to debate this matter, and I will wait outside in the sunshine while you do so.'

He turned to leave the building, but was stopped by a swift interjection by the tribune he had gone toe to toe with earlier.

'There's no need, Rutilius Scaurus. I think I speak for all of my colleagues when I say that none of us was given any choice but to remain silent while our centurions ran amok and brought shame on the guard. And none of us has any intention of attempting to protect the men that did so.' He looked about him questioningly, but not one of the gathered officers had anything to say. 'We will find the men who butchered Pertinax and bring them to justice, and we will parade our men to swear loyalty to Septimius Severus, as you demand. Unarmed.'

Scaurus nodded decisively.

'Good. Be ready to refuse any further orders from Julianus. And when the time comes for the changing of the guard, the outgoing watch is not to be relieved other than for a single century to act as gatekeepers and keep out the baser elements among the citizenry. Those men will be commanded by you, Tribune, and the watchword will be "blood and honour".'

The officer nodded slowly.

'Blood and honour. I will see you later, I presume?'

3

Scaurus met Senator Cilo in front of the curia several hours later, he and his men now dressed and equipped in the uniforms of the praetorians they had so recently been. Scaurus looked every inch a senior guard officer, while Marcus and Dubnus, dressed and equipped as guard centurions, radiated a veiled menace that made the forum's passing citizens instinctively give them a wide berth. Senators were streaming into the building in twos and threes, their bodyguards walking away into the forum in search of somewhere to wait close by rather than remain close to the knot of hard-nosed praetorians in front of the senate house. Cilo looked Scaurus up and down with a knowing expression.

'Well now, here you are looking just as angrily superior as the real thing. I presume, given the lack of screaming and bloodstains on the steps of the curia, that Didius Julianus either didn't attempt to set his dogs on my colleagues or was told to forget any such idea?'

Scaurus shook his head.

'He tried. The guard very sensibly refused, after having the likely consequences for them and their families pointed out. And their refusal to comply with the order was unequivocal.'

The dignified messenger from the Palatine Hill, a lictor bearing the rods and axe that were the symbol of his station, had been outraged to have his message container smashed under the heel of a hobnailed boot as a signal of non-compliance. His angst had been somewhat increased when he had then found himself ejected from the fortress onto the road outside in an undignified sprawl.

'I see. In which case I think the soon to be ex-emperor has just signed his own death warrant. I'm just about to go back in there'

– he gestured to the curia – 'and suggest to the city fathers that we would all be well advised to vote Severus into the role he'll be taking for himself in less than twelve hours, with or without our blessing. So I suggest that you take your party of cut-throats into the palace and deliver the sentence.'

He waited for a moment, then raised a questioning eyebrow at Scaurus's look of distaste.

'Surely you're not squeamish, Rutilius Scaurus?'

The younger man shook his head.

'I've spilled more than enough blood for Rome that one more life in the cause of a swift resolution to this matter isn't going to trouble me. Even if Julianus wasn't actually responsible for my uncle's murder he might well have connived at it, and he only has himself to blame for being idiotic enough to buy the throne and put himself in this position. He chose to ride this tiger, he cannot be surprised when it decides to eat him.'

'But . . . ?'

Scaurus watched the senators making their way back into the chamber for a moment.

'It's easy for you. You cut and ran, and only came back when the threat of your death was lifted. And now you'll whip the senators up to declare Severus imperator before fading back into the pages of the history books. Whereas I, you suggest, have only to commit a single act of murder to finish this whole thing off tidily and wrap it up with a ribbon for the new emperor to enjoy opening tomorrow. You will be back in the shadows, while I will be standing in public view with a bloodstained dagger, so to speak.'

He smiled wryly at a memory, and Cilo frowned at the expression.

'There is something amusing in all that?'

'I used to have a comrade in arms called Cotta. A former centurion with the Third Gallica in the east. I got to know him after his retirement from the service. And the circumstances of his having left the service, some years before the completion of his term, were that he was both gifted and unlucky enough to be selected by a legion legatus, and assigned the task of assassinating a legatus augustus who had taken the apparently insane step of declaring himself emperor.'

Cilo nodded knowingly.

'Avidius Cassius, in Aegyptus?'

'Yes. Cotta managed to bluff his way into Cassius's headquarters and decapitate the great man. After which he was given enough gold to fund a comfortable lifestyle and sent on his way. And that, one would have thought, would have been that.'

'Instead of which . . . ?'

'He spent the next ten years looking over his shoulder. Constantly hunted by the men of Cassius's legions, who wanted revenge for the death of the man they had thought was going to make them into dives miles.'

Cilo laughed quietly.

'They would have been rich soldiers indeed, had he managed to actually take the throne. So your concern is with revenge?'

'No, Senator. My concern is the notoriety that comes from taking on the title of regicide just as surely as night follows day. Cotta told me that from the moment he took Avidius Cassius's life he was a marked man, forever wondering who would be the next one to try to take his life to prove themselves the better man.'

The senator nodded.

'Understandably. But then you have a significant advantage over your former centurion. You will be anonymous. Just another guardsman among hundreds of others who come and go from the Palatine every day of the year. You will go into the history books as "a praetorian", nothing more.'

Scaurus nodded.

'That much I had already worked out for myself. But I'm quite sure that the seductive possibility that nobody will ever know who killed the poor fool is counterbalanced by something I am quite sure is real.'

'Which is?'

'The unerring ability of such a deed to haunt the perpetrator in the future. Either in this life, or the next.'

Cilo nodded, a hint of sympathy in his otherwise untroubled expression.

'Ultimately, I suppose, you can console yourself with the hard fact that you have very little choice in the matter. Do you? But let me make it easier on you. By the time you've found Didius Julianus and done what needs to be done, you will be obeying the legal orders of the senate. Because just before the vote to name Severus as emperor there will be another, declaring Julianus to be an enemy of the people and condemning him to death. I will send word to you when it is done, and you can proceed to do the city's will with a clear conscience. And with the blessing of the gods who watch over the city.'

The guards on the forum gate snapped to attention as Scaurus and his men approached up the final part of the switchback ramp that climbed the Palatine Hill's side, designed to allow an emperor to ride down to the senate house if he chose to do so. In contrast to the bustling city below, the palace environs were deserted, with none of the coming and going that would usually have been the case as dusk deepened and the palace's daytime functionaries made their ways home.

The duty centurion stepped forward, saluting Scaurus with a wary eye on his companions, especially the barbarian Arminius, who was revelling in the chance to roam the palace unchecked.

'The watchword, Tribune?'

'The watchword is blood and honour, Centurion. Is your commander already in the palace?'

The junior officer nodded.

'Yes, Tribune. He left word that he is to be found in the audience hall. He also left strict instructions that no one else is to be admitted without your express permission.'

'Wise of him. Thank you, Centurion. Send word to me when Senator Cilo's messenger comes to the gate, will you? He will give you the watchword and leave, and I simply need to know that he has done so.'

The centurion snapped to attention.

'We will do what is ordered, and at every command we will be ready!' He shot the palace's stone bulk a meaningful glance. 'Just don't expect to find the place lit up in the usual manner, Tribune. The slaves have all retreated to their quarters in expectation of the usual trouble that happens when an emperor is overthrown.'

Scaurus turned away with a meaningful glance at Marcus.

'Wise of *them*. Usually it's the men set to guard them who take advantage of moments like these.'

They walked into the palace's western wing, the formal and more public palace of Domitian that had been added to the older and more homely palace of Augustus over a century before, making their way through the peristyle garden into the great audience chamber where the praetorian was waiting for them. In the absence of the usual bustle of slaves to keep the great chamber's lamps lit, it was gloomy, with deeper shadows in the massive room's corners, from which oversized effigies of the gods glowered down at them. The tribune was sitting beneath a massive statue of Hercules that had been commissioned by Commodus with his own face as the god's representation, and he got to his feet and waited for them at the deity's feet.

'Ah, Rutilius Scaurus. You're here to—'

'Better you don't know.'

The younger man nodded his understanding.

'I don't envy you. But it has to be done, I suppose.'

Scaurus waved a hand at the audience hall's darkened but still grandiose chamber, towering columns of red Aegyptian marble supporting the huge roof under which yet more giant statues of the deities stared down inscrutably from alcoves built into the walls.

'The last time I was here it was filled with the so-called elite of Roman society. They had been called here by Pertinax, who was forced to conduct a grand sale of the previous emperor's possessions in a desperate attempt to put some money into the imperial treasury. Commodus's clothing, weapons, chariots and all manner of other precious items were sold that day, purchased by the rich for the purposes of showing their peers how wealthy they were. They bought slaves too, children among them, and we later found it necessary to save one young boy from an obvious paedophile.'

The other man nodded, clearly uncertain as to the story's relevance.

'And when the sale was done, with millions pledged in gold and buyer's remorse probably already setting in among the bidders, not that any of them could back out of their purchases without losing face, the emperor retired into the consilium over there' – Scaurus pointed to a heavy wooden door into the emperor's private council chamber – 'to tot up the day's takings. At which point the men who had conspired to put him on the throne did their very best to walk away with as much of that money as they thought theirs of right, which was to say most of it. They were the men behind the throne, they reckoned, and they deserved a substantial reward for their risk in overthrowing the tyrant Commodus.'

The praetorian nodded with a carefully neutral expression, unsure as to where the story was going.

'I see.'

'Do you? My point is this: they're all the same. Commodus was a monster, although we'll all be praising him soon enough, I expect, but his one virtue was that he kept the senators in their place. Because the men of honour among their number are now like rare gems scattered on a rubbish pile, few in number and almost impossible to make out from the dross around them. Their preoccupation is for the most part how they can turn the situation to their own advantage, and get back to the good old days before Augustus put them in their place. The lack of an effective emperor can only result in untrammelled greed on the part of the strongmen who rise and fall among the city's elite and, if the history books are any guide to the future, the same succession of bloody civil wars that killed millions in the last days of the republic.'

'And Severus is the only alternative?'

Scaurus smiled sadly.

'Severus is the only man with sixteen legions at his back and less than a day's march from the city. Niger has six and is at the other end of Mare Internum. And Albinus, who is worse than either of them in my opinion, has just three, and is currently sitting on his backside in Britannia. Severus is the only option, and it is our job to make his assumption of power as trouble-free as possible. Even if that means regicide.'

He turned to leave the hall.

'And you believe that a civil war can be avoided?'

The note of hope in the younger man's voice made his lips twitch into a smile as he turned back.

'I very much doubt it. If Niger gives up his claim to the throne, journeys to Rome and throws himself on Severus's mercy, then perhaps he might be spared, but how likely is he to seek an early death?'

He turned as the centurion from the gate walked into the hall, walking up to the two men and saluting.

'Tribunes, a messenger from Senator Cilo has come to the gate and given the watchword.'

'Gods below, Cilo wasn't exaggerating when he said it would be the work of moments to persuade the city fathers to condemn Julianus.' Scaurus turned to his men. 'Come on then, let's go and do this distasteful task, shall we?'

They walked through the dark, silent palace as quietly as was possible given the scrape and click of their hobnailed boots on the marble flooring. Moving through the wide, open halls of the Domus Domitiana, built a century before, they progressed into the Domus Augustana's more intimate warren of interconnected rooms, which had housed the first emperor and his family at the empire's birth a century before that.

Entering the peristyle garden at the heart of the older palace, Marcus saw a lone slave working in a flower bed on his hands and knees, either unaware or uncaring of the threat that had caused his peers to take refuge in their cells. Looking up at the sound of their footfalls, his eyes widened as he realised that death was stalking the palace corridors. Leaping to his feet, he made a dash into the palace on the other side of the garden, tossing aside the trowel with which he had been weeding with a clatter of iron on stone.

'Hold!' Marcus put a hand out to restrain Dubnus, who was poised to give pursuit. 'It doesn't matter if he warns Julianus we're coming. There's no escape from this golden cage.'

He looked around the gardens, recalling the time he had spent effectively incarcerated within its luxurious confines while he had waited for Commodus to call on him to fight for his life in whatever new and deadly scenario caught the emperor's fancy.

'All of the conspirators against Commodus are dead. His concubine Marcia, her lover the chamberlain Eclectus and the praetorian prefect Laetus, all murdered by Julianus to prevent them siding with Severus . . . I wonder if that little shit of a maior domus survived?'

As if to answer his question, a slight figure appeared in the doorway through which the gardener had fled. Raising his voice to be heard across the garden, he walked out into the open space, demonstrating remarkable courage for a man alone in the presence of so many armed and hard-faced intruders.

'I was wondering where all the praetorians had gone, but now I see the reason. You're here to murder the emperor, aren't you . . .'

He trailed off as he got close enough to make out their faces beneath the helmets whose cheek plates both disguised them and lent their faces a brutal aspect.

'By the gods! *You*?'

Scaurus stepped forward with a grim half-smile.

'Yes, us. And yes, we're here to—'

'No.' Sporus pointed at Marcus with a look that combined horror with contempt. '*Him!*'

Marcus nodded, walking forward until he was within arm's length of the palace butler.

'Greetings, Sporus. I could say that it's a pleasure to see that you've survived the upheavals of the last emperor's death, but I'd be lying.' He matched the maior domus's hate-filled stare with a level gaze. 'I should have known that a man like you would find a way to come through these difficult days without as much as a scratch.'

The butler glared at him in disbelief.

'Quite how you can be *so* brazen I have no idea! Have you come to murder your second emperor in less than a year?'

Marcus reached out an arm with the speed of a striking snake, taking a grip of the servant's tunic and dragging him up onto his toes.

'I'm not the only man here who's connived at the death of a man wearing the purple though, am I?'

'What do you mean? It was one of *your* men who struck the fatal blow that killed Pertinax, a centurion of the guard!'

He winced as the grip on his clothing tightened, pulling him so close to Marcus's face that all he could see was the Roman's eyes boring into his own.

'Tausius killed Pertinax, that's true enough. And it's a crime he'll be paying for all too soon. But you were a key part of that plot, weren't you? You were in league with the so-called "Saviours" who put an unarmed emperor to death without any thought to the implications of their crime. They planned to kill him at a poetry reading in the city, and when he changed his mind about going and stayed in the palace, you told them where they could find him. Didn't you?'

He waited for the butler to attempt a denial, nodding grimly when the other man's eyes widened at hearing the truth of his betrayal.

'As I thought. It won't surprise you to learn that the "Saviours" are now prisoners awaiting execution. They will all die when Septimius Severus enters Rome tomorrow.'

Sporus laughed humourlessly, throwing his defiance back in Marcus's face.

'*Another* emperor? That'll make four this year if I include poor Commodus. I have to say that I'm getting used to introducing them to the palace one after another. How long will this one last, I wonder? Long enough for me to tell him the story of how a seemingly harmless gladiator was brought to stay in the palace, and ended up being the man who murdered the only lawfully appointed emperor of the four of them? After all, as part of the familia Caesaris I have a duty to ensure that he knows—'

Marcus pulled his pugio from the sheath on his hip, raising the blade in front of the butler's face.

'One swift cut and I can remove that potential problem from my life.'

'Coward! But then how like you to take your knife to a defence-less—'

Sporus fell silent as Marcus released his grasp of the maior domus's tunic, gripping his right arm before the other man could pull away from him. Smiling tightly, he slipped the blade's last inch under the four strings of coloured beads tied tightly around the other man's wrist, each one of the tiny ornaments adorned with a minute aquila symbol embossed in gold leaf.

'Do you remember when you told me what these were all for? Blue for the slave quarters. Purple for the emperor's private quarters. Yellow for his bedchamber. And green to be allowed to come and go from the palace.'

Sporus stared at him in horror, his head slowly shaking from side to side in silent entreaty.

'So yes, I could take your life. You've earned that punishment for betraying Pertinax. But there are two very good reasons why I won't kill you here and now. For one thing I'd be murdering you in cold blood, and that would make me just as much at fault as you are.'

Sporus quailed as he realised what his nemesis intended.

'No. *Please*—'

'And the other reason is that it's so much more fitting for you to have time to realise just what it is that you've lost before your life ends. Consider this the price of your treason.'

He flicked the knife's blade, severing the strings and sending the multicoloured beads in all directions. They bounced across the stone flags with a rattle that died away as they came to rest in the flower beds and the gaps between the flagstones.

'No!'

Marcus released his arm and pushed him away, gesturing to Dubnus.

'Take him to the gate and have him put outside. Tell the centurion that he is under no circumstances to be readmitted.'

'No!' Sporus's voice had risen to an alarmed shriek. 'No no *no!* You cannot do this to me! Take my life, but do not cast me out onto the streets, I—'

The Briton punched him in the face hard enough to momentarily silence his alarmed protests, then took one arm and hustled him away back towards the forum gate, leaving a trail of blood spots across the paving stones from his bleeding nose. His renewed shouts faded as he was hurried away, leaving Julius and Scaurus looking at Marcus with various expressions of surprise and appraisal.

'It would have been kinder to kill the man.' Arminius shook his head at his friend's unexpectedly harsh judgement. 'You know what he'll be subjected to on the streets.'

Marcus nodded grimly.

'Yes, and I'm not proud of such an act. But he threatened me one time too many. And this time he would have had the means to have us all executed by simply telling Severus that it was me that killed Commodus. You saw the way that our new emperor is already positioning himself as Marcus Aurelius's son and Commodus's brother, so he wouldn't have any choice but to avenge him. And this way, if Sporus's absence is noticed, we can all swear to any god he chooses to name that we had no part in his death.'

Scaurus nodded slowly.

'I see your point. Very well, gentlemen, let us go and do what we have been sent here for.'

They found the former emperor waiting for them in his private quarters, a dagger lying on the bed on which he was sitting. He looked up as Scaurus opened the bedroom door, and the look of relief on his face was momentarily disconcerting.

'Thank the gods. I was afraid that my former brothers in the senate would send the mob in here to tear me to pieces. Although I suppose that would mean that Severus would arrive to find the place nothing more than a burned-out shell. And that would clearly *never* do.'

He stood, opening his arms before him to demonstrate that he was unarmed.

'You have been sent from the curia, I presume, to carry out a sentence of death. I am declared an enemy of Rome, of course?'

Scaurus nodded without speaking.

'And who do they send to end my life but the stone-eyed killer who used to stalk around after Pertinax. Here for revenge, are you? And happy to murder an unarmed man?'

The younger man shrugged.

'I find the deed distasteful, Didius Julianus, but nothing more than that. I watched my uncle fall under the swords of praetorians who less than one night later had sold the throne to the biggest fool in the city. And I find it hard to believe that your opportune purchase wasn't prepared in advance. A discreet exchange of messengers, perhaps, asking whether you would be willing to consider the guard a more fitting power in the city to bestow the throne on its next occupant than your fellow senators?'

Julianus laughed bitterly.

'If only it had been so carefully considered, I might have had the sense to turn them down. The truth of it is that I was in my cups when the tribune knocked at my door and offered me the chance to bid for the throne. My wife egged me on, telling me that this was my one chance to find glory in this life, as if I wasn't already rich enough. I knew it was a disaster from the moment I woke up in this bed the morning after, and that feeling of dread only got worse when the plebs started calling me a parricide and throwing stones at me. Which was of course the guard's cue to run amok and make the whole thing a great deal worse than it already was. After that I knew that I was on borrowed time, because the first man with an army to reach Rome was going to murder me with the support of the people and the senate, and probably those same praetorian bastards too. And now here you are, right on cue.'

He sighed.

'You'll make it quick, I hope?'

Scaurus nodded.

'And as painless as possible. A dagger blade pushed into the space behind your collarbone will render you unconscious within a few heartbeats, and death will follow soon after. Unless you wish to fall on a sword?'

He tapped the hilt of his own weapon with a questioning look, but Julianus shook his head with a dismissive expression.

'That's all very well for the battlefield, when there's a statement to be made about one's undying loyalty to Rome in the most extravagant way possible, but I'll take the less painful exit from life, thank you. And my body . . . what will be done with me afterwards?'

Scaurus unsheathed his pugio, gesturing for the other man to pull away his toga to enable a clean kill.

'You're worried that the senate might have voted for you to be dragged around the city with hooks?'

The former emperor nodded, shrugging off the heavy garment.

'It is the depth of disgrace. I realise there's no point in a damnatio memoriae edict, as I have neither statues nor inscriptions to be defaced, but there might be those envious of me who would seek to demonstrate their hatred by despoiling my corpse and persecuting my family. And the gods know that Severus would be in favour of such barbarism.'

Scaurus shook his head.

'There is no such sentence on you. And your family have been ordered to attend the palace to collect your body. As long as they have the sense to cremate it and leave no trace, I would imagine that there will be no further action taken against them.'

'Very well.' Julianus sank to his knees in the folds of the discarded toga's pristine white cotton, looking up shamefaced as Scaurus stood over him with the blade of his dagger raised for the death stroke. 'I am sorry about the death of your uncle. Pertinax was a decent—'

The pugio stabbed down into the base of his neck, Scaurus twisting it as he withdrew the blade to ensure that the artery beneath the skin was severed. He stepped back, watching as the dying man realised what had happened, opened his mouth in a vain attempt to protest at the lack of warning, then toppled forward onto the carpeted floor and lay motionless with blood streaming from the deep wound. Scaurus wiped his knife blade on the toga and then sheathed it with a sigh.

'So ends the rule of a man who was hopelessly inadequate to the task. We can only hope that his successor can put an end to this constant cycle of death and terror.'

'You found Didius Julianus and carried out the sentence prescribed by the senate?'

Scaurus nodded, bowing his head momentarily.

'Yes, Imperator. The pretender is dead.'

The party had slipped out of the city in the quiet hours after midnight, and had made their way along moonlit roads to where the army lay restlessly encamped like a sleeping tiger dreaming fitfully of the blood to be spilled in the morning.

'And Fabius Cilo did exactly as he was commanded?'

'He followed your instructions to the letter, Imperator. The senate were quick to vote for you to be declared imperator, and for Julianus to be executed.'

'I expected nothing less. And what of the body?'

'It was decided to allow his family to take it for a quiet private ceremony. It seemed reasonable, under the circumstances, although I specified cremation rather than burial.'

'To avoid any lingering trace of his illegal regime. Good thinking. And will there be any resistance when we arrive at the city's gates?'

Scaurus shook his head firmly.

'The guard will parade as you have commanded, in their ceremonial tunics and completely unarmed other than for their daggers. They will be told that they are to take the sacramentum to bind themselves to their new emperor.'

Severus got to his feet and paced across the tent's flap, looking out towards the east where the first faint blush of the sun's impending rise was just touching the horizon's blackness with a hint of the darkest blue.

'I wish that we were on the march already.' He turned back to his gathered generals, who had gathered to hear Scaurus's news. 'Wake the army. By the time they're ready to march there'll be enough light for a cautious advance.'

Julius Laetus laughed tersely.

'I doubt it will take the legions more than half an hour to break camp and be ready to move. From what I've seen they've been unable to sleep for the most part.'

His amusement was proven justified, the legions' centurions having to do little of the usual shouting and wielding of their vine sticks to have their men paraded and ready to march, their tents and cook-pots swiftly packed away onto carts in preparation to move. With Laetus's men in their usual vanguard position, the army took to the road one legion after another, deliberately sacrificing the usual caution on the march for speed in the approach to the waiting city. At Severus's command Scaurus and his familia rode ahead of them with a cavalry escort of a decurion and thirty horsemen, taking the shortest direct route to the praetorian fortress. Vorenus met them at the gate.

'It's as you predicted. Our remaining prefect has gone missing without trace, doubtless knowing that he'll be marked for death when Severus takes the throne.'

'And what of Pertinax's killers?'

The tribune smiled thinly.

'Let's just say it's been a busy night for the senior centurions. They've been hunting down Tausius and his accomplices ever since you made them the offer of an honourable discharge in return for surrendering the men who killed Pertinax.'

'And?'

'The last of them was dragged up the hill an hour ago, Tausius himself, shouting that they had no right and that every man inside the fortress shares the responsibility for what he did.'

Scaurus shrugged.

'Not entirely untrue, but hardly relevant under the circumstances. I would suggest you have him gagged when the time comes.'

The praetorian nodded.

'They'll all be bound and gagged. It wouldn't do for the new emperor's triumphant return to Rome to be marred by a lot of screaming and shouting, would it?'

At Scaurus's command the waiting guardsmen, just as sleepless as Severus's army, were marched out onto their parade ground, watched by the familia from the vantage point of their horses' saddles. The praetorians were clad, as ordered, in the ceremonial uniforms that they would usually have worn for holidays and feasts, their armour replaced by red tunics and the wreaths of laurel leaves customarily worn for celebrations. Stripped of their swords, spears and shields, the size of the purses worn on their belts was noticeable, made larger than the usual soldier's purse to carry the gold they had been paid to bestow the throne on Didius Julianus.

'They seem cheerful enough, don't they?'

Marcus considered the column of men marching out onto their parade ground for a moment before replying to Dubnus's knowing question.

'They're happy enough to let those men among them who conspired to murder Pertinax take the punishment coming to them if it gets the rest of them off the hook. A few men die, the rest of them keep the gold their treason earned them and go back to the old ways. Why wouldn't they be cheerful?'

The Briton grunted in reply, watching as cohort after cohort streamed out of the fortress equipped as if for a holiday, their demeanour more suited to a coming day of celebration and feasting than a solemn transfer of power, men surprised but happy by such a propitious turn of events. As the last of their ten cohorts marched out of the fortress the gates were closed behind them, an action noticed only by a few men at the column's rear. Dubnus grinned as the news rippled slowly through the assembled guardsmen, the first looks of disquiet creasing faces into worried frowns.

Scaurus was watching the marching men intently for any sign that their sullen nervousness might turn into aggression, if they realised the nature of the trap into which they were marching.

'Let's be clear, gentlemen, if they get skittish I want no heroics. At the first sign of any trouble we ride away and leave them to it. Let them take on Laetus's legion with nothing more than their pugios if they're that keen to bathe in their own blood.'

But if the assembled guardsmen were disquieted by being shut out of their own fortress they didn't seem to have the appetite to fight, simply waiting in their ranks under the watchful eyes of their officers. After a few moments of inactivity the long silence was broken by the appearance of the first men of Severus's vanguard, the first cohort of Laetus's Fourteenth Legion, as they came up the road from the east at the ferocious battle march pace.

'I have to admit it, those bastards make me nervous, and I'm not going to be looking down their spears.'

Marcus followed Julius's stare and found himself forced to agree. In a calculated piece of theatre, the leading cohort was composed of the legion's combat veterans, men who had been young in the last hectic years of the German wars that had ended a decade and a half before. There were greybeards among their number, but there was no doubt that every man among them would have seen battle, killed enemies and seen friends die, hardening those who survived with their lives and sanity intact into trained and blooded killers. Scarred faces were evident in every row of the advancing column, the inevitable mark of combat, lending a fearsome aspect to their already bellicose advance, and looking out across the ranks of praetorians it was evident that the guardsmen were just as perturbed as Julius was impressed.

Muttered comments and sidelong glances were a clear sign of their nervousness at Severus's army's arrival.

'Reality seems to be starting to dawn, it seems.'

Scaurus was staring up at the fortress's walls, where the figures of armed and armoured legionaries were appearing all along the rampart. As the last of the praetorians had marched out, the rear gates had been opened to admit a cohort of men who had marched by a circuitous route to take the fortress in a bloodless victory, cutting the increasingly worried guardsmen off from the weapons that they usually used to hold the city in an iron grip. Some among them were shaking their heads and casting dark stares at their officers, and Marcus wondered just how many of them would seek vengeance against the men who had led them into an iron-jawed trap.

As the waiting praetorians' muttering increased in volume to a low-level hubbub of worried conversation the veteran soldiers marched past them, splitting into two columns each two abreast and swiftly encircling the parade ground. The cohorts following behind them repeated the manoeuvre, until the waiting guardsmen were surrounded by a continuous wall of soldiers arrayed eight deep around them. As the rap of their hobnails died away to silence, Julius Laetus walked through a gap opened in his men's line, followed by half a dozen legionaries carrying a wooden tribunal, which they placed in front of the praetorians.

'Men of the Praetorian Guard!' Absolute silence fell at the general's shouted words. 'You have been gathered for three purposes!'

He turned and gestured to the podium as Severus, clad in his ceremonial armour and purple cloak, walked through the ranks of his soldiers and mounted the rostrum, the men of his bodyguard filling the space between the tribunal and the guardsmen, their swords drawn and shields raised, staring impassively at the praetorians over their shields' iron rims.

'Firstly, you will swear the sacramentum to your emperor!'

Led by their officers, the assembled praetorians took the oath of everlasting fealty to Rome's master, their words spoken grudgingly but clearly enough. When it was done Laetus nodded grimly at them.

'You are now bound irrevocably to the service of the Imperator Caesar Lucius Septimius Severus Pertinax Augustus! Any man who breaks that oath will forfeit his own life and those of any of his fellows who abet his crime in any way! And now, as a reminder of the oath's meaning, you will witness the punishment of those among you who are guilty of the crime of regicide!'

The centurions who had murdered their former emperor Pertinax were led forward, shackled and gagged to prevent them from crying out, and only able to express their terror by the horrified urgency of their stares and, in more than one case, the urine soaking their boots.

'That's my cue.'

Scaurus climbed down from his horse and walked forward, pulling his pugio from its sheath as he moved to stand next to the group's ringleader Tausius. Laetus nodded to him, gesturing to the waiting members of the emperor's bodyguard to take their places beside the other conspirators.

'Centurion Tausius and his fellow conspirators committed the gross crime of invading the emperor's personal quarters, and putting him to death when he chose to reason with them! And then, when it seemed they could sink no lower, they sold the throne to the highest bidder! The pretender Didius Julianus has already been executed, and now Tausius and his associates will meet the same fate!'

He nodded to Scaurus, who put the tip of his pugio under Tausius's jaw and gripped the shoulder of his tunic with his other hand to ensure the death stroke would be clean.

'I swore to see you dead for killing my uncle. That oath is now fulfilled.'

He slashed through the helpless praetorian's neck to open his arteries, stepping back to allow the slumping centurion to fall to the ground. His face was speckled with the blood that had flown from the wound his blade had opened, but he made no effort to wipe it off. The other men of the bodyguard followed suit, and within seconds the conspirators were all dead or twitching in their last moments of life. Scaurus turned away and remounted his horse expressionlessly, while Laetus surveyed the white-faced guardsmen before him with satisfaction.

'So die all traitors! Their bodies will be cast out of the city for the carrion birds, and they will not be given any burial. Their spirits are doomed to wander the Earth for eternity, forbidden to enter the underworld! And any of you could share that fate, if you choose to disobey the commands of your emperor!'

He paused for a moment to allow the hard reality to sink in, before gesturing to Severus.

'And your emperor will now make his wishes clear to you!'

He turned and nodded a command to the senior centurion standing next to him, and the leathery-faced veteran bellowed a terse command.

'Fourteenth Gemina! Spears!'

The legionaries surrounding the praetorians moved as one, dropping their spear points from the parade rest into the fighting stance, and taking a step forward to present the closest of the guardsmen with a forest of iron blades all pointed squarely at their faces.

'Praetorians!'

All eyes turned to the waiting purple-clad figure, and Severus stared back at them for a long moment before speaking again. His voice was harsh, his tone derisive, and at his first words a collective shiver seemed to run through the assembled guardsmen, as his contempt for their actions was made clear.

'Centurions and tribunes of the guard, come forward!'

At the prearranged signal the praetorian officers marched forward and assembled before his rostrum with a line of armed soldiers between themselves and the emperor, and more men moving to separate them from their guardsmen. The praetorians stared wide-eyed, expecting, Marcus guessed, to see their leaders made into a bloody example of Severus's justice.

'You officers have been guilty of the crime of allowing your colleagues to indulge in the crimes of both regicide and a form of maiestas, diminution of the majesty of the Roman people, in their bearing of arms against the Roman state! It was your failure to lead them as required by your oaths of duty to the throne that resulted in the murder of an emperor and the disgraceful sale of the empire to the highest bidder. I could sentence you all to death without a second thought as to the legality of doing so!'

He stared hard at them for a moment, and Marcus wondered momentarily whether he intended to honour his offer of honourable discharge in return for the surrender of the fortress and its occupants. The guardsmen watched intently, some nudging their comrades in expectation of a swift and one-sided bloodbath.

'But you have obeyed my instructions to the letter, and so as agreed I dismiss you all, with honour, from this moment on. You may leave, and are free to remain within the city. Use the years that remain to you to reflect upon the mercy displayed to you today, and be careful never to come to the throne's attention in any way! Do not mistake this magnanimous act of mercy for any lack of resolve, or you will swiftly come to regret the error!'

The officers were directed to leave through a gap opened for them in the ring of soldiers, and Severus turned his attention to the men of the guard, who were, for the most part, looking relieved by their officers' escape from the harsh penalty that might well have been applied to them. But from the first word the emperor spoke to the remaining praetorians, it was apparent that he harboured no such merciful intentions towards them.

'You men of the guard swore an oath to protect your emperor! And it was not the oath of a man based on the frontier who will never see the emperor unless a campaign brings his master to the province in question, and only then from a distance! You swore the oath of men whose daily routine took them into the palace! Into his private quarters! It was the oath of men entrusted with the sacred duty of protecting the most important man in the world! You didn't just kill a man, you took your swords to the empire itself! And if that were not enough, you then sold the throne to the highest bidder, more like money-grubbing stallholders than guardians of the city's honour!'

He paused to allow that to sink in.

'You are no more worthy of Rome's trust than the most hostile of her enemies. And if you cannot be trusted, you can no longer occupy the role that has been yours since the days of the Divine Augustus!'

Severus gave the assembled guardsmen one last contemptuous stare and turned away, his bodyguard closing ranks behind him. A deathly silence fell across the parade ground as his words sank in and the implications of the ranks of spearmen surrounding them sank into the stunned cohorts. Scaurus turned in his saddle and smiled tightly at Marcus.

'I'd say that's a fair description of what they've done to the empire. Let's see how much they like what comes next.'

Laetus played a bleak smile across the dumbfounded praetorians.

'Former guardsmen, you are from this moment dismissed from your service. But not from your oath of loyalty to the emperor. You will be allowed to leave this place one man at a time, placing your daggers, your belts and your purses on the appropriate pile as you leave. You will leave the city immediately, without entering it for any reason. Further, you are also forbidden from coming within one hundred miles of Rome, on pain of instant execution without either trial or the right of appeal.'

He waited for a moment while the sickening nature of their fall from grace became all too obvious on the faces of the men staring back at him over the helmeted heads of his legionaries. Exiled from the city and stripped of their gold and the belts that marked them as soldiers, they were instantly reduced to penury, and fit only for manual labour far from their homes and families, whose fate would be equally uncertain.

'As many of you as possible will be subjected to a thorough search before you are allowed to leave, and any man found to be hiding gold anywhere about his person will be severely punished. Return what you stole from the empire and you will be allowed to leave without violence, and with your worthless lives intact. And be grateful that you have been spared that much!'

'You should have seen their faces, Imperator! It was sublime! I swear I could hear them grinding their teeth as they were forced to drop their purses and walk away. A few of them refused to surrender the trappings of their previous lives, and had to be forcibly stripped of their boots, belts and purses, which was of course all the excuse my men needed to give them a beating. And you'd be surprised at the number of them that tried to smuggle their gold away in the only obvious place!'

Laetus was sprawled on a couch in the palace of Domitian's massive triclinium, the formal dining area, overlooking the city. His place adjacent to Severus's own couch emphasised his place in the imperial retinue, the closest to the emperor of all of his personal circle who were present. Scaurus and Marcus were standing guard on the dinner party along with a dozen of the emperor's former legion bodyguards, men who had taken up the praetorians' weapons and armour to transform themselves into the guardsmen that the emperor had decreed would be their role henceforth.

'The most priceless moment was when one of their cavalrymen couldn't persuade his horse to stop following him away, and was forced to kill the beast with his dagger! For a moment I thought he'd realised that either the horse had to die or he did, but then he cut his own throat as well, he was so upset by the whole thing. I tell you, the looks on their faces!'

The two friends exchanged glances at this further proof of Laetus's brutal nature, but Severus simply nodded, unaffected by the story.

'I wish I could have stayed to enjoy their discomfiture, but I had more important tasks to be performing.'

'Quite so, Imperator.' Laetus dipped his head in recognition of his master's point. 'And the senate were appropriately respectful?'

Severus snorted.

'The senate were the usual nest of vipers. They'll do as they're told for the time being, but I know them all too well. They'll be at dinner in a dozen places this evening, all fixated on plotting. Some of them will be minded to follow me, for the time being at least, waiting to see how I fare against Niger and Albinus. After all, I have over half the empire's legions in my pocket, and Rome under my boot. That makes for decent odds, I'd say.'

Laetus nodded, all too well aware that his master's entry to the city had been one calculated to inspire fear and obedience in the populace no matter what their social rank was. Although he had changed out of his general's armour into a toga at the city's gate, and continued into Rome on foot, he had been accompanied by his entire army, legions and cavalry, with the former trailing the praetorians' standards in the dust in an unmistakable signal of their supremacy. At his command they had been quartered all over the city, in public buildings of all sorts including temples and shrines, and their overbearing behaviour and refusal to pay for produce and other goods taken from the city's merchants had inspired exactly the fear in the populace that he'd wanted to achieve.

'But you believe there will be those who choose otherwise?'

The emperor shrugged, with a knowing look.

'Of course. Niger is well supported among the plebs, and Albinus is a canny enough politician. They will both have their supporters, and of course they will know that I'll have to move on one of my two rivals soon enough. And so they'll bide their time, and wait for me to leave the city and take my praetorians with me, I'd imagine. In the meantime I'll do my best to disarm their urge to resist.'

'Oh?'

Severus raised a wry eyebrow at his general.

'I know, your choice in my place would be a good-sized purge to bring the gold in and put them in their place, but that's not my calculation. Not yet, at least. Tomorrow I will address the senate and I will assure them that there will be no such persecution.

Indeed I have it in mind to tell them that I will always consult with them before executing any of their number. I will also order a state funeral for Pertinax, to give the man the honour he deserves for his attempt to steer the empire back onto a straight course. And in doing so I will, incidentally, as will be noted by all sensible historians, link myself to the man's honesty and probity – and of course, indirectly to the man whose example he revered, Marcus Aurelius.'

'Clever of you, Imperator.'

Severus ignored the sycophantic comment.

'I need to chart a course through these next few months that will enable us to hold on to power while we put Niger in his place, which is to say communing with the spirits of his ancestors. Speaking of which, we need to start planning the campaign to dig him out of his hole in Antioch. Once we've got his head I'll make sure that's one city that won't forget its disrespect for a long time to come.'

'Disrespect, Imperator?'

Marcus wondered if he detected a slightly sardonic note in the question, but if Severus realised that the question was intended to draw him out on the subject, he was too eager to vent his irritation not to follow the cue.

'They were unwise enough to make sport of me in public when I was governor of Syria for a short time, after Pertinax's removal from the position several years ago. They knew I wouldn't be there any longer than it would take for a fast warship to deliver my successor, and they certainly made it clear that they didn't have any respect for a temporary role-holder. When we retake the city they're going to find out that the price for disrespect of a Roman legatus will make the fun they had with me all those years ago a very expensive pleasure indeed!'

He put his plate down and stood up, a signal that the meal was over.

'I've no appetite for poetry tonight. You can send the entertainers away, I'm going to have my first decent bath for a month and get to bed. Tomorrow after the morning acclamation we'll have an initial council to work out our next steps.' He shot a glance at the waiting praetorians. 'Make sure you're there, Rutilius Scaurus, you've earned your place in the room in the last few days. We might well have use of your campaigning skills in the months to come.'

4

'At least you get to see your uncle receive the decent funeral that he was denied at the time of his death.'

Scaurus nodded at Julius's sober sentiment, looking across the forum at the shrine that had been erected beneath the raised platform of the rostra, at the foot of the Capitoline Hill. Lavishly decorated with gold and ivory, it contained a funeral bier of equal opulence that housed a wax effigy of Pertinax dressed in the full ceremonial uniform of an emperor celebrating a triumph. The replica's facial features had been modelled so closely on those of the man whose life was to be celebrated that even he had to admit that it perfectly captured the dead emperor's likeness.

'I could wish that such extravagance was unnecessary, but I cannot fault the sentiment.'

The forum was packed with the men of the senate and their families, with hundreds of men from Severus's newly formed praetorian guard carefully arrayed to control the event. There was a large crowd of the usual hangers-on, rich members of the senatorial and equestrian classes and their clients, and the new prefect of the guard was taking no chances that one of their number might be an infiltrating assassin in the pay of either of the two factions rivalling the new ruling group.

At the sounding of a mournful horn note Severus led the senators forward, Cilo on one side and Laetus the other. The men in the crowd following them had their togas turned inside out to hide the purple edging that signified their rank, while the women were wearing suitably muted clothing and had only their wedding rings for jewellery, to signify mourning. A pair of guard centurions flanked the imperial party, alert for any sign of trouble and clearly ready to drop their silver-tipped vine sticks and draw their swords.

Severus knelt on one knee before the shrine for a long moment and the entire body of the senate emulated the gesture, although – as the result of prior discussion, Marcus suspected – they went down on both knees, as a gesture of respect to their fallen emperor. At length the emperor rose and approached the bier alone, spending some moments communing with the dead man's spirit before stepping back and turning to face the crowd, raising his voice to be heard above the inevitable susurration of whispered comments.

'Helvius Pertinax gave his life for Rome! And so we will show him the utmost respect for his sacrifice! I have taken his name, in his honour!'

'And not because it makes him look like some sort of avenger then?'

Julius smirked from his place in their line, maintaining the facade of his new rank as a praetorian centurion even while passing comment on the emperor's feigned grief.

'And now we honour our fallen brother, and praise him as a Roman hero whose murder has robbed the empire of a favoured son, a great man whose only desire was to lead his people to new glory! Let us send him to commune with the spirits of the emperors who have gone before him to the underworld, so that they may know the great honour he brought to the city!'

At another note from the horn, a parade of palace servants bearing the busts of great Romans from the republican and imperial past processed past the shrine.

'The divine Julius . . . the blessed Augustus . . . Vespasian . . . Trajan . . . Hadrian . . . Marcus Aurelius . . . they're bringing out all of the great men to welcome my uncle to the underworld, aren't they?'

Scaurus's muttered comment reached Julius, who snorted a mirthless laugh.

'Too soon for Commodus, though?'

'Give it time.' The tribune's gaze remained level, but his response was acerbic in tone. 'Severus is already talking about himself as Commodus's brother, so as to wrap himself in shared glory.'

The busts of famous men of the city and those of other countries were paraded past the shrine, followed by a salute by the massed legion cavalry in a none-too-subtle hint at Severus's military power, children rushing out with baskets to collect the dung dropped by the hundreds of horses as they passed. The lament was then delivered by a choir before the careful placing of funeral gifts at the bier's foot. With this the commemoration of Pertinax's life was declared to be complete all but for the eulogy, which Severus delivered at some length. Concluding his oration with the fervent wish that Pertinax's spirit might fly over the city like a majestic eagle, to look down on all the good work he had done in his short reign, Severus turned to the waiting priests and signalled that his address was complete.

'Is that it? My feet feel like they've swollen to twice their size just from standing here.'

Scaurus laughed at Dubnus's complaint.

'We're only just getting started.'

Deconstructing the shrine with swift, practised skill, the priests passed the bier to the waiting equestrian pall-bearers, who shouldered their burden and set off for the campus martius with emperor and senate following close behind. Some of the senators beat their breasts in a display of grief and shame that they had allowed so great a man to fall to an assassin's blade, while others played a haunting dirge on flutes, their music echoing from the stone buildings around them in a discordant wail that set Marcus's teeth on edge. On a piece of open ground close to the Mausoleum of Augustus a towering three-storey-high pyre had been built in readiness for the dead emperor's cremation, topped with a shining gilded chariot that Scaurus recognised as one which his uncle had used a couple of times during his short reign.

The bier and its accompanying funeral gifts were placed inside the pyre with impressive speed, Severus and the most notable dignitaries kissed the wax effigy, and then the year's consuls lowered lighted torches to the oil-soaked kindling carefully placed to have the structure ablaze in short order. As the first smoke rose, black and greasy from the burning oil, a man standing close to the familia pulled on a thick cord to perform the ceremony's last piece of showmanship. Freed from its cage inside the pyre, an eagle flapped free and climbed on the fire's first wave of heat, flying up into the clear sky before stooping down on a flock of doves conveniently released at the right moment.

Severus turned to the senators as the bird of prey tore down through the scattering birds, taking one in its claws and beating away across the river to consume it at leisure away from the pall of smoke rising from the pyre.

'You see! He is deified, and like an eagle his divine spirit descends to seek vengeance on those responsible for his death! He is telling me not to let his murder go unavenged, and all those who encouraged such a base act will not go unpunished!'

Scaurus nodded knowingly.

'See what he did there? He won't name his rival in public, but he just put Niger on trial in absentia and declared him guilty without any hesitation whatsoever. And all we have to do now is fight our way through six legions to bring the guilty man to justice.'

The Domitian palace's consilium was a good-sized room, but the number of Severus's senior officers who had been summoned to join his inner council meant that it was barely large enough to accommodate them all. Uncertain why the emperor had specifically invited them to attend, Scaurus and Marcus placed themselves by the room's door, where they could hope to go unnoticed, praetorian officers simply doing their duty. Marcus, recognising a familiar face across the room, directed Scaurus's attention to the newcomer.

'It turns out that Fabius Cilo read his future with great accuracy. He is indeed part of Severus's inner circle. I see he's even matched his beard to the emperor's favoured style.'

The senator had indeed made a change to more closely align with his master, his beard no longer one shaggy mass but oiled and combed to form two spiral-shaped clumps that fell from his chin. He met both men's eyes in turn, nodding his recognition in a slightly regal manner.

'Gentlemen!' The chief lictor called the meeting to order, casting an imperious gaze around the room until all conversation had ceased before nodding to the doorway, where his master was waiting. 'The emperor!'

Severus swept in, taking a seat at the head of the table and waving a hand for the council members to be seated. He waited for them to take their places before speaking.

'We are here to plan the military defeat of the pretender Pescennius Niger. So . . .' He looked around the table. 'Rossius Vitulus, you have control of the treasury for the expedition to the east. Are we in a good condition to prepare to march?'

'Indeed, Imperator. Donations from the senate have been brisk, under the encouragement of our new colleague Aquilius Felix.'

The emperor turned to the former centurion, who had been allocated a place closer to his own seat than might have been expected to be granted to a man of such apparent lowly status.

'You are to be congratulated, Felix. None of my former colleagues saw fit to decline the opportunity to fund a war against Niger, a man many of them secretly hoped would be their emperor?'

The centurion smiled, shaking his head.

'I simply suggested that they should each consider this very moment, Imperator, when you ask me which of them were forthcoming with their gold. I also invited them each to reflect on the disfavour they might experience for being the only man who failed to make a suitable donation to our shared cause. Given that every other man asked had of course been both swift and generous in his support.'

Severus smiled broadly.

'Ha! I presume you did the rounds of the men known to support me first?'

'Of course, Imperator. With a hundred senators and more already committed, it would have taken a brave man to be the first to decline. And of course we also have the significant amount of gold that was confiscated from the praetorians, which further fattens the purse available to you.'

'Very good. Very good indeed. I'll have other tasks for you, I expect.' Severus's attention shifted to his next associate. 'Fulvius Plautianus, what news do you have for us?'

Marcus and Scaurus exchanged a glance. Plautianus, the emperor's cousin and lifelong friend, elevated to the rank of praetorian prefect, was known to be totally ruthless. His reply confirmed his reputation.

'I have good news, Imperator! My agents have in the last week taken hostages from the families of several of Niger's leading supporters, including his general Asellius Aemilianus's sons. And last night we took the greatest prize of all, the pretender Niger's own children!'

'Excellent!' The emperor, who would already have heard such good news and planned this exchange to make the most of it in the meeting, clenched a fist and slammed it down on the council table with a resounding crash. 'That will give him pause for reflection as to the course he is taking! He can still step back from the brink of disaster, if he sees reason. But since Aemilianus had the nerve to imply that he might side with us for a time before throwing in with Niger, I will have his fucking head whether he surrenders or is taken alive!'

He turned to Cilo, who drew himself up in his seat in anticipation of some sort of honour for his part in the events that had seen Severus ascend to the throne.

'You, Fabius Cilo, have been a stalwart of my cause. You managed to guide Commodus's corpse to a safe and dignified burial thanks to your membership of the priesthood of Hadrianus, and you were instrumental in making sure that my sons evaded any threat of capture by the agents of the usurper who throng the city. And with my own sons safe, while we now have such powerful

hostages we have the decisive advantage if the need should arise
for such leverage. And that is before we come to your masterful
handling of the senate, keeping them quiescent while we entered
the city and took control. I shall issue a proclamation that from
now on you are to be titled Comes Imperatoris!'

Cilo bowed his head in recognition of the compliment.

'I am honoured to a greater degree than any deed of mine has
earned, but I will endeavour to earn the title of Companion of the
Emperor, and will always be at your service, Imperator.'

Severus inclined his head fractionally in acceptance of his lieutenant's vow of loyalty, then looked around the table at the other
members of the council.

'So, gentlemen, we have the gold we need to go to war. And we
have the advantage over Niger that we can exert familial pressure
on both the pretender himself and his leading general, who is also
the most eminent man supporting his doomed bid for the throne.
And Albinus's army in Britannia has been neutralised by the simple and cheap expedient of giving him the meaningless title of
Caesar. Let that fool believe he will inherit the throne when I die
for as long as he stays gullible, and we will have all the time we
need to settle matters in the east before turning on him at our leisure. All we need to do now is to decide how to go about defeating
Niger!'

Julius Laetus, having not yet been consulted, clearly felt it was
his place to have an opinion.

'Imperator, I—'

But if the emperor heard him start speaking, he showed no signs
of recognising his lieutenant.

'And so this is what I have decided!'

He looked at Cilo, who stiffened in his chair in anticipation of
his reward.

'The latest reports from our spies in Antioch tell us that the
usurper plans to cross the straits of the Propontis, and secure
them from being crossed by our armies. He will of course occupy
and fortify Byzantium, with the plan of using it as the anvil on

which to swing the hammer of his army, if we are foolish enough to commit to a full siege. And so while we will march east deliberately and in strength, an advance guard of a single legion will be thrown ahead of our main force with all possible speed, to disrupt his preparations.'

Laetus's face took on the beginnings of a guarded smile at the news that a legion was to have the honour of leading the army against Niger, with the expectation that it must surely be his own Fourteenth Gemina. But his satisfaction was short-lived. Severus continued, his face a hard, expressionless mask.

'The legion I have chosen for so distinguished a task will be the Fourth Flavia Felix, whose legionaries arrived some days ago from Singidunum. And I have decided that as his reward for securing my children from the usurper's agents, and making clear to his fellow senators that there was nothing to be gained in resisting my procession to the throne and much to be lost . . .' He paused, and the colour seemed to drain from Cilo' s face. 'I name Lucius Fabius Cilo as their legatus! He will lead the Fourth Legion into battle in my name, and frustrate our enemies' designs by forcing them to deal with an attack much sooner than they will have expected!'

Laetus's smile faded, but in his eyes Marcus wondered if he could see a hint of relief. A legion recently arrived after a fifty-day march from the province of Moesia would be less than happy to be turned around and marched back in the other direction without a lengthy rest, and a chance to enjoy all that Rome had to offer that the other legions from the Danubius were already enjoying. Severus looked around the table, as if challenging all present with the task of managing such a difficult situation. From the studied neutrality of his expression, Cilo was far from satisfied with the emperor's decision, but also knew there was no good way to challenge him on it. The senator inclined his head with grave dignity.

'I thank you for your trust, Imperator. Neither myself nor my legion will let you down.'

'I know that only too well, Lucius.' Severus smiled thinly. 'And now to discuss the disposition of our main army.'

Laetus's look of dissatisfaction smoothed over in an instant, in clear anticipation of some reward for his part in the triumphant march of the Pannonian legions from Carnuntum, but the emperor turned to another man at the table with his next edict.

'Tiberius Claudius Candidus, you will in turn take command of the province of Pannonia's four legions and their supporting auxiliaries.'

Scaurus snorted soft amusement.

'That's every legion that marched south with him. No pressure then.'

Severus stood and walked around the table to where Candidus had been sitting quietly and with the look of a man who was comfortable in his role as one of Severus's legion legates.

'You will form them into an army that we will call the exercitus Illyricus, and your title will be Dux Exercitus Illyrici. While other legions pin our enemy in place, your army will be the hammer we use to break his strength!'

The newly promoted Candidus looked surprised for a moment, then got quickly to his feet and saluted.

'As you command, Imperator, so I will deliver it!'

'I know you will, Legatus Augustus. And now, let us consider the map, and discuss the details of how we will take this war to the pretender's front door!'

Any amusement that Scaurus might have felt at the predicament into which Cilo found himself unexpectedly pitched was swiftly extinguished by Severus's parting comments to the Fourth Flavia Felix's new legatus, as the meeting of his consilium drew to a close. Cilo bowed, repeated the gratitude he was probably far from feeling at his new command, and was making his way from the room when the emperor called to him, having waited until he had reached the door, where Scaurus and Marcus were standing.

'Oh, and Lucius?'

The senator turned back, his face already carefully composed.

'Imperator?'

'It is how long since you commanded a legion? Fifteen years?'

Cilo conceded the point with a small nod.

'Almost, Imperator. I commanded Fourteenth Flavia Firma before becoming your neighbour as the governor of Gallia Narbonensis.'

If the reminder of their joint status as provincial governors a decade before was intended to make the point that a legion command was beneath his expectations, it evidently failed to have any impact on the emperor's chain of thought.

'In Syria, as I recall?'

'Indeed, Imperator.'

'A Syrian legion, with all that implies.'

From the look on his face, Cilo was only too well aware of the reputation for indolence and indulgence that the eastern legions had among the army of the empire's western provinces. While not necessarily based on fact, the cultural differences between the two ends of the Middle Sea were mercilessly exploited by the western armies whenever the opportunity provided itself. The clear if unspoken implication being that he would have learned little of the art of war from such a soft posting.

Severus smiled indulgently, flicking a glance at Scaurus.

'Given that lengthy gap since your last military experience, and the nature of your last command, I have decided to provide you with some officers whose experience of commanding eastern legions in combat is more recent. Rutilius Scaurus!'

Scaurus snapped to attention, already quite sure of what it was the emperor intended.

'Imperator!'

Severus walked across the consilium chamber until they were eye to eye.

'I chose you to be the messenger I sent to Fabius Cilo for two reasons. Can you guess what they were?'

'Assuming that neither of them was based on the trust of long experience, Imperator . . .' Realising that he might well be on thin ice, he pressed on swiftly. 'I would imagine that you wanted to send in a man who wouldn't be afraid to confront the praetorians, or to execute Julianus for that matter. That would be one of the reasons I assumed was behind the honour of your selecting me for the task.'

Severus nodded slowly.

'Perceptive *and* ruthlessly honest. And the other reason?'

'I did not see it until you asked the question, Imperator. You wish me to accompany the legatus to the east with his new command, and to assist him in bending to his will a legion that may well be resistant to making the return journey so soon.'

Severus nodded, his eyes on the younger man.

'I see that you are indeed a man to watch. If you manage to survive the next few months, that is. You do understand the Fourth Legion's proposed role, as Niger and I jockey for position at the gateway to Asia?'

'I do, Imperator.' Scaurus looked the emperor in the eyes, unafraid of any implied challenge. 'You wish the exercitus Illyricus to have as much time as it needs to come to full fighting strength. Four fully manned legions and their auxiliaries make for a brutally powerful hammer, if swung at the right moment. And when that blow falls you want it to be composed of forty thousand men who are as hard as iron. Which means that Claudius Candidus will need time to bring them to peak condition.'

'As I said' – Severus regarded him levelly, his expression unreadable – 'you are an intelligent and, I hear, a resourceful man. Exactly the right person to assist my old ally Lucius in what, from some perspectives, could seem to be something of a suicide mission. Sending a single legion against the entire strength of the east could easily end in disaster, even if it will indeed provide us with enough time to ready our main force.' He swept both men with the same hard stare. 'As the Spartan women used to say to their husbands and sons, gentlemen, come back with your shields or on them! You have the chance to write a glorious chapter in the Fourth Legion's history, or to bring lasting disappointment upon its name. In the event of the outcome being the latter, I'd suggest that neither of you comes back.'

*

An hour later, having left the palace and made their way through the crowded streets, made doubly busy by the number of soldiers wandering the city, apparently still adapting to the astonishing size and scale of Rome's seemingly endless streets, the familia were approaching the Viminal Gate.

'Look at them, wide-eyed and clueless!'

Dubnus nudged Arminius in the ribs, indicating a tent party of legionaries who had just come through the gate and were standing staring down the Vicus Patricius with the look of men who were struggling to adjust to its grandeur.

'Poor bastards.' The German shook his head dismissively. 'They've been expecting to find the streets paved with gold cobbles and all they've found is a fresh coating of shit. Like getting a beautiful woman into bed only to discover that her tits are nothing but padding and her teeth began their life sticking out of an elephant's face.' He breathed in deeply. 'Although to be fair, they have been lucky enough to smell her delicate perfume.'

'What, that subtle combination of horseshit, slaughterhouse blood and dead dog?'

Arminius nodded cheerfully.

'That's the one. It's no wonder the emperors all wear perfume.'

Morban spoke up from behind him.

'I'll wager two for one that this emperor doesn't use the stuff. A brisk rub under his armpits with some rough soap and a chin-scrape with a dagger will be enough for a man like that!'

'Not a chance.' Dubnus half turned to send the former standard-bearer a disparaging glance. 'Once that gang of plucked and painted hermaphrodites that run the palace get hold of him they'll have him smelling like a cross between a rose bush and a whore's crotch scarf before he's had time to realise what they're about.'

Walking a few paces behind the squabbling soldiers with Scaurus and Marcus, Cilo was still bemoaning his recent downturn in fortunes, as he perceived it.

'Did you know Severus was going to give me this poisoned cup to drink from?'

Scaurus looked at him before replying, a note of disbelief in his voice.

'A legion command, Legatus? Poisoned?'

The senator raised a jaundiced eyebrow at the younger man.

'Don't pretend you don't know what I mean, Rutilius Scaurus. I would have been better off with a pat on the back and the suggestion that I might return to my position as an influential member of the senate. A position of honour suited to a man of my age and seniority, membership of the Arval Brothers, perhaps, or something equally prestigious requiring no real effort and posing no significant risk. I thought my soldiering days were long behind me.'

'Instead of which you find yourself with the unenviable task of having to take a legion of unknown capabilities all the way to Thrace, and from there more or less straight into battle. I do see your point.'

'But what am I to do?'

Scaurus shook his head in feigned incomprehension at the senator's question.

'You can only obey the emperor's orders, surely?'

Cilo's anger flashed to the surface of his previous careful composure.

'That's easy for *you* to say, Tribune! You are the hero of any number of battles against the odds, I believe? Whereas my own military service was sadly lacking in any such opportunity for glory. And while I would have welcomed the opportunity as a younger man, I am no longer sufficiently . . .'

'Foolish?'

Cilo caught the sardonic note in the younger man's voice.

'Enthusiastic, shall we say?' Scaurus allowed the following silence to lengthen until Cilo had no choice but to be the first to speak. 'But now I'm just an ageing politician. Without the first idea as to how to go about this job that Severus has dumped on me as the reward for my loyalty. Or any appetite for it. Which is presumably why he . . .'

'Dumped me on you as well?'

'Putting it a little harshly, perhaps, yes. You were born for this.' Scaurus nodded.

'I can see your point. And I am willing to assist you in more ways than a mere tribune would usually dare to suggest. But this only works one way. You have to delegate your authority to me *completely*. There can be no picking and choosing which of my commands you decide to approve.'

Cilo laughed softly.

'And if I agree to that condition and then renege on the agreement, if the moment comes when I believe your decisions will get us all killed?'

'Then you, Legatus, will be the first of us across the river to the underworld. We will be alone, without any support for hundreds of miles, and that means that if we are to survive we'll have to be both cunning and lucky. If you make any attempt to undermine my orders that I believe will get men killed unnecessarily, then I will have no choice but to kill you and take formal command, be under no illusions. It's your choice. I'll run your legion for you, and discharge the emperor's orders the best way I know how, but in return you will make it my legion in all but name. You may take this offer or leave it, as you see fit. But either accept the offer with a full understanding of its conditions, or reject it and find your own path to death or glory.'

Their legion's camp was at the far end of the legions' encampment, the Fourth having arrived last, furthest from the river, and Marcus was interested to see the condition of the legionaries through whom they were walking to reach it. Men were sprawled on the ground around their tents, many of them apparently the worse for wear after the previous night's alcoholic and sexual heroics.

'This all looks very relaxed. They seem to be spending the emperor's gold in anticipation of actually receiving it.'

Julius laughed acerbically.

'That's putting it mildly. They look like they wouldn't put up a decent fight against a gang of twelve-year-olds, never mind Niger's legions.'

As if to underline his point, a white-faced legionary staggered out of his tent and vomited copiously across the grass beside it, drawing a chorus of abuse from the men around him, more than one of whom looked as if they were hovering on the edge of following his example.

'Your new command isn't going to be in any better condition than these animals.' Scaurus looked at Cilo with an uncompromising expression. 'And they're not going to want to go to war having only just arrived, especially with the Pannonian legions showing no signs of moving *and* half their number having just been turned into guardsmen with all the benefits that will bring them. Which means that we're going to have to be somewhat brutal with our boys.'

'And?'

'And, Legatus, it's a long way from Rome to Thrace. Any commander willing to beast the poor fools back onto the road is going to be nobody's favourite. You've been commanded to put your head into the lion's mouth. Now do you see why I'm only willing to take this task on if I have complete freedom of action?'

They had reached the Fourth's praetorium, a cluster of headquarters tents that had been erected in a somewhat haphazard manner without any apparent regard to the usual military fixation with neatness and order. There were no sentries to be seen, only a few men sitting around and eyeing up the newcomers with little interest and what appeared to be a good deal of quiet derision.

'Right, there it is. Your new command. And it's time to decide – how do you want to do this?'

Cilo nodded briskly, looking almost as queasy as the soldiers they had passed earlier.

'They're all yours, Tribune.'

'*Senior* Tribune. You will always address me as Senior Tribune, and my centurion here' – he beckoned Julius to his side – 'as First Spear.'

The senator frowned.

'But surely the legion will already have a senior centurion.'

Scaurus smiled thinly.

'He's not much in evidence, is he?' He turned to the waiting Briton. 'All yours.'

Julius looked over at the grinning legionaries, who were assuming from his uniform that he was a praetorian.

'What happens if I break one or two of them?'

Scaurus shrugged.

'We'll have to get some more to replace them. But try not to break too many, eh?'

The Briton nodded, starting forward with his face set in an intimidating scowl.

'You want a hand with that?'

He looked back at Dubnus, who was grinning at him knowingly, then turned back with a nod.

'Actually, you could help me. Hold this, will you?' He passed the disgusted Briton his vitis. 'In case I need to use both hands for a spot of vigorous disciplining. I'll let you know if I need anything else. For the time being just do what you do best.'

'Which is?'

'Fuck all, obviously.'

He strode across to the legionaries, who promptly stopped their sniggering and tried to put on an approximation of solemnity.

'Right, who's first?'

The biggest and most self-assured of the soldiers was the first to speak.

'First for what, Praetorian?'

'Well volunteered!'

The big man reached down and took a handful of the speaker's tunic as he replied, effortlessly pulling him to his feet and then punching him hard in the gut and dropping him retching to the ground.

'Who's next?'

One of the choking soldier's comrades, still taking Julius for the praetorian his equipment indicated he was, decided that he wasn't going to wait to receive the same treatment.

'What the f—'

Pivoting at the waist, Julius delivered a powerful uppercut to the chin of the speaker as he was scrambling up, lifting him off his feet and sending him reeling back onto their tent, which collapsed under his weight. The remaining three soldiers backed away, casting nervous glances at the Briton's first victim, who was showing no signs of getting off the ground.

'I can keep doing this all afternoon, and if I get bored there's always that big oaf over there to take over from me!'

'Oi!'

Ignoring Dubnus's protest, he held a hand out for his vine stick. Having received it, he stepped forward, considering the soldiers predatorily.

'I am a centurion! So the next man not to use my title and show some fucking respect will be getting the same treatment as they did!'

Realising their mistake, the three men came to a sloppy attention, while Julius examined his knuckles.

'The second bastard had a nasty pointed chin.' He gestured to the headquarters tent. 'Shall we, gentlemen? If I find their eagle unguarded I swear I'm going to kill someone.'

Scaurus stepped forward and gently pushed him to one side.

'In which case it'll be better if I'm the man to make that discovery. Far better for a tribune to administer that sort of justice than a centurion, wouldn't you say?'

Julius nodded and gestured to the tent's open flap.

'After you, *Senior* Tribune.'

Scaurus stepped into the tent to find a centurion standing at the parade rest in front of the legion's sacred eagle standard, four other officers standing behind him guarding the legion's pay chests. He was bare-headed, his immaculately polished helmet at his feet, and his hair was clipped close to his skull to reveal a scalp that was scored by a long white scar.

'Centurion.'

The officers snapped to attention at the sight of a tribune's polished bronze armour.

'Sir! We will do what is ordered, and at every command we will be ready!'

'Good man. You can start by telling me why it is that you seem to be the only officers in the camp, and why you're the ones standing guard on the most sacred symbol of the trust the empire places in your legion?'

The centurion's answer was clear and straightforward, and delivered with a level gaze that did him credit, under the circumstances.

'When the legatus and his tribunes decided to abandon us and go off to their homes in the city the other centurions mostly wanted to follow them into Rome, none of them ever having seen it before. The few of us with more sense decided to stay and guard the praetorium, to keep the eagle and the pay chests safe.'

Scaurus inclined his head in respect.

'Understood. And you have the thanks of your new legatus for such devotion to duty.'

'Begging your pardon, Tribune, but who—'

Scaurus shook his head.

'You'll find out in due course. In the meantime you can leave us to take your place while you go and gather the legion's centurions. All of them.'

'Ah . . . they're . . .'

'In the city, I know. And before you try to tell me that they have permission to be off duty, their new legatus has just rescinded it. So if you need something to motivate them with, just spread the word that any man not back in camp by nightfall who doesn't have proof of prior formal permission to leave the camp will be reduced to the rank of legionary. Other than yourselves that is, because I suspect you'll be hunting them down well after dark. Off you go.'

The officer saluted, and fell back on the legions' customary expression of obedience once more.

'Yes, Tribune! We will do what is ordered, and at every command we will be ready!'

He picked up his helmet and went to leave, but Marcus smiled and raised a hand to halt his departure for a moment.

'What's your name, Centurion?'

'Justus, Tribune.'

'Well met, Justus. Tell me, before you leave, what was it that put the scar across your head?'

The centurion smiled wanly.

'A spear, Tribune. I didn't have time to find my helmet when the Germans attacked our camp in the middle of the night, and I didn't quite manage to duck in time.'

'You can forget my formal title, Justus, we are all warriors here. And the man behind the spear?'

'Sleeps in the German mud.'

Marcus nodded, stepping out of his way.

'Not many of your men remember the Germanic Wars, I'd imagine?'

'Fewer every year.'

'And with every year standards slip away just a little?'

Justus nodded.

'I can't deny that. And with every year I look forward to completing my twenty-five a little more.'

Marcus smiled slowly.

'In that case I have some good news for you. This legion is now under new management. And the management in question doesn't consider that sort of backsliding acceptable. Feel free to warn your fellow officers . . . not that it'll make much difference, I expect.'

The Fourth's former legatus walked into the camp shortly before nightfall, messengers sent to his house on the Quirinal Hill, high above the city's stinking slums, having delivered a letter from Cilo suggesting his return.

'Lucius Fabius Cilo! Of all the people I'd have expected to be replaced by, you have to be just about the least likely! Surely you must have hoped for something a little less . . .' He smiled, clearly not at all put out at losing his command and if anything simply amused, '. . . demanding?'

Cilo inclined his head in recognition of his fellow senator's point.

'You're right, of course, colleague. You can only imagine my own surprise when the emperor decided to hand me this duty. But a man has to do his part for the empire, does he not? It's a bit of a lucky escape for you though, isn't it?'

His fellow senator had the good grace to look rueful.

'I can't deny that being retired to enjoy the comforts of my home will make a pleasant change from life on the frontier.' He shot a glance at the ranks of centurions gathered on the open space in front of the praetorium, thirty or so of the legion detachment's forty officers having already returned, still dressed in their tunics, boots and belts and all, crucially, unarmed. Their first spear was standing in front of them, his expression best described as combative, clearly waiting for an opportunity to vent his spleen on someone. 'And I won't miss them either. You might not be aware of it, but I was a tribune with the Sixth Victrix in Britannia ten years ago, so I know what a well-commanded legion looks like. And, despite all my encouragement, this is not what I'd call a well-commanded legion. Your first spear in particular is a man best described as venal. Not to mention lazy, which is worse.'

Scaurus, who had been listening, broke into their discussion with the ease of a man who knew that he was going to have to clean up the outgoing officer's mess.

'Forgive the bluntness of my question, Legatus, but could you not simply have replaced your legion's first spear with a more suitable man? After all, the fish usually rots from the head down . . .'

Shooting a hard stare at his supposed junior, the senator was clearly disquieted to find himself already the recipient of an equally uncompromising regard in return. Cilo spoke into the silence, an amused note in his voice.

'I should introduce Gaius Rutilius Scaurus. He is a veteran of Britannia, Dacia, Parthia . . . I could go on, but I suspect you'll be familiar with the name. And he's been appointed by the emperor to provide me with the appropriate guidance to avoid getting my legion destroyed in its first battle.'

Scaurus smiled tightly.

'Which means, Senator, that while you might like to have me beaten for my insolence, you're in no position to do any such thing. And I'll repeat my question – why not simply end the career of the one man in a position to make improvements but failing to do so, and put a better candidate in his place?'

The other man laughed tersely.

'The garrison legions can be a law unto themselves, Tribune. If I'd retired dear old Festus there I'd have had another man just like him proposed as his replacement by the legion's centurionate, with some not-so-subtle hints that failure to agree to his promotion wouldn't be "popular with the men". And since the centurions control the legionaries, I have no doubt the threat was an effective one, in a roundabout manner.'

Scaurus nodded knowingly.

'Ah. So *that's* the way it is. Thank you for the clarity, Senator.'

He waited for the niceties of the handover of command to be completed, and the outgoing legatus to make his way back towards the city, before issuing the command the men standing around the group of officers were waiting for.

'Light the torches!'

With sunset close, and the sky already turning purple in the east, an alternative form of illumination had been organised, dozens of torches ringing the impromptu parade ground, and at Scaurus's command they were lit. Calling for silence, and waiting patiently until the hubbub of commands and the bustle of his order being obeyed had died away, he addressed the surly group.

'Centurions of the Fourth Legion, I am Senior Tribune Gaius Rutilius Scaurus. As of today your legion has a new commander, Lucius Fabius Cilo! The emperor has thanked your former legatus for his service and excused him from further service! Why has he done this at this time, you might well be wondering? The answer is simple: we will be marching for the east at dawn the day after tomorrow, acting as the vanguard legion . . .'

He stopped speaking as a growing grumble of discontent reached his ears, and waited in silence until it died away, the assembled officers realising that he was staring at them in silent disgust.

'Gentlemen, the next man to open his mouth unless I invite him to speak will be disciplined! If you can't behave like officers then you will be treated like common legionaries. *Harshly!*' He nodded to Julius, who signalled Dubnus to step forward, flanked by his hulking axemen. 'Now, where was I before I was so unwisely interrupted? Ah yes, we will be marching east as the emperor's vanguard legion! The Fourth will have the honour, indeed the privilege, of being the first men into battle against the pretender Niger's eastern legions!'

He paused, waiting for any response, while Dubnus and his men scanned the centurions' ranks with open hostility.

'Does nobody have anything to say? No expressions of zealous delight at the emperor's faith in you? No? Very well, let's get down to business then!'

He walked up to the scowling first spear and looked the man in the eye.

'First Spear Festus, is it?'

The senior centurion, seeing the opportunity to vent his frustration, nodded furiously.

'Yes, Tribune! And I must complain in the strongest of terms about the way—'

Scaurus raised a hand to silence him, putting his open palm within inches of the discomfited centurion's face.

'I'll stop you there, Festus.'

His expression was unchanged, but even though he spoke quietly his voice had taken on a frosty note that left the centurion facing him under no illusions as to the state of his temper.

'I asked you a question, which you answered adequately. When I want you to comment further, I'll ask you to do so. Understood?'

Festus's jaw rippled with his efforts to keep his temper under control.

'Yes. Tribune.'

'That's Senior Tribune to you, First Spear. And just in case you've forgotten how a legion's command structure works, I'm the one who tells you what to do.' Scaurus stepped in closer, putting his face within inches of the older man's, wrinkling his nose at the stink of wine on his breath. 'If I order you to take your own life, your only question of me should be whether I want you to cut your own throat or just fall on your sword. Understood?'

The senior centurion nodded, his bluster seemingly having evaporated.

'Yes, Senior Tribune.'

'Good. You do retain at least a rudimentary grasp of discipline then. And yet that doesn't seem to extend to your control of your men, does it? I ordered your officers to be back in camp by nightfall, and yet a good quarter of them aren't to be seen. I presume they all have official leave to be absent, recorded in the daily orders?'

Festus frowned.

'The daily orders?'

'The daily orders, *Senior Tribune*. Don't make me remind you again. It is usual, indeed it is mandated under imperial military regulations, that no man should be allowed to leave the legion's camp or body of march without formal permission, recorded in writing by the legion clerks. If you want to send men to hunt wild beasts it has to be recorded. If you allow a man to go home to visit his family, it has to be recorded. And, First Spear, if you decide to allow your men to go drinking and whoring in Rome, it has to be recorded! So tell me, where are those records?'

The senior centurion, unwisely, chose to make attack his defence.

'If I had been allowed access to the administrative tent I—'

'You would have retrospectively written up the permissions required for thirty-four of your forty officers to be absent without record?'

'What?'

Scaurus leaned in closely, almost whispering in the senior centurion's ear.

'You have two choices right now, Festus. One is to continue to lie and bluster, and to deny the obvious truth that you have allowed the men behind you to absent themselves without any hint of control. Which, given the evidence to the contrary, will see you summarily tried, sentenced and executed. The other is to admit to your error, making your officers' lack of cooperation with your commands not to leave their duties without permission very clear, at which point I'd imagine I can persuade Legatus Cilo to reach a reasonable conclusion as to a more lenient penalty. Your choice.'

He straightened up, and raised his voice to be heard by all.

'First Spear Festus, would you like to say anything before I ask the legion clerks to show me the evidence as to whether you and your centurions had formal permission to leave the camp?'

The senior centurion dithered for a moment, saw the absolute certainty in Scaurus's eyes, and decided not to gamble.

'Senior Tribune, I have to report a gross lapse in discipline. In the absence of our legatus, who had ridden into the city with his staff officers, I allowed my centurions to leave the camp without formally recording their names and expected dates of return. I would have insisted that they go through the correct procedure, but they were all in too much of a hurry to listen to me.'

The men behind him were shaking their heads in disbelief, but as the first voices were raised in protest Scaurus roared a command at them that made Festus flinch, such was its ferocity.

'Be! *Quiet!* The next men to so much as breathe loudly can have an advance taste of the scourge!'

He turned back to the first spear.

'Do continue.'

The abashed senior centurion shook his head, his eyes fixed on the ground.

'There's nothing more to say, Tribune, sir. I know that I was weak, but they didn't allow me to do the right thing!'

One of the men behind him stepped forward, bunching his fists, his face contorted with rage.

'You fucking liar! You fucked off into the city and left the rest of us to—'

Dubnus stepped in and punched him to the ground, putting a hand on his dagger to forestall any action by the fallen centurion's comrades. Scaurus shook his head in disgust.

'A gross breach of discipline! Take him away, give him a dozen lashes and then bring him back for sentencing along with the rest of them!'

Dubnus signalled to two of his axemen, who stepped in and effortlessly hauled the dizzied officer to his feet, dragging him away with his boots scraping across the grass. His fellow centurions stared at each other in dismay as the realisation that they were in deep trouble sank in. Scaurus turned back to the first spear.

'First Spear Festus, you have by your own admission been guilty of a quite astonishing breach of imperial regulations. Your failure to control your mutinous officers resulted in the legion's camp being abandoned by all but a very small number of loyal officers, without whose presence the legion's eagle would have been left unprotected along with the pay chests. I will now consult with the legion's new legatus to decide upon your fate, and that of the men you command.'

He walked back to join Cilo, beckoning Julius to join them.

'If we're going to do this then it has to be done hard and fast. There are no half-measures possible with undisciplined animals like those, we have to dig out all of the rot or it will continue to fester and poison the legion. And I don't want to wake up with some disaffected officer's dagger in my guts. So here's what I've decided you need to order.'

'You want what, Grandad?'

The prefect in charge of the main armoury looked down at Morban with an expression that combined superiority with disdain for such an obviously lesser mortal. The brick-built warehouse and the workshops that supplied its contents were a sprawling hive of activity, with cartloads of wood and iron being delivered to feed into the production of swords, spears, knives and other staple items of a legionary's fighting kit. Having waited in line until several other officers, all centurions, had spoken with the prefect and left, seemingly empty-handed, the former standard-bearer had made his opening gambit, ignoring the other man's dismissive tone and replying with a single word.

'Spears.'

Marcus was reasonably sure that without his own forbidding presence and that of a grinning Arminius behind Morban, the Briton would already have been ejected from the prefect's office. The wooden-walled space was just big enough for a chair and desk, and its windows looked out onto the warehouse's racks of weaponry intended for the equipping of the empire's new soldiers.

'You want spears, do you? Even assuming that letter of authority is genuine . . .' He raised a hand to point at the scroll on his desk, and seemed to be about to cast doubt on its authenticity when something in Marcus's face changed his mind. 'Look, we just don't have any spare equipment. Haven't you heard, every legion from the northern frontier is in town to put a new man on the throne, and every one of them is now recruiting for a war in the east against another man that wants to take his place!'

Marcus decided to assist in moving the discussion on to the point at which Morban's skills would be of more value in dealing with the man with whom they needed to do business.

'And every new recruit needs to be equipped, right?'

'Exactly, Tribune! Every bloody legion legatus thinks that all he has to do is send a shit-kicking centurion down here to hold my feet to the fire and I'll just cough up the equipment they need out of thin air. Helmets and armour and swords and shields and boots and tunics and cloaks and cooking pots and—'

'Spears?'

'Yes! And spears! Two spears per man and some more to replace the ones the stupid bastards managed to bend so badly that they can't be thrown any more! And they think all they have to do is sign for them so that the palace can accept the expenditure, and that's all it takes! I've had legates in here telling me that if they don't get what they want then they'll report me to Severus, like that's going to magic the kit they want out of thin air!'

Morban smiled knowingly, picking up the thread of what the prefect hadn't yet realised was a negotiation.

'And if you offer them auxiliary equipment they don't take the disappointment well, am I right?'

'Oh, it's not the legates, they wouldn't know the difference between a legion spear and their own pink asparagus. It's the blasted centurions!' He affected the deep and slightly stupid-sounding voice of an imaginary centurion. 'The legion-issue pilum must have shanked iron heads of no less than a foot long from the wooden shaft. The purpose of this design is to improve penetration and also make the spear harder to remove from a shield once it's been thrown. The spears you are offering us do not have shanked heads, but are just spearheads riveted to wooden shafts, which are not fit for legion use! Issue me my legion pila and be quick about it!'

He shook his head in disgust.

'I've got thousands of perfectly good spears, properly made wooden-shafted hastae with foot-long blades, evil things that'll stop a charging horse, but will they take them? Will they buggery!'

Morban grinned up at him.

'So a load of proper German-made legion pila might be of interest to you?'

The prefect's eyes narrowed.

'How many and where did you steal them from? I haven't got any use for anything that can be traced back to the original owner, because it's honey-cakes-to-gold-coin odds that the original owner will come for replacements and realise that I'm trying to sell them their own property!'

The Briton shook his head with a serious expression.

'No, these are the property of the legatus who's authorised me to sell them to you. Eight thousand, three hundred and fifty-seven iron-shanked legion-issued pila, which you can have straight away. For the right price.'

'You want me to sell me your legion's spears? Has your legatus gone completely mad? What are you going to do when you get into battle?'

Morban grinned insouciantly.

'I'm not going to do anything, because I won't be there. But this one behind me and his ugly barbarian mate will be, commanding men equipped with the wooden-shafted hastae that you're going to give me as part of the deal.'

The prefect shook his head in disbelief.

'*Part* of the deal? You think I'm going to give you my hastae and then pay you for your pila? Not a chance! At the very best I'll do an exchange, and even then I'll want to sort the pila by quality, weed out the bad ones—'

'Very well.' Morban turned and walked away, beckoning Marcus to follow him. 'We'll sell them to your competition and then you can deal with them instead.'

'Wait! What competition?'

Morban winked at Marcus and turned back to face the prefect.

'What, you think you're the only buyer of spears on the market?'

The officer contorted his face in disbelief.

'Of course I'm the only buyer of spears! Who else is going to be interested in them?'

The Briton shook his head.

'Under normal circumstances you'd be right. But these aren't normal times, are they? Everybody wants pila, and you don't have any! Which means they're not just pila, they're a commodity! I can sell my eight thousand, three hundred and fifty-seven pila to someone who sees them as an investment and who'll give me a good price to own them now, while demand is high. And you, you'll be left to deal with the imperial officers who'll come to see why you don't have the pila that the centurions all want! After all, you'll have taken the money required to get them made, and this emperor is that very dangerous thing, a man with a short temper, an eye for the detail and a liking for an exemplary execution. They'll go over your accounts like ticks settling in for the summer, and if there's anything wrong with the way you've been doing business, they'll find it alright. Good luck!'

'But selling imperial weapons is an offence punishable by death!'

Morban shrugged.

'I didn't give you a name. Which means that I can inform on you for cheating the army and you can't lay a finger on me! I'll just sell my spears to my friend Petrus the Greek and you can buy from him at whatever inflated rate he fancies, when you realise that having some pila is the only way to give the legions what they want and keep the palace off your back.'

The prefect shook his head with a sick expression.

'How many hastae do you want?'

Morban smiled.

'Four thousand, five hundred.'

'What, you're going to re-equip a whole legion with second-rate spears?'

Marcus shook his head.

'They're only second-rate if you don't know how to use them.'

'And what do you want for the pila?'

Morban shrugged.

'Shall we say one aureus apiece for every ten?'

'Two and a half denarii each?'

'We could make it one aureus for nine. Or even eight. You choose.'

5

The legion's officers waited as Julius strode briskly through the camp towards their tight group at the column's head, his vine stick beating out a marching rhythm only he could hear against his right calf. The Fourth's legionaries were standing in the march formation with their new and unfamiliar hastae over their shoulders. Each tent party was waiting in the empty spaces where their tents had been pitched, ready to move out one at a time in a precise sequence that would put the entire legion detachment on the road in less than an hour, if performed flawlessly.

'Ah, here's First Spear Julius. Are we ready to march, I wonder?' Cilo watched his new senior centurion's progress for a moment, smiling at the way even the hardiest of his men avoided making eye contact with him. 'Gods, look at the man. He's every legionary's nightmare made flesh!'

Marcus nodded at the legatus's almost awed statement, noting that the three other narrow-striped angusticlavi tribunes who had joined them since the legion's change of command were also watching their first spear with something approaching amazement. All three were young men whose fathers were Cilo's amici, and who had requested that he take their sons to war in order to put their feet on the first step of the cursus honorum. In the usual run of things the legatus would have been concerned to ensure that at least one of his narrow-stripe tribunes was a relatively experienced soldier, preferably with a spell in command of a five-hundred-man auxiliary cohort under his belt. He had however readily agreed that in this case, with Scaurus serving as a broad-striped laticlavius tribune, and Marcus and a still-reeling Justus as the other two narrow-stripes, there was no such need, and he had therefore been happy to grant such favours. Scaurus smiled knowingly at the sight of Julius, back in armour and with an iron grip on his vitis.

'It's all effortless, of course, Legatus. He's had leather lungs for so long now that even a few years of retirement hasn't slowed him down.'

'He was retired?'

Scaurus turned to look at the youngest of the tribunes, the son of a noble family whose place in Rome's glorious history was beyond reproach. He nodded gravely, with the feeling that his life experiences since he had been the younger man's age made the real age gap between them a good deal more than a dozen years. Lucius Furius Aculeo could trace his line back to the earliest days of the republic almost seven hundred years before, and was not shy in making sure that everyone around him was aware of that supposed superiority. To Marcus's eye he bore a striking resemblance to a man he had known in Britannia a decade before, with hints of the same strength in his body, even if it were yet to mature into the bull-like frame of the Furius he had encountered during his first campaign.

'We all were, Tribune Furius. After we defeated the empire of Kush in Aegyptus, we realised that returning to Rome would be a death sentence. And so we stayed there.'

The younger man's eyes widened.

'Kush? The legendary kingdom? It actually exists?'

Scaurus ignored the younger man's informality.

'Yes, it does. Catch me at the right time and I'll tell you all about how we held a fortress on the River Nilus against a hundred thousand fanatics. But as for here and now, you need to remember that I am a senior tribune. When you address me you must call me sir, and show the appropriate respect.'

He laughed at Furius's expression of doubt.

'Yes, I know, no one's ever dared to address you like you're an equal before, or at least not in a way that wasn't a kindly attempt to make you more like a normal person and less like a child whose every whim was to be indulged. Your father's maior domus might have called you by your first name, and you might have been encouraged to accept that familiarity, but everyone else would have been wary of you at best. But as of now, that all changes. Each of you young men will be assigned to the oversight of a senior centurion commanding a cohort, and I have explicitly ordered those men to tell you if you're doing something wrong, albeit with the degree of respect appropriate to the situation.'

The young man frowned, presented with something he genuinely couldn't comprehend.

'Appropriate to the situation? Surely I should be treated with respect at all times?'

To Marcus's surprise, the newly promoted Justus answered the question. Still looking deeply uncomfortable in a bronze muscle cuirass, his hands continually fretting for the vine stick he was no longer entitled to carry, he was gradually adapting to the fact that he was now a member of the equestrian elite, thanks to Cilo's agreement to Scaurus's decision to socially promote him, a decision that the palace hierarchy had been swift enough to endorse.

'Allow me to illuminate the question from recent experience, colleague. If it's a simple matter of military practice, and we're not in battle, your centurion will probably have a quiet word in private. Nobody wants to be the cause of upset, after all. But if we're in battle, or if whatever you've ordered looks likely to cause loss of life, then he may be forced to correct you somewhat more swiftly, and quite likely publicly. It's just how it has to be, sometimes, to avoid men dying needlessly.'

Furius's frown deepened to something closer to incredulity.

'But what if I'm not prepared to *accept* such a lack of respect?'

Marcus smiled tolerantly.

'Respect doesn't come from who you *are*, it comes from what you *do*. Stand alongside your men in a battle line, when the enemy are thrusting spears at you from four feet away and screaming about cutting your balls off, and if you can keep from shitting yourself then you'll be on the way to earning respect. Until you've shared that experience with your men the best you can hope for is obedience, at least to your face.'

The tribune looked at Cilo for some form of backup, only to find the senator shaking his head.

'Take it from me, Tribune, nobody in this entire legion is going to show any of you young gentlemen very much respect other than that due to your position until you've earned it. Fear, yes. Subservience, undoubtedly. But respect will come later, once we've met Niger's legions and gone toe to toe with them. If we survive the experience, that is. Ah, First Spear . . .'

Julius saluted, taking care to address both Cilo and Scaurus.

'The Fourth Legion is ready to march, Legatus. Although I'm not convinced that it will go as smoothly as we hope, given the number of new centurions we have.'

Marcus snorted a mirthless laugh.

'You're not having second thoughts, are you, Julius? The organisational revisions were your recommendation, after all.'

Cilo's orders two days before had been every bit as ruthless as Scaurus had mandated when it came to disciplining the legion's lax centurionate. Every officer who had effectively left his century to their own devices to go into Rome had been charged with deserting his post, albeit with the usual death sentence commuted to an administrative punishment of thirty lashes apiece, the least that Scaurus considered suitable under the circumstances. With the corpses of a pair of older men who had failed to survive their scourging still draped over the whipping posts, the remainder had been led away, staggering and dripping blood, their backs lacerated into ruin.

'Have them treated by the legion medics and then dismissed with enough money to survive the journey back to Singidunum.' The senior tribune had shaken his head sadly at the sight of so many officers summarily dismissed, while knowing that the effect on his command would be immediate and powerful. 'And let's get on with swearing in the new centurions, shall we? This legion isn't going anywhere until we have officers I can trust to do their duty.'

He had watched with grim amusement as the best-regarded chosen men in the legion, amazed at such a swift and unexpected turn of fate, had been sworn into their new and godlike roles. Their selections had been based on recommendations from Justus and his few remaining colleagues, who were for the most part also promoted to command the detachment's eight cohorts as first spears. Justus himself had been at first amazed, and then simply bemused, to be promoted to the exalted position of tribune, granted equestrian rank and equipped with the finery expected of a Roman senior officer. He had stared in disbelief at Scaurus when called to the command tent to hear the news of his promotion.

'But will I even be capable of such a role, Tribune?'

Scaurus had smiled grimly.

'That depends on which part of the role we're discussing, *Tribune*. I doubt very much that you'll make much of a peacetime officer, at least to start with. And I certainly won't be asking you to recite any poetry at a formal dinner any time soon. But as a man to command a cohort in battle, and to have the respect and obedience of your men when the time comes for us to make the best of the difficult orders we've been given, you'll do well enough. And I have no doubt that you'll do better than any number of well-educated young gentlemen.'

Cilo turned to Scaurus, who was mounted on a horse beside his own, every other officer having been instructed to march on foot to get their feet accustomed to hard going. He extended a hand to gesture at the road away from the camp to the north.

'Very well, Senior Tribune. Shall we get on with discovering whatever fate it is that the emperor's orders have in store for us? I'm keen to see how well all these new officers do at putting a legion onto the road. It is something of an art, and it's a long road to Thrace, which means I don't want to lose an hour's marching time every morning while they sort themselves out.'

Scaurus nodded at Julius, who turned, put his whistle to his lips and blew a single long blast, raising his vine stick and then slashing it down in the signal to commence the legion's deployment. He gave the two men a knowing look and then turned away, ready to visit his ire upon those of his new officers with whose performance he was less than satisfied. But by the time half a dozen centuries were on the move it was clear that, whatever their fighting capability might or might not be, they were at least sufficiently well practised in the manoeuvres necessary to get the four thousand men of the legion's detachment to Severus's army marching in an acceptable time. Julius nodded reluctant agreement when Marcus made a favourable comment on their abilities, as the two men marched alongside the leading century.

'It's not pretty, but it's good enough that we don't need to bring them all back and make them do it all again. I'd go so far as to say that some of those new centurions are almost acceptable, which isn't what I'd expected to be saying at this—'

He fell silent at the piercing note of a cornicer's horn from the rear of the column, and looked back to see a horseman trotting up the long line of marching centuries.

'An officer? Are we expecting any more snot-noses?'

The two men reined in their horses, waiting as century after century of men strode past them, Julius taking the opportunity to bark terse instructions at those soldiers still struggling with their equipment. They fell in with the command group just as the horseman caught up with it, and the veteran centurion shook his head with a world-weary sigh as it became clear who it was who had joined the column of march.

'I should have known it. And right on cue, eh? Obviously you'd be along for the glory-hunting, because since when have you ever been able to control that urge to try to get yourself killed, eh?'

Varus winked down at him, evidently delighted to be reunited with his friends, then saluted Cilo and made the purpose of his unexpected appearance clear.

'Legatus, sir! I bear a message from the imperial staff! Your orders have been changed!'

He held out a message container, and Scaurus shook his head ruefully.

'I wonder why it is that I feel a premonition of impending doom whenever I see your face, Vibius Varus.'

He looked at Cilo questioningly, and the legatus gestured to the proffered wooden tube.

'Be my guest, Senior Tribune. Let's see what it is that the emperor has in mind for us now.'

Scaurus broke the tube's wax seal and pulled out the scroll inside. He read the closely written order inside with an expression of growing amusement.

'Go on then, if it's that funny you can share the joke with the rest of us!'

Scaurus looked down at Julius with a smirk.

'Oh trust me, Centurion, you're going to love this. Do you recall a ship by the name of the *Victoria*?'

The Briton stared at him for a moment and then shook his head again, looking even less impressed than he had with Varus's unexpected arrival.

'Oh joy. All the fun of the fleet, eh?' He shot a meaningful look at Varus. 'And I presume we're going to be burdened with yet another *senior* tribune to tolerate as well?'

Varus leaned out of his saddle and clapped him on the shoulder with a broad smile.

'I know you've missed me, Julius, so yes, you'll be delighted to know that I am indeed ordered to accompany the Fourth to the east. Who knows, perhaps I'll surprise you with some of the things I've learned while you've been sunning yourselves in Aegyptus.'

Julius nodded, pursing his lips in apparent agreement.

'Perhaps you will, Tribune. After all, I do hear that the frontier garrisons are *especially* fond of their livestock.' He switched his attention to Scaurus. 'Right, I'd better get this lot stopped and turned around, hadn't I? Given that we're probably not marching north any more?'

'Gods below but this shithole smells worse than Rome, if that's possible.'

Julius looked out across the small inland sea that was separated from the main bay of the Misenum naval base by the bridge towards which they were marching. Behind them the legion's long snaking column was stretched out over several miles of the road south from Neapolis, the city outside which they had camped the previous night. In the distance to their left the looming bulk of the volcano Vesuvius was a dark silhouette against the blue summer sky, its barren slopes still covered in ash. Ptolemy had taken great pleasure the previous night in relating to them the way in which, a hundred years before, its eruption had buried the cities of Pompeii and Herculaneum and their inhabitants in the space of a single day, making great play of the suddenness of their deaths. The veteran centurion shot the mountain another unhappy look.

'You're absolutely sure that thing's not going to blow its top off again? The Sparrow was very clear in his storytelling last night that if it does we'll all be flash-roasted in an instant.'

Marcus shook his head, exchanging a knowing smile with Varus, who was riding alongside him.

'What he omitted to tell you was that there were a large number of earthquakes before the volcano erupted a hundred years ago. We'll get plenty of warning if the gods below the earth decide to vent their wrath again.'

Julius stared at the giant peak for a while before speaking again.

'I still think the fleet should have come to Ostia to collect us, rather than our having to march all this way south to get to them.'

'The emperor's war planners were very clear on the subject. They wanted us to leave Rome on foot and *not* heading for Ostia, because that would be like sending Niger a message to tell him we were taking the sea route and will be in his face in less than half the time he'll be expecting. And besides, fleets aren't like horses, First Spear. You don't just leap on a ship and head off wherever it is that you want to go. There are crew to recruit and train, masts to be repaired, ropes to be made . . .'

'And seamen to be dragged off the local whores, more likely. At least they have plenty of ships ready though.'

Looking out to their left into the harbour, they could see fifty or so vessels riding at anchor, while the quayside that was coming into view was lined with another dozen major warships.

'There's the *Victoria*, I'd know that ship anywhere!' The officers followed Ptolemy's pointing finger, looking at each other, none the wiser. 'See her finely drawn bow – and there, the fleet standard is flying from her mast!'

Julius nodded slowly.

'I think the Aegyptian midget has the right of it.'

He ignored Ptolemy's outraged indignation, managing to shut out the stream of complaints that the former palace scribe was venting at anyone prepared to listen.

'I'm not listening to your quacking, Sparrow, so you might as well save your energy.' He looked across the bay at the ship Ptolemy had indicated with a thoughtful expression. 'I wonder if that gnarled old bastard of a butcher's son is still prefect of the praetorian fleet?'

Scaurus turned and spoke over his shoulder.

'Tribune Varus! Who is it we're ordered to report to on arrival at the port?'

Varus turned his attention away from his discussion with Marcus.

'We are to report to Prefect Titus on board the flagship *Victoria*, and he will arrange for embarkation and shipment to the east!'

'Thank you, Tribune. And there you are, Julius, your question is answered. We are indeed going to be shipping with our old friend Titus once more.'

Ptolemy spoke up again, quite undeterred by his previous rude treatment.

'Do you mean to say that the prefect commanding that fleet is the son of a butcher? I do find myself wondering just how it is that a man of such lowly birth could ever have progressed to such a—'

'Someone tell him, before I'm forced to throttle the curiosity out of the little bastard.'

Scaurus laughed tersely at Julius's plea.

'That's easy enough to relate. He worked his way up from sailor to navarchus on simple merit, then was appointed his former tribune's stand-in for a while, after the man got himself killed leading his marines into battle alongside us at the siege of Nisibis. After which, it seems, your former imperial master the chamberlain Cleander was quick to see the opportunity he offered. His unlimited power as chamberlain allowed him to arrange any number of schemes to defraud the imperial purse in the provinces controlled directly by the throne, working through men of the equestrian class he had appointed to their roles, but he needed a safe way to bring the proceeds back to Rome. And Titus was the ideal fleet commander to carry the spoils to him without exciting any suspicion. After all, who could be more upright than the prefect of a praetorian fleet? Being able to demonstrate to Commodus that he had promoted a man who wouldn't be influenced by the senate, with whom the emperor was at daggers drawn by that point, was just an additional bonus.'

Ptolemy nodded his understanding.

'I would imagine that he's going to be surprised to see us, after all this time. He must have written us off as dead years ago!'

They marched the first cohort onto the dockside, leading the legion up the stone-surfaced mole past a succession of moored warships until the leading century reached the last berth in line. Scaurus shouted an order for the column to halt, then turned to look up at the *Victoria*'s command bridge, raised above the vessel's stern, to see the praetorian fleet's commander looking back down at him. He raised a hand in salute and called out a greeting to the sailor.

'Greetings, Prefect! The Fourth Legion has been directed to march here and take ship with you to the east!'

The dark-faced officer stared down at them for a moment, his face unreadable, then nodded and spoke briefly to his officers before climbing down from the ship's bridge and walking forward to the plank gangway that connected ship and shore. He walked down it and towards the group, saluting Cilo as he came to a halt. With a face weathered and tanned to a dark shade of brown by years of exposure to sea and sun, his hair an iron-grey and clipped close to his skull, his eyes were darker still, expressionless in all but the intensity of their stare.

'Legatus. I am Prefect Titus, commander of the emperor's praetorian fleet based here in Misenum. I have orders to ship your legion and essential supplies to a landing point in the east of the empire, where you will be disembarked in a position of advantage in the war with the pretender. But I had no idea that you would be travelling in the company of these men.' He shot a piercing stare at Scaurus. 'Tribune Scaurus. Of all the people I never expected to see again. It seems that my fate in life is inextricably bound to your own.'

Scaurus inclined his head in recognition.

'It's good to see you again, Titus. Hopefully we find you in good health?'

The sailor grimaced.

'As good as can be expected. My wife and children are all dead, and so I dedicate my life to the fleet. And my fleet is in excellent condition.'

'I'm sorry to hear that. Was it the plague?'

'They were taken from me without warning.' The sailor raised a hand in negation of the subject. 'But enough of that. My orders from Rome in turn incorporate fresh orders for your legatus.'

He raised a message cylinder whose wax seal had already been broken, and Cilo stepped forward, his face tense with expectation.

'What exactly *are* your orders, Prefect?'

'I am commanded to sail with all possible speed, once your cohorts are loaded into my vessels, and to plot a course through Mare Ionium and Mare Aegaeum. And when we reach the northern end of Mare Aegaeum, I am commanded to disembark you within a few days' marching distance of Perinthus, on the Thracian coast, and then to make a swift withdrawal in order not to jeopardise my command. I am commanded that on no account am I to pass through the Hellespont, to avoid the risk of an enemy fleet bottling us up in the Propontis.' He handed Cilo another, sealed, message container. 'And here are the fresh orders for you from Rome, Legatus, delivered only yesterday.'

Cilo took the scroll from Titus, broke it open and read the emperor's instructions with a grim face.

'It is as you say. We are commanded to disembark as close to Perinthus as is possible without your risking losing your fleet to enemy action, and then to advance with all speed to attack the city.' He looked at Scaurus in dismay. 'But that all seems very hasty. Surely it would make more sense to introduce us to the campaign in a more careful disposition?' He shook his head with a look of perplexity. 'I had expected us to be ferried to somewhere like Thessalonica where we would be able to procure transport and supplies before marching east. Surely attacking with such haste and throwing the legion ashore so close to an enemy-held city will carry a much greater risk?'

Scaurus shook his head, looking out to sea past the *Victoria*'s bow.

'Severus has decided to make this legion into what the Jews would term a sacrificial lamb. We are to risk our own destruction in the common good. I can only imagine that he plans to use our threat to Perinthus to take the pressure off the Moesian legions as they besiege Byzantium, and to distract Niger's generals from his main army's advance and buy time for him to bring forward his main threat, the legions of Candidus's exercitus Illyricus. It might well prove to be a masterstroke. But it might well also result in the destruction of this legion.'

With the process of loading the legion onto Titus's vessels completed, and having left the horses to the tender mercies of the port authorities due to the fleet's inability to ship them, they put out to sea without delay. They turned to the south-east to run down the Italian coast under sail, the oarsmen sitting idle at their benches playing knucklebones and dice to pass the time while their passengers started familiarising themselves with their new homes.

'They'll have an easy time of it until we pass the Strait of Messana with the wind at our backs, and the Ionium Sea should be straightforward enough, but they'll have to earn their rations once we turn north into the Aegaeum, and take the prevailing wind right on the prow.'

The usually taciturn Titus had come down from his command deck on the *Victoria*'s stern to look out at the passing coastline with the legion's officers, once the complexities of getting sixty vessels out of the tight harbour entrance and out to sea had been dealt with. The Fourth's men had been divided up between the ships by centuries and told to stay in their places on deck, called forward to exercise and perform their toilet over the ship's side one tent party at a time. The remainder of their time was to be spent, Julius had decided, in the never-ending busy work every soldier hated, and he was making his expectations clear to the century that had been unfortunate enough to be selected to board the flagship.

'If you're not exercising or hanging your arse over the side for the fish to laugh at the size of your pricks, then your armour, sword, dagger, spears and brightwork all need polishing! And when you've finished polishing that lot you can start on your leatherwork! After that you can either find something to do that'll keep me from taking you for a shower of lazy bastards who need a few hours on the rowing benches! And yes, I can see they're not rowing, but you fucking will be! The entire legion will be inspected when we disembark tonight, and any century I find that's not gleaming is going to be feeling very sorry for itself by the time I'm done with them! And no, feeling like you're about to puke up your arsehole does not excuse your duties! You're legionaries, not the kind of weak-minded soft-footed flowers that have to ride everywhere!'

More than one of the new tribunes shot their First Spear a surprised glance, swiftly looked away when they realised that he was staring straight at them. He paused for breath, and the sound of centurions and watch officers shouting orders and berating the slow, lazy or seasick was audible across the water from the closest vessels. The fleet commander smiled at the imprecations they were using to motivate men who had been expecting an easy day of it.

'He has not changed, I see. You will be wanting to land your men early enough in each day to allow him to subject them to training, I presume?'

Scaurus nodded his agreement.

'Either that, or we delay sailing until they've been given at least two hours of drill. They might look like legionaries, but they're not ready for a real fight.'

They decided to go for the option of morning training, reasoning that the legion's soldiers would be easier to manage if they boarded the warships having been properly exercised. Julius had grinned when asked the question.

'Can I wear them out in two to three hours? Just watch me.'

The next morning, he assembled his cohorts on the beach up which the ships had been dragged for the night, Scaurus and his tribunes standing by to witness what it was he planned to do. Gathering the legion around him and raising his voice to a parade ground roar to be heard over the surf, and with an amused audience of sailors sitting in the prows of their beached ships, he told the assembled soldiery what it was that he had in mind for them.

'Right, you men have done nothing but march for the last six weeks! So we don't need to get you fit, but we do need to keep you fit! Besides which we're going to be spending the next month or so camping by the sea every night, without either the time or the space for a lot of road marching!'

Marcus could see that the men closest to where the officers were standing were smiling and nudging each other. Arminius leaned in and whispered to him conspiratorially.

'I don't think they've woken up to what a bastard he is yet, have they?'

Julius continued, a smirk lighting up his face and giving the closest soldiers to him cause to wonder what it was that he was finding so funny.

'And I am reliably informed that nobody in this legion has fought anything harder than a vicus pimp since the German wars, so anyone here who took part in that goat-fuck is probably so old that they've forgotten it ever happened, never mind what it was they had to do. And so, you delicate barracks blossoms, what we're going to do, rather than worrying about getting you to the battle, is work on what we're going to do when we actually have to face the enemy. Who, let me remind you, are just the same as us! They wear the same armour! They carry the same weapons! They use the same tactics! So we're not going to beat them with superior equipment, and you can poke all that horseshit about them being effeminate easterners that the imperial pronouncements would have you believe right up where the sun doesn't shine!'

He walked down the ranks of suddenly very attentive legionaries.

'Why do I say that? Because I, and your senior tribunes, have fought alongside the bastards! We had to rough them up to get them ready for it, but our one legion fought a whole army of Parthians ten times our strength to a standstill! And it's easy for men who'll never get within a thousand miles of the fighting to call them soft!'

He looked about him at the ranks of silent soldiers.

'But you men, you'll be seeing what I mean soon enough, and you'll be seeing it from three feet away! It'll be a man just like you, trained like you, equipped like you and just as keen as you are to make his emperor the *only* emperor, and make himself rich! And he'll be crouching behind a shield just like yours, with a spear ready to put through your face!'

He fell silent, allowing the silence to work on them.

'Me? I don't plan on dying just yet! And certainly not because I couldn't get a gang of ugly bastards like you lot to put up a decent fight! So, what we're going to do is this!'

He put a hand out to Dubnus, who passed him a spear whose iron blade was shining in the sunlight.

'I know, you've been pulling faces at these ever since they were issued to you! This is a hasta! It's an old-fashioned spear, a much older design that the pila that the legions use! And it's what the auxiliaries use, because they're not as important as the legions and don't get the best toys! But it is also much more useful in a fight than the pila that you're used to, because it's not a single-use weapon! When you throw a pilum you are saying goodbye to your spear, because you won't get it back until after the battle and even then only if you win!'

He lowered the weapon to a fighting position, aiming the long iron blade at one of the watching legionaries.

'When you fight with this you can kill with it as many times as you are presented with a target and still have the strength to wield it! You can outreach a swordsman by at least three feet, and carve him a new nose while he's still wondering how to get through a forest of these! And you can lose a battle and still walk away with it, if you have the guts for a fighting retreat! It is the better weapon for the sort of war we'll be fighting – with only one disadvantage! Who can tell me what that is?'

A legionary in the front rank, his beard shot through with white and his face marked with the unmistakable scar tissue of a veteran, answered the question.

'We'll have to stand and take a volley of pila or two before the fighting starts, Centurion?'

'Yes! That man gets a night off guard duty for having the guts to shout out an answer! The only problem with this is that you have to stand up to one or two volleys of spears from the enemy before you can start slaughtering them with your extra reach! So we're going to teach you two things over the next few weeks! how to fight with the hasta and cut an enemy's front rank to ribbons! And how to take a volley of pila without getting one in the face!'

The legion's men, like soldiers everywhere, swiftly adjusted to their new daily routine. With an hour of daylight remaining, Prefect Titus's chief navigator would select a section of shoreline well away from any settlement and the fleet would run in to beach itself, sailors and legionaries alike leaping over the side to drag their vessels out of the surf and anchor them firmly to the shore above the expected high-tide line. The soldiers would gather driftwood from the beach and swiftly forage the coastal land beyond for anything either combustible or consumable, their hopes of happening upon either fat calves or farmers' daughters, however, forever unrequited. Each tent party would cook their evening meals on beach campfires and then, exhausted by the previous day's exercises and constant polishing of their weapons and armour, bed down for the night.

Julius's morning training routine also quickly became second nature for the men of the Fourth, who were in any case used to being woken at first light. Having slept in their cloaks and blankets, they were chivvied onto whatever open ground was available, using the beach's difficult footing if necessary, to undertake incessant battle drills in the cool of the morning before the sun rose high enough to make the exercise too onerous.

'It looks like we're training our men to fight like the phalanxes of old.'

Marcus, watching from the top of a dune, shook his head at the young tribune who had spoken, a young man from a less exalted family than his overly self-assured colleague Furius Aculeo, and who by comparison seemed thoughtful and respectful in nature.

'I'd say it's more a cross between a phalanx and a traditional legion. Why don't you go and get as close to one of those practice battle lines as you can without getting stabbed and tell me what it's like to face?'

Unable to train man to man with sharp iron, and lacking wooden practice weapons, Julius had settled for incessant practice of tactical manoeuvres and swift changes of formation across the varying types of ground they found at each beach, making use of the difficult sandy footing to work on their stamina. And with every formation change he pushed his centurions to repeat the same three tactics time and time again. Marcus watched as the closest cohort tramped past him along the beach, their four deep lines filling the sandy expanse from the dunes to the water, another cohort following fifty paces behind them. Julius was walking ten paces in front of them bellowing the same repetitive commands that the legion's men were having drummed into them time and time again.

'*Shields!*'

At the shouted command the front rank squatted and pushed their shields forward, thrusting the layered boards as far from their bodies as possible so that a thrown pilum's iron head penetrating the shield would have empty air to cross before striking the man behind it, angling the shields to deflect the spear upwards, and turning their heads to put a layer of helmet iron between their skulls and the enemy. At the same time the second rank raised their shields and overlapped them with the front rank's boards, bending their upper bodies away and turning their heads.

'*Spears!*'

The legionaries stood and raised their spears, the rear ranks pressing in close to present as many spear points as possible, facing an enemy with a constant threat of taking one of the long leaf-shaped blades in the face or neck.

'*Rotate!*'

The front-rankers turned to the right, still holding their shields towards the notional enemy, then took a sideways step to the rear at the same moment that the men behind them turned to their left and took a matching step forward, turning to use their shields to protect both themselves and the men they had just replaced.

'*And keep doing it!*'

The senior centurion walked up the dune to join Marcus, looking down at his legion's labouring men.

'It takes one sort of staying power to march thirty miles in a day, and another to fight a battle where the most critical need is to be able to run and fight when you're already exhausted. What I'd really like is to get them working in the heat of the day, but we simply don't have the time if we're going to comply with the emperor's orders.' He turned to shout abuse at the centurion of a century that was supposed to be practising the testudo formation, his men in sad disarray with spears protruding at a variety of angles. 'What the fuck is that? You pricks look more like a fucking hedgehog than a tortoise! Get it sorted!'

The big Briton shook his head in disgust as the officer in question belaboured his men with his fists, boots and vine stick, cajoling them into some semblance of the desired formation and roaring at them to advance with their spears level.

'If they can manage to keep formation when their feet are six inches deep in sand, they shouldn't have any problem with doing it on firmer ground.' He turned away, having caught sight of the following cohort, which, attempting to obey the horn signal to redeploy from testudo into line, had disintegrated into chaos.

'You, the centurion with the crest about to fall off your helmet! Get your men back in a straight line before I'm forced to come and do it for you!' He turned back to Marcus, hefting his vine stick in readiness to use it on the backs of the offending legionaries. 'What I'd give for one decent battle to sort the wheat from the chaff here. This is like death by a thousand cunts!'

Marcus left him to it and went to find the familia, who were exercising in a grove behind the beach. Lacking armour and shields for the most part, they were sparring with the practice swords they habitually carried with them. Taking up one in each hand, he signalled to Arminius and his protégé Lupus, who, knowing what was expected, took up positions on either side of him, nodded to each other and then attacked simultaneously. The three men fought in silence other than the grunts of their exertions and the clack of the wooden blades, Marcus holding the barbarians at sword's length rather than going straight for the kill.

After a few minutes of sparring Arminius, his face sheened with sweat, held up his blade.

'I'm not as young as I was! He's all yours, Lupus.'

He tossed his sword to the Briton, who caught it neatly, grinned, and raised his eyebrows in silent question at Marcus, who, long accustomed to their routine, nodded back at him.

'As ever, if you can best me I'll give you an aureus to irritate your grandfather with.'

The younger man set himself and went for his mentor with real purpose, their blades blurring with the speed of the fight as neither man held anything back. For a while it seemed as if they would still be fighting when the time came to embark, but to the knowing eyes of the familia, long accustomed to their sparring, it was obvious that Marcus was holding back, still fighting just within his abilities rather than at the ragged edge where errors were inevitable, while the Briton was railing at his defence with all he had. At length Lupus started to tire and his attack laid him open to a lightning-fast touch of Marcus's outstretched blade on his chest, and both men stepped away.

'That was better than any other time. You will have the beating of me, if you can just learn to slow your pace a fraction and fight with this' – Marcus tapped his head – 'rather than those.' He pointed a sword blade at the younger man's crotch. 'Now let's go and watch the soldiers sweating, shall we? Not to mention the sight of a fifty-year-old legatus pounding up and down the beach to get himself fit to march. Fabius Cilo might have gone soft with all that comfortable living, but he seems to recognise the facts of his situation. I might run with him for a while.'

Exercises completed, and with the legionaries glowing from their exertions, they boarded the ships, whose crews then carried out the unwieldy task of getting a fleet of seventy vessels off the beach, turned around and headed south down the Italian coast in some semblance of order. While the soldiers wolfed down their morning ration, flatbread with cheese and dried meat, Scaurus called a meeting of his officers in the shadow of Titus's command deck.

'Today we will be passing through the Straits of Messana, then turning left to sail up the coast to Tarentum before we cross the bottom of the Adriaticus to Nicopolis. We did discuss making the crossing to Patrae in one jump, but it's a four- or five-day voyage and the risk of losing half the legion in a storm is too great, so we'll have to sail around the northern edge of the Ionium Sea instead. But either way we're running short of some essential provisions, so this is our chance to resupply.'

His words were inevitably overheard by the soldier Sanga, who was, it was universally acknowledged, the most adept of the familia when it came to the lurking and listening aspects of the informer's art. They were then swiftly communicated to Morban, the veteran soldier's partner in crime whenever there was money to be made from the unsuspecting. The former standard-bearer then promptly went about running a book among the soldiers aboard regarding the odds of the fleet docking that day, while already knowing full well that such a possibility had already been discounted.

This of course resulted in a good deal of hopeful eyeing of the shore by men whose time in Rome had been curtailed by their being ordered to sail east so soon after their arrival, an expectation that led to a good deal of money being wagered on a port visit that day, and at seemingly generous odds. But it was not to be. The fleet swept through the strait without even a hint of diverting into the port city of Rhegium, the soldiers staring forlornly out to the flagship's left at the tantalisingly close shore. Insult was added to injury, it seemed, when a detachment of military freighters peeled away from the mass of ships and headed in to collect fresh supplies, leaving the soldiers to watch them sail out of sight as the flagship made the long turn onto a north-easterly heading.

Marcus found the former standard-bearer standing at the rail with Sanga, making an unconvincing attempt to look equally disappointed and ignoring the disgruntled looks that the legionaries were casting at them. Saratos, a Dacian with considerably more common sense than either, and the closest thing Sanga had to a friend, was standing beside them. He was counting his winnings from having known to bet against a wager Morban had chosen to favour with odds that were indeed too good to be true, and dropped the money into his purse as Marcus approached, giving him a knowing look. The tribune, having been acquainted with both Morban and Sanga for a decade, felt no need to stand on ceremony.

'Look at you both, grinning like you woke up this morning to discover your pricks had grown to double their former size overnight.'

'I don't think even the most accommodating of whores could cope with twice the size of this piece of—'

Waving a hand to silence Sanga before he had chance to wax lyrical on the subject, to Saratos's evident relief, Marcus continued in the same tone.

'I'd imagine you would both be somewhat less happy were the men you've just defrauded to find out what we already all know all too well. You two knew that there was no way we were going to risk the flood of desertions that might result were we to stop anywhere other than an empty beach, didn't you?'

The two men looked at each other, each willing the other to reply, but the tribune beat them to it.

'I saw you lurking at the rail while the tribune was briefing us, Sanga, and I saw you go rushing off to make your proposition to this sticky-fingered purse ferret. Doubtless the two of you have made a tidy profit from your inside information, but then I'd imagine men have gone over the side for less?'

Morban looked up at him with an expression that combined the distress of being found out with the cunning of a man who could be relied on to turn any situation to his own best advantage.

'Taking that obviously unwarranted slur at face value, Tribune, what is it that you might want from me . . . from *us*?' He shot a hard stare at Sanga to pre-empt any attempt on the veteran's part to sidle away. 'That is, we were guilty of any such attempt to benefit from inside knowledge, which of course neither of us would ever even consider—'

Marcus raised a hand, shaking his head wearily.

'Stop. Just stop talking, you'll give me a headache with your unending flow of mendacity and deceit.'

'Mendacity?'

The Dacian, whose vocabulary had expanded significantly during their long sojourn in Aegyptus, interjected helpfully.

'This means that you are a lying bastard, I think?'

'Thank you, Saratos, and you . . .' Marcus put a finger in Sanga's face. 'Shut your mouth and keep it shut. Let's just assume, for the sake of argument, that I have a point. Or, worse than that for you two, that it doesn't matter whether I'm right or not. Because were even a hint of your knowing that we're never going to dock today to reach the ears of the men you tempted with such generous odds, you'd both be facing a rather robust challenge before dawn tomorrow. Or should we put that to the test?'

Both men shuffled their feet and, at length, admitted that the tribune's argument had some basis in fact, looking, if not guilty, at least a little concerned as to their officer's expected recompense. Morban shot a look down at his purse, perhaps wishing he'd found a way to offload some of his recent gains, but Marcus shook his head with a jaundiced expression.

'Unlike you, Morban, I'm not interested in money.'

Looking relieved, the older man muttered something about that being no wonder given his privileged start in life, which Marcus chose to ignore other than to skewer him with a penetrating stare.

'What I *am* interested in is your silence with regard to a subject I'm just about to explain to you. And my expectation that you're going to do exactly what I tell you, no matter what it is. And that you're going to swear an oath to the Lightbringer that you'll keep that promise no matter what profit there might be in breaking it. Do I have your agreement, or do I have to start explaining to the men of the first century why it is that they have so much less gold this evening?'

Two days after the fleet made the turn to the north-east to beat its way up the Italian coast towards Tarentum, with the wind on their left beam forcing the navarchus to sail the ship with its sails so close-hauled that the rowers were put back to work to keep the vessel moving at an acceptable speed, Marcus was looking out at the passing coastline when the young tribune Furius Aculeo announced his presence beside him with a cough. Ignoring what under military etiquette was effectively without meaning, he ignored the attempt to gain his attention, only turning to face the younger man when he felt his sleeve being tugged.

'I wish to discuss the question of your—'

Marcus shook his head, restraining the temptation to laugh at the younger man's look of discomfiture.

'If you want to talk to a superior officer, Furius Aculeo, it is customary to indicate the intention by announcing your presence in a respectful manner, and requesting permission to engage in conversation. Man to man I'm happy enough to be addressed by my name, if combined with the proper respect. But coughing to gain attention, as if seeking to make a point to an inattentive slave, especially in the manner of a man who expects everyone around him to be hanging on his every word, is not acceptable. It will simply result in your being ignored by men who will assume either that you actually have a cough or are badly in need of a lesson in manners. And' – he raised a hand to forestall Furius's reply – 'tugging a senior officer's sleeve will undoubtedly earn you a reprimand under the wrong circumstances, although I am willing to overlook it this once.'

The younger man thought for a moment.

'I see. In that case, Senior Tribune, I wish to speak with you on a difficult but unavoidable subject.'

'My parentage?'

Furius frowned.

'Yes. How did you know?'

Marcus smiled, showing his teeth but without any genuine humour.

'I knew because you've been staring at me when you think I'm not looking ever since you joined the legion. Which tells me that your father, who has never met me and whose social standing was insignificant until he was lucky enough to hitch his fortunes to Severus's rise to power, told you to watch out for me before you left home. I'd imagine he said something like, "Aquila's father was a traitor, and the apple never falls far from the tree, so wait and watch him and you may get the chance to denounce him and take his place." Words that, were I ever to hear them, would result in a great deal of unhappiness for him.'

The young tribune blinked at his superior's unexpected vehemence.

'But your father *was* executed for treason.'

'My father and my uncle were executed for the crimes of having massive fortunes and a villa outside Rome that Commodus coveted for his summer palace, away from the stink of the city. They were falsely accused by the chamberlain of the day and murdered by a gang of killers who sold my mother and sisters into a cult of rapists and murderers. I have had my revenge on everyone involved, but I can never restore the honour that my family had ripped from it. So, Tribune, can you see why I might be a little short-tempered with foolish comments about my father's *treason*?'

Furius nodded, but while he was clearly abashed he maintained eye contact with Marcus in a way that bespoke a strong spirit.

'I see. There was another matter that my father mentioned.'

'Something to do with the death of a relative of his, in Britannia?'

The tribune blinked again.

'Yes. A cousin of his, Gracilus. He wrote a letter to the imperial authorities stating that he had identified a fugitive from justice by the name of Aquila who had taken refuge with the cohorts on the Wall, but he died before he could do anything to apprehend the man. Natural causes, my father heard, but he was never convinced . . .'

He stopped speaking, his eyes widening at the murderous look on Marcus's face and the hard edge in his reply.

'Your father's cousin was the sort of man who could take pleasure in rape and murder. Which was an unwise thing for him to attempt with the woman I loved. And so he died, with a legion surgeon's verdict of natural causes in the absence of any evidence to the contrary. The result being that there was one less animal to trouble the innocent. The letter of denunciation he wrote before he died was enough to bring the frumentarii after me, but

I managed to avoid their clutches too. And now, thanks to the brief and unhappy reign of Pertinax, I am somewhat restored in the world. Exonerated, and allowed to continue going about doing what I've chosen as my calling in this life. And so you have to ask yourself whether *any* of that has anything whatsoever to do with you, Tribune? I think you would be wise to concentrate on the fight that we're sailing towards, and being ready to play your part to the emperor's satisfaction, don't you?'

Furius looked at him for a moment in silence, then nodded and turned away without speaking again. Marcus watched him return to the group of his peers without a backward glance, and showing every sign of having accepted the warning; but his every instinct was telling him that the matter was shelved rather than forgotten.

6

'This is all still Roman, right? We haven't sailed off the map into a land full of dog-headed men and fire-breathing lizards? Oi, I saw that, you big ugly bastard!'

While Ptolemy had merely smiled at Sanga's question, as a group of Scaurus's familia had stared out over the ship's side at the coast less than a mile distant, Lugos's response had been a less tactful shake of his massive head and a snort of amusement. The giant Briton grinned at the insult, an expression fearsome enough in itself that some of the watching oarsmen shivered and turned back to their preparations for the afternoon of hard labour.

In the days that followed their passing Sicily the fleet had sailed on, first making its way up the southern Italian coast until the gulf of Tarentum had opened up on the ships' left side, then crossing the seventy-mile stretch of open sea, in a single day that saw the rowers exhausted by the time land was reached on the far side. Two days later they had crossed the Ionium Sea to Buthrotum in Epirus, then continued south down the coast of Greece to its southernmost point, the kingdom of Sparta, which had once been militarily pre-eminent in the region. Now the rowers were glumly readying themselves for the fleet's impending turn north and the long slog up the peninsula's chaotic coastline.

'All that time you had to improve yourself while we were at leisure in Aegyptus, and what do you have to show for it?'

Sanga's friend Saratos leaned forward to venture an opinion in response to the Briton's question.

'Seven children, by my count. Several hundred women who will remember him with gratitude for the speed and short duration of the acts he paid them to perform, and—'

His comrade shook his head with feigned incredulity.

'Whose fucking side are you on, you Dacian donkey?'

Saratos shrugged.

'Big man asked a question, and it seemed to deserve an answer.'

The Briton shook his head at his comrade.

'I've told you before not to encourage either him or the dwarf!'

Ptolemy bridled at the soldier's customary insult whenever his intellect was called into question, but Lugos was the first to reply.

'This is Greece, which was conquered by Rome hundreds of years ago. It was once the home of the world's greatest warriors, traders and thinkers, but of course Roman rule has reduced its people to being concerned mainly with the availability of baths and wine. You would fit in here perfectly.'

The Briton grinned.

'Too right I would! From what I hear about the Greeks, there must be a lot of women that need a proper seeing-to!'

'If what you say is true then it is indeed a good thing that you're here.'

Sanga frowned, unsure as to why Lugos, long since his sparring partner, would be agreeing with him.

'Yes . . . because . . .'

He waited for the big man to interrupt him with an insult, and was on the brink of continuing when his expectation was proved correct.

'Because you bring Saratos with you.'

'What?'

Lugos winked, further discomfiting the closest oarsmen.

'Saratos. I hear he's the man who closes the deal for you, so to speak.'

The officers ignored the sounds of bickering reaching them from the prow, Titus pointing over the *Victoria*'s left side at the Greek mainland.

'Now my men will earn their coin. It will be rowing all day and every day from here to the Hellespont, because the winds in the Aegaeum, the etesiae, will blow from the north every damned day.

Even with the sail furled we'll make no better progress than fifty miles a day if we're lucky. It is a happy wind for the return journey, but a powerful impediment for us now.'

When the reduced pace of their progress north up the Greek coast became painfully evident, and with his men having by this point formed relationships with the ships' crews with whom they sailed every day, Julius went to Scaurus with a suggestion.

'Our men might be getting better at drill, and that'll be essential when it comes to a fight, but all this sitting around isn't doing them any good. Plus the oarsmen will be totally worn out after a few hours, and putting our men in would give us more speed and get us on the ground in Thrace earlier.'

'So we'd either be rushing to our doom or gaining the advantage of possibly beating Niger's men to the punch.'

'One of those things, yes.'

The tribune thought for a moment.

'Do it. But make it worth their while. Promise them a day on the beach with wine and hogs to roast before we disembark and go looking for trouble. Plus you can run that competition you were talking about.'

With the promise of a day's indulgence as the reward for their labour the legionaries were keener on the idea than would otherwise have been the case, and Titus was happy enough to go along with the idea, albeit with some modifications.

'You let them just jump onto a rower's bench and they'll cause chaos. Putting the others off their stroke, dropping their oars into the sea and all sorts of other nonsense. You can put some of them in alongside my lads to give the rest time to get their breath back and let this infernal wind dry their backs, and once they've learned how to row we'll see which of them we trust to actually wave an oar around, shall we?'

And so it was that Julius challenged his cohorts to see who could produce the most men trusted to take control of an oar, with the carrot that the most successful cohort would be allowed a whole day off all duties when the time came for the promised day of rest. And such was the excitement engendered by the competition that few of the legionaries gave any thought to the fact that they were hastening the fleet towards their disembarkation into the teeth of an enemy. Nor did they stop to consider why it might be that while Morban was doing brisk business each evening in accepting wagers on the rowing skills of each cohort as seen from the flagship, and as judged for him by a panel of experts – his new friends aboard the *Victoria* – he was conspicuously absent from any gambling around the swordsmanship competition that Julius had announced would be held on the day of the celebration.

'You want to send a party into Thessalonica?' Prefect Titus's expression made it clear he considered the request unnecessarily risky at best. 'We need to consider this enemy territory, or at best disputed. There will probably be enemy spies in the city, and our presence may well alert them to the presence and intentions of my fleet and your legion.'

Scaurus conceded the point gracefully. The port city of Thessalonica was out of sight from the fleet's current position, tucked away in a sheltered bay at the top of the Thermaic Gulf, and, having replenished their supplies by detaching merchant ships to call at each port as they had sailed up the Greek coast, Titus had already decided to steer well clear of it. His stated plan had been to cross the gulf's mouth a good fifty miles from the port, in order to avoid providing any more of an advance warning of their presence than sightings by the inevitable fishermen, whose catches the fleet's roaming Liburnian scout ships purchased to supplement their rations.

'I understand.' The tribune acknowledged the point without abandoning his request. 'And in recognition of that risk it wouldn't be me going ashore, but rather a selected few men who can be trusted not to vanish into thin air at the first sight of a woman. What better way is there to find out what we might be facing once we get the legion's boots on the ground? But the real reason for us to get some men into the city is the need to find out what the land we'll be wading ashore onto is like. Nothing fancy, all we need is whatever the local geographers have written about the coastline. My Aegyptian scholar went looking for the information in the usual sources, but all that Strabo, Herodotus and Pliny have to say about the coastline in question is more to do with which tribe commands the beaches we might land on, rather than what those beaches would be like in terms of shelving depths, the violence of their surf and all the other useful things we need to know.'

The potential for the port city to have the information they would need had been Ptolemy's idea, and while Scaurus had suspected that he and Lugos were desperate for more books, having read everything they'd brought with them twice over, he'd been forced to agree that it was a good one.

Titus looked out over the ship's side at the Greek coastline with a calculating expression.

'I must admit that there is some business I could do in the city. It will take two days for us to row in against the wind, do our business and then sail out again, while the fleet crosses the gulf and proceeds east along the coast towards the Hellespont, but the time might be well spent. If, of course, we can avoid the attention of enemy informers. Who would you send to perform such a task?'

Scaurus gestured to Marcus.

'The tribune here, obviously. Ptolemy to find the books we're looking for and Lugos and my man Arminius to make sure that he doesn't get robbed in the street, and my Hamian centurion to keep an eye open for any sign of enemy informers.'

Titus nodded decisively.

'Very well, just those five. I'll signal for one of the smaller Liburnians to come alongside and take us in. Be ready to board, and make sure you don't stand out as soldiers.'

The familia watched Marcus divest himself of his elaborately decorated belt and the swords that customarily hung on both of his hips, strapping a plain leather belt in its place. Sanga sidled up to him with a look that combined hope and expectancy, rolling his eyes in dismay when he was firmly rebuffed.

'We don't have the time for your usual method of intelligence gathering, I'm afraid.'

The soldier turned away, grumbling bitterly that some people got to go ashore to indulge their favourite pursuits while the best spies in the familia were yet again condemned to sit on their arses and watch. He was about to comment further when he was interrupted by the soft but authoritative voice of Qadir, who was wrapping his bow and a dozen arrows in canvas to disguise the weapon's distinctive shape.

'You're good enough, Sanga, but there are two men on this ship who have more skills when it comes to the informer's craft. For one thing Saratos is less likely to be distracted by the sniff of a tavern owner's apron, or by the alluring scent of his wife for that matter, and for another there is a man aboard who taught you most of what you know.'

The Briton shook his head at Qadir.

'All due respect, Centurion, but when did you last live in a gutter watching out for the mark for a week?'

The Hamian smiled indulgently at his former pupil.

'I've always believed in the principle of a horse for a course, Legionary. If there is a gutter to be squatted in to watch a house, you are by far the best qualified of us in terms of both aroma and appearance. Truly you were born to sit in a gutter, and indeed you are the master of the art of doing nothing except beg and stare at every passing woman for days at a time. But when it comes to simply following a comrade at a distance, ready to intervene if they are accosted and without ever having been seen before the intervention is required, then I am *that* man.'

Sanga watched with a downcast expression as Titus, Lugos, Arminius, Marcus, Qadir and Ptolemy boarded the small and fast Ligurian *Neptune's Trident*, which had run up alongside the flagship at the prefect's command, heading away to the north towards the port city. Aboard the small vessel the four friends enjoyed the spectacle of the dozens of vessels arrayed across the ocean behind them, while Titus stared about him critically at the state of the ship's rigging and cleanliness. After a while, with the fleet having disappeared over the horizon behind them, they turned their attention to what Ptolemy informed them was the ten-thousand-foot-high peak of Mount Olympus looming over the coastline to their west, and when that palled they settled down to rest in the shade while the rowers laboured to drive the vessel north into the gulf.

Later that evening, with the small vessel beached in an uninhabited inlet close enough to the port city for an early arrival the next morning, they sat around a fire and ate fish purchased from a passing fisherman an hour before. He had sailed a small boat with a distinctive black sail; his skin had been the colour of copper, and his face had borne testament to a lifetime spent on the water. And while he had reassured them that Thessalonica remained loyal to the emperor in Rome, it was a statement that Marcus was inclined to take with a pinch of salt when he then promptly agreed with the deliberately provocative assertion by Qadir that Pescennius Niger was indeed a great man and ruler of the world.

'How much easier to be a man like that.' Marcus nodded at the Hamian's musing, Ptolemy and Arminius already being asleep and Titus engaged in discussion with his sailors on some nautical topic or other while Lugos sat and listened in silence. 'With no concept of the squabbles of great men, and owing his allegiance to the sea and little else. I would imagine that Titus might consider the chance to change places with him as a serious proposition, to be the master of his own destiny and beholden to no man.'

'Baked in the sun, battered by the wind and soaked by the rain? I doubt it's a life for an old man.'

The Hamian shrugged.

'Not having to worry about who's emperor, or what danger their whims might place you in? It is the very life we had in the palms of our hands, until that cursed storm pulled us back into this life of violence and constant risk of our very lives.'

Marcus nodded his agreement.

'That was our aim, but the life you describe is not my destiny, that much is clear. Twice now we have taken the chance to step back from the events that drive the empire's fate. And twice the gods have chosen to deny us that peace, and drawn us back into the storm that constantly rages over Rome's destiny. There seems to be no escaping it, and so I have resigned myself to accepting that it is my life, and making the best of it. And who knows, since the gods are so insistent that this is our course in life, perhaps we might yet still serve some higher purpose than simply slaughtering the empire's enemies?' Marcus stretched. 'But to more pressing matters – what do you plan tomorrow, great master of the informer's art?'

Qadir smiled at the prospect of the next day's subterfuge.

'As to that, once we are ashore you will not see me until there is a need for me to intervene. I look forward to being the ghost of Hamah once again, a role I have not played in many a year.'

When pressed on the apparently self-appointed title he declined to elucidate, rolling himself in his cloak with the canvas-wrapped package by his side, leaving his friend to ponder afresh the twists of fate that had torn him from the illusory promise of a life safely distanced from the machinations of empire.

They left the beach with the first pink flush of dawn, rowing up the gulf in the still of the morning and making the right turn into Thessalonica's wide sheltered bay an hour later. Docking at the main quay, Titus announced himself to the harbour master as conducting an advance reconnaissance for an imperial fleet that was still two weeks distant, delayed in sailing by problems with the readiness of its warships after so long a period of peace. He had explained his intended ruse the previous evening, based on the hope that the fleet, passing fifty miles to the port's south, would remain unreported prior to their arrival.

'It'll give them pause for thought if they're wavering in their loyalty, and explain our presence without compromising our mission.'

The official shrugged, showing no sign of being at all perturbed by their arrival, and expressed his complete loyalty to the throne in fulsome terms. He invited the honoured prefect to join him in a tour of the harbour's facilities, while the august imperial officer's companions were free to take advantage of the city's many and cosmopolitan facilities in the meantime.

'There will be racing in the hippodrome later this afternoon, or, if you prefer, the scenic view out over the city and the bay from the acropolis is quite a panorama. This will also enable you to take the measure of the city's defences. We are without a garrison at the moment, of course, as the cohort has been called away to serve with the imperial army.'

Having established that he had no idea whose army the troops had been called away to serve, Marcus and his companions took their leave and headed into the city, Qadir fading into the background as expected. Marcus, Lugos, Arminius and Ptolemy meandered slowly through the streets with the demeanour of tourists everywhere, deliberately delaying their search for a bookshop in order to first ensure that they were not followed. The Roman was grateful that Sanga was not with them as a succession of temptations were laid before them with every brothel and tavern they passed, although Arminius, his hair released from its plait to hang free over his shoulders, had to be persuaded more than once to stop grinning at the women and patting his crotch.

'Will you ever give up hope that they won't want to be paid?'

The German grinned back at him, clearly in a playful mood.

'Surely they must be aroused by the presence of such an exotic northern barbarian. It amazes me that they have the willpower to resist!'

At length, and after an hour of studiedly nonchalant wandering around the streets while Ptolemy puffed and sighed with impatience, they came across a bookshop.

The Aegyptian, unable to control his eagerness to be among the collected knowledge of ages, darted between the neighbouring vendors' trestle tables, laden with meat on one side and fruit on the other, waving away the clouds of flies, and almost threw himself into the emporium, Lugos ducking under the shop's lintel behind him. Marcus took a look around before following, seeing nothing more than a typical street scene with a few shoppers picking at the various vendors' displays with feigned disinterest, while passers-by hurried along the street towards their destinations.

'Keep a watch on the street, Arminius? Qadir will be somewhere close by, but I'll be happier with you looking out for trouble as well.'

Inside the gloomy shop, the light of a single lamp doing little to improve on the doorway's dim illumination, the walls were lined from floor to ceiling with neatly organised scrolls. Ptolemy was already engaged in discussion with the bookseller, an avuncular and expressive Jew who had clearly recognised the diminutive scribe as his chance to make a big sale and close up for the day.

'We have them all, my friend, all of the greats that a man as intelligent as you is looking for! The Greek philosophers, the Roman historians, even books written by men of the barbarian north where you would imagine no man ever learns to read, much less put his thoughts on his wretched land onto paper.' He turned to gesture at a shelf loaded with scrolls, oblivious to Lugos's angry glare at his throwaway comment. 'We have the latest volumes of the *Deipnosophistae* by the renowned Athenaeus of Naucratis . . .' He smiled at the sudden excitement on Ptolemy's face. 'Or perhaps some of these, writings by a man whose name will become famous I think, a student of the law and jurisprudence who seems to have an unending output? His name is Aemilius Paulus Papinianus, and he is quite brilliant! See this, his book *Quaestiones*, in thirty-seven volumes. I will make you a special price!'

While this was much to Ptolemy's taste Lugos was more inclined to history, which led to a tour of shelves dedicated to the great recorders of events. The shopkeeper picked out book after book, extolling their virtues as if to a new reader until, having been the recipient of a glowering look from the big man, he wisely left the Briton to peruse the stock for himself.

'And you, Tribune, what can I find for you to read?'

Marcus controlled the urge to take him by the throat, and smiled the smile of a man surprised to have his profession so easily deduced.

'Is it that obvious?'

The Jew smiled indulgently.

'Your boots are utilitarian, but of the highest quality. Your clothing is fashioned in a somewhat military style, but again made with durable and comfortable materials. And your hair is cut short, in the manner of a man who routinely wears a helmet. I had another customer much like you until recently, the commander of the local garrison, and he displayed the same giveaways. A good customer. I can only hope he returns safely from the civil war that must soon blaze across this land—' He raised an apologetic hand. 'Please forgive my impertinence. I am forever risking the ire of my customers with such snap conclusions. It goes with the trade I suppose, forever looking out for men who would like to read without paying for the pleasure. Tell me, what can I find for you to feast upon, so to speak?'

Marcus smiled again.

'I am no great intellectual, unlike my friends. But I do have one great interest, in geography in general and in coastlines in particular. Not just maps, you understand, but in the make-up of a coast, the cliffs, the headlands and the beaches. And I am interested in the local area, say from here to the Hellespont.'

The shopkeeper nodded his understanding.

'A simple enough interest to satisfy! But are you sure that something from my *special* collection wouldn't make an intriguing addition to that worthy study?' He indicated a section of shelving protected from casual perusal by a gauzy curtain. 'It caters to those men who might be missing the company of women – or indeed men – and is a cornucopia of the erotic writings of the last few hundred years. No cheap filth, of course!'

'Only expensive filth?'

The Jew laughed uproariously.

'You I like, Tribune! A man like you would make good company over a jar of wine! I only stock the most tasteful of erotica, some of it exquisitely illustrated by artists whose visions must have been based on the strongest of lusts, to judge from their realism and, shall we say, lifelike depiction of the act in all its forms. And I do mean *all*. Men and women, men and men, women and women, satyrs with both of the sexes . . . ?'

He looked at Marcus enquiringly, but the Roman shook his head with a faint smile.

'A book on the geography of the coast between here and the Hellespont would satisfy all of my needs, although I thank you for the offer and will recall your shop when I need anything of the nature you describe.'

The Jew shrugged and reached up to a high shelf.

'You know your own mind, Tribune, and that is a gift in times like these! Very well, here is what you need. You must forgive the expensive nature of the book. For one thing we don't sell very many by this author as it is somewhat specialised, and it contains many maps that must be laboriously hand-drawn . . .'

Having taken a fat scroll down from its shelf, he passed it to Marcus, who opened it and swiftly scanned the first chapter. The author had either commissioned an artist to draw a map of the coastline his work described or had done so competently himself.

'This is perfect. How much?'

Once his purse was open, he was unsurprised to find both Ptolemy and Lugos at his side with their intended purchases held out. Taking the three books that Lugos had carefully selected, he passed them to the Jew, who was looking at Ptolemy in surprised delight, then turned back to admonish the Aegyptian, feeling like a parent whose task was to explain to an eager child the price and number of honey cakes that were to be purchased.

'You can barely carry so many books, and how will you protect them from the elements? You can choose the same number as Lugos, who has managed to make a selection that is both varied and sensibly composed of long reads.'

He raised a finger to forestall any argument, shooting the bookseller a look that told him that any pleading on the scribe's behalf would not be tolerated, then waited while the dismayed Ptolemy made his choice, stretching the patience of all concerned by changing his mind half a dozen times before settling on his final choices.

'I wasn't at all surprised that you chose the latest work by Athenaeus, and I don't think you'll regret it,' said Lugos, who was leading them out of the shop, having eventually been impelled to assist the scribe with his selection. 'I've always found his writing to be so—'

Reaching behind him without looking back, he swept the Aegyptian to the ground and underneath a stall laden with freshly butchered meats, tossing his books to the sprawling, winded scribe.

'Hold these!'

A pair of nondescript men dressed in threadbare military tunics were waiting for them on the street, both with an infantry shortsword drawn, the looks on their faces bespeaking the slightly bored mien of the professional killer. Looking for Arminius, Marcus realised that the German was motionless on the ground behind them, bleeding copiously onto the street's cobbles. Lacking room to attack two abreast, the two men advanced down the narrow aisle between the meat and fruit stalls in single file, the leading swordsman sizing up the Briton speculatively. Not allowing his would-be assailant to take the initiative, the giant grasped a sheep's leg from the butcher's stall and pivoted at the hip, swinging the solid piece of meat and bone in a blurring arc just as the first attacker made his move. The impact smashed him sideways, knocking the sword from his hand and throwing him headlong across the fruiterer's wares. The table on which the fruit was arrayed collapsed instantly, dropping him to the ground, where he lay momentarily stunned. Pointing a finger at the helpless assassin, Lugos stepped past him and barked a single word.

'Yours!'

His dagger already drawn from beneath the cloak that had concealed it, Marcus waited for the fallen man to reach out for his sword before stooping to put the pugio's long blade into the flesh under his outstretched arm, the expert killing stroke thrusting the foot-long dagger in to its hilt. Wrenching it free, and ignoring his fatally wounded victim, he swapped the knife to his left hand and picked up the gladius with his right. Straightening up again, he saw Lugos, having sidestepped the second man's hurried thrust, grasp the outstretched sword hand and then break the attacker's arm at the elbow like a twig. Opening his mouth to scream, he was rudely silenced by the giant wrenching his head two-handed, breaking his neck and dropping him bonelessly to the street's cobbles.

Advancing past the Briton as he too picked up his victim's sword, the Roman looked up and down the street, finding it unsurprisingly empty of anyone but another half a dozen men, all armed. The biggest of them was advancing to their right with three more at his back, all of them wielding short throwing javelins with grim-eyed competence.

'You fuckers are going to regret that!'

Marcus looked for and found Qadir, who was looking at him questioningly from the street's far end to the friends' left, twenty paces beyond the two men with the meaty build of gladiators blocking any swift exit in that direction, their attention riveted on the action to their front. He nodded wearily at the Hamian as the killers' leader pulled his spear back with his gaze fixed on Lugos, spitting his fury at the big Briton as he prepared to hurl the deadly missile.

'This is what happens when—'

With the hiss of an angry viper an arrow flicked past the Roman's face, close enough for him to wonder if the kiss of its flight feathers had been real or imagined, burying a foot of its length in the spearman's chest. While the men behind him were still working out what had happened a second shot took the next closest of them down, prompting the remaining pair to turn and run for safety that they were never going to reach. The first fell with a shaft protruding from his back, and the second dropped to his knees, choking on his own blood as he scrabbled at the iron head of an arrow that had transfixed his throat.

Seeing that the remaining two men, clearly having been set to guard the other end of the street, were caught between the Hamian's deadly bow and the vengeful Lugos, Marcus hurried to where Arminius was lying in the street, face down in a pool of blood that was trickling towards the gutter from the deep wound in his back. He turned him over to see the big German's face slack and lifeless. Closing his friend's eyelids, he pushed a coin into the dead man's mouth, and then turned to the men lying along the street's length.

The closest of them, the spearmen who Qadir had taken first, was lying on his back with the arrow's shaft pointing at the sky, panting swift shallow breaths. When the Roman came into his field of view he snarled weakly, his body jerking as the captured gladius stopped his heart. The next man was already dead, the arrow having pierced his chest from back to front, and the man behind him was so close to death as to make the swift thrust of the blade a mercy killing, but the last of them was lying on his side with the shaft that had dropped him protruding from his back.

Marcus squatted by his head and put the dagger to his throat.

'The arrow went in low. It's in your liver. Which means you'll die whether I give you peace or leave you to struggle for a while. Give me a name and I'll make it easier for you.'

The wounded man nodded, having watched his own death approach with that of each of his comrades.

'One of you . . . a Roman . . . his name was . . . Sartorius.'

Marcus cut his throat and turned away, walking back to where the last two men were cowering under the threat of Lugos's fury, their weapons kicked into the gutter. He walked out in front of them with the gladius raised and his dagger held low and out to one side to draw attention to the blood dripping from its blade. With their weapons taken from them both men were clearly caught on the horns of a dilemma, neither fight nor flight offering any hope of escape, their identical blue tunics giving him a clue as to what they were.

'I don't have time for anything fancy, the vigiles will be here soon enough, so let's get this over with quickly. You're gladiators, aren't you? All that muscle and flesh you're carrying is a dead giveaway, not to mention the matching tunics. I wonder how your lanista would take the news that you're moonlighting on him, breaking your oath and putting his investment at so much risk? I don't even have to kill you, just disarm you and take you back to the ludus, for him to make an example of you for the rest of his fighters.'

He grinned mercilessly at them, nodding as he saw the confirmation in their faces.

'There you go – you chose to gamble, now you have to pay the price for picking the losing side! So, here's how it works. I know who ordered this, and whoever can tell me where to find this Sartorius gets to walk away. Eventually. The other one dies here.'

The shorter of the two raised his hands in a gesture of surrender.

'I'll tell you whatever you want!'

'You fucking—!'

His comrade, realising that he was being abandoned to his own fate, turned and lunged at him with raised fists, only to stagger and then collapse to the ground with Marcus's sword in his side. The Roman kicked him off the blade and raised the captured gladius in an uncompromising gesture.

'Start talking! The city watch will turn up soon enough, and I have no intention of being here when they arrive.'

The gladiator raised his hands in an attempt to place the blame for the attack elsewhere.

'We were nothing to do with it. They were the men who took the coin to take you!' He pointed at the scattered bodies littering the street. 'They're a gang, deserters the lot of them! They just brought us in for numbers, and to keep the street empty!'

'So who gave them the orders? Who's this Sartorius?'

The terrified captive shook his head, his eyes wide with the need to prove his relative innocence.

'I don't know!'

Marcus shrugged.

'You're not much use to me alive then, are you? At least dead you send a message to the city that traitors will be punished with the loss of their lives.'

'No! I can help you!'

The Roman shrugged.

'Yes, by being seen to be punished.'

He raised his sword, but before he could strike the gladiator was on his knees, begging for mercy in a babbling gush of entreaty.

'I can help! I know where they planned to take you. They had orders to deliver you, just *you* and none of the others.'

Marcus looked down the blade at him.

'Where? And how do you know?'

'There's a hideaway in a cave close to the Acropolis. I heard them say they were going to take you back there.'

'It sounds to me like someone's exercising some good judgement in their orders of who to kill and who to capture?'

Qadir joined Marcus by the captive. He had wrapped his bow in the canvas bag he had used to conceal it as he tracked them around the city. The Roman nodded.

'And you can take us to this lair? If you lie to me and I find out that this is a trap, or that you have no idea where it is, I'll hamstring you and leave you crippled for life, and then leave word at the ludus where you can be found.'

'On my life, it's true! I'll take you there!'

Reasoning that leaving by either end of the street risked running into the urban watch, Marcus led their captive back to the bookshop, whose proprietor was watching from his doorway. Tossing a generous handful of coins to the butcher and fruiterer to compensate them for losses that were minor at best, in the hope of gaining their silence for a short time at least, he gestured at the shop's shaded confines

'You have another way out of here?'

The Jew pointed to a doorway at the rear of his premises, so low and narrow that it looked almost too small for the Briton to squeeze through. Marcus held up another coin, glinting in the lamplight.

'A gold piece should be enough to buy your silence, and that of your neighbours?'

'Of course, Tribune. And here is a gift for you, for the entertainment you have provided.' He handed Marcus a scroll. 'You'll thank me later.'

They emerged in a narrow lane behind the shops, hurrying away up the roads that led towards the Acropolis, the gladiator's left arm firmly held in Lugos's unbreakable grip. Following the road that curved around to the right of the base of the fortified hillside, their reluctant guide took them up into the hills behind it. The rocky ground was studded with boulders, some with stunted olive trees growing around them, while a low scrub and the scattering of trees provided ground cover that made it hard to see much more than fifty paces. Qadir looked about them with an unhappy expression.

'This is far from the ideal ground to advance into without any previous scouting. There could be a century of enemy spies out here and we would never know they were there until they had us surrounded.'

Marcus nodded at the Hamian's misgivings.

'A single man must go forward, and see what can be discerned from observing this gang lair.'

He started forward but found his way blocked by the Hamian.

'You are not the right man for such a task. They would hear you coming from a hundred paces, despite all your efforts to be silent. I must do this.'

'The ghost of Hamah?'

Qadir smiled.

'It is many years since I was that man, but yes. Let us see what there is to be seen, and heard, by a patient and quiet man.'

He vanished into the undergrowth and after a few moments was lost to sight, his stealthy advance undetectable. Marcus turned back to the cowed gladiator, whispering in the discomfited captive's ear with the dagger held up for him to see.

'We must wait in complete silence for him to return. And of course you will be tempted to call out, in the hope that they will both free and reward you. Be sure that you understand what will happen if you make the wrong choice in that moment of decision.'

'No!' The other man's whisper was frantic, as Lugos leaned in close to stare at him forebodingly. 'I would never . . .'

'We both know you would sell us out in a moment if you thought you could get away with it. So just be clear that were you to do so, I would make it my last task to put my dagger into your guts and wrench it around a time or two to make your last few days of this life truly hard to endure. Low down, to avoid the risk of nicking your liver and giving you an easier exit from your agony. If you choose to shout a warning you will be condemning yourself to a death that could take two or three days of excruciating pain.'

The gladiator raised his hands to fend off the blade's threat, his terrified whisper barely audible.

'No! I swear on the altar of Pluto himself that I will not make any such effort! Only spare me and I will dedicate one half of my future winnings to his name!'

Marcus took the dagger from his throat, but kept it in sight and ready to use.

'You're not really made for your chosen career, are you? You bought all that talk of your being a valuable asset, never once stopping to think what might happen if your lanista needs a man to use as the tethered goat in demonstration of a better fighter's skills, didn't you? You should buy yourself out, if you have the means, because you will never live to receive your wooden sword with fear that obvious.'

Qadir crawled to within fifty paces of the cave's presumed location, moving the stones in front of him as far as he could to either side to avoid dislodging them and causing a noise that might betray him. Judging the distance remaining from his proximity to the steep rock face, he slid noiselessly into the cover of a stunted olive tree and listened intently, without the sounds of his body

sliding across the dusty hillside's stony terrain to distract his sharp
hearing. The sound of voices was intermittent but unmistakable,
coming and going as the wind gusted across the hillside. Two or
three men were speaking, their words unintelligible beneath the
hiss of the breeze over the dusty ground.

He thought for a moment, then reached down and eased his
penis out from under his tunic, and urinated into a dip in the
ground. A good-sized puddle formed and, scooping handfuls of
dust into the liquid, he stirred the viscous mixture with a finger
and then brushed in more dust, continuing the process until a
thick ochre-coloured mud had formed. Taking a handful, he wiped
it across his face, not stopping until a coating of the dun-coloured
mixture was in place on his exposed skin, then rubbed more of the
dust into the parts of his tunic that he could reach until its dark red
wool was effectively disguised from casual view.

Crawling forward with infinite care, he moved slowly towards
the sound of the voices until he was able to hear what was being
said.

'. . . much longer we have to wait for those idiots to bring a single man up from the city, I wonder?'

The voice was authoritative, and the question clearly rhetorical,
since it went unanswered. Easing forward a few more inches, the
Hamian found a line of sight to the speaker and watched through
the gap in the scrub, unconsciously holding his breath with the
drama of the moment. Equipped in the finery of a legion centurion, albeit with a black tunic beneath his armour, he was holding
a ceremonial hasta pura in one hand, the spear's ornate head made
broad enough to sport an eye-sized hole on each side of the exag-
gerated leaf-shaped blade. Watching the officer pace back and
forth with evidently mounting irritation, Qadir was certain that
the gleaming ornament hanging from his belt would be a miniature representation of the spear's ostentatious badge of rank. One
of the men sitting around him said something that the Hamian
was unable to hear, but if his words were indistinct the officer's
response was all too clear, and his accent at once familiar.

'Do I think the fisherman was pulling our pissers to get himself some money?' He shook his head emphatically. 'No. His description was too strange to be made up, and too specific, for that matter. Too much like what we have been looking for, a sign of Rome's power approaching by sea as well as by land. A man looking to get paid and then vanish with the gold might have told us that five men had come ashore, and perhaps added the detail that one of them was a naval officer and another looked like a legion tribune, and left it at that. But what was it that he told us? That the sailor went off with the harbour master, and that the officer was accompanied by a giant, a barbarian and a squeaking bookworm? It's just too strange a description to be invention. No, the information was genuine. Add to that the fact that he claimed to have sold them fish last night and it's solid as stone as far as I'm concerned. It's not the fisherman that's the problem, it's those fools we hired to take them prisoner!'

The next comment was equally inaudible, but the centurion's answer was both clear enough to be heard and a warning note to Qadir, as he raised a sand glass that appeared to be more than half empty.

'How much longer do we wait? Not long. If those idiots don't appear with the legion officer by the time this has run out then my patience will have run out with it.'

Backing away with slow, careful movements, the Hamian retreated back down the hill until he was sure that there was no risk of being seen, then cautiously got to his feet and carefully, still crouched over, retraced his steps back down the slope to where he had left his comrades waiting for him. He found the gladiator still crouching under the threat of Marcus's pugio, while Ptolemy and Lugos had both opened scrolls and started to read, the intellectual equivalent of a legionary's urge to sleep whenever a moment of peace presented itself. Putting a finger to his lips, Qadir pointed back down the hill towards the city, ignoring the wrinkled noses of his companions at the acrid scent of his impromptu camouflage. Two hundred paces back down the slope, standing in the shadow of the towering fortifications and washing the mud away with water from a stone trough fed from the city's aqueduct, he was finally willing to speak.

'Our escape was narrower than you might imagine. There is a Roman up there, a man of the great city itself. And it seems to me that he wouldn't have been minded to let you live, had those cut-throats taken you to him.'

'A man of Rome? Are you sure of that?'

Qadir nodded.

'As sure as I can be, having heard enough of your people speak over the years. He had the accent of the slums, that fast way of speaking and turn of phrase. One of them called him Centurion, and I am fairly sure that he is from the same mould as that man who has become the emperor's enforcer, the former centurion Felix.'

'You think he is a grain officer?'

'That or something alike, whichever way they name such a man in the east. I listened to him from perhaps thirty paces distant, and to me he sounded as if he had the same ruthlessness and total air of superiority that so much power in such an apparently lowly rank can give a man. It seems he and his men have infiltrated the city with orders to search for any sign of an imperial army being shipped here from Italy, and that they were alerted to our presence by the fisherman who sold us our dinner last night. I saw his boat in the harbour earlier without making any connection, until I distinctly heard the officer tell one of his men that the "fisherman" had described us well enough that the gang they employed to abduct you should have been able to follow us from the docks easily enough. An officer, a barbarian . . .' He paused for a moment at the reminder of Arminius's death, the wound of his loss still fresh. '. . . a giant and a small man, which implies that the fisherman was away to tell them of our arrival before I disembarked once you were gone from the port, which is why he missed me.'

Marcus nodded, ignoring Ptolemy's bristling anger at being described as small.

'So the man we bought fish from last night was the traitor? Which means that the main question is whether he saw the fleet passing to the south, or believed that we were just a single vessel scouting the way for an army's future arrival?'

The Hamian shrugged.

'Nothing that was said gave any clue as to that, but either way we need to be away from here. There were a number of them waiting in the cave, and it didn't sound as if their leader was a patient man. Putting down a few brigands is one thing, but fighting a running battle through those streets with as many men as I suspect they have in reserve would be a different matter.'

'Agreed. You' – Marcus turned a hard stare on the gladiator – 'will accompany us to the dockside, and as long as you make no attempt to betray us, you will live to spend another day terrified in the arena. Try to run, call out or in any way make the mistake of thinking you can do anything other than keep silent, and your death will be both public and unpleasant in the extreme.'

They hurried down to the docks with as much haste as was seemly, finding Titus waiting for them by the Ligurian with the look of a man who was just as keen to be away.

'Business all done? Where's the German?'

Marcus nodded tersely, indicating the waiting ship.

'He's dead. Killed by hired killers set on us by Niger's agents. I'll show you what we found once we're on our way back to the fleet, but for now just accept my assurance that this is the one place we don't want to be!' He turned to their captive. 'You can go, and if you have even an uncia of sense you'll run back to the ludus and keep your head down about this whole thing!'

The gladiator needed no encouragement to turn on his heel and head for the safety of the dockside gate while the party boarded the Liburnian, and the Roman watched him vanish through it as the ship's master ordered his men to cast off and man their oars to get the vessel turned through a half circle so that the sails could be spread. With the etesiae wind on their right side, and blowing from the rear quarter, the ship heeled over slightly as the sails filled and took it out across the water at the speed of a cantering horse, the vessel's master steering for the bay's entrance with the look of a man who was happy simply to be back at sea.

Looking back, Marcus saw a small group of men in red tunics emerge onto the quayside, a spot of blue among them betraying the presence of the gladiator. He raised a hand to point at the receding ship, and Marcus shook his head in disbelief at the man's stupidity.

'The fool. There's no way they could have identified him as an accomplice in our abduction if he hadn't sought them out in hope of some reward. Instead of which their only sensible action must be to silence him.'

Qadir moved to stand beside him, his excellent eyesight allowing him to watch as the distance between ship and shore opened swiftly.

'No more days in the arena for him then.'

Marcus shook his head, unable to feel any sorrow for a man who had chosen to betray them and yet still wincing as the red tunics closed in around the hapless gladiator.

'No.'

The enemy soldiers turned and left through the dockside gate, leaving a single blue tunicked body on the stone quay behind them. Reaching the bay's entrance, the ship's master pushed his vessel into a sweeping left turn to run south into the gulf, ordering all sail to be raised for maximum speed as they ran before the wind in their pursuit of the now distant fleet. And when an hour later, and with the story of their escape from Sartorius's trap told, the fisherman's distinctive black sail came into view on the horizon, Titus strolled over to the master and pointed it out, his orders blunt and to the point.

'Run that boat down. That bastard sold us out, so he can go into the sea and become food for the fishes. No man can hope to betray the empire and live when his treason is discovered.'

An hour later, with no sign of any pursuit and the Ligurian running south at a brisk clip with the wind on her left rear quarter,

Titus left her master to his own devices and walked across the deck to where Marcus was looking back over the rail in search of any sign of another ship behind them.

'The masthead lookout will see them before you do, not that anyone's going to try to chase us down. For one thing I reckon they're guessing we have a fleet out here, and for another it's all very well to skulk around the city looking for spies and another thing entirely to do it on the sea. Especially now we've dealt with their spy. So, let's have a good look at this map of yours.'

He took the book that Marcus had purchased and turned the scroll slowly, considering each port and beach in turn.

'Too far from where you want to be . . . too risky a landing . . . ah, perhaps here?' He pointed at the map with a broad finger. 'Aenus.'

Ptolemy perked up immediately.

'Aenus? A city founded by the ancient Greek hero Aeneus. He, of course, was the father of Cyzicus, who was the founder of the city of the same name, and—'

Marcus interrupted him in a kindly but firm tone.

'Ptolemy, go and read your books with Lugos, before you irritate the prefect more than you already have?'

The Aegyptian sniffed and walked away, Titus following him with a dark and forbidding stare.

'You tolerate too much from the men of Scaurus's familia. I could wish I still had a family to bestow half as much indulgence on.' He glowered at Marcus, making the Roman wonder what had befallen his wife and children. 'Anyway . . . Aenus. That's the best place to land your legion, to judge from what the writer has to say.'

Marcus stayed silent, and after a moment the sailor continued in a thoughtful tone of voice.

'A long beach, long enough to take the whole fleet in one landing. And just as well, because the harbour can only be reached by means of a narrow entrance, and lies on an estuary bay so shallow that I fear half of my ships would ground before they could land their men. The beach itself must be impossible to attack from the land, because he says that it is backed by an uninterrupted salt marsh, which means that even if there are three legions waiting for you they wouldn't be able to get to you while you were landing.'

Marcus looked at the map and saw a thick group of symbols indicating what could well be marsh grass running along the whole length of the beach.

'So how do we get onto solid ground?'

'There.' Titus pointed at the hand-drawn map to indicate a thin line through the marsh. 'You see? A path through the marshes. Wide enough only for two men to walk abreast at best, I would imagine.'

Marcus thought for a moment.

'The city must have hundreds of occupants. Perhaps thousands?'

'Which is ideal. Quite apart from it being a major port for the movement of goods, this man names it as a fishing port. They supply fish and roe to the surrounding lands, using salt from the sea to keep it edible. Take the city and you'll have enough food to keep your legion fed for a few days while you advance on Byzantium, and the carts to carry it as well. Aenus has to be the best option you have.'

'My point is what's to keep them from sounding an alarm? A fleet coming over the horizon will surely be visible long before we can get ashore and bottle them up inside their own walls. One man on a horse could be all it takes to raise the alarm and bring their legions down on us.'

Titus nodded.

'Under normal circumstances, you are absolutely correct. Anyone watching from their walls would see us coming the moment the first ships come over the horizon. Which means we'll have to land you at a time when there's nobody watching the sea, doesn't it?'

7

Scaurus took the news of his freedman's death at the hands of the enemy spy's men stoically, but Marcus knew that he was deeply affected even if his friend was able to contain most of his reaction.

'He died quickly?'

Qadir answered, his voice muted by the grief they were all feeling.

'He was stabbed in the back with a gladius. I had already real-ised that something untoward was happening from the number of men on the street, but I was unable to get his attention. His back was to me, and he was lost in contemplation of a passing woman. I doubt he even knew what it was that killed him.'

The tribune nodded sadly at the easterner's words.

'Typical of the man, always much more at home in the forests and marshes of his homeland than in our cities where he could never resist the temptation to demonstrate his manliness. I will miss him more than I would have thought before this moment, with his constant offering of unwanted advice and opinion and unbreakable belief in his own superiority. And you will need to break the news to Lupus with care, Arminius was practically the father he lost ten years ago.' He took a deep breath. 'I will pray for him. And now tell me the story of how this came about, and how you eluded capture. It sounds as if you had a lucky escape. Tell me everything about this mysterious officer Sartorius you saw, Centurion.'

They had rejoined the fleet just as the sun sank below the west-ern horizon, running ashore in the gloom alongside the beached warships. Titus, having agreed with his deputy where the war-ships would land each night, had guided them straight to a long beach on the island of Thasos, where they found the legion already ashore and Scaurus and Julius conferring beside a fire that was being coaxed into life by Sanga and Saratos.

'There is little more to tell you, Tribune.' Qadir had recounted the story of his infiltration of the enemy camp to Marcus twice, racking his memory for any more detail, but had been unable to dredge up any more facts than had been immediately forthcoming, which he recounted in a matter-of-fact way. 'I got close enough to be able to see the man, as he stood outside the cave in which they were waiting for their hired swords to bring them our comrade. His uniform and equipment were military, and there was no doubting that he was a centurion or that his men were legionaries, from the respect they showed him. Or, for that matter, that he was impatient in his pursuit of what he saw as interlopers in the city. Whether he was also a frumentarius is perhaps debatable, but his status as an agent of Niger's army seems indisputable. For one thing he was holding a hasta pura, and for another his belt order contained a miniature representation of the same symbol of power.'

Scaurus nodded his agreement with the Hamian's opinion.

'If he was carrying a ceremonial lance then he has to have been someone's beneficiarius. Quite possibly Niger's, when he was governor of Syria before taking the purple. A beneficiarius consularis, perhaps, and a man of some particularly specialised skills, it seems.'

Cilo, who had been sitting and listening, nodded his agreement.

'It sounds likely. He must be a man of known abilities who suddenly found his master elevated to the rank of emperor, and who took full advantage of that good fortune to advance his own rank. And who has now been ordered to scout forward for any trace of an army being sent around their left flank by sea. Which means that we might just have betrayed our presence to them by sending your men into Thessalonica.'

Scaurus sat down, gesturing for his companions to do the same.

'We had little choice, if we were to find the right spot at which to put the legion ashore. You're sure that the fisherman you killed was the man who betrayed your presence in the city?'

Marcus's answer was equivocal.

'It seems likely. We saw no other fishermen the evening before we went into the port, and he headed away to the north when we bade him farewell, heading for the city. The odds that he was being paid to watch the approaches to the port, and that this man Sartorius knew we were coming even before we arrived in the harbour, must be good. It's possible that Prefect Titus ordered the murder of an innocent, but I doubt you reach the rank he has without the ability to harden your heart to that sort of possibility.'

The tribune nodded.

'And no degree of questioning his guilt is going to bring the man back.' He gestured to the scroll in Marcus's hand. 'So, what did you bring back? Do you have a beach for us?'

The younger man unrolled the book to the page that Titus had selected in the long hours of the Ligurian's stern chase of the fleet, passing it across to the tribune.

'Here . . .'

Scaurus looked at the section of the book presented to him and nodded slowly as Marcus described the advantages that Titus had laid out in assessing the potential landing spot.

'It looks like the perfect landing ground, and about as close to Perinthus as it's possible to get without the risk of Titus taking the fleet through the Hellespont into a potential trap, which he has explicit orders to avoid . . .' He pondered the book for a moment. 'The only real risk being that someone from the city gets away before we can surround it, and raises the alarm inland.'

He handed the book to Julius, who took one look at the hand-drawn map and shrugged.

'It looks as good as anywhere. How far distant is it?'

'About fifty miles.' Titus had joined them, having taken a moment to relieve his deputy of command of the fleet. 'It's a good choice, with only one problem to be dealt with.' He looked around at them, waiting for anyone to comment. 'No? There's nowhere to beach for the night within twenty miles of the place where we could land without the risk of word getting out the next day. If you want to achieve surprise we'll have to spend the night before the landing at sea. Which means that if you're planning on rewarding your men with that day on the beach you've been talking about, then it's tomorrow or never.'

Marcus shot a glance at Sanga, who was close enough to have heard the exchange as he pretended to tend a fire that was already well alight.

'If you know what's good for you, Legionary, you'll keep your mouth shut on that subject. And besides, if you give me any reason to be unhappy with you then I won't be inclined to give you this . . .'

He opened another scroll, the one given to him by the bookseller when they had used the man's shop as an escape route from the urban watch the day before.

'See? I'd imagine you'd be quite keen to receive this as a gift.'

The soldier leaned closer, unable to see clearly in the fire's flickering light, his eyes lighting up as he realised what was drawn on the paper Marcus had unrolled before him. He reached out to take the book, but found his hand closing on thin air as it was pulled out of his reach.

'No, you can only have it if what the prefect just said stays a secret until we officially announce it tomorrow. If the legion get wind of a day off the camp will be in ferment all night, and I'll be forced to burn this rather than give it to you. Do we understand each other?'

'I can't believe he's dead. If I'd gone with him he'd be alive now.'

Lupus was still in a state of grief, hollow-eyed at the loss of the man who had been the closest thing he had to a father after his own father's death in a rebellion along the frontier in Britannia.

'If you'd gone with him you'd both be dead now. The men who were hunting us were veteran soldiers, and they attacked him while he was doing what he enjoyed the most.'

The younger man's half-smile was poignant in the firelight.

'Don't tell me, I can guess. He was talking to some woman or other about what a stallion he was, right?'

'So it seems. There were eight of them, and I doubt he ever saw them coming.'

Lupus blew out a long breath.

'At least it was quick. I don't know what I'll do without him though.'

'I do.' The Briton stared at Marcus questioningly. 'From tomorrow you are no longer under tuition. With Arminius's death the tribune needs a bodyguard to replace him.'

'I could never—'

'Replace him, yes, I know. But from tomorrow you can start trying your best to do so. Report to me at daybreak and we can introduce him to the idea. Now get some sleep while I go and find Julius.'

The beach sentries directed him to the highest ground overlooking the beach, where the big Briton, having dismissed the lookouts, had taken over the duty himself. The full moon was serene in a cloudless night sky above them, reducing the blaze of stars to a shadow of their usual splendour.

'Is there no peace to be had, even here?' The big centurion's smile belied his gruff tone, and he kept his eyes on the horizon as Marcus seated himself on a rock. 'You can't sleep either?'

The Roman looked over the moonlit sea for a moment before replying.

'There'll be time enough to sleep tomorrow. Tonight my mind can't stop working on how close we came to being overwhelmed by a gang of former soldiers and gladiators. If they'd had the sense to take us in the bookshop they could have overwhelmed us with sheer weight of numbers in such a confined space.'

Julius shrugged.

'Then be grateful that they didn't think it through, or just arrived too late to take advantage.'

'Yes. But the fact that the enemy has spies out this far west of the Propontis isn't a good sign for us. Where there's a spy there's likely to be an army not too far behind.'

'Very likely. And it's more than possible that we'll be facing two or three times our own number within a few days. But I'll tell you one thing. The day I don't have to get back on that fucking ship and spend all day shouting at bored soldiers to polish their armour for the ninety-ninth time will be a *really* good day. Just to have solid ground beneath my feet and the opportunity to put this legion on the road for a proper battle march, that's what I'm looking forward to.'

Marcus nodded.

'You think they'll have a decent fight in them?'

The big man laughed softly.

'Every retired centurion ever to carry a vitis has always told anyone who'd listen that the legions are nowhere near as good as they were when he was serving. Because every centurion ever has always believed that he and his mates had the biggest balls ever when they were young.'

He smiled, his teeth a white bar in his heavily tanned face in the moonlight.

'And every centurion ever was full of shit. These men are no worse and no better than any other legion there's been since the Divine Julius took on the Gauls so that he could write a book saying what a great general he was and get the women wet and paint his face red for yet another parade. Some of them will be shit-scared, and have to be kept in line by their officers with violence. Some of them will be monsters, and have to be restrained from going at the enemy on their own. And most of them will be like we always were – present company notwithstanding, given you had to be saved from the enemy more than once when you waded into them with your iron singing blood and death. They'll screw up their courage and fight like men, because what else can they do this far from home? So yes, they'll have a decent fight in them. Whether it'll be enough will depend on what the enemy have to offer.'

He looked out over the moon, which was touching the southern horizon and starting to sink beneath the sea.

'At least tomorrow they'll have a chance to drink a cup of wine and eat some good roast meat, rather than the constant diet of fish. And the entertainment of watching their champions go at each other with practice swords. Will you be taking part in the competition?'

Marcus shook his head.

'No. I think it's better if someone from the legion wins the prize, and not an officer who's been with them for less than a month.'

The following day's sky was empty of clouds, and Julius decided to get the day's competitions out of the way before the sun's unobstructed heat made the exertions impractical. Each cohort put forward its champions in the disciplines of sprinting, boxing and swordsmanship to compete for the title of legion champion, and the much more important prize of an amphora of wine for their century for each winner. Morban, his instincts twitching with the urge to make money from the innocent, watched Marcus with an expression of sorrowful regret as the Roman steadfastly refused all attempts to persuade him to take part in the swordsmanship competition. His angst was hardly improved by the sight of Sanga and Saratos doing a brisk trade in pornographic images, drawings cut from the book that Marcus had promised them in order to keep the day's competition a secret until the day dawned, having first retained their own favourites for later perusal.

Smiling knowingly at the frustrated former standard-bearer, the tribune instead appointed himself as the swordsmanship competition's arbiter, the judge of the matches that would reduce the competitors from ten to five plus the man he decided had been the best loser, then to three plus another deserving loser, and then to two for the final match. Two hours later, with the first of the semi-finals fought, and the winner strolling away to the awning where each round's victors took shelter from the sun while awaiting their next match, Dubnus nudged Marcus. He tipped his head towards the triumphant fighter whose men were still cheering his latest victory.

'See that one? Bet you weren't expecting him to even enter the competition, never mind be halfway decent with a sword.' He barked out a laugh. 'And there was you not wanting some recently arrived officer carrying off the prize, eh?'

With the penultimate qualifying match completed, and one bout remaining before the final fight, which would determine who would be crowned as the legion's best swordsman, the two men were as surprised as the rest of the legion that the man on whom all the serious money was now being wagered was not a legionary, or even a chosen man or centurion, but one of the legion's new tribunes. Marcus had at first simply been nonplussed to learn that Furius Aculeo was to be his cohort's champion, rather than any of the soldiers serving under the young officer. He had watched with what had at first been no more than professional interest, as the tribune had despatched his first opponent with ease while displaying hints of an unexpected skill, seemingly fighting well within the abilities that his easy victory hinted at.

Entering the ring of men with shields that defined the arena for each bout to judge the tribune's second match, he had initially suspected that Furius had met his match in a rangy and scarfaced chosen man, whose combination of skill and aggression had made his own first-round match little more than a formality. A brief flurry of action had swiftly dispelled any such expectation, although the hardened soldier had at first merely been discomfited by his opponent's unexpected ability to evade his initial onslaught. The chosen man had swiftly been stunned, however, by the ease with which the younger man had turned seemingly effortless defence into a blisteringly swift attack. Slipping his sword's tip through the other man's crumbling defences to make the required three touches of the wooden blade that ended the match as swiftly as it had started, he had turned away from his crestfallen rival with an expression that bespoke little more than the delivery of a firmly held expectation on his own part.

But it had been the third match that had shown the man's true abilities. He had been matched with a legionary who had been a gladiator in the legion's home city of Singidunum and who, belatedly realising the somewhat hazardous nature of his profession, had chosen to enlist with the Fourth under a false name on the day the legion had marched south in support of Severus. The recruiting centurion, recognising a good thing when he saw it, had turned a blind eye to what was effectively the theft of a lanista's property, purporting not to know who the new recruit was and tacitly recognising, given they might all be dead soon enough, that the matter of the man's ownership was quite likely never to be an issue. Something of a celebrity as a result, the new legionary had proven unbeatable by any of the men who he had been matched with in the previous rounds, and had approached each fight with the swagger and bombast of a man who believed himself unchallengeable. But if he had expected to add the young man facing him to the list of those he'd humiliated with his assured blade-work, his awakening had been both prompt and spectacular.

Going at Furius with everything he had, wary of allowing a man he took for a competent if not expert challenger a look-in and risking falling to some fluke or piece of bad luck, he found his attacks foiled and evaded with the same ease he had previously enjoyed against less skilled opposition. Frustrated, he had attempted the use of physical intimidation in the form of a shield charge, only to find himself on the ground with his ankle smarting from the sword stroke delivered by Furius as he had rolled his body around the attack, grinning at his opponent with an expression that clearly indicated he knew all the gladiator's tricks and more. Neither had switching to defence saved him from further humiliation, the young tribune carving through his attempts at blocking with the ease of a veteran to score the remaining strikes required to win the match with consummate ease.

Leaving his defeated opponent to the jeers of the assembled soldiers, Furius had returned to the awning under which the victors of each match took shelter from the sun as they awaited their next bout, now empty as the remaining two contenders prepared for their own, seemingly irrelevant, match. Marcus nodded in recognition of Dubnus's point.

'I can't deny that I'm impressed by his ability with a sword. I'm curious to find out where he gained that sort of skill.'

He strolled over to where Furius was taking a drink of water before the last match, nodding his respect to the younger man.

'You have the skills of a master swordsman, Tribune.'

Furius nodded, his face impassive in the face of the praise.

'I know. I was inspired as a boy of seven by a visit to the Flavian arena in the company of my father. It was my first games, and I was fortunate enough that it was a day that went down in history, the day that a gladiator by the name of Corvus overcame odds of three to one to become an instant hero for the crowd. I can still see him standing among the corpses of his fallen foes with two other men at his side, after they defeated nine opponents in less time than it would take to tell the story. My father told me that I had seen the birth of a new star, a gladiator who was destined to be as famous as Flamma the Great, and yet he never appeared on the sand again. Not that it mattered to me, because I was at once and forever devoted to the gladiatorial arts from that day.'

'And you started training with the blade?'

Furius took a wooden sword from the rack, stretching forward into a practice lunge before coming back to a standing position.

'I was already training to be a soldier. My father was set on sending me to the army when I came of age, in accordance with family tradition, but that training was nothing like as exciting as what I'd seen in the arena. The sheer joy of watching a master swordsman like Corvus dance around his opponents, his two blades flickering like the fangs of a striking snake, made me reconsider what I wanted from life. After that day in the arena I didn't just want to be a swordsman, I wanted to be *the* swordsman, the master swordsman of my day. And so I practised for hours every day with a succession of tutors, until by the time I was fifteen my father could no longer find anyone I couldn't beat after a few matches to work out their style, unless they resorted to using their greater strength to overcome me.'

Marcus nodded.

'And then as you became a man and worked with weights to put on some muscle even that wasn't enough to beat you. And you discovered the only problem with being known as the best at what you do, didn't you?'

'Yes. Men would refuse to cross swords with me, knowing the outcome was already decided. And every time I went blade to blade with a man whose skill was sufficient to give me a workout I found that I wasn't enjoying it any more, just working out how to manoeuvre them into the best position for the touch that would end the match.'

'You no longer enjoy the thing that has come to define you.' Furius looked up at him with a knowing expression, tacit recognition of Marcus's point. 'There is no joy in it for you, as you are always expected to win by all involved, including yourself. What you expected would be the source of your pride has become little more than work for you, with every man that matches his skills against yours only fighting to survive or for the chance to say that he crossed blades with you. Welcome to the rest of your life.'

He turned away and went to rejoin Dubnus by the shield-bearers, who were holding their boards over their bare heads to protect themselves from the sun.

'It's like looking at myself ten years ago. He has achieved what seems to be the pinnacle of his chosen craft only to discover that it is a lonely place, stripped of the pleasure he expected to find in becoming the best at what he does. Flamma warned me as much when I was striving to master the skills he was employed to teach me. "Be careful to find something else to live your life through," he told me, "or you'll end up like me, with nothing more meaningful to live for than the empty adulation of the mob, with no true friends and a million fickle worshippers all waiting for the next man to make the subject of their devotion." Being the best man you know at what you do is the end of the journey, but it can be a disappointing destination to reach. It was only finding the comradeship of you and the other members of our familia that gave me any purpose. That, and my wife and son . . .'

The Briton snorted a laugh, attempting to divert his friend from thoughts of the past.

'Him? The best? Not likely! You could have that boy on his back without breaking sweat!'

Marcus shook his head.

'What would be the point? He already hates me, because he knows I killed his uncle. The last thing we need is for him to be brooding at my back when there's a war to be fought. And in any case there's no way for us to find out without crossing swords, which is definitely not my plan. Now do me a favour, go and tell Morban exactly that, to prevent him from taking bets on the idea of the two of us fighting a match.'

He turned away and summoned the other two semi-finalists, a pair of centurions who fought out a protracted match that neither of them was sufficiently skilled to end quickly. The fight, between two closely matched men, both in peak condition, and fought in temperatures that were already high enough to soak their tunics with sweat within the first few minutes, swiftly deteriorated into the spectacle of two exhausted fighters battering at each other's shields with ever-increasing weariness. Marcus was about to step in and pause the bout when one of the centurions stopped fighting, dropped his sword and leaned on his shield panting for breath.

'I'm fucked, Tribune!' He breathed hard for a moment before continuing, waving a hand at his equally exhausted fellow officer. 'This prick can take on the young gentleman if he thinks he has the beating of him, because I'm pretty sure I don't!'

Marcus nodded and turned to the other competitor, reaching for his sword hand to raise it in victory, but the centurion was having none of it.

'No you fucking don't, begging your pardon, Tribune! I've no more chance of beating that young man than he does. He can have the prize as far as I'm concerned and that's that.'

Recognising that neither man was in any state to fight another bout, Marcus accepted their joint resignations with good grace, and invited Furius to return to the ring of shields to be named as the champion swordsman. But the young tribune's reaction was not the one he had expected. Raising both hands, he declined the title with a solemnity that Marcus suspected was a mask for a different motivation entirely.

'I cannot accept a prize that I have not won! Since there is no other man of the right skills to face me in the ring, we'll just have to declare the championship of the legion as a vacant chair until someone comes to the fore who can dispute with me for the crown. Unless, of course' – he turned an outwardly innocent gaze on Marcus – 'there is someone else with the sort of skill with a blade who could be persuaded to cross swords with me?'

With no intention of being deprived of their entertainment, and already cheerful from their first issue of wine, the soldiers needed no encouragement to take up his cause, shouting, 'The legion needs a champion!' and 'Show us your skills, Tribune!' until Marcus nodded good-naturedly and agreed to a match to settle the matter. Amid the cheering and shouting of encouragement he heard Morban shouting the odds for this new and unexpected bout, and realised too late that his warning to the notorious odds-fixer had fallen on stony ground. Turning, he found Dubnus at his shoulder, looking over at their comrade with an amused expression.

'So what if he fleeces a few of them? They could all be dead inside a week, and us with them!'

Accepting the brutal logic of the Briton's argument, he nevertheless took a moment to walk over to the veteran standard-bearer, who was standing in a crowd of soldiers with Sanga keeping order. Beckoning Morban to join him, he whispered a warning in his ear that turned the older man's face grey.

'Careful what odds you offer – who knows, I might just have to lose this match to teach you a lesson.'

'You wouldn't, surely . . . ?'

Marcus smiled ruthlessly at Morban and at Sanga, who had walked up behind the veteran soldier and was listening intently.

'It would be a refreshing change to have someone else as the object of all that "Two Knives" nonsense.'

He turned away from the horrified odds-maker and walked back to the awning under which the fighters had sheltered from the sun, and where Furius was waiting for him. A rack of wooden practice swords had been set up in the shade, and he took a few moments to choose a well-matched pair of the weapons before turning back to the ring and looking questioningly at the younger man.

'You're sure you still want to do this?'

Furius stood up and went to the rack, selecting a second rudis to match his opponent's choice of equipment.

'What, you thought that fighting dimachaerius style might have put me off? Not likely, I'm as accomplished with two swords as with one.'

Marcus shook his head.

'No, I was asking if you're sure you want to do *this*?'

Furius frowned in mock confusion.

'Do I want to cross blades with the man who killed my uncle? With me the master of every swordsman I've ever been matched with?' He shook his head in apparent incomprehension. 'Tell me, Valerius Aquila, what part of "a chance to humiliate my family's greatest enemy" is it that do you not understand?'

Marcus shrugged, suddenly very much aware of the gap between their ages.

'I just wanted to be sure what it is you hope to gain from making such an extravagant gesture. Come on then, let's get this over with.'

He walked out from under the awning and crossed the sand to enter the ring of shields with Furius hurrying to catch him up, his face hard with anger. Signalling to Dubnus to close the ring, he waited while the Briton ordered the waiting half-dozen soldiers to move into position, presenting an unbroken wall of wood and iron around the two men.

'Competitors, are you ready?'

Both men raised their swords, edging closer to each other and touching blades to indicate their willingness to fight, then both took a single step back.

'*Fight!*'

Furius stormed forward with both swords raised, first swinging one blade to draw a defensive block and then darting a lunging sword low at Marcus's forward knee, only to find his attempt slicing thin air as the older man stepped neatly away from the attack. He reset and went forward again, employing a different ploy by mounting a driving attack, a series of lightning-fast lunges intended to overwhelm his opponent's ability to defend with his other blade ready to capitalise on any sign of weakness, but Marcus simply stepped back and parried the first three stabs before attacking into the fourth and forcing Furius back onto the defence. But then, just as the younger man tensed, expecting his opponent to push his advantage, Marcus stepped back and resumed his defensive posture, encouraging his opponent to come at him afresh.

The two men fought their way around the circle by fits and starts, Marcus backing away and fending off a series of attacks in a seemingly effortless gradual retreat while his opponent railed fruitlessly at his defence. The legionaries gathered around them and – other than the odd curse from one of the many who had bet on Furius as yet another attack died on the wall of his opponent's steadfast resistance – watched the skills on display in rapt silence.

When Dubnus called the first break both men were wet with the sweat of their exertions, but where Marcus, who had been fighting within himself, was relatively fresh, Furius was breathing hard and had the slightly wide-eyed look of a man whose race was already well run. Having counted to thirty, the Briton signalled to the soldier with the timing glass to turn it over, but, having led Furius out into the middle of the ring for the restart, Marcus kept his blades low and made a comment to his opponent pitched low enough to reach his ears alone.

'The art of the blade isn't as easy as it seems when every opponent is bought and paid for, or one of your own men.' Furius, who had been looking at the sand and mulling his next attack, stared at Marcus in silence as he continued. 'Learn this lesson, Tribune. The next man you face with a sword in his hand won't be an instructor, or have any reason not to want to put his own iron right through you. And while *that* man might not have your skills, you're going to find the battlefield a great leveller when it comes to ability. Because a man who kills an enemy in the way you're capable of doing will make himself a target for another dozen men in the same instant.' He hefted his swords. 'Now, do you want a little longer or are you ready to go again? You look as if you could do with a little time to get your breath back.'

Furius bridled, his face a mask of anger.

'I don't—'

But Marcus was already moving, the points of his practice swords weaving a sinuous pattern before him as he went from defence to attack, speaking all the while as he took the fight to his young opponent.

'You learned your swordcraft from a succession of instructors.' He lunged in and drew the parry, watching Furius's eyes as the tribune defended himself. 'I can see each of them in your technique.' Another attack, a lunge followed by a sweeping cut that sent the younger man back, his face a mask of concentration, intent on resisting the unexpected assault. 'You are the predictable and almost perfect product of your training. But there was never one great swordsman to tie it all together for you, and to gift you with the unpredictability that goes with the experience of fighting a champion gladiator. And I was trained to fight by Flamma himself.'

He went on the attack again and, unlike the previous sallies, his last attack was unceasing, flowing through a dozen relentless strikes that drove Furius backwards around the circle of shields, barely able to parry each thrust and cut before the next was in the air and needed to be stopped. The soldiers were watching in awe now, realising that the unregarded officer they had assumed was past his prime was in fact still very much at the peak of his powers. And then, unexpectedly, just as the younger man's defence was starting to crumble and Marcus's victory was looking ever more assured, he stood back and looked at the panting tribune over the points of his swords. He spoke, his voice lowered to reach only the ears of the man to whom he was speaking.

'Flamma taught me more than just how to use a sword. He instructed me in what it means to be a man with the ability to beat any opponent, and how to wear that ability in such a way as to avoid making enemies at every turn. So I'll make you an offer. Let's respect each other's skills and call this a dead heat, with neither of us able to best the other. That way all the bets that my man the odds-maker has made with inside knowledge will be null and void, saving our comrades who gambled with him from the sight of his ugly grin as he pockets their coin. We can share the wine out among the soldiers who've sweated to hold their shields up all morning, and most importantly you and I can remain colleagues, rather than there being a continuing spirit of enmity between us. After all, I spared your uncle's life until he made the mistake of trying to rape my wife.'

He waited for Furius to reply, watching as the emotions of the decision played across the younger man's face.

'But why not just end it? We both know you could finish this match at any time you like.'

Marcus shrugged.

'A decade of war will tend to teach a man, over those years, that victory and defeat are just two sides of the same coin. And that the difference between the two can be so small as to be imperceptible. We're both skilled with the blade, and my only advantage was years of tuition from a man who died in the arena to save my life, and taught me the value of making friends rather than enemies. So . . . ?'

Furius nodded and lowered his swords.

'I accept your offer. And thank you.'

Marcus lowered his weapons and spoke out, loudly enough to be heard by every man present.

'Tribune Furius and I have decided that we are perfectly matched. And that any further contest would simply be a waste of our sweat. And so we jointly declare this match to be a draw!

All bets are void, and the prize will be shared among the men who have competed and the men who held the shields that made up the arena!'

The puzzled faces of the watching soldiers turned into broad grins, for the most part, and Morban found himself the instant and unwilling centre of attention as men gathered around him to reclaim their stakes. Marcus ordered the shield-bearers and defeated competitors to join him and Furius as they broached the amphora and, having poured a joint libation of the first cups poured onto the sand, both pronounced the wine drinkable. Ignoring rank, the two men stood and drank with their fellow soldiers, Marcus listening with amusement to the increasingly heated complaints from the legionaries surrounding Morban.

'Go and make sure they don't have to turn him upside down and shake the money out of him.'

Dubnus nodded knowingly and downed his wine with a wince.

'Oh for a cask of beer. And yes, I'll stop the idiot from being lynched. But tell me . . .' He leaned in to speak in a low and conspiratorial tone, casting a glance at Furius, who was standing in a knot of centurions who were competing to praise his abilities. 'Why was it exactly that you spared that boy's blushes? You let him off the hook just when you had him at your mercy.'

Marcus thought for a moment before replying, smiling wanly at the memory he had recalled to momentary and bitter-sweet life.

'Do you remember Antenoch?'

'Yes, I remember him. An excellent centurion's clerk, and a fighter as well. And I remember that he died saving that idiot Morban's grandson's life. If not for Antenoch Lupus wouldn't be sitting over there drinking wine with Lugos and the Sparrow and wondering what the fuck it is they're quacking on about.'

'All true. And do you recall the first day that I met him?'

The Briton smiled ruefully.

'Yes. The day he pulled a knife on you, and you lied to save him from execution.'

'Something you didn't understand at the time.'

'True. I thought you were mad to risk losing Uncle Sextus's favour for the sake of getting one idiot soldier on your side.'

Both men smiled at the memory of Sextus, the first spear who had preceded Julius in command of the First Tungarian cohort in which they had both served.

'And later . . . ?'

'Later it was clear to all concerned that your gamble had paid off. But I still think the risk you took was too great. And I feel the same way about that young idiot.' Dubnus raised his hands in mock surrender. 'I *know*, it's your risk to take.'

He walked away, pushing his way through the throng of men surrounding Morban.

'Back off, you animals! I'll make sure he pays you all out!'

Marcus was still smiling when a discreet cough behind him caught his attention. He turned to find Furius, who followed up his deliberately informal greeting with a salute, a good deal more respect in his demeanour than had previously been the case.

'Forgive the attempt to humour, Tribune?'

'Forgiven, Tribune. What can I do for you?'

The younger man looked at him for a moment before replying. 'I came to the legion with two instructions from my father. He told me to earn the glory that would be the key to a successful senatorial career, and to find some way of restoring the family honour that you had traduced by killing his brother.'

Marcus nodded.

'And now . . . ?'

Furius grimaced.

'While the first of those instructions remains valid, the second feels . . .' Marcus waited while the tribune tried to find the right word. '. . . irrelevant.' He took a deep breath. 'Talking to my centurions a moment ago, I realised that they're all just as uncertain about what happens next as I am. And that the only people in this legion with the first clue as to what we're going to do once we land on enemy soil are you and Tribune Scaurus's other men. And I found myself wondering how I could have been so idiotic as to want to humiliate you.'

He looked at Marcus expectantly, and when the older man failed to respond he spread his arms wide in acceptance of his caution at such an about-face.

'Yes, I do appreciate that this is something of a swift change of view. Less than an hour ago I wanted nothing more than to crush you in front of these men, and have as much revenge on you as possible without actually taking iron to you.'

'And now?'

'Now . . . ?' Furius reached out and tapped one of the wooden practice blades racked close to them. 'Now I realise that you could have killed me in the ring with one of these, and nobody would ever have put it down to anything more than an accident in the heat of the fight. After all, we've already buried three men on the way here who got unlucky in training. Or you could have broken one of my kneecaps or an elbow with equal ease, and sent me home when this fleet lands the legion and turns back. Instead of which you chose to allow me a graceful way out. It's not what I was expecting, or even something I thought I'd need, but I'm enough of a gentleman to be both gracious and grateful.'

'And later? When the battle we're sailing towards is fought, and either lost or won? If we both live through the storm of iron and blood, what then? Will I have to go back to watching out for you again?'

The younger man raised his hands in a subconscious gesture of surrender.

'It's a fair question. And to be honest it wasn't my choice to come after you, but my father's instruction to take vengeance for his brother. And my uncle wasn't a man I particularly liked, to be honest. So if we both survive the next few weeks intact I'll swear an oath to whichever god you choose that our blood feud has been settled to my satisfaction.'

Marcus smiled knowingly.

'Won't that place you in a difficult position with your father? Presumably *he's* sworn an oath to have revenge. And after all, it was his doing that you're as skilled with a blade as you undoubtedly are. Surely you owe him the service of your sword arm?'

'Yes. He swore that oath, when the news of his brother's death was conveyed to him. But I didn't ever swear to take vengeance for him, and if he asks I'll tell him that military duty and my own sense of honour prevented me from doing as he wished.' He grinned conspiratorially. 'And if I fall in battle you can tell him so yourself with my blessing.'

Marcus nodded.

'If you die with honour in whatever is to come then I will be sure to make sacrifice for you, and bear the news of your deeds back to Rome if I survive.'

The words earned him a wry smile.

'If you survive . . . ?'

The older man shook his head slowly.

'You have much to learn, and your first battle will be a rude awakening if you expect the face of battle to be anything other than terror, blood and violent death from all quarters. Including, if you're not careful, from the men at your back, when the blood is flying and it's all too easy to put a spear through a comrade in error. Sharp iron doesn't differentiate between friend and foe. So forget about any thoughts of glory and acclaim, and start thinking about staying alive for long enough that you might have a chance of making sense of the whole bloody mess the next time it happens to you.'

'Not quite as cheerful this morning, are they, Tribune?'

Scaurus smiled at Legatus Cilo's slightly sardonic opinion as both men watched the fleet's preparations to sail. The legion's soldiers had sat around their campfires until late into the previous night, drinking whatever remained of the wine that had been distributed to them earlier that day and accustoming themselves to the fact that they would be going to war the next morning.

'Some of them have headaches from drinking all that rather primitive wine. And all of them are pondering what the next few days might have in store for us all.'

The legionaries knew the morning routine by heart now, and each century was gathered close to their allocated vessel, ready to board once the ships had been warped out into the shallow water next to the beach by means of the ropes mooring them to the sand being loosened while men on their sterns hauled them slowly out along the cables connected to their sea anchors.

'And what do you expect we're sailing into?'

Scaurus contemplated the question for a moment.

'That very much depends on our opponent. If Niger has gone on the offensive and thrown his legions across the Propontis to occupy Thracia and Macedonia, then we could find ourselves facing a very unfair fight within days. If, on the other hand, he's decided simply to hold the crossing point at Byzantium, we might find that we have the free run of the land around it and face no battle but rather a series of skirmishes with his scouts.'

A horn sounded, and the legionaries obeyed the command to begin their boarding of the vessels, which had long since ceased to be anything other than a mind-dulling routine, filing down the beach and climbing over the ships' sides.

'Do you think that likely? That the man who seeks to conquer the western half of the empire might simply look to prevent us from crossing into Asia at the narrowest point?'

Scaurus shook his head.

'It's not the course of action I'd take. And Niger will have enough experienced generals on his side to be very clear that if he exercises his usual caution in this case then he'll end up surrendering whatever initiative he has. It's not his usual style to be quick to come forward, but even he must realise that to allow Severus to occupy everything up to the gates of Byzantium is to invite disaster. I think we'll find ourselves with at least one legion in our faces and quite possibly one or two more, if they're serious about some sort of forward defence of the crossing. Which is why what worries me most about this whole venture is our complete lack of any ability to scout the countryside around us.'

Cilo nodded, but it seemed to Scaurus as if he was recognising the point without truly understanding its implications. He sighed, deciding not to press his concerns given their complete inability to rectify the deficiency. The process of loading the legionaries onto their transports was proceeding as smoothly as could be expected after more than a month of daily practice, with only the occasional shout of abuse reaching the two men as one of the hungover soldiers fell into the surf, or took too long to clamber over a ship's side.

'So, Legatus, all you have to do is issue the command and we're ready to sail. Titus will take the fleet out to sea where we can't be seen from the shore, with the land only visible from the masthead, then row east until darkness falls. By which point he expects us to be within ten to fifteen miles of our landing point.'

'And we're really going to spend the night at sea?'

Scaurus grimaced, sharing his superior's evident disbelief despite the fleet tribune's breezy assurances of the previous day.

'Apparently it's nothing out of the ordinary, if the sea is calm enough, and the weather seems to be set fair as far as the sailors who understand these things are concerned. The wind is from the north-east, so there's no risk of running aground, and there's very close to a full moon tonight, so Titus assures me they'll be able to keep station with each other while it's dark.'

'And then we go ashore at first light.'

The younger man pondered the simplicity of his superior's statement, not for the first time envying the legatus his air of insouciance, the result of having effectively surrendered his command to his deputy.

'It all sounds simple enough. Whether it will prove to be quite such plain sailing is yet to be proven.' He gestured to Lugos, who was standing close by with the cage he had protected from hungry legionaries the previous evening, within which the disconsolate-looking cock was awaiting its fate. 'Shall we go and entreat the gods to grant us the favour of gentle winds and calm seas? That fine fellow has been crowing since first light, as if he knows it's his last day.'

Cilo nodded portentously, recognising a way to contribute with his priestly skills, and patted the knife at his waist.

'I think I can assure you that the omens will be good. And given that this is such an important sacrifice, I think I'll make a personal contribution.' He tapped the heavy gold bracelet on his right wrist. 'Commodus himself gave me this bauble ten years ago, which makes it more than suitable as an offering to Neptune, wouldn't you say?'

Scaurus inclined his head in respect for the proposed addition to their sacrifice, enough gold to buy a man a dozen formal togas and the fine footwear to accompany each of them.

'Indeed I would, Legatus. As long as we can prevent half the legion from diving in after it.'

8

'When I tell you to get ready to land, get on one knee so that you don't go arse over tit when the ship beaches! When I tell you to disembark, you get over the side at the front of the ship where the water will be shallow! Do not ponce about trying to decide whether it might be a bit cold, take it from me that it'll be fucking freezing and just get on with it! Get your arses over the side and onto the beach! Do not collapse on the sand as if you've been shot by an archer, get up the beach as if there's a tavern at the top with the beers poured and the barmaids oiled up and waiting for you!'

A few of the soldiers gathered around Julius tittered, looking at each other to share their amusement. Any mirth was drowned out by the rhythm that the rowing master was pounding out on his drum, and the accompanying song of encouragement that his apparently tone-deaf deputy was roaring out at the rowers, a vivid evocation of the ship's speed and power. The fleet, having lined up far enough offshore that the pink-tinged hills were only visible from the *Victoria*'s masthead, was now rowing in towards the beach at maximum speed, with the oarsmen, being all too well aware of the fleet's vulnerability to lurking enemy vessels so close to the shore and working their oars for all they were worth. Julius cast a disgruntled stare at the singer, raising his voice to be heard over the harsh notes of his song.

'Fuck me, but it'll be a pleasure to hit dirt just to be out of earshot of that bastard's dirge!' The men around Julius grinned even more widely, momentarily forgetting the beach that the fleet was racing towards, less than half a mile distant. 'When we hit the shore, each cohort's standard-bearer will find the right position to form a column down the length of the beach! The ships aren't staying, so don't hang around waiting to pull them up onto the sand, get your arses out of the waves and follow the eagle to the head of the column! And if you can't see the eagle, just follow the sound of shouting!'

The legionaries grinned at each other again, knowing that the legion's standard-bearer would have Julius at his shoulder from the instant he went over the ship's side, while the man in question kept the straight face that was expected of his exalted position. The grizzled senior centurion continued, ignoring their amusement even though the levity of his instructions was clearly intended to lighten their mood.

'While we're getting our shit into a neat pile you will see a party of men heading off to the nearest settlement.' He gestured to Marcus and the rest of Scaurus's familia, who were already waiting in the *Victoria*'s bow, ready to disembark and carry out their orders.

'Do not attempt to follow them! They will not have discovered the location of any pay chests, pig farms, taverns or brothels! They will come back very quickly if there are any enemy forces in the area, because they're not looking for a fight, just to find out what's waiting for us behind the dunes, and to steal whatever horseflesh the local barbarians haven't already eaten or fucked to death.'

The soldiers were grinning at each other now, as completely distracted from the impending landing on an unscouted enemy shore as the senior centurion intended.

'Once we have you in a nice tidy line, and you can't hear me shouting any more, get ready to march, and for the love of all the gods, stay on the track! This shithole we're landing at only has one good road off the beach! Any other path you see will lead straight into a marsh in which all the armour you're wearing will pull you down and drown you like you'd fallen into the sea, so step out lively and let's get on to better fighting ground as quick as we can! We land, we form up and we fuck off!'

The first century were nodding, recognising these as the sorts of instructions that were easy to understand and which had a clear objective.

'Isn't the plan a little more complex than that?'

Marcus turned to find Lupus at his shoulder, the young warrior's face a study in confusion.

'Yes, of course. But Julius knows that his men aren't interested in the finer details, they just want to be told where to go and what to do. And by making them laugh he takes their minds off the risk that they might have to fight their way off the beach, if the enemy has somehow predicted this landing.'

The line of warships was sweeping in towards the beach, now barely a hundred paces distant, and at the navarchus's command the rowers lifted their oars from the water to avoid thrusting the flagship onto the sand so hard that they would need to be towed off.

'Get ready to land!'

Marcus went down on one knee, nodding approvingly as Lupus did the same. With the usual harsh grinding of sand beneath the warship's keel the *Victoria* was ashore, her panting oarsmen lowering their oars back into the water and rowing slowly in order to keep her from being pulled backwards off the beach by the undertow.

'Come on!'

Marcus and his companions went over the side and into the thigh-deep water, splashing ashore and hurrying away up the beach while the first century took their places at the ship's rail, goaded on by Julius's roared command.

'Disembark! *Move!*'

The standard-bearer jumped over the side with more athleticism than a man of his age would usually display, shouting at the century to follow him. The century poured over the rail after him, and Scaurus walked forward from the vessel's stern to take his place behind them with Varus at his side, trailed by the legion's other officers, whose excitement at the novelty of a beach landing was obvious.

'Very well, gentlemen, shall we go and join the first spear on the—'

The tribune turned at a tap on his shoulder, and found the fleet's prefect standing behind him.

'Ah, Titus, come to make sure we all leave?'

The naval officer stared at him impassively.

'There are some things I need to tell you, Tribune. Might be best if the rest of your officers got on with their jobs while I do it?'

Scaurus nodded equably, gesturing to Varus.

'Take the young gentlemen and start getting our legion into shape for the march, will you, Vibius Varus?' The tribune nodded and led his juniors away, leaving only Marcus and Cilo beside him. 'Now, Prefect, what is it that you have to tell us? Some new orders you were told to save for this moment perhaps?'

The other man's face changed in an instant, his former imperturbability falling away like a mask that he had been wearing ever since first seeing Scaurus in Misenum.

'I waited five years to see you again, you bastard, never once expecting ever to do so!'

'Wait . . .' Cilo raised a hand, his expression one of confusion. 'If this is some sort of personal matter this is hardly the time or place to be discussing it!'

Titus waved a dismissive hand.

'Go about your business, Legatus. The fact that I will never see you again makes me indifferent to your words. And I will speak with this man before he goes to his fate.'

The senator nodded grimly.

'Make it quick then, Prefect. And enjoy the moment, because I'll have you dismissed and flogged for that disrespect!'

Scaurus nodded slowly.

'Your family? This has to be about your family, I presume. Something to do with Cleander?'

The prefect nodded, his face set as hard as stone.

'You will recall that we took you to Alexandria under his orders, years ago. During which journey I confided in you that my fleet was being used to smuggle the profits of his embezzlement back to Rome. Within a day of your arrival you accused the prefect commanding the province of exactly that embezzlement, in league with Cleander.'

Scaurus nodded.

'I did. It was the only way to save my familia from becoming Cleander's sacrifice. We would have died in Aegyptus without that leverage to force him to release the troops I needed to perform my orders.'

'Your familia?' Titus waved an angrily dismissive hand. 'The price for your familia's survival was the loss of my wife and children!'

'Cleander took your family?'

'I was ordered to the palace, when we docked in Misenum at the end of that journey. Arrested by the praetorians. Stripped of my uniform at spear point. Thrown into a dungeon and left to stew in my own piss for a few days, then hauled out and dressed in my uniform again. It had been washed, and smelt of rose oil, while I stank of my own filth. They took me to Cleander, who told me the mistake I had made in confiding in you. That I had shown myself to be unreliable. He had ordered you to your certain death, he told me, and my honesty had allowed you to escape that fate. And in return for that mistake, I was to be shown the error of my ways.'

'Let me guess. You told him to do his worst, and he declined to damage even a hair of your head?'

Titus gritted his teeth, looking out across the line of beached ships.

'I was too valuable to be executed, he said. A fleet commander who knows the underbelly of every port around the Middle Sea makes for the perfect smuggler when there's illicitly obtained gold to be transported. Unlike, he told me, my family. And then he had them brought in. A praetorian stood behind me with his dagger at the back of my neck, and two more dragged my wife and children into the room. I could see that she had been misused simply from the look in her eyes, and my children were terrified. They tried to run to me, but the guards held them back.'

He fell silent and stared at Scaurus.

'I'm sorry. If I had known . . .'

Titus shook his head, evidently barely restraining his fury.

'How could you *not* have known that your threats to reveal the chamberlain's schemes would result in my punishment? And you surely knew Cleander well enough that he would never throw away a man as useful as I was, when there were other ways to punish and coerce me. He told me that the price of their being spared would be my total and unswerving loyalty. And that they would be executed immediately if I failed to serve faithfully, and to keep my mouth *shut.*'

He spoke through a clenched jaw, his words barely intelligible.

'And so I kept my mouth shut. For three years I did as I was told. Praying every day for his death, so that I could free my family. He would mention them every now and then, and say things like "your son has learned his letters" and "your daughter is such a pretty thing now that she is ten years old". Giving me hope and keeping me in an iron grip.'

Scaurus nodded sadly, saying nothing. Even Cilo's look of outrage at such insubordination had faded to disbelief.

'When Cleander was executed by Commodus I hurried to the praetorian fortress and begged to see the prefect, so that I could secure their release. But he was adamant that they were not in his custody. He told me to forget them, and that they had probably died soon after the last time I saw them. That I could consider it Cleander's revenge on me for your survival.'

'And you cannot avenge them, Cleander already being dead.'

Titus nodded.

'I am unable to avenge myself on the man who ordered their death. But not on the man who caused it. You threaten me with dismissal, Legatus, but you do not realise what a waste of effort it is to threaten a man who is already dead in his heart.' He handed a small flat piece of metal to Scaurus, and Cilo stiffened as they both recognised it for what it was. 'Take this, Gaius Rutilius Scaurus, and read it when you have the time to fully appreciate what it is that I have asked the gods to do to you. May they see fit to visit my misery on you a dozen times over. Now get off my ship!'

*

Marcus led his men up the beach at a brisk trot until they reached the top of the slope, and the sand gave way to a mixture of dune scrub and salt marsh. Hunched over the desolate landscape a good two miles to the north was a walled town built on the only defendable ground close to the sea, its walls a barely visible pale shade of pink in the early dawn light.

'This is when we get to find out if the enemy have been astute enough to garrison the likely landing points.'

He led them along the edge of the dunes, searching for the track shown on the map, a narrow ribbon of firm ground through the marshes that lay behind the beach to the city's rocky perch.

'Here!'

Dubnus looked dubiously at the opening in the dunes' scrub, perhaps six feet wide, then across the marsh whose stench of rotting vegetation was a giveaway as to just how impenetrable it was likely to be.

'You're sure this is it?'

Marcus looked at the map in the dawn's thin light.

'It's in the right place, and it looks too well trodden to be anything else. We'll find out soon enough though.'

They hurried along the path, leaving Lupus at the entrance to direct the still-forming legion to follow them, their gazes fixed on the city's walls as they trotted ever closer along the sinuous track's turns. The sounds of the legion forming up to march faded behind them until the only sounds were the wind ruffling the marsh grass and their panting for breath as they pounded along the track, laden down by their weapons and armour. The brooding hump of the hill on which the city was built loomed ever larger before them until they ran, breathless and with heaving chests, to the point where the path's uneven sandy surface gave way to a cobbled road. Marcus raised a hand to stop his men, allowing them a moment to regain their breath now that they were concealed in the deeper shadow at the hill's base. Breathing hard, Dubnus looked up at the walls above them, the higher stones glowing in the dawn's slowly increasing light.

'The fleet has to be visible from up there. All it takes is for one man to be up and about early, or for them to have sentries on the walls, and this could go wrong before we even get to the gate!'

As if the gods had been listening to his apparent determination to tempt fate, the party heard a scrape of leather on stone, and looking up saw a man craning over the wall's edge to stare out across the marshes to the beach, where Marcus realised the masts of the fleet must be visible over the dunes. After a moment of silence the sound of his shouts reached them, and the scrape of hobnails on the wall's stone walkway as he raced to raise the alarm. Marcus shook his head in frustration at the timing of the landing being detected.

'Run! We have to get to the gate!'

Abandoning their previous cautious pace, the party ran hard around the hill's base, hearing horn blasts as whatever presence it was that Niger's forces had within the city walls came to life. Rounding the wall to come within sight of the city's gate, they were just in time to see a horseman gallop through it and away up the road to the north-east, a track that Marcus knew was a direct route to the town of Claudia Aprensis. Qadir raised his bow to take a shot at the distant rider, but lowered it with the arrow still nocked to the weapon's string.

'It is too far for a shot to reach.'

They trotted on, reaching the city's gates to find them closed, half a dozen nervous-looking men in old but serviceable armour staring down at them. One of them called down, his voice tremulous.

'Who are you, and what do you want?'

Marcus laughed softly.

'They sound about as worried as I would in their place.' He raised his voice to be heard on the other side of the wall. 'I am a tribune of Rome! And I have been sent here to accept your oath of continued loyalty and service to the one true emperor, Septimius Severus! You might have been tempted to throw your lot in with the usurper in Antioch, but I would invite you to take a look over your eastern wall at the legion that will be knocking at these gates very shortly.'

The helmeted man leaned out to address them.

'I am the magistrate of the city of Aenus! We have been visited by representatives of the emperor Gaius Pescennius Niger, and warned as to the consequences if we collaborate with his rival, the pretender Severus!'

'I see . . .' Marcus allowed the silence to drag out for a long moment. 'Tell me, the man who came to threaten you with "consequences" if you dare to show loyalty to the true ruler of Rome, and a man with sixteen legions to Niger's handful, was he a centurion by the name of Sartorius, with the emblem of a beneficiarius hanging from his belt?'

'Yes, he told us that Niger had granted him the power of life and death over our city's people. He came to us ten days ago, and warned us that there is a fleet headed this way as the advance guard of Severus's army! And he told us that—'

'If you were foolish enough to cooperate with us then there would be a dire retribution visited on the city when Niger wins the war? The confiscation of all wealth and most of your food, the sale into slavery of your sons and daughters, etcetera and so on and so forth?' Marcus looked up at the disconcerted official. 'Am I right?'

'Yes. His warning was very specific. And he did not sound like a man given to empty threats.'

'And nor is he, from my experience of his methods. The only problem for you right now being that he's not here and we *are*! So let's get all talk of vague and unspecified consequences out of the way, shall we? Either you open the gates to your city now, and make your food stores available to us, or we will have no choice but to burn you out. Your position and power come from *Rome*, Magistrate, not from Antioch, and it is Rome that will have you executed as a traitor to your oath, today, if you force me to such an act of barbarism!'

'I will consult with the city elders and—'

'You will open the gates now! If you do not, then when the legion reaches these gates, the only decision my superiors will have to make is whether to smash them in and allow his men to make free with your people and their possessions, or simply to burn your city to the ground as an example to your neighbours! I will give a count to ten to make your choice!'

The magistrate stared down at him with hatred for a moment and then turned to shout down into the street behind him.

'We will comply with your command, albeit under protest!' He vanished from the wall and walked out through the gates as they swung open, his sword held by its blade with the handle held out to Marcus. 'I surrender, Tribune. I hope that you can keep your part of the bargain that we have just struck, and protect us from the wrath of the emperor we have just betrayed?'

Scaurus and Cilo arrived on the scene at the head of the leading cohort a short time after the surrender, halting the column and walking forward to join Marcus. Both men were minded to magnanimity despite the eager looks on the faces of their men, who were more than ready to sack the city after over a month at sea.

'We can't afford to leave an angry town at our backs, so we either have to kill them all or spare them, and tell them it's the will of the emperor that all good citizens should be allowed to reconsider oaths sworn to Niger under duress.'

Scaurus turned to Julius and issued an order that he was well aware had the potential to go badly wrong if not carefully policed.

'First Spear, have the best-disciplined of your centurions take a tent party apiece into the city and search for their food stores. Make sure they choose men they can control – we can't afford for this to turn into a free-for-all or we'll have the rest of the legion desperate to get in there after them. Tell them we're looking for whatever stores of food can be found, and the means of transporting it. We'll requisition half of everything they have and see if that's enough to keep us in the field for the next week or so. And warn them that any complaints from the locals about the requisition of anything other than food will be thoroughly investigated, treated as looting, and that the thieves in question will be executed to set the right example to their fellow soldiers. Up to and including the rank of centurion, Julius.'

The Briton saluted and turned away, calling out to where Justus was standing beside his cohort's centurions and staring at his own senior centurion's vine stick with a wistful expression.

'Tribune Justus sir, your assistance with stopping these crooked bastards behind you from getting themselves executed would be of enormous value, if I might ask for some of your precious time to assist me?'

The newly promoted tribune smiled more broadly than Marcus had seen since his elevation to the equestrian class, and started choosing the centurions and men who would accompany him into Aenus.

'That's a smart move by Julius, I couldn't have picked a better man myself. Now let's get the legion camped outside these walls, and close enough that their presence keeps the men of the city cowed into submission. And while they search for supplies, you and Varus can go and look for the one thing we need more than food, if we're to have any chance of avoiding marching straight into the jaws of Niger's legions.'

The two tribunes walked into the city at the head of a party comprising most of Scaurus's familia, the sight of the giant Lugos enough to cow even the most bellicose of the city's men, who were in any case already visibly shaken by the appearance of the piratical-looking legionaries on the streets of their home. Thus it was that the friends were quickly directed to the prize that they were looking for, the small city's main livery stables, and it was equally swiftly apparent that the ostler had no intention of risking his life to dispute the beasts' change of ownership. They reported back to Scaurus with the five horses that looked suitable for a day's hard ride, leaving the remainder for the task of pulling requisitioned carts in the legion's supply train. The tribune's mood lightened when he saw the beasts.

'Very good. At least now we might have some warning of whatever force their messenger manages to bring down on us.' The tribune drew Marcus aside. 'But before you choose your companions and ride out, we need to discuss something that has arisen unexpectedly.'

He explained Titus's abrupt change of demeanour, and the vehemence with which the fleet commander had confronted him at the moment of disembarkation.

'And I can hardly blame the man, in all good conscience. After all, I did use information he gifted me to deal with the governor of Aegyptus, and it did land him in the deepest of water with Cleander. Who seems to have had revenge on him by murdering his family. He gave me this.'

Marcus looked at the curse tablet for a moment before taking it and holding it up to the sunlight, reading aloud the spidery writing scratched onto the thin lead leaf's surface.

'"Gaius Rutilius Scaurus, may you be cursed that at the moment of your greatest victory you will meet your death in disgrace and ignominy."'

Scaurus nodded slowly.

'Clever, isn't it? He can't be accused of treason, because I have to have won a battle for his curse to take effect.'

'The inscription still looks fresh, as if it were engraved no more than a few days ago. That must have been what he was doing in Thessalonica. I'd assumed that he was sending a report back to Rome. Presumably this is just a copy of the original.'

'Yes. Apparently there's one just like this folded twice and wedged into the brickwork of the mithraeum in the city. He found out enough about me to place the tablet where it would be the most likely to have the desired effect, and where better than in the wall of a temple dedicated to the god I serve?'

'But surely your priesthood in the service of the Lightbringer will protect you?'

Scaurus grimaced.

'I very much doubt it. A well-founded curse like this one with the loss of loved ones behind it, and freighted with all the hatred that he spilled over me back on the beach, must be a powerful thing indeed.'

'And you weren't tempted to kill him?'

'To what end? The poor bastard has been robbed of everything he ever loved and left as a shell of the man he was. And if his men hadn't simply beaten me to death for killing their prefect, where would my honour have been then? I would be facing a sentence of death for the unlawful murder of a fellow officer, curse or no curse. No, the only way to deal with this is to serve the empire to the best of my abilities and wait to see what comes of it. After all, we both know that there is frequently no response from the gods to such entreaties. We'll just have to wait and see. And in the meantime I suggest that you choose carefully as to who it is that will accompany you to the north, to find out exactly what it is that we're facing here. Now that the fleet has withdrawn, we're inextricably committed to making the best of this hopefully surprise appearance in the enemy rear.'

'This land is colder than a Druid's nuts. I thought the whole idea of being this far south from the icy barbarian wastes was to at least get some sun on your back?'

Marcus smiled wryly at Dubnus's emphasis on the word icy.

'I take it you missed Ptolemy telling anyone who would listen about what he read about Aenus in a book called the *Deipnosophistae* then?'

Dubnus shook his head with a terse laugh, pointing to his throat.

'The day you catch me taking any interest in that fool's twittering, you can put the dagger right here! But go on, what did he say? And what the fuck is this book he's quacking on about?'

'*Deipnosophistae* is Greek for "the dinner table philosophers". The story is that a number of learned men come together for a dinner that lasts several days, and in the course of it talk extensively about the arts, and places, and even subjects like sex. There are over a dozen volumes now, and he keeps turning them out, it seems. Ptolemy and Lugos are quite taken with it. And the point is that when he comes to describing the cities of the east, and in some detail, he writes that Aenus has eight months of cold and four months of winter. Which seems apt.'

The Briton nodded.

'Bloody right it does. Perhaps my blood's got thinner with so long spent in the warmth of Aegyptus.' He shook his head. 'The very thought of going back north to Britannia starts to sound less and less like a good idea.' He sighed. 'So, our mission is to ride north until we bump into the legions coming the other way, right?'

'Not exactly.' Marcus looked about him at the surrounding landscape, rolling hills covered with an endless carpet of neatly tended olive trees and scrub. 'There are two routes from Aenus to Byzantium. Either we can march north up into the interior of the province, using the road from Aenus to Hadrianopolis, and then strike east for the Propontis using whatever tracks we can find. That approach will take at least eight days, and run the risk that we run out of food and can't find sufficient resupply to keep five thousand men fed. Or we can take the obvious road and head east along the southern spur of the road from Italy to the Propontis, the Via Egnatia, joining the main road after two days and then marching for another day to reach the sea at Rhaedestus. We could hopefully resupply there, and then it's a day's march from the city to Perinthus, and another from there to Byzantium.'

Dubnus grimaced at the comparison.

'So it's either eight days of marching and hoping not to be detected, and possible starvation before the battle that could decide whether we live or die, or five days along the main road from Rome to the Propontis with no chance of avoiding being seen if there are enemy scouts out. It doesn't sound like much of a choice to me.'

'You have the nub of it.' Qadir leaned back in his saddle and stretched his back. 'The main road from Rome to the Propontis isn't likely to be undefended. And this trick that Severus has decided to play isn't such a stroke of strategic genius that a competent opponent couldn't predict it, even if they didn't have spies out looking for us at all the major ports.'

The Briton shrugged.

'We're going to have to fight them at some point before this act of idiocy is done with, aren't we? Why not get it done while the legion still has full bellies and boots that aren't falling to pieces?' He turned to Marcus. 'And since we're riding east, I presume that the tribune is of the same mind?'

'He and the legatus decided to go by the shorter route, even if it is more obvious. It's a five-day march for the legion, if they push hard enough to do thirty miles a day, and it might just be the trick that gets us to the gates of the city without being intercepted by Niger's forces. If they've been deployed further to the west in anticipation of a landing somewhere back down the coast, and we can get around them, that is.'

Dubnus nodded doubtfully.

'But do you really think we can march five thousand men through this never-ending olive grove without being detected? In the forests of Germania, perhaps, but here the legion will raise enough dust to be seen from miles away. If I were commanding them I'd have my legions waiting in reserve somewhere close by, ready to strike out in either direction, and I'd have all the roads properly scouted, with men clever enough to see us coming without our seeing them.'

Marcus gestured at the landscape around them, shallow hills uniformly covered with olive trees as far as the eye could see.

'All true. Which is why we're out ahead. We're scouting for their scouts, and we're not here to smile and wave.'

The friends rode steadily to the east until past noon, skirting the southern side of a range of hills that overlooked Aenus before turning to the north-east. Proceeding with caution, checking each stretch of countryside from cover before crossing the open ground, they rode through a low valley and then headed for a towering hill in the middle distance. Reaching the lower slopes as the sun was dipping towards the horizon, they left their horses under the care of Sanga and Saratos, while Marcus, Dubnus and Qadir climbed to the top of the prominent feature, but only after Dubnus had taken the precaution of confiscating the two soldiers' shared purse.

'You can have it back when we come back down. I just want to be sure that you two won't have made yourselves scarce by the time we've been up and back. The fact that there won't be a drink to be had within fifty miles that won't either leave you blind or impotent wouldn't stop the pair of you, and it'd be a shame to have to track you down and kill you for desertion.' He held out a hand. 'I'm not joking. Hand it over.'

Saratos shrugged as he slipped the leather pouch off his belt.

'Probably wise of you. It can be hard to control him when he thinks he can smell wine.'

Sanga shot his comrade a disgusted look.

'There'll be a farmer somewhere close with a few jars of the good stuff that he's made for his own use.'

Dubnus turned away with a shrug.

'Quite possibly. And he'll never know what a lucky escape he just had. Get yourselves around to the eastern side of this nice big piece of cover and gather enough wood for a fire. There could be wolves in these mountains, and besides that I'd like to avoid freezing my balls off overnight. Just make sure it can't be seen from the plain to the west, heh?'

The three men climbed five hundred feet up the side of the valley through which they were riding, ascending the hillside with due care not to disturb the tree's foliage or kick up dust, but when they reached the top of the slope and looked around them, there was little to be seen. In the warmth of the late afternoon the surrounding land was wreathed in shadows and coloured amber by the setting sun, and the flat plain that stretched as far as the glinting ribbon of river that reached the sea at Aenus's harbour was devoid of anything resembling military activity. The olive groves that covered every piece of ground that wasn't too steep to climb formed a sea of pale green that covered the landscape, through which the dirt road at the hill's foot ran a mile or so to the north to meet the indistinct but unmistakable path of the Via Egnatia, in its long course from the Dyrrachium on the Adriaticus to the very edge of Asia. Smoke rose from scattered olive farmers' dwellings, but of the usual hallmarks of a legion's progress or presence there was no sign whatsoever. Dubnus stretched and took a drink from his water bottle while the other two men stared out across the silent land.

'No dust from cohorts on the march, no smoke from cooking fires . . . we might just manage to pull this off.'

Qadir shook his head at the Briton.

'It's too early. That messenger won't have reached the next settlement of any size, Claudia Aprensis, yet, even if he's riding the poor beast he escaped on to the point of collapse. I don't expect we'll see anything of note today, or probably tomorrow either, unless they're very quick off the mark with their scouts.'

They descended the slope without waiting for darkness to fall, reasoning that the possibility of seeing anything of note was strongly overmatched by the need not to jeopardise their mission by any of them incurring a serious injury in the dark. At the foot of the hill the two soldiers had lit a small fire, and the party sat and ate the dried fish that had been the main foodstuff in Aenus's storehouses in the warmth of its flames, listening to the yipping calls of a pack of wolves that were hunting the slopes for rabbits and other small animals. With nothing else to distract them, and leaving Sanga, once again relieved of his purse, to stand the first watch, they rolled themselves in their cloaks and slept as well as could be hoped for under the circumstances.

The next day was a repeat of the first, the party eschewing the road and taking care not to be seen as they picked their way through the landscape to its south, making their way through a low valley before climbing the last of its hills on the southern side, barely two hundred feet above the plain it looked out on. The open ground was nestled in a more-or-less unbroken circle of the same low hills, little more than two miles across and perhaps five miles long, the Via Egnatia running across it from west to east. On the far side of the open space a fortress had been built into the rising ground overlooking the road, and the three officers looked across the gap at it with shared unease.

'High ground on three sides and dominated by an enemy camp big enough to hide a cohort. If I had to find a piece of ground on which a legion could be bottled up and slaughtered I doubt I could do better than this.'

The other two men nodded at Marcus's gloomy sentiment, and Qadir considered a verdant valley that under less martial circumstances would be land to answer any farmer's prayer.

'Indeed. Once an enemy had marched into it all you'd have to do would be put a blocking force on the western end, your archers on the high ground to either side, along with some legionaries to stop an enemy from climbing out over the hills, and you'd still have a nice clear path in from the east to allow a decent-sized army to swing the hammer on that anvil. You're right, let's be sure to avoid coming anywhere near this death trap.'

'That's easy enough to agree with, but hard to do.'

Marcus pointed at the fortified settlement on the valley's far side.

'That fortress is there for a reason. It dominates the road to Rhaedestus from the east, and the only way to avoid it is to go the long way around to the north. And it gets worse if you go another fifteen miles along the road to the east, because there is a major town on the road, Colonia Claudia Aprensis.'

Dubnus nodded gloomily.

'A colonia? So it's a military town.'

'Founded by veterans at least, so likely to have some sort of garrison. Which makes it look like a very unattractive road for us to take. Although you might argue that nobody would expect a force of only one legion to attempt such an audacious attack. It's like a single thief trying to kick the door of a banker's office open without knowing whether his bodyguards are waiting inside or down the street in a taverna. Which might make it the unexpected choice.'

Qadir looked across the wide valley again, and shook his head unhappily.

'But surely any half-competent enemy will have prepared for us to take this road?'

'I agree. And so we will have to hope that this enemy is less competent than we fear. Perhaps we should have a closer look?'

Marcus and Dubnus settled down to watch the fortress, Qadir having suggested that he and the two soldiers scout forward to see if there was any sign of military traffic on the road. They had divested themselves of their armour and wrapped their cloaks around themselves to conceal their military-issue daggers before walking away down a handy track towards the road.

'Anyone they meet is going to know they're soldiers just from their boots. And that's before Sanga finds a taverna and starts shouting the odds at the locals.'

Marcus smiled at the image, rolling on his back to stare up at the clouds above the two men.

'One look at that fortress is enough to start me wondering if trying to attack Byzantium by this route is really the wisest choice. And makes me reflect on what a defeat here would feel like.' He turned a serious gaze on his friend. 'Has it ever occurred to you that we've never actually been on the losing side of a fight in all these years? From that first dirty little scuffle in a village on the far side of the wall in Britannia to that last desperate defence of an abandoned fortress in the far south of Aegyptus, we've never met an enemy that was capable of defeating us. I know I was captured by bandits in Germania, but that was just me and not an actual defeat.'

Dubnus kept his gaze locked on the brooding fortress on the valley's other side.

'True. We've fought a dozen times and never yet showed an enemy our backs. But then we've always had the best of the strategy. The tribune always made sure of that.'

'And the tactics. Remember when we waited on that hill in Parthia and let the Persians' heavy cavalry come at us at the charge? Their hoofs were like the thunder of the world's ending, and the smell of all those horses will be with me to the day I die. I was convinced that there was no way we could stop them, and yet . . .'

'And yet we ate like kings that night, on meat cut from all the poor beasts those fools had driven to their destruction.'

'Yes.' The Roman rolled back onto his front. 'We have lived charmed lives when it has come to the battlefield. And yet in all that time I've never had quite such a strong feeling that we're staring defeat in the face. Although where the enemy might be remains a mystery.'

They found the legion in the process of digging out a camp on the other side of the hill, close by the lake from which they had refilled their water skins that morning. Marcus was pleased to note that the sentries were on their mettle, and that there were men stationed on the slopes above them as they rode up to the camp's north-facing gate. They found Scaurus and Cilo considering a copy of the map in the command tent, both men eager to hear what it was that the scouts had discovered.

'We've little to tell you that's especially informative, sir.' Marcus pointed to the map. 'At last light yesterday there was no sign of any enemy activity to the west, as far as the eye can see. There were no troop movements on the Via Egnatia and no obvious signs of large bodies of men encamped in the immediate area.'

Scaurus pursed his lips thoughtfully.

'That's good. And what about the road to the north of here?'

Qadir stepped forward and saluted.

'I took our two best infiltrators up the hill to the fortress that overlooks the road.'

The tribune leaned forward, his stance betraying both a hunger for information and a deeper anxiety as to what might be awaiting them on the hill's far side.

'And . . . ?'

The Hamian's usual air of quiet self-confidence was for once not in evidence.

'The vicus on the ground below it was about as quiet as any I have ever seen. No beggars, no children playing in the streets, and so few people to be seen that I would question whether it was even populated if I hadn't been served a cup of wine in a taverna. My fellow spies were equally uncomfortable, even with drinks in their hands.'

Dubnus had scoffed at Sanga when the three men had returned to the overlook.

'What's the matter, Sanga, you look like you lost your purse and found a dog egg!'

But the usually combative soldier had merely muttered something unintelligible, and left Qadir to explain what it was that had so clearly spooked him.

'The fortress's vicus had the feeling of a man holding his breath and waiting for something. There was a kind of . . . tension in the air that it was impossible to put my finger on, but it was palpable, Tribune. Of course the taverna owner was friendly enough, but even there I was left in doubt of what I was seeing. He had no wife, for one thing.'

Cilo looked puzzled.

'And that implies what, Centurion?'

'A man of your exalted rank will not be familiar with the ways of the world of the street, Legatus, but it is an article of faith for the kind of man who buys a taverna that he will need a wife to oversee the cooking of the food he sells and to keep the serving girls in order. A bar owner without a wife is like a man with one arm. But there wasn't a woman to be seen, which was what unnerved my companion Sanga. And the landlord himself was something of a specimen, muscled in a way I've never seen on a man with the run of his own private wine shop.'

'Hmm. Of course one out-of-place muscle-man does not necessarily make a conspiracy. But what are we to infer from this, gentlemen?'

Scaurus answered Cilo's question.

'The fortress's vicus was empty for the most part, with only a very small presence of men, who all looked like they were of military age, am I right?' Qadir nodded. 'And the fortress was devoid of any of the usual business of military life?'

'No soldiers, no shouting, no sentries on the walls or men coming and going. And the taverna owner just served us and went back to talking to another man who looked like he could lift his own weight over his head. His apparent complete lack of interest in us was almost painfully studied. I'd say he was an active-duty centurion, someone bright enough to be picked out to watch out for spies, while his companion looked like every long-serving chosen man you've ever met, not clever enough to earn the cross-crest but with that look of brutality and cunning they all have.'

'Shit.'

'Tribune?'

Scaurus turned to Cilo.

'Ever since Centurion Aquila's narrow escape in Thessalonica I have been wondering just how much Niger's intelligence apparatus knows about our mission to capture Byzantium. After all, we know very well that Rome is a nest of informers at the best of times. And now we have the proof of it. Were it just the empty fortress I would be less perturbed, because the cohort based there could well be away with either of the armies depending on how loyalties have played out here. But the absence of life in the vicus and this whole empty landscape is what concerns me. It tells us that our worst fears may very well be about to be visited upon us.'

The legatus replied, his tone that of a man who did not really want an honest answer to his question.

'You think that the enemy are aware of our presence here, and of our mission?'

The tribune's answer was edged with steel, that of a man who had already understood a drastic change in circumstances and was busy working out how best to deal with their new situation.

'I think that the enemy are expecting something very much like the task we have been set to perform. After all, our departure from Misenum was hardly conducted in conditions of secrecy, and a legion boarding such a fleet will not have gone unreported. The fact that there were men waiting for us in Thessalonica indicates either that we were detected beforehand or that some bright individual on Niger's staff predicted our potential arrival and sent out detachments to wait for us to make just such an incautious landfall. And so I think we can deduce from this latest piece of information that they have adopted a posture of readiness to deal with us wherever we come ashore and wherever we then go, with their intelligence net spread wide.'

'And so what do you propose that we do?'

Scaurus smiled bleakly.

'We have two choices. Either to bow to the inevitable and find a defensible position in which to await the arrival of a force that will probably be several times the size of our legion. Or to make the most of what might just be a fleeting window of opportunity, and march on our objective with all speed, with the aim of striking before whoever is in command on this side of the Propontis regroups his forces and comes after us.'

'And your choice?'

The tribune looked at the hand-drawn map on the desk in front of them, then stabbed his finger down at it decisively.

'My choice is to move fast and throw our enemy off balance, Legatus. Because any other course of action will be little better than surrender.'

9

'So we're going backwards to go forward? Really?'

The Briton looked over his shoulder at the officers riding behind the familia's men at the head of the legion's column, his expression at once managing to combine disdain and supplication. Marcus smiled at the disgruntled question, but Qadir beat him to the punch in answering. The cohorts had marched back the way they had come for several miles before being directed to the south onto a track that was now climbing the lower slopes of a thousand-foot-high hill.

'In reality we are going both sideways and upwards to go forward . . . eventually. You will doubtless recall how deserted the garrison town was yesterday?'

The Briton shrugged, his unease of the previous day clearly forgotten.

'Made getting a drink right easy.'

Saratos added to the Hamian's attempt at explaining the legion's reversal of course.

'You are making it too difficult for him to understand. It needs to be simple enough for a small child, or perhaps a dog.'

'Oi!'

The Dacian ignored the look that Sanga was giving him.

'You will recall, Sanga, that we were served our wine by a man who looked every bit as nasty a bastard as Julius? No insult intended, Centurion.'

The man in question, riding a commandeered horse alongside Marcus, waved a dismissive hand.

'Oh, none taken, Saratos. In fact I'll take it as a compliment. Tell us more about this prime specimen of military prowess.'

The soldier shrugged.

'You know the type well enough, Centurion, all muscles and shout, with rocks in his head and a voice like gravel being poured through a sewer grating.'

Julius turned and raised an eyebrow in silent comment to Scaurus, riding behind him and alongside Legatus Cilo.

'Your description is vivid, *Watch Officer*. And I suggest you leave it at that before I *do* take offence and accidentally demote you back to legionary, and in doing so drastically reduce your income.'

Saratos nodded in an untroubled manner, knowing the big Briton well enough to be clear as to how far he could push his luck.

'Yes, Centurion. Anyway, Sanga, you recall this man?'

'I recall the wine. Too much water, and what wine there was in the cup tasted like piss.'

Julius leaned out of his saddle and tapped Saratos with his vine stick's silver-capped tip.

'And while we're establishing what's acceptable in the telling of this seemingly endless story, let's not let it get in the way of covering ground, eh? Keep the pace up, or I'll sound the horns to give the legion a run up this hill at the battle march for a few miles, and tell anyone that asks that it was down to you two fools!'

Saratos shot Sanga a glance and upped the pace just enough to keep the centurion off his back, looking up at the hill's crest two miles distant and hundreds of feet above them.

'Anyway, this tavern owner, as I told you at the time, was no more a tavern owner than you will ever be, and—'

Sanga bridled, having realised what his comrade was getting at.

'Oi, that's my fucking dream you're stamping on!'

'Ah, so *now* you listen! And it was obvious that the real owner was probably hidden out the back while this man was in his place to look out for men like us.'

Sanga was clearly unimpressed.

'So you and Qadir said at the time. So we're expected. Big fucking surprise, given we sailed past a dozen ports on the way here, and never went ashore for as much as a single night! Doesn't explain why I find myself sweating like a bastard to climb a hill that's taking us in the wrong direction though, does it?'

Scaurus spoke out from behind them.

'My apologies for not making the time to give you a private briefing, Watch Officer Sanga! Allow me to elucidate!'

Sanga looked blankly sideways at Saratos.

'It means to explain.'

'Thank you, Saratos, I forget that your colleague never bothered to learn any more Latin than was required to order beer and insult his officers when he thought they weren't listening! Anyway, Sanga, we're marching up this hill because I want to put it between us and the men who, as Saratos has explained, I strongly suspect are looking for us. And I plan to use all the hills between here and Rhaedestus as cover for our approach, avoiding the Via Egnatia for as long as possible. With scouts out in front of us to make sure we won't blunder into any ambush that might be set for us! Speaking of which . . .'

He signalled to Marcus, who beckoned Qadir to join him.

'I think your eyes are going to be essential for such a task, colleague. Look for the agreed signal, Tribune.'

The two men rode to the top of the hill at a gentle trot, knowing they couldn't afford to tire their horses too soon in the day. Cresting the ridge a thousand feet higher than their starting point on the plain below, they looked out over the mass of olive trees below them, and the sea beyond them to the south. A single lonely ship was just visible on the water's expanse, while away to their left they could see for ten miles along the spine of the ridge they had just climbed.

'There's nothing that looks like military activity. Or at least nothing that I can *see*.'

Marcus nodded at his friend's pronouncement and unsheathed his swords, holding them crossed over his head in the prearranged signal that would keep the legion climbing towards the summit rather than falling back to prepare for battle on the plain below. He waited for the horn call confirming that the signal had been spotted, then sheathed his weapons and gestured at the road in front of them.

'In that case I suppose we should go and make sure that there's nothing waiting for us that's well hidden enough to elude even your sharp gaze.'

They rode out ahead of the legion down the hill, turning left when a track heading east presented itself on its lower slopes.

'Of all the desperate missions we've ever been tasked with, this seems to be most desperate of all.' Qadir leaned forward in his saddle to stretch his back. 'Which is ironic when I consider that several of them were actually intended to kill us, whereas this one seems to be a clever but cynical sacrifice of a legion on the emperor's behalf, rather than an act of outright malice. Can we even hope to get as far as Rhaedestus, never mind Byzantium, before whatever force has been gathered by Niger to deal with us hunts us down?'

Marcus pointed to their left to indicate the ridge they had just climbed, now sloping gradually down as it ran from west to east.

'If the grain of this country runs in the same direction as that ridge line then we have a decent chance of at least getting to Rhaedestus without being detected, by using the hills for cover. And if we can take Rhaedestus, and resupply the legion with enough food to keep marching for a few more days, then perhaps, just *perhaps*, we can press on to Perinthus, and take that too and clear the way to Byzantium.'

'And then?'

The Roman smiled sadly.

'And there was me thinking that you were the philosopher of our party. There is a chance that we can take Byzantium, although it will require outrageous good fortune to enable us to elude detection, or, if we are detected, to defeat whatever force Niger sends against us. It will mean having to force the road at both Rhaedestus and Perinthus, and then breaking through whatever walls might have been erected at Byzantium itself. But then what? By then I'd imagine that we'll be somewhat lighter in manpower than we are now, due to the men we will lose in the fighting that will be required. And by taking the city we'll have tied ourselves to a location and allowed the enemy to manoeuvre as he sees fit to defeat us. There can be no way for the rest of the army to arrive soon enough to rescue us, which means that we must eventually be defeated, and either killed in battle or its aftermath or, if we're lucky, taken captive and shipped off to wherever the enemy deems the best place to let us rot. And the best result we can hope to achieve is to disrupt the line of communication back to the east, although I'd imagine that it will be easily enough re-established elsewhere.'

'As I thought. And my lack of understanding is not with the likely outcome, which has been clear to me since our orders were announced, but rather with the reasons behind them. Why throw away a legion in this way? Surely we'd have been better used as part of the army that will be advancing to invade Thrace and bring Niger's army to battle?'

Marcus nodded his understanding.

'I asked the tribune the same question, and I suspect it was the same as the one he probably asked the legatus.'

'And his answer was . . . ?'

'That there was little of any military value in the idea of throwing a single legion forward in such a bold gesture. Perhaps the forces distracted from massing to strike at the advancing army coming east will be disproportionate to the strength of the single legion sent to distract them. And perhaps the enemy general will be sufficiently discomfited by our presence in his rear to allow that distraction to have some practical effect. Although it seems that neither of them is all that convinced that this is any kind of masterstroke that befits the loss of the Fourth. Or even that Niger's army will be far enough advanced to the west that we'll actually arrive in their rear rather than present ourselves in front of them.'

Qadir shook his head in bafflement.

'In which case why issue such a pointless command? Why condemn four thousand soldiers to death, or imprisonment? I assume you asked that question as well?'

Marcus nodded.

'I did. And the answer wasn't one I was expecting. Not strategic advantage, and not even some wild throw of the dice, but rather the product of the emperor's need not to be challenged. Cilo, it seems, believes that he has all too clearly become a man of importance to be allowed the power of an army command, or to enjoy a simple retirement back to his country estate. An army commander might dream of imperium, and be tempted to murder his master, declare the death a sad accident and turn all those legions back on Rome to take power. Better to have the army commanded by a relative non-entity like Tiberius Claudius Candidus, who might also make a competent general, than let someone like Laetus or Cilo have the chance to wield the power of four legions. And were he to retire to his estates then he would be much closer to Rome than Severus, while the emperor is on campaign here in the east, and able to use his influence with his fellow senators to his own ends. Which seemingly would make him a threat to the emperor's throne.'

'So this command is intended to neuter any threat he might present. But all the same, a whole legion?'

'I know. But we both know the mindset of the sort of man who takes the throne. Why worry about a single legion when there are plenty more in the army? Sending Cilo to fight an inevitable battle against impossible odds is a far more "honourable" way of disposing of a potential rival than execution, and removes the risk of a relative seeking revenge given that the death can be declared a tragic but unavoidable loss and commemorated with great ceremony, especially if it can be argued that some benefit resulted. It may not be militarily sensible, but for a man like Severus it's simply a logical way to deal with a perceived threat.'

'And if it gets the rest of us killed that won't trouble him even a little?'

Marcus laughed aloud.

'Would our deaths trouble a man like Severus? I very much doubt it! And now I suggest that we give up all thoughts of his motivation in entrusting this suicide mission to us, and go about proving what an excellent command he's running the risk of losing. The more carefully we look for signs of the enemy the more likely we are to have the chance to make that supremely futile gesture in front of the walls of Byzantium.'

The legion camped in the shadow of the ridge that night, Marcus and Qadir having chosen a spot where the hill above them was still high enough to hide their presence. They sought out the tribune to make their report as the sun was sinking behind the hill and burying the camp in deep shadow, finding him deep in discussion with Julius and Cilo. Scaurus met them with a wry smile on his face, an expression that told them that not all was well. Lupus was walking close behind him with his hands close to the hilts of his swords, clearly taking the role of bodyguard he had inherited with Arminius's death very seriously.

'Greetings, gentlemen! As you may have guessed from the worried look on the face of my new guardian' – he flashed a quick smile at the young Briton – 'it seems that the legion is close to revolt at the perilous nature of our situation. The legatus and I have decided to discuss the matter with our senior centurions, and to make the realities of the situation quite clear to all concerned.'

He ordered Julius to gather the officers to a command briefing as the sky above them was starting to darken, and once they were assembled he looked around the group, finding their faces grim and their apparent collective outlook equally dour.

'I see the reality of our position has sunk in! Yes, gentlemen, we really are a thousand miles from any reinforcement, with only three days of somewhat disappointing half-rations remaining and another five days, march ahead of us before we reach our objective, even if we were to go the whole distance at the battle march. And there are quite likely to be enemy legions waiting for us somewhere close by in these hills. Our position is, on the face of it, hopeless. But we are the emperor's chosen few! We are the men he chose to send forward in the pursuit of this outrageous mission, to provide him with a victory whose name will echo down the centuries! And we will remain true to his faith in us, whatever it takes!'

He looked around at them again, seeing backs stiffen and hands tighten around the shafts of their vine sticks at the challenge implicit in his words, and nodded his understanding of the concerns he knew were doing the rounds of the camp even as he spoke.

'And yes, we could probably avoid a great deal of bloodshed if we were simply to march out of these hills and present ourselves at the closest military camp. You might even be expecting myself or the legatus to do just that! After all, surely we men of the ruling class have more in common with each other than with our men? And doubtless we would find an eager welcome among our colleagues leading the men hunting for us, since we are such a tightly knit faction?'

The truth of what he was saying was written across their faces, guilt at such a bald statement of their unspoken concerns and fear that they might yet be proven to have been well founded. He laughed softly, looking around the group and meeting each man's stare in turn.

'It's true, we could slip away from here, ride up to the gates of Colonia Claudia Aprensis and receive a warm welcome from the man commanding there. Enjoy a bath and some wine. Eat some relatively good food and put any thought of your plight out of our minds. Except for two things that you might not have considered. Firstly, the legatus and I are both wedded to the service of the emperor with shackles that, although they only exist in our minds, are like chains of the strongest iron. Fabius Cilo has sworn an oath to the imperial god Hadrianus, and to Rome itself, to see this mission through, and were he to break that oath he would instantly become an outcast among his own people, and not welcome among his ancestors in the underworld when his time comes to join them. And I, brothers, am a priest in the cult of the Lightbringer, Our Father above, and I too have sworn a holy promise to see this through, with a sacrifice on an altar dedicated to his name and on which his eyes always stare. I have sworn that oath in the presence of the god I serve, and to break it would be to undergo the uncertainties of the death of an unbeliever!'

He lowered his voice, forcing them to lean in to hear him.

'And so you see that neither of us has any choice but to follow this path to its conclusion. However grim, however glorious, and however triumphant. And we are asking you to follow that path with us, and to bring your men with you.'

Tribune Justus spoke first.

'You said that there were two reasons why we should forget any fears of your abandoning us?'

Scaurus smiled at him.

'Indeed. And to know what the second of them is, just take a look at each other and tell me what you see.'

'I'll tell you what I see, Tribune.' The commander of the Fourth Legion's sixth cohort, a muscular man with a ropey scar running the length of his right arm, stepped forward. 'I see men like myself, soldiers since we were little more than children. Men who have only ever known this life, and who worship no other god than Mars. Men who will follow our appointed leaders to the gates of the underworld if they command it.'

'And men who will never forget, or forgive, if we were to betray you, am I right?'

The centurion nodded.

'We would bear that grudge to a man for the rest of our lives, us few here and many others besides.'

Scaurus opened his hands to Justus and inclined his head in indication of a question answered.

'And there you have it, colleague. If my oath, and my love of Rome, did not keep me true to her service, then you can be assured that the certain knowledge that several thousand betrayed soldiers would be praying for my death and plotting my murder would be more than enough to ensure my loyalty. I already have one curse hanging over me, and my desire for a thousand more is every bit as low as you might imagine.'

He raised his voice to be heard by the closest of the soldiers bedding down for the night.

'So tell your men this! Your officers will be faithful to Rome, and them, unto death! And any man who chooses to steal away in the night might escape a miserable fate, or possibly deny themselves the chance of eternal glory, but either way they will find themselves cursed for ever as oath-breakers, and outside of Rome's protection until the days of their deaths. Because no matter whether they swear a new oath to the usurper Niger or simply try to hide in this province and avoid justice, they will be sought once the empire is united again under the one true emperor. And when they are inevitably captured they will be treated to the only penalty Rome has for the deserter. A death far worse than any that might result from the next few days of our mission!'

He looked about them, seeing new resolution in their faces.

'So go and tell your officers what I have told you, and have them tell their men. And then get them bedded down. Tomorrow is going to be a long and difficult day.'

The centurions turned away and went back to their cohorts in the failing remnants of the daylight, and Scaurus turned to Marcus and Qadir.

'A disaster hopefully averted. And now, gentlemen, join me for a light supper of dried fish and tell me what you have discovered as to our route tomorrow, will you? Hopefully we can concentrate on hiding behind the mountains rather than having to climb over any more of them!'

The Fourth was moving again shortly after dawn, its officers reporting mercifully few desertions overnight as they assembled their men and got them onto the track in the usual two-abreast formation. A chilly mist had sprung from the ground overnight, adding a spectral quality to the landscape as the sun rose above the horizon and turned it into a grey curtain, enveloping the soldiers in rippling curtains of moisture.

'I don't envy Julius his task of getting them onto the road without any of them blundering off unnoticed or heading off in the wrong direction.'

Marcus laughed softly, cautious even in the absence of any enemy.

'Oh, I expect there's a section in the book of regulations with specific reference to movement in restricted visibility. It probably involves a lot of shouting.'

The two friends had resumed their roles as the legion's only scouts, Qadir grimacing as they crossed a shallow saddle of land between the now almost imperceptible ridge that had concealed them the previous day and the next terrain feature, a shallow valley in which it might be possible to march a good distance out of the view of the fortresses on the Via Egnatia.

'And besides, this mist might well be salvation for us. We may be a dozen miles from the Colonia, but a low sun can betray a legion on the march as effectively as lighting a signal fire. Reflections from polished iron, the long shadows of marching men catching the eye . . .'

They rode cautiously forward down a long sloping track until they reached a river, the two men at once both delighted at the chance for the legion to refill their water skins and worried that it might be an impassable obstacle, but the track took them straight to a ford. Splashing through the shallow water, Marcus looked down at his horse's legs, making an assessment based on his long experience.

'It's only two feet deep, and moving slowly enough that we won't lose men to being washed off their feet. Perhaps this is meant to be.'

Qadir looked at him with a hint of amusement.

'I always thought that I was the most superstitious of the tribune's familia, until you were awakened by that German priestess. But now you're the man who looks for omens and portents.'

'It's not so much that I actively consider the signs of divine favour, more that my life seems to be lived under the protection of . . . some deity I cannot name, but whose influence is as pervasive as the very air we breathe. Think back to the times when we have faced odds no man would ever choose to gamble on, and then consider our good fortune in winning despite those odds.'

'And that couldn't be because the tribune himself is a master of both strategy and tactics? Or because my goddess the Deasura watches over us?'

It was a long-running subject of good-natured debate between the two men, and Marcus raised his hands in mock surrender.

'It could be either of those factors or one of a good deal more. But whatever or whoever is guiding our path today could not have done much better than to provide us with mist to conceal us and a fordable river to ease our passage and fill our skins. All we need now is a field of a hundred prime sheep to fill our bellies with something other than dried fish!'

They scouted forward, leaving an agreed sign in the form of broken branches laid on the track's verge in the shape of an arrow to indicate which road to follow at a fork in the road two miles after the ford. The path took them to the south of a shallow hill with a higher peak to their right and, leaving their beasts tethered in a grove that could be seen from the top, they climbed it to take advantage of its elevation, taking their helmets off and swathing their armour in their cloaks to avoid reflections from the rising sun. The view from the summit was unobstructed all the way to the road, the morning mist having burned off other than along the river's course to their east, and the Via Egnatia's cobbled ribbon was visible as a faint line across the landscape.

'I can see a cart moving from the west to the east, but other than that, nothing.' Qadir was shading his eyes and staring intently out across the open landscape. 'And the fortress at the Colonia is clear enough, but we're too distant to see if its walls are manned.'

'So there is no sign of pursuit, but no proof that there are no pursuers out there hunting for us.'

'Yes. Whoever it is that protects us, whether the Deasura, your German goddess or just the Lightbringer, must be fond of a joke. I can only imagine what—'

He fell silent, staring intently at the olive trees that crowned a lower hill in the middle distance.

'What is it?'

'I thought I saw movement. Just for an instant, and even then in the corner of my eye. But now that I am looking directly at the spot I can see nothing out of place.'

He remained stock-still for another long moment before looking away from the patch of trees that had caught his attention.

'It might have been nothing. A bird alighting on a branch or a creature of the forest hunting for food. But it might have been something more sinister. Perhaps we should act with caution.'

They returned to the horses and led them into the grove on the path's north side, far enough to be invisible from the path. Qadir took his bow from its place in his quiver and fitted an arrow loosely to the weapon's string.

'We must find somewhere where we can watch the path without being seen. If what I thought I might have seen was a scout, and if they saw us up on the hillside, they might well work their way north with the aim of following us along the path, or just wait for the legion to arrive. Either way, if we wait here we will have the best possible chance of detecting them.'

He advanced carefully back towards the path until they could see it through the trees, then looked about him until he found a suitable place in which to take cover.

'We won't be seen from here. All we have to do now is wait.'

They settled into the concealment of a knot of scrub, Qadir showing Marcus how to use the dusty soil to mute the white wool of his tunic.

'It strikes me that you're very proficient at this sort of thing.'

Qadir smiled at the whispered comment.

'For a while "this sort of thing" was what I did all the time.'

'When you were the ghost of Hamah?'

Another smile.

'Yes, that was in those days.'

Silence fell between them, and Marcus knew that while his friend would probably answer the question if asked directly, to do so would subtly change the nature of their relationship. After a pause so long that he had come to expect no further response, the Hamian spoke again.

'I was what you might call a street fighter.'

The Roman held his silence, knowing that whatever it was his friend was going to share with him would be best emerging at whatever pace suited him.

'My father was a rich man, as rich as any Roman senator, but his wealth did not come honestly. He was the leader of a large and influential gang of smugglers and thieves, and he brought me up to be his successor. He taught me the ways of street justice, where the only real arbiter is the blade of a knife. And I was a willing student.'

'You don't have to tell—'

Qadir's interruption was out of character, even if delivered in the most even of tones.

'My friend, you have asked the question, if only silently, and I trust you well enough to know that I can tell you anything without being judged for the deeds of my past. And those deeds were, as you can imagine, very much on the wrong side of the law, whether Roman or our own. I became my father's trusted lieutenant as I entered manhood, and performed the tasks he needed to be able to deny all knowledge of. He pointed me at his enemies, and I removed them from his path. I learned the skills of an informer and an assassin, and I used them to hunt down and murder anyone that stood in his way.'

He sighed.

'My father told me that I would live that life for the rest of my days, have my own sons and raise them in the same way, but of course the Deasura saw his hubris and decided to punish him for imagining that he could expect to foresee the future. The Roman governor realised that smuggling was damaging his tax revenues, and decided not to tolerate it any longer. He set the vigiles on us, removing all constraints on them, and they burned my father's operation to the ground in days. After he was taken by them I chose to fight, rather than surrender to them. And so I fought, and I lost, and I was captured in the same way, betrayed by an informant.

'My father was executed, and like all of his men I was given a choice, to either be executed or join the Roman army, and of course I chose the latter, reasoning that there was nothing the army could do to me that would in any way be worse than the streets. But it turned out that—'

He fell silent.

'What is it?'

'Watch.'

Marcus stared out through the bush's spiky camouflage and waited for whatever it was that Qadir had heard or seen to become obvious. He was on the verge of telling his friend that he must have been mistaken when something moved fractionally in the undergrowth next to the path. The Hamian's bow sang and shot an arrow into the undergrowth, and whatever had moved in the shadows of the grove let out a high-pitched squeal and fell to the ground with an audible thump.

The two men hurried down the shallow slope, Qadir with another arrow nocked to his bowstring and Marcus with his swords drawn, but when they reached the spot they discovered that what the Hamian's shot had hit was not, as suspected, an enemy scout.

'A deer.'

The beast was still panting, unable to rise from the bloodied ground where it had dropped, and Qadir gave it the mercy stroke with a swift prayer for forgiveness.

'We cannot eat it, as we have no time to cook the meat and in any case to do so would be a betrayal of our comrades' monotonous diet of fish. And so I ask the Deasura for her pardon for killing without purpose. And if there were enemy scouts that I saw momentarily, they will be long gone by now. I suggest we do the same.'

They returned to the horses and resumed their path to the east, following the track all morning and into the early afternoon as it led up the northern side of the valley and along the flank of higher ground to their north that would protect the legion from detection as it marched on Rhaedestus. Leaving a confirmatory sign every mile or so, they pushed along the ridge's southern side until the range of hills came to an end with one last summit, a little higher than the others.

The view from the top revealed what Marcus had expected. In the shimmering distance, looking over a succession of successively lower hills, they could see the sea; and on the coast perhaps ten miles distant, its buildings seeming to ripple in the haze, was a city.

'Rhaedestus?'

The Roman nodded.

'If the map is to be believed.' He looked to the north, and the familiar straight line drawn across the landscape by the Via Egnatia. 'Let's go and have a look at the road that will take us there, shall we?'

They rode cautiously up the eastern side of the hill for another mile or so until the road itself came into view, the usual carefully engineered arrow-straight strip of massive polygonal paving stones worn perfectly flat by centuries of traffic. It was quiet, with a few travellers visible in the distance in either direction and a farm cart rumbling towards the two men, driven by a lazy-looking man whose donkey had the appearance of not being long for the world. The farmer nodded as the cart passed, seemingly untroubled by the presence of a pair of centurions at the roadside, and the two men watched as it rumbled on down the road to the city.

'A cart with no load? Why bother to make the journey, I wonder?'

Qadir nodded, equally thoughtful.

'Let's have a look at the road, shall we?'

The Hamian got down on his hands and knees and examined the surface carefully, blowing away the sand from the cracks between the paving slabs until he found what he was looking for.

Standing, he offered his findings to Marcus, who looked at them for a moment before dropping them into his belt purse.

'It may mean nothing, or it may be a sign that we ignore at our peril. Very well, I think I've seen enough.'

They retraced their steps back to the hill that had been their vantage point, at the valley's end, and decided that the combination of flat ground, the presence of a stream for the legion to refill their water skins, and proximity to the city while still having an escape route back to the east, made it ideal as a camp for the evening. The marching column came into view after a further hour's wait, and after a brief conversation Scaurus agreed with their suggestion and ordered Julius to settle his men down for the night.

'Don't bother gathering firewood, we're too close to the city to risk alerting any patrolling enemy scouts. And tell them it's one last meal of dried fish – tomorrow night we'll be eating whatever it is they have in the granaries and warehouses of Rhaedestus. And now, gentlemen, why not show me the view from up on that hill?'

They climbed into the late-afternoon sun, Scaurus remaining silent until the three men were standing on the flat ground at the top of the slope. He looked out to the west at the distant city, then north at the road, still visible in the early evening's amber glow.

'So that's the city. And no more than four hours' march distant. It seems as if this wild gamble on the emperor's part might just be about to pay off, if we really have got this close to it without being detected.' He turned back to look at his silent companions. 'But what is it you wanted to tell me? The pair of you have the look of men with something on your minds.'

'For one thing we might or might not have spotted an enemy scout this afternoon, although we lay in wait without seeing anything more. And we went for a look at the road when we got here.'

Marcus fished in his purse and dropped three small pieces of iron into his friend's hand.

'Hobnails?'

'We found them in the cracks between the paving stones. That many nails, and none of them rusted – which means they haven't been there long – must mean that a large force has passed in the last few days. And we saw what looked like a farmer heading into the city, except his cart was empty and it looked a lot like the sort of cart we use to carry our cook-pots and tents on campaign.'

'So you think he was an enemy spy?'

The younger man shook his head.

'I don't know. He looked like a farmer, slightly ragged and not all that clean, but then he could have swapped places with Sanga and you wouldn't have known the difference.'

Scaurus laughed, breaking the tension.

'I can just see Sanga riding a cart and cursing the order that had him there while his mates were doubtless away drinking and whoring. But seriously . . .'

'I know. We're quite possibly bringing far too much paranoia to a simple situation.'

'Possibly. Or you might be showing me the warning signs of impending disaster.' The tribune pondered for a moment. 'Which is hardly the happiest position to be in. Of course the nails might be from Niger's legions marching west to attack Italy before Severus can do the same to Antioch, have you considered that? We might just be the only legion in eastern Thrace, which would make this seemingly suicidal mission a masterstroke by the emperor. The road to Byzantium might be wide open, with nothing more to stop us taking the Golden Horn than an auxiliary cohort or two. But there's only one way to find out.'

They went down the hill again and the tribune went into a huddle with Cilo and Julius, explaining their scouts' findings and forebodings. In the end the discussion boiled down to their simple lack of choice in the matter, Cilo of all people hitting the nail squarely on the head.

'We can fall back from here to who knows where, with no idea where the enemy actually is since we have no cavalry to go and find them. Which would mean abandoning our mission and our duty to the empire. Or we can sit here and wait for them to appear, from whatever direction, surrendering any initiative. Or, as we all know to be the right approach, we can go forward in the direction ordered and do our duty, which might actually end up being the way to save our own skins as well.'

He looked around at the men who were ultimately his officers, even if Scaurus was effectively in command, smiling in a way that endeared him to the watching Marcus more than his words, the epitome of patrician duty to Rome.

'I have sacrificed to Mars, and to Victoria, and have every confidence that they are watching over our fortunes. But ultimately this war will be won by the courage and confidence we bring to it, and by that alone. So let us take the only path allowed to us by our duty, but take it gladly. And while I can't speak for you men, I'm happy to share the fact that another meal of that awful dried fish would have had me eyeing my sword, and wondering if it might not be preferable to fall on it than take another mouthful of the stuff. So it's death or glory for me, gentlemen, and I can only hope that you choose to join me when I march out to attack Rhaedestus.'

After a moment of silence Julius stepped forward and saluted.

'The Fourth Legion will be at your back every step of the way, Legatus. We will do what is ordered, and at every command we will be ready!'

Cilo patted him on the shoulder, drawing an astonished look from the usually dour centurion.

'I know you will, First Spear, because I know that you understand your duty to the empire just as well as I do. Even if that duty is founded on a different rock, we both stand on the solid certainty of what is expected of us both. Expected of all of us, gentlemen!'

He smiled once more and then turned away, leaving the familia to consider his words. To their collective surprise, it was Sanga who spoke first.

'Well, if it's good enough for the likes of him . . .'

And that seemed to be the feeling among the men of the legion as they bedded down for the night, their guts filled with the last of the fish and with only their cloaks to wrap themselves in against the cold of a cloudless night. Marcus and Julius took the first watch, and with no rampart to walk chose to climb the hill that the two scouts had ascended the previous afternoon. The full moon was just starting to wane, providing sufficient illumination for the two men to have a clear view of the sea, whose waves rippled like the shine of a polished and oiled mail-coat under its silver light.

'So it's what, fifteen miles to this city, right?'

Marcus thought for a moment.

'Probably more like twenty, given the dog-leg to get to the road, and the fact that we can't march in a straight line to get there once the Via Egnatia starts weaving around the hills.'

'So we'll arrive outside the gates in the middle of the day, if I push the legion along at the battle march with minimal rest stops. Which is going to leave us a bit fucked if they decline to surrender and we can't just smash our way in without being peppered with arrows or set on fire with oil.'

The younger man nodded, and Julius continued.

'That's the gamble Severus took on our behalf, isn't it? That our unexpected appearance in the enemy rear, and the threat to their line of communication from Asia through Byzantium, would cause their resistance in Thracia to collapse. His strategy is to chase them down as they try to get back across the Propontis to safety before his main army can bring them to battle. That way he secures Thracia at the very least, and bottles Niger up in his Asian provinces, and with any luck he'll be able to get his army across the Propontis into Asia before the enemy army has had time to find its feet again.'

'So now all we can do is go and find out what the numbers are on the dice he rolled for us.'

'Yes. This is the day we get to find out what fate he's condemned us to enjoy.'

Julius looked out over the darkened landscape for a moment before speaking again.

'If there are men out there waiting for us I have to give full respect to them given that we haven't as much as caught sight of them.'

They watched over the sleeping legion until Qadir came up the hill to relieve them, and Marcus rolled himself in his cloak to get some sleep. But his dreams were no respite from the pressures of the previous days, a chaotic mix of sailing and marching as if his mind were reprising the events of the previous month. Close to dawn, as he was starting to stir, a new dream overtook him. The shadowy presence he occasionally recalled on waking, a woman's voice that came to him unexpectedly and without any precedent in the day that he could ever discern, spoke in his ear, her words brooking no argument.

'This is a day for you to endure! Endure, until the eagle takes you under his wings!'

He woke at a touch on his shoulder, and found Dubnus standing over him.

'You were talking in your sleep again, some nonsense about an eagle. It's time to be up and ready to move.'

Untangling his legs from the cloak's folds, he rose and belted on his swords by touch in the darkness, hearing the sounds of men doing the same thing around him, their voices quiet so as not to wake their tent-mates who had stood watch and were still sleeping. The day was barely begun, the eastern sky shifting from black to purple with the sun's imminent rise, and in the half-light the two men made their way to the stream and washed their faces and necks. Dubnus laced the cheek guards on his helmet closed, grimacing at the acrid smell of stale sweat from his still-damp arming cap.

'A cup of wine and a decent sweat in a legion bathhouse would be just about perfect right now. Instead of which I have to go into battle smelling like something a badger would turn its nose up at.'

They found Scaurus drinking water from a cup, his expression pensive in the dim light of the dawn.

'Gentlemen. I trust you slept well?'

'I did, thank you, Tribune, or at least until Two Knives had one of his goddess dreams.' Dubnus shot an amused glance at Marcus. 'I can always tell, you start babbling nonsense like you've had too much wine and can't get your tongue around the words.'

'She visited you again. Was it an omen?'

Marcus shook his head at Scaurus.

'Not that I can tell from the little I remember. This oaf woke me up just as she started telling me something . . . something about having to endure, and an eagle.'

Scaurus smiled wanly.

'No detailed advice on our deployment in the event of a battle then? Perhaps it means that there are friendly legions close by, although I can see no way for that to be the case. But given that she has chosen to visit you today of all days, and with such a message, this might very well be a day that will demand endurance from all of us.' He turned and saluted as Cilo walked up to the small group. 'Ah, Legatus, you've dressed for the occasion!'

The patrician had emptied out the box that had been transported on a cart all the way from Rome and arrayed himself in his ceremonial armour, a magnificent bronze chest plate and greaves with a gold and silver decorated helmet whose workmanship was little short of perfection.

'I decided that if there was ever a day to wear my grandfather's armour then it's today. Whether we face the greatest battle of our lives or just another day of marching, I will at least be ready for any eventuality!'

Julius gathered his centurions with three swift blasts of his whistle, waiting until all sixty men were gathered around him in expectant silence until he spoke. Raising his voice loud enough to be heard by them all, and the soldiers immediately behind them, he raised his voice to a gruff parade-ground bark.

'This is the day, my brothers! This is the day when all that dancing on the sand might just pay us back! Today is the day we march on the city of Rhaedestus! Today is the day we *take* the city of Rhaedestus! And if your men need no other motivation, just tell them that if we don't take Rhaedestus then we won't be eating anything tonight other than what's growing in the fields around the city!'

He paused to let that sink in for a minute.

'And tell them that if that's not enough to have them on their mettle, then they need to be aware that there might be an enemy army hunting us! Just because we've seen no sign of any soldiers doesn't mean that they're not out there! So from the moment that we leave this camp we're going to be doing everything possible to make it difficult for that enemy, if they do exist, to catch us with the latrine sponge between our legs!'

He paused, waiting for the chuckles to die away.

'We march at the battle pace! I know you'll all be cursing me five miles from here, but not being where the enemy thinks you're going to be is the best way to throw his plans out of the window, and to make him respond to you. And you, my brothers, are the cream of the Danubius legions. So if it comes to a fight we need have no fear! Go and gather your men, get ready to march, and tell them that tonight we will feast on the spoils of a victory that will shake the usurper's pretend empire to its foundations!'

The centurions did as they were ordered, and while Scaurus and Cilo waited for the legion to be ready to march, Marcus and Qadir mounted up to ride up ahead of the legion.

'North to the Via Egnatia, then turn east and go as far as it takes to get eyes on the city.' Julius stared up at Marcus and raised an admonishing finger. 'No risk-taking, right? And no putting yourself into any position that might be impossible to get out of under the wrong circumstances. If there are legions waiting for us out there, you're not going to be any use face down with an arrow between your shoulders! Right, on your way,' he shouted as a parting comment as the two men turned their mounts to ride out, 'and remember to look twice before you go anywhere that might conceal an enemy!'

The two men rode north to the road, stopping to look down the cobbled pathway in both directions for any sign of a military presence. Just as had been the case the previous day, the road seemed almost empty, a farm cart the best part of a mile away to their left being the only thing of note on a main route that would normally be expected to be a busy link between east and west. It was Qadir who put his finger on the sense of unease Marcus was feeling.

'What bothers me most is not seeing the sort of traffic I would have expected to find on the main route from Rome to Byzantium. It was empty yesterday, even if it was late in the day, and it's empty now an hour after dawn. If it's this quiet in another hour or two then I think we can safely say that there's something not quite right.'

They trotted their mounts east, scanning the high ground to the north intently but never seeing anything to give them any concern. The road turned to the right, hooking around a piece of higher ground to its north, and after a cautious initial reconnaissance on foot the two men relaxed as they found the next stretch of cobbles as empty as that which had gone before. After less than a mile it turned back to the left, heading east again, and when they hobbled their horses and went forward cautiously once again there was nothing out of the ordinary, other than the apparent lack of travellers that was starting to perturb them both. The high ground to their left was lightly wooded, and in the middle distance a rudimentary structure was huddled by the side of the road, a one-room olive farmer's house like others they had seen. Qadir looked at it dubiously from the cover of a bush, shaking his head unhappily.

'There's something just not right here. Let's stop to smell the air properly.'

They squatted in the bush's cover in silence, and Marcus looked down the road to the point where it vanished around a bend to the right a mile distant.

'I know what you mean, I feel the same unease, but there's nothing to—'

'Exactly! There's nothing. No birdsong. No farm dogs barking. Nobody in the fields. This isn't farmland, it's a battlefield laid out and waiting for us to blunder onto it.'

Marcus listened carefully for a moment. The silence was complete, uninterrupted by as much as the song of a lark.

'You're right. And those trees' – he looked up at the ranks of olive trees marching away up the hill – 'aren't any sort of obstacle to a surprise attack down the hill.'

'If they came at us down the hills in enough strength to outflank us on both sides then the only way to escape would be that way.' Qadir pointed down the shallow slope at the sea's distant sparkle. 'They could push us straight down the hill and into the water, and put us to the sword on the beach.'

Marcus looked back down the road to Rhaedestus.

'That farmhouse. If this is where they plan to attack us then it could well be the hiding place for whoever's going to call in the enemy, if they're waiting on the far side of the hill.'

The two men looked at the ramshackle building, and after a moment Marcus nodded decisively.

'We can't prove any of this, and we can't take it back to the tribune without that proof. If we halt a battle march without good cause we could be throwing away the only chance we'll get to take the city without a fight. Which means we have to go and find out. But not by knocking on the front door.'

They returned to their horses and remounted, turning south off the road into the olive groves, down a farm track that took them out of sight of the Via Egnatia within fifty paces. Qadir turned and looked back, unable to make out the road's cobbled ribbon through the intervening trees.

'This is perfect ambush country. You could muster a cohort two hundred paces from the road and it'd be impossible to see them until they started advancing.'

The two men tied their horses to trees, drew their swords and ghosted through the olive grove in a direction roughly parallel with the road until they spied the farmhouse through the foliage. Moving as quietly as they could, unable to prevent the faint crackle of twigs snapping underfoot, they crept up to the house's wall, crouching in its cover and listening intently. The smell of woodsmoke and burning fat was in the air, making Marcus's stomach clench at the thought of eating.

'By now there should be at least one dog going wild at our scent, or whining at the cook.' Marcus nodded at Qadir's whispered statement. 'There is no dog, because there is no farmer here.'

A voice reached them from the other side of the wall, muffled enough to have come from within the house. The words were indistinct, but audibly harsh and guttural, Greek spoken by a man whose first language was an eastern dialect. Another man answered, so close to them that he could have been sitting with his back to the wall. His voice was more cultured, and instantly recognisable from his accent as being from Rome, most likely a son of the city sent east to serve with one of the legions facing the Parthians or dominating Judea.

'I know, you have to wonder just how long it takes to cook a sausage! Get them burned and on the plate, Demitrios, I've not eaten since noon yesterday and my stomach thinks my throat's been cut!'

Marcus and Qadir looked at each other, the Hamian pointing at the wall and raising his eyebrows in silent question. The Roman thought for a moment and then nodded and pointed at the house. He drew his swords one at a time, careful to avoid the scrape of steel on the scabbards' metal throats, while Qadir readied his bow and uncovered the arrows in his quiver, putting one to the weapon's string and holding another, with the hand drawing back the first to almost the bow's full tension.

They crept down the wall to the gate, which was slightly ajar, and Marcus crouched low to look through the gap into the farmyard. A fire was burning in a partially visible brazier, and a morose-looking soldier was squatting close to it with a frying pan, a legion-issue signal horn lying on his cloak close by. The Roman pointed to the gap, and Qadir peeped through it and nodded his understanding as Marcus whispered in his ear.

'I'll go first. The man tending the fire is their cornicer, so shoot him first to stop him blowing his horn. Then kill whoever comes out of the farmhouse. I'll deal with the Roman, because we need him alive.'

He took a long, slow breath, set himself ready to attack, then shouldered the gate wide open and went through it with the Hamian close behind.

10

The legionary cooking the sausages died without ever really realising what was happening, Qadir's first arrow punching through
his armour and killing him instantly. He fell forward onto the
fire, his greasy tunic and hair igniting in an instant to swathe his
body in flames with a *whoof* of combusting grease. The officer
sitting with his back to the wall was still gaping in amazement as
Marcus, having kicked the gate open, ran at him with his swords
raised, and his own blade was barely clear of its scabbard when
it was smashed from his hand by the Roman's first strike. Swinging his gladius, he hammered the flat of the blade into the side
of the other man's head and bounced him off the wall, knocked
senseless by the blow.

Turning to face the house, he was just in time to see a centurion burst through the door with his sword drawn before the officer
went sprawling full-length in the dust, Qadir's second shaft in his
right thigh. Rolling onto his back and stiffening in agony, the officer
opened his mouth to bellow a warning to whoever was behind him
in the house, but Marcus, already running at the doorway behind
him, chopped his spatha's blade down into his throat and silenced
him without breaking stride. Another man appeared in the doorway,
dithered for a moment at the sight of his officer being murdered,
turned to run and then arched backwards in agony, staggering back
into the house with an arrow's shaft protruding from his back.

Marcus shouldered him aside as he went through the doorway with his blades held ready to fight and Qadir at his back.
In the single room's cramped confines a man was getting to his
feet from the floor on which he had been asleep after standing a

night's watch. The Roman raised his spatha and pointed it at the hapless soldier.

'Stand down now or die!'

The other man hesitated, caught between fighting and surrender, and Qadir stepped out from behind Marcus with an arrow nocked to his bow and the string taut. Realising that the fight was already lost, the legionary dropped his sword and fell to his knees, quailing as the Roman stood over him with his bloodied spatha ready to strike.

'*You* can live, but you have to tell us what we need to know.'

'I don't know any—'

'Which legion do you serve with?'

The legionary looked from Marcus to Qadir, who laughed tersely as he slung the bow over his shoulder, his usually cultured voice deliberately harsh.

'Don't look at me, boy. Answer the question or don't answer it. What's one more corpse to bury?'

'The Sixth Ferrata!'

'How many other legions are there waiting for us here?'

'Two! Twelfth Fulminata and Third Gallica!'

'How many cohorts?'

The soldier shook his head desperately.

'I don't know! Perhaps two legions' worth?'

'And where are all these men?'

The legionary pointed at the sloping ground on the other side of the road, visible through the farmhouse's open window.

'Up there, on the other side of the hill! They're waiting for us to give the signal!'

Marcus nodded at Qadir as he turned away.

'You know what to do.'

The soldier shrank away in horror as the Hamian stepped forward, but all Qadir did was bind his hands behind his back and then tie his ankles together. He finished the job by stuffing a handful of wool into the bound man's mouth from his dead comrade's tunic.

'Someone will find you eventually. Count yourself lucky you had the sense to surrender.'

The two men left him lying on the floor and went out to see what state the officer Marcus had stunned was in. He had recovered his consciousness but not his wits, and was still so dazed that the two men had to assist him back into a seated position.

'What . . . ?'

He stared at Marcus glassily, trying to work out who the strange newcomer was and taking time to connect the pain in his head with the man standing in front of him.

'You . . . hit me . . . with your sword.' He shook his head as if the pain he was suffering could be shaken off. 'Thought I was going to die.'

'Not today.' Marcus pulled the dagger from his captive's belt and tossed it down beside the concussed tribune's sword. 'Not unless you try to raise the alarm. What's your name?'

'Gaius Antius Calpurnius. My father is Marcus Antius Calpurnius and he's going to—'

'Save it. This is an interrogation, not an invitation to you to tell me what a big mistake I'm making in not washing your feet and sending you on your way.' The younger man's poorly concealed start at his captor's abrupt forcefulness told him everything he needed to know as to his state of mind. 'Which legion do you serve with?'

'I can't—'

'You're not keeping any secrets I don't already know, Antius Calpurnius. It has to be the Third, the Sixth or the Twelfth, I know there are detachments of all three out there in strength, just waiting for us to stroll into this trap, and I just want to know which legatus to return your head to if you keep playing it dumb.'

The younger man looked at him for a moment.

'You're not joking, are you?'

Marcus snorted a hollow laugh.

'This is a civil war we're fighting, not some sort of child's game of hide-and-seek. You were waiting here so that you could signal once we were too far down the road to escape, to bring those three legions over the hill and bottle us up like rats in a trap! The result of which would have been that the best part of twice our strength would have had their spears at our throats and pushed us into the sea. It would have been a slaughter, and *you* would have been the man to get it started!'

He softened his voice, picking up the other man's pugio and examining the blade's edge.

'So no, Gaius Antius Calpurnius, I'm not joking. You can answer my question, or you can be the fourth man I kill today. So, one *last* time, which legion is it that you serve with?'

Something in his voice made the tribune look up at him with a look of horrified realisation that the threat was both real and final.

'I'm a tribune with the Third Gallica.'

Marcus smiled.

'Tell me, do the Third's officers still use a villa in the hills that the legion's men call the Honeypot to while away their spare time, or is there some semblance of military discipline among your colleagues?'

'How could you know that . . . ?'

'I know that, Gaius, because I used to be one of those officers. It was the man commanding your enemy today who led the Third to victory at Nisibis almost a decade ago!'

Calpernius's eyes widened.

'That was *you*?'

'That was *us*. We unpicked the lock of Parthian military supremacy on their own ground, and showed them what it means to take liberties with the empire. And now we're here to do the same to you. Your usurper of an emperor will—'

'He's here.'

Marcus stared down at the younger man in amazement.

'Niger? Is *here*?'

The tribune nodded.

'He's been promised a battle of annihilation against your force. His man Sartorius has set up the whole thing, with spies in the ports you sailed past and fast messengers relaying the news of your progress. Ever since the news of your landing was received there have been scouts watching you and guiding in the legions.'

'This man Sartorius being Niger's beneficiarius?'

Calpurnius shook his head.

'He's more than just a beneficiarius. Much more. He was a grain officer, until the emperor elevated him to the position of chief informer and set him to work. The man's a genius.'

Marcus shrugged.

'Genius or not, he got one thing wrong.'

'What's that?'

'He didn't manage to entice us all the way into his trap before we detected it. Which means that this is going to be a proper fight, rather than a one-sided slaughter. Come on, you're going to be in the best seat in the arena for this show.'

They found the legion marching along the Via Egnatia, close to the point where the road made its turn to the right. Julius barked the command for the column to halt when he saw the two men cantering back along the road with Calpurnius seated behind Marcus, walking forward to meet them with Dubnus and Scaurus.

'He looks a bit cleaner than the average grunt, and that tunic's clearly high-quality. Is that a prisoner or have you got a new boyfriend?'

The captive glowered at him from his place behind Marcus while the Roman dismounted, unable to follow suit with his hands tied behind his back. He had been compliant with their commands once he'd been assured that he was in the hands of a fellow Roman gentleman, and on being addressed by the bluntly spoken centurion he assumed the haughty mien of a man sinned against.

'I am a Roman officer, Centurion, and you have no—'

'He's the man who was set to spring a trap on us not far down the road from here.'

Marcus shot a hard look up at his captive, who sniffed and looked away in disgust at being interrupted. He pointed to the hill overlooking the road to the north.

'There are strong detachments of the Third Gallia, Sixth Iron-clad and Twelfth Thunderbolt lying in wait behind that high ground. Their plan is to let us get close enough to the city that there's only a few hundred paces between the road and the city walls and the sea. This tribune and his men were tasked with sounding the horn call that would have sprung the trap.'

'They planned to pen us up for the slaughter.' Scaurus looked up at the hillside. 'But surely they have men up there watching us?'

Qadir shook his head.

'Once you're in the heart of the grove it's impossible to see anything without the risk of being seen yourself, Tribune. I think one of their scouts got too eager yesterday and almost betrayed his presence.' The Hamian gestured to the captive Calpurnius. 'Which is why this man was positioned to sound their horns once we were past their hiding place and too far into the trap to avoid being bottled up, pinned up against the sea and forced to surrender. If they even planned to let us surrender, and not just to kill us to the last man as a demonstration of their ruth-lessness.'

While he was speaking Marcus helped their prisoner down from the horse's back.

'His name is Gaius Antius Calpurnius, and he's one of Niger's inner circle. He says that Niger himself is up there, come to take the glory of destroying one of Severus's legions as the result of a plan set up by his man Sartorius.'

The tribune pondered Marcus's words.

'Well now, isn't that bold of him? And he might well yet cel-ebrate that victory, but he'll have to pay a high price in his own dead if he wants to take our eagle. First Spear!'

Julius snapped to attention.

'Tribune!'

'You heard all of that. What is your recommended tactical dis-position?'

The grizzled Briton looked about him, then pointed up the hill to the north.

'The enemy are going to come over the hill and down that slope, once they realise that we're not playing their game. It's downhill all the way to the road, and then the ground rises again over there' – he pointed to the olive grove on the right-hand side of the road – 'and that looks like the only defendable ground that's available to us. I'd say we either make a run for it and risk being hunted down when the lack of food leaves us without the strength to march, or else we fortify the treeline opposite their direction of attack, put a cohort at right angles at each end of the defence to stop them flanking us, and take them on in a fair fight while we still have some chance of giving a good account of ourselves, here and now. That way we have the best chance of fighting them to a standstill, and having as equal a voice as possible if it comes to discussing terms. If we kill enough of them they might just decide it'll be easier to let us go.'

Scaurus considered the cleared strip of ground beyond the road, bare earth with a scattering of hardy scrub that ran thirty paces to where the ranks of olive trees rose up the higher ground to their right.

'It's not much of an option, but it's better than any of the alternatives. Very well, deploy your men and prepare them to fight!'

Julius stepped to the column's side and gave the hand signal for the legion's officers to join him for a briefing, pumping his fist to emphasise the urgency. The centurions came up the line of men at a run to cluster around him, while their men watched with the stolid discipline that was founded on the collective knowledge that whatever their fears as to what was to come, the reprisals for any loss of control would be swift and brutal. The Briton looked around at his officers, assessing the determination on their faces.

'We have a battle to fight! The enemy will come over that hill' – he pointed at the higher ground to the left of the road – 'and try to overwhelm us with numbers. Which means we need to set up a defensive position from which we can kill enough of them to make them think again. So when I blow my whistle you will turn your men to the right and take them to the edge of those trees.' He pointed at the edge of the grove to the right of the road. 'Get them lined up and then turn them round and back them up five paces. I want a four-man-deep battle line facing the road just inside the treeline, with the lead and rearguard cohorts deployed to secure the flanks at an angle you can choose to suit the ground you're on.'

He nodded at their dubious expressions.

'Yes, I know this is less than ideal. Fighting from a forest is well up the official list of bad ideas, as we'll be scattered for good if we have to retreat. And going four men deep will restrict our front- age, before anyone says it. But this isn't going to be over quickly, so I want to be able to rotate fresh men into the fight and give the rest of us time to get our wind back before we have to go back in. Plus we'll have casualties to cope with. The good news is that the trees will stop them dropping arrows on us, the bad news is that I won't be able to see very much of what's happening once we're engaged, so it'll be down to horn calls. I'll keep the first cohort as a reserve in the centre, and the only signal we'll use is one long blast if you're literally at breaking point and need reinforcement. Don't blow without good reason or I'll kill you myself to save the enemy the trouble, but if you do have to give the signal, keep giving it so that the centuries I send can find you!'

He looked around at the serious-faced men gathered around him, their expressions ranging from sombre realism to stone-faced denial of their own fears.

'You are going to have men wounded! A lot of wounded! If they can still fight then tell them how lucky they are and put them back in the line. If they can't fight then get them out from underfoot, pull them clear of the line and leave them to it. Your bandage-carriers are going to be needed in the line, and there'll be too many casualties for them to deal with in any case. We can worry about the walking wounded after the battle, and do the decent thing for those that are going to die but haven't gone to the underworld yet.'

The veteran officer grinned mirthlessly at their serious expressions.

'Cheer up! Today you have the honour, the privilege, of becoming members of an exclusive brotherhood. After today you'll be able to look down on all those other bastards in the army who haven't seen the elephant yet. That, or you'll be dead and past caring. Either way, this is the defining day of the rest of your lives! Don't let your men down, don't let me down, but most of all don't let *yourselves* down!'

He turned back to Scaurus and Cilo.

'Anything to add, sirs?'

To Marcus's surprise it was Cilo who stepped forward, looking every bit the Roman general in his pristine armour, speaking with a calm, straightforward demeanour intended to instil confidence in his men.

'The emperor will be in our debt for what we do today, gentlemen! We will deliver a mighty blow to the usurper's fighting strength whatever the outcome of this battle! And I look forward to celebrating that result with you all soon enough, and toasting our victory and the honour of every man who puts his life at the service of Rome today!'

Julius stepped forward again, looking grateful for the senior officer's brevity.

'Thank you, Legatus. Right, get your men deployed when I sound the horn and be quick about it. Dismissed!'

His officers headed back to their centuries, those at the far end of the column running back to their men, each of them turning to look back at Julius in readiness for his signal.

'Tribunes!'

The legion's young gentlemen gathered around the gruff centurion, Marcus and Varus standing to one side to show that as experienced officers they were not the subjects of the first spear's attention.

'I wasn't joking when I said that once we're deployed it'll be hard to see what's happening along the line, and that's where you come in. There are six of you, and I'm going to allocate you out to the furthest three cohorts on either side. Link up with the senior centurion and watch the battle with him. Do *not* give in to the temptation to dive in and start fighting, because you're no good to anyone dead! When, and *only* when, it looks like your part of the line might be about to collapse, you can authorise the call for help. If the cornicer's dead then blow the horn yourself – nothing fancy, just a long hard blast to let us know you're in the shit, and if we have any reserve left I'll send it to you. If no one turns up when you blow it'll be because we got overwhelmed somewhere else, and you'll just have to do your best with the men you have left. Now, are you ready for war?'

The officers stared back at him, collectively stunned by the sudden turn of events, but if his intention was to roar the question at them again in the traditional style, a waved signal from the rear of the legion's column caught his attention instead, telling him that the rearmost cohort's senior centurion was back in his place and the legion ready to be ordered to their battle position. Turning to the officers standing close by, he nodded tersely as he raised his whistle to his lips.

'On your way, gentlemen, because this road will be knee-deep in enemy soldiers before you know it!'

At the whistle's shrill command the legion's cohorts and centuries turned to their right, obeying the bellowed commands of their officers, then hurried towards the edge of the olive grove, a wave of iron washing across the open ground and up to the treeline. Julius watched them moving towards their new position from the road's slight elevation, gesturing for the tribunes to take up their positions with their cohorts.

'Go on then, and remember to stay out of the fight until there's no other choice!'

'Should we too perhaps join our command, First Spear?'

Julius turned back to answer Scaurus's question.

'Apologies, Tribune, yes, you and the legatus need to get behind the cover of a cohort too, by the eagle please. I'm going to wait here for long enough that I can see what we're facing.'

The tribune nodded, knowing better than to argue with something that his senior centurion had made his mind up to do.

'Very well. Stay with him please, gentlemen.' He turned away and ushered Cilo towards the trees in the wake of their legionaries. 'He might need convincing to do the sensible thing and retreat back behind his men before the enemy scouts part his hair with an arrow.'

Marcus gestured the remaining officers to follow.

'Dubnus and I will stay with him. I'd quite like to see what Niger has managed to bring to this party.'

The three men walked forward until they were close enough to the trees to see up the hill in the gaps between them, squatting to get as close to the ground as possible for the clearest view. They waited in silence while the clamour of the legion's redeployment reduced, the centuries settling into the four-man-deep line that Julius had ordered.

'They're not bad, are they?'

Dubnus nodded, turning back to watch as the legion's centurions and chosen men pushed their troops into place.

'Like I told you before we landed, they're the same mixture of frightened kids, dumb farm boys and madmen we've commanded before. Once they have an enemy hammering at their shields we'll find out if they have the collective balls to fight them off. Ah, and speaking of the enemy . . .'

He gestured to the hillside above them, where a line of advancing men could be seen through the foliage.

'Legionaries, as advertised.'

'And they look tidy enough too.' Julius shook his head glumly. 'I was hoping that this was a massive bluff, but it looks like we're going to have to fight for our lives.' A flicker of movement caught their eyes as a scout flitted down the slope from one piece of cover to the next, a bow in his hands. 'Come on then, let's put some men with shields between us and them before their equivalent of Qadir starts putting arrows between our shoulders!'

Taking up their position behind the centre, most of the seven cohorts in the main line, with Julius's first cohort in reserve close behind them, they watched over the legionaries' heads as the enemy force took up position on the open ground behind the road some fifty paces distant. Expanding slowly but surely with the addition of each new cohort, the opposing force first matched and then exceeded the strength and length of the defenders, the enemy centurions shouting and pushing their men into place just as their own had moments before. Once Niger's men were fully deployed a familiar figure walked out in front of them, his black tunic identifying him as the man who had sought to capture Marcus in Thessalonica, and the Roman nodded at Qadir's confirmation of his identity.

'So there's the master strategist.'

Sartorius cupped his hands to his mouth to amplify his shouted greeting.

'Permission to approach is sought! I have a message from the emperor for you, Lucius Fabius Cilo!'

Not waiting for permission to be given, the master spy stalked forward alone, looking up at the waiting legionaries as he advanced until he was within ten paces of their positions. Putting his hands on his hips he looked up and down the line of cohorts with an affected expression of sadness.

'It seems that all my efforts to end this matter bloodlessly have come to nothing!'

'If I might, Legatus?'

Cilo gestured magisterially to Scaurus, who called out to the waiting beneficiarius.

'I have a score to settle with you, Sartorius!'

The other man stood in silence for a moment before responding, ignoring the threat.

'You have played a strong game with what you've been given, but you do realise that you stand *no* chance of surviving this battle? We are the best part of three legions strong, and your men must be as hungry as street dogs after so long on the march with so little to eat! This fight will be over inside the hour, and every one of you will either be dead or running for his life. Our cavalry's lances will reap a grievous toll of the survivors, chasing down every last one of you . . . unless of course we just stand here and wait for you to surrender from hunger!'

Scaurus laughed tersely.

'If that's the message you want to send the rest of your army, that you were too timid to defeat a force one third your own strength, go right ahead! But once night falls, who knows what might happen? I'd imagine that five thousand men attacking out of the darkness could make quite a mess of your legions!'

Sartorius laughed, sounding genuinely amused.

'Oh we'll come up there for you soon enough! But let me appeal to reason one last time. The emperor – the real emperor, of course – asked to be remembered to you. He has fond memories of your part in his victories in Dacia and Gallia, and he specifically asked me to offer you an honourable surrender, with no confiscation of weapons or executions. If, that is, you'll swear an oath to leave Thrace and take no further part in this campaign.'

Scaurus pushed his way through the line of shields protecting him from enemy archers, taking one from a legionary and raising it to stare through the gap between the shield's rim and his helmet's brow guard as he stepped out onto the open ground and stood close enough to Sartorius to speak conversationally.

'You can save your crocodile tears for the men you're about to lose in battle, Sartorius. Yes, we know your name. Some of my centurions have personal experience of your attempts to *avoid* bloodletting in Thessalonica, although the only man you succeeded in killing was my freedman. A man I had known for half my life, and who was worth a dozen like you. So I'd suggest you stay well clear of any actual fighting today, because there are a number of men here sworn to see you die today who will be on you like flies on shit.'

He waited for the beneficiarius to respond, but Sartorius only shrugged.

'That was war, Rutilius Scaurus. You *are* Gaius Rutilius Scaurus, I presume? I've been looking forward to meeting a man with your reputation for being every bit as much the schemer as I try to be! A war that your man on the throne started. And men die in war, as you know better than I do. And what should I tell the emperor? That his offer of peace is declined due to the death of a former barbarian slave?'

'Tell Gaius Pescennius Niger that Fabius Cilo is regrettably unable to accept his offer, having already sworn to serve one emperor to the death, but that the fact of his kind regard is appreciated.'

'Really? You'll just throw away your last chance to save five thousand men from death?'

The tribune shook his head.

'No. What I just threw away was your last hope of dealing with this incursion deep into your territory without losing at least five thousand men of your own! If not a good deal more. So farewell Sartorius, say hello to your master from me, and point out to him that little surprises like having to deal with a legion appearing in your rear area are the least of what he can expect from Severus once the army's main force arrives. I almost feel sorry for him, having to face such an accomplished master of the dark arts of both politics and warfare. And now you can leave, before I decide that you have overstepped the civilised bounds of negotiation and have my archers put a few arrows into you.'

He stepped back through the Fourth's line, handing the shield back to the man he had taken it from. The spy nodded and turned away, calling a parting comment over his shoulder.

'You will soon enough regret such bold behaviour, Tribune! Ready yourselves to suffer the anger of the true emperor's faithful legions!'

He walked through the enemy line, legionaries stepping aside to allow his passage without any order being given, and, after a pause, presumably to allow time for Niger to be briefed, the waiting legions' horns brayed the command for them to attack. The attacking line lurched into motion, crossing the road and beginning to climb the shallow slope towards the waiting defenders.

'Will you give a command to fight?'

Julius answered Cilo's question on Scaurus's behalf, raising his voice to be heard over the tumult of the approaching enemy.

'There's no need, Legatus! Our centurions will know when to start the battle wherever it comes to us first!'

The easterners were close enough that their eyes could be seen over the rims of their shields, their faces betraying the same combination of determination and terror that Marcus knew from long experience they would be seeing in the men facing them. A man facing the line in front of the command group was panicking loudly, fighting to escape from the soldiers around him whose advance was remorselessly pushing him ever closer to the defenders' waiting spears. With the strength gifted to him by terror he managed to turn his body and set his feet to push back, but he might as well have been resisting the strength of a ploughing ox for all the good it did. His boots slid backwards through the verge's scrub as the enemy line ground closer to the defenders, the men around him ignoring his panicked screams. The centurion standing behind them barked an order for them to attack and, as the front-rankers reflexively drew their spears back ready to throw, Julius, recognising the command, shouted the same warning to his men that his centurions were issuing all along the line.

'*Shields!*'

Reacting instantly to the long-practised command, the Fourth's front rank took a half-pace forward, thrusting their shields out away from their bodies to put empty air between the layered boards and their armour and crouching into their protection, lowering their helmeted heads to protect their faces. The men behind them raised their own shields to intercept thrown weapons with a higher trajectory, huddling close to the front rank to maximise their mutual defence. The legionaries facing them shouted a disciplined roar and hurled their weapons almost as one, with a deadly rippling cascade of dull thuds and metallic clangs as the spears hammered through the wooden boards or glanced off their iron bosses. Here and there men screamed as the knife-like spear heads, mounted on long iron shafts, punched through their shields to find the exposed skin of a face, a thigh or an arm, the men behind them dragging them out of the line and taking their places to re-form the wall of shields facing the enemy before they had the chance to regain their forward momentum.

'*Spears! Get ready for them!*'

Men with shields weighed down by spears hanging from them, the iron-shanked weapons impossible to dislodge without exposing themselves to attack, rotated back into the packed ranks of men behind them, their places taken by the second-rankers while they fought to pull the encumbering weapons free and rejoin the line. The front-rankers hefted their stabbing spears and readied themselves for the inevitable attack, the men behind them taking hold of their belts and talking to them, partnerships readying themselves to fight for their lives. With another bray of horns the easterners drew their swords and came forward up the last ten paces of the slope, and the Fourth's men braced themselves for the onslaught, the two armies sizing each other up for a moment like fighting dogs going eye to eye before sinking their teeth into each other's bodies.

With a collective exhalation of effort from the attackers as they ran the last few paces the fight was on, and the chaos of a full-scale battle descended on what had been a relatively ordered affair until the moment that the two sides went blade to blade. Looking out across the battlefield from their elevated position, all Marcus could see were two lines of almost indistinguishable helmets opposing each other, the simplicity lent to the scene by distance deceptive as to the murder being done at the point of contact where the two armies were grinding bloodily against each other. The enemy soldiers were pushing to get into sword's reach of the line, while the Fourth's men were obdurate behind their shields, using their spears' greater reach to stab out at the faces and legs of the men facing them to inflict wound after crippling wound, sending their victims staggering away to seek assistance to stem the flow of their blood. Scaurus pointed at the enemy soldiers facing them, calling out a warning to Julius.

'They're going straight for the throat!'

In the fight happening in front of the familia's position the enemy legionaries were being driven forward by their officers, their gazes fixed on the prize of the Fourth's eagle standing proud above Cilo's head. They were attacking and dying at a ferocious pace, the attack relentless in its apparent determination to capture the legion's symbol of imperial pride. The legionaries defending the position were fighting hard but already flagging in the face of such a fierce onslaught. Fresh troops were being pushed into the line facing them as fast as their comrades were sent staggering away with horrific face and leg wounds or dropped, dead or dying, onto the blood-soaked ground between the two lines.

Julius nodded agreement with Scaurus's opinion, leaning close to Marcus's ear to be heard over the battle raging not ten paces from where they stood.

'Let's not risk it working for them! Take a century in and re-inforce those poor bastards!'

Marcus turned and walked the few paces to where the first cohort's senior centurion was waiting for him with an expectant look.

'We going in, Tribune?'

'One century only, First Spear! We just need to convince them that the eagle's not interested in a relationship just yet!'

The older man grinned at the black humour.

'Fair enough, I'll—'

'Not you. Give me a centurion I can trust to go at them like a wild dog so we can put them on their arses!' Marcus laughed at the officer's look of disappointment. 'Trust me, your time will come soon enough!'

'And when it does I'll wish it hadn't, I know. I've heard enough of your stories to tell me that. Decimus!'

One of the centurions who had fought each other to a stand-still in the beach tournament stepped forward from the waiting officers.

'First Spear!'

'Go with the tribune here and show these eastern arse-eaters how soldiers from the Danubius fight! And don't come back without a new crest for your helmet, that one looks like a crow's arsehole!'

The officer grinned and called his men forward, listening to Marcus's commands as the legionaries hurried to him.

'There's no time for making this tidy, just get your men into that fight!' The Roman pointed at the melee raging in front of them. 'And make it savage – we need to make them back off before they get the idea they might just win the battle here!'

Decimus turned to his men, raising his sword over his head and then pointing at the struggling legionaries who were starting to be forced back, step by step.

'We're going in there to make sure no bastard gets their hand on that!' He pointed up at the legion's eagle. 'And I'll give a gold aureus to any man who brings me a fresh crest for my helmet taken from one of those cunts! Get in there and fight!'

His men piled into the fight, shouting in the exhausted defenders' ears to rotate and allow them to take their places in the line. The arrival of fresh spear arms had not come a moment too soon, the men coming out of the melee staggering a few paces back before standing bent over and panting to get their wind back, and looking around them to see which of their comrades had survived the vicious combat, casting sideways glances at the growing number of corpses and seriously wounded that were being dragged out of the combat. Marcus turned to Julius and pointed to the savage fighting that was raging only a dozen paces from them, shouting over the cacophony of yelled commands, screams, blown whistles and the scrape of iron on iron as the two sides jockeyed for an advantage.

'I need to go in there and look the other side in the eye! If they have the will to push hard enough we're going to need to put more men in there!'

The big man nodded and waved the other members of the familia forward.

'Our brother wants to go and play in that' – he gestured to the fighting, so close that the coppery stink of spilled blood, underlaid by the smell of involuntarily ejected faeces and urine, was like an assault on the senses – 'so go with him and make sure he doesn't end up as food for the crows! Go!' He reached out a hand to stop a grim-faced Ptolemy from advancing with his friends. 'Not you, you get to stay here and ready yourself to either die gloriously in the last stand under the angry chicken or write the story afterwards.'

Ignoring the scribe's wounded stare as the veteran soldiers gathered around him, Marcus picked up a shield and spear dropped by one of the badly wounded men dragged out of the fight, rubbing the blood running down the weapon's shaft from its gore-slathered iron head into the wood's grain. He gave his companions a grim smile, seeing on their faces the anticipation of combat in its various forms, Sanga and Saratos's weary resignation, Qadir's calculation of the odds, Dubnus's glee at the prospect of a battle after so long and, for the two barbarians, Lugos and Lupus, a simple stoic readiness to fight. He beckoned them in close and raised his voice to be heard.

'Nothing fancy, brothers, I just want to see whether these men will still be coming at us when half of them are dead or dying and we're down to the game of last man standing. Stay on my shoulders and try not to get killed!'

A few long strides took him to the back of the fight, and the centurion Decimus, whose men had joined it a moment before, startled to find a tribune at his shoulder.

'I'm going in for a look! Come with me if you like!'

'Wha—'

'*Rotate!*'

Marcus slapped a rear-ranker on the shoulder and stepped into his place as the legionary obeyed his training, turned to his right and stepped back, Dubnus and Qadir taking their places beside him while the others stepped in behind them, the giant Lugos looming over them at the rear. Dubnus gave him a knowing look as they prepared to go deeper into the fray.

'You just can't stay away from flying blood, can you?'

Marcus acknowledged the truth of the statement with a shrug, then tapped the man in front of him.

'*Rotate!*'

The legionary gave up his place behind the fight with a look of bafflement that became consternation as Lugos dragged him effortlessly to the rear and out of the familia's way forward.

'You can fight soon enough, little man!'

'*Rotate!*'

The next legionary was holding on to the belt of the front-ranker in front of him, keeping him upright while he battled against the identically equipped men facing him, stabbing out with his spear while using his shield to fend off the swords stabbing at his face. Before Marcus had the chance to repeat the command and take the second ranker's place the front-rank man, clearly tiring, took a gladius thrust in the throat from a man who had dodged his spear and stepped in close to make the kill before raising his shield to fend off the inevitable retaliation. Staggering backwards against the man behind him, the dying legionary crumpled, taking them both out of the fight. Seizing the moment, Marcus pushed past them and stepped into the line, the men facing him baying across the six-foot gap between the two battle lines at the sight of the fine equipment that marked him as an officer.

Inclining his spear downwards and taking a quick pace forward, he attacked before the enemy soldier had time to take guard, stabbing the spear's long blade down into the victorious legionary's booted foot while he was still exulting his success, then shield-barging him back into his comrades. The opposing line of legionaries were thrown into disarray for long enough that Dubnus and Qadir were able to haul the dying man and his comrade out of their way and step in alongside him, restoring the line. Seeing the crest of a centurion's helmet close behind the enemy line, Marcus shouted to the men around him and then attacked again.

'The officer!'

The legionaries facing them died without ever really having the chance to set themselves for the renewed fight, having barely pushed their wounded comrade off their shields before the three men lunged in and speared them, Marcus putting his hasta's long blade over the shoulder of the man facing him to kill the legionary behind him while Qadir darted his long blade into the front-ranker's throat in the moment of his distraction. Taking a step forward into the space vacated by the fallen enemies, they struck again, hearing the screams and involuntary exhalations of breath as the men behind them stepped up and finished off the wounded with swift economy. Lugos's voice boomed over the battle's din, as loud as a trumpet call and every bit as unnerving to the men facing them.

'*Follow Two Knives! Attack!*'

With the centurion behind him bellowing at his men to follow where the officer was leading them, Marcus went forward again, stabbing at a man who had only a moment before been watching the fight from behind two ranks of his comrades. The legionary raised his shield to deflect the blade, but dithered for a moment and paid dearly for the hesitation, Dubnus stabbing in with his spearhead to put the long iron blade through his thigh. While the crippled enemy was still drawing breath to scream Qadir lunged in and thrust his spear into his face, drawing an anguished wail that shocked the men to either side of him for an instant. While they were still gaping at the horror that had been inflicted on him Marcus flicked his spear up into an overarm throwing grip, hurling it at the enemy centurion as the officer turned back from calling the next wave of reinforcements forward. The weapon's blade took him in the throat, the outrage in his eyes fading as the spearhead's impact snapped his spine and his head lolled back, his body dropping into the blood-soaked mud that had been churned up by the two armies' booted feet.

Dubnus and Qadir attacked on either side, their spearheads darting in and out with furious speed, forcing the men facing them onto the defensive while Marcus drew his swords and went forward again. With the men of Decimus's century pressing in behind, the familia forced a path to the centurion's body, the legionaries facing them backing away from the furious assault until the Roman was standing over the fallen officer. Knowing that it would only take a moment for the enemy centurions to react with fury at the loss of one of their own and send in fresh men, he wasted no time in hacking his gladius down into the corpse's neck, severing the helmeted head from the centurion's body and snatching it up by the helmet's crest, held in place by the leather cord fastened under the dead man's chin. Brandishing the prize over his head, he stared defiantly at the eastern legionaries for a moment, the enemy line seeming to recoil at the sight of a seemingly blood-crazed enemy officer holding aloft the bloody prize of their centurion's head.

He stepped back, the familia's line closing behind him, and turned to toss the prize to Decimus, smiling mirthlessly at his amazement at what he had just witnessed.

'Here's your new crest, Centurion! You owe me a gold!'

The other man nodded mutely, then turned to his men and raised the head for them to see.

'If a tribune can do this to them then you animals can hold them off all day!'

He waved them forward, and Marcus stepped back, waiting until the blood-spattered familia had been relieved by Decimus's men, breathing hard and with their faces betraying the same twitchy aftermath of combat that he was feeling. With the last of them out of the fight unharmed, he turned and made his way back to the command post to share what he had learned with Julius, only to find a huddle of men gathered over one of the command party, a pair of booted feet all that he could see through the press of their bodies. He pushed forward to look down at the stricken man, closing his eyes as he realised just who it was.

11

'What happened?'

Scaurus turned to him, his usual imperturbable expression replaced with blank-faced shock and his voice little more than a shocked whisper.

'They got lucky. The arrow must have deflected off a branch to have hit him at that angle.'

Julius was on the ground with the last six inches of an arrow's shaft protruding from the bare flesh inside the collar of his armour, staring up at the sky through the branches above them. He saw Marcus bending over him and managed a weak smile, wheezing out words that were so close to whispers that the younger man had to crouch by his head to hear them.

'*Here it is then. The moment we all fear. This is me done.*' Marcus nodded sadly, unable to ignore the blood bubbling around the arrow's shaft. '*You'll look after them, Annia and the children.*'

'Like my own.'

The dying man's lips parted in a faint smile at the irony in the promise.

'*I know you will. Tell her I died quickly and without any pain.*'

Marcus nodded again, tears pricking at his eyes.

'*Now make it true.*'

The Roman looked down at his stricken friend, unable to find any words with which to answer the plea for the mercy stroke.

'*Do it. Win or lose, there's no way I'll live this day out, is there?*'

Marcus turned to look up at Qadir, who was standing behind him. The Hamian shook his head. He had seen enough arrow wounds over the years to know that his friend was fatally injured. He touched a hand to the hilt of his dagger, but the Roman shook his head in grateful rejection of the offer and looked back into his comrade's face.

'*You'll do it for me. You never yet failed a friend.*'

Unable to speak, he simply nodded.

'*You will say the words, when the time is right?*'

The dying man was looking up at Scaurus, who was kneeling beside Marcus and bending his head to hear his friend over the battle's tumult only a few yards distant.

'I will commend you to Our Father and assure your passage to the underworld, my friend.'

Julius nodded fractionally, every gesture clearly shooting fresh pain through his body.

'*Then let's get it over with. You have a battle to fight.*'

Marcus nodded and drew his dagger, putting the blade under his friend's throat.

'Go to your ancestors, my friend. It was a long journey, and you were the best of companions.'

He put the knife's tip in the flesh under Julius's throat and tugged it across his neck, looking down into his friend's eyes as he smiled and then died, his blank stare staying fixed on the sky over their heads. After a moment Marcus wiped the dagger on his tunic, before resheathing it, then picked up his dead friend's vine stick and stood up. Scaurus spoke, his voice hoarse with grief.

'And now all we want is for all this to go away. But it isn't going to. And without leadership we're all dead.'

'Yes.' Marcus tore his gaze from the dead centurion's corpse and matched Scaurus's stare. 'And we both know the best man to take his place.'

The tribune nodded, and turned to the waiting familia, their faces reflecting his shock at the unexpected turn of events.

'The first spear is dead, and must be replaced! I name Dubnus as the man to carry the burden of command!'

The big Briton stared at him aghast, shaking his head in protest.

'What? I can't—'

Marcus raised a hand to silence his friend.

'From the first day I met you you've tried to be an outsider and stand above all this. But you're as much a part of everything that makes this legion work as he was. So accept your fate! Unless you want to see me condemned to carry this?'

He raised Julius's gold-capped vine stick, and waited for the faint amusement to light his friend's tear-stained face.

'You? Carry that?'

Marcus nodded, smiling through his grief.

'I know! He's bellowing a protest, wherever he is!'

He held out the stick and the big Briton stared at it for a moment, desire and reluctance fighting in his expression. Marcus was on the verge of speaking when he reached out and took it, looking up at the sky for a moment before turning back to the battle. The fighting had slowed from its initial breakneck pace to a steadier but still brutal game of wits between the two battle lines. The easterners' greater numbers were being offset by the longer reach of the Fourth's spears and their desperate determination, the long blades flickering out to strike time after time, while the enemy's shorter swords required them to expose themselves to the danger of a hedge of spears two and three deep to come to close quarters.

'It's your battle now, First Spear! What should we do?'

The Briton looked back at Julius's corpse lying among the olive trees.

'Just what he would have told us to do. We keep killing them until they either kill us all or get bored and piss off to bother someone else!'

For Marcus, following Dubnus's instruction to roam the line with Lupus and Lugos for backup, looking for sections of the defence in need of reinforcement, the battle became a series of momentary impressions that he later realised he would never be able to banish from his memory.

The first came early in the fight, and was a moment of such horror that it was to define a level of ferocity for which the battle of Rhaedestus was to become infamous. Patrolling the rear of the legion's right wing, Marcus realised that an enemy cohort was being driven forward by its officers up the shallow slope and into the defenders' line so hard that the four-deep defensive formation had started to thin as it was pushed backwards into the trees. Sensing the weakness with each retreating step the defenders took, and that victory might be at hand, the easterners started singing their victory anthem as they drove forward, heaving at the shields in front of them with rhythmic pushes in time with their song.

Running towards the point of the enemy incursion with the two barbarians at his heels, he shouted a command to the men of the adjacent cohort.

'*Rear two ranks, with me!*'

He led the reinforcements at the right flank of the straining enemy legionaries, grabbing a fallen spear and shield as he ran. Singlemindedly driving forward into the flagging defenders, few of the easterners had seen the approaching wave of spearmen, and the frantic warnings of those that did went unheeded, muffled by the roared anthem, until it was too late.

Reaching the rear of the Fourth's line, stretched so thin that he was able to push his way into a gap and set himself to fight, Marcus could feel the pushing of soldiers behind him and see their spearheads levelling to either side of his head, ready for overarm thrusts into the mass of the enemy legionaries. The singing among the men closest to him was faltering, as the enemy soldiers realised that they were helpless under executioners' blades, pinned in place by the men being thrown into the fight from behind.

Marcus picked a legionary, their eyes meeting for an instant as he thrust the spear into the gap between armour and helmet, ignoring the hot sprinkle of his victim's blood on his face as the legionary's expression changed from terror to outrage at the helplessness of his death. He pulled the spear back and struck again, and now the men around him were reaping the same bloody harvest, a chorus of terrified screams from the soldiers trapped under their blades failing to halt the crush of the comrades piling in from behind the slaughter.

On the far side of the enemy intrusion into the line a similar horror was playing out, and over the easterners' heads Marcus could see Justus urging his men on in the same grim murder of enemies who were unable even to raise their shields to defend themselves, so tightly were they packed into the cauldron that their advance had created. Those pushing in behind belatedly began to realise what was happening, their feet sliding backwards on ground pounded to a slick foam of red mud as the life blood of dozens of dying men flowed back down the slope, and their anthem completely petered out, the song's harsh strains replaced by calls for the soldiers in front of them to retreat.

Not waiting for orders, the legionaries behind the press of immobile and helpless victims began to pull back, shouting at the men behind them to do the same, and as they started to back away the bodies of the men who had been speared slumped to the ground in their wake. The legionaries who had been pushed back into the trees surged forward across the litter of dead and dying soldiers, the second-rankers stabbing down with their spears to deliver death strokes while the men in front of them continued the massacre and the soldiers behind them dragged the enemy casualties out from under their feet. Marcus ordered the reinforcements back to their own cohort and walked along the back of the re-established line to find Justus supervising the stacking of their corpses in a separate place to the bodies of his own men.

'That was close. Well done for seeing the danger and reacting.'

The former centurion nodded, the whites of his eyes and his teeth bright in the mask of a face spattered with the same sprays of blood that Marcus knew were the match of his own equally grisly appearance.

'If ever I had any idea that battle was going to be a noble matter, that was just beaten out of me. That was just slaughter, plain and simple.'

Marcus gestured to the eastern cohorts still trying to re-form on the lower ground in front of them, centurions belabouring their men with their vine sticks and the flats of their swords, while the legionaries bore their abuse with stoic disinterest.

'They won't try that again for a while though.'

He clapped his fellow officer on the shoulder and moved on, watching the fight for any signs that another section of the battle line might be in danger of collapsing. The enemy legions attacked in imperfectly coordinated waves, and one cohort might be fighting for their lives while another stood alongside them with nothing to do but watch, Marcus cautioning the senior centurions not to weaken their cohorts when another attack by the men to their front might be imminent.

With a sudden blare of horns the enemy line pulled back from where it was still engaged, and Sartorius walked through them and came up the slope under a flag of truce. He stood a few paces from where Scaurus and Cilo waited beneath the legion's eagle and looked up at them, his previous levity replaced with an expression of entreaty that looked a little forced to Marcus.

'Gentlemen, I—'

'No thank you, Beneficiarius Superbus.' The messenger blinked at the naked insult in the use of the word 'arrogant', but managed to retain his facade of unconcern as Cilo continued. 'We won't be accepting an offer of a truce unless the terms have changed somewhat. If you still expect us to swear not to return to the war as the price for being allowed to walk away, the answer remains no.'

'I see. You realise that there's no way you can triumph here? And from the look of it you've lost a good portion of your strength.'

The legatus shrugged.

'And I grieve for every one of them. But we've killed three of yours for every one of ours who has fallen, so presumably at this rate it'll be just Niger and me facing off amid a sea of corpses, if that's what your emperor wants.'

Sartorius nodded.

'Very well, the battle continues. I presume you'll allow us to retrieve the corpses of our fallen before we recommence fighting?'

'No.' Scaurus stepped forward alongside his legatus. 'Let them lie where they fell, to encumber your advance and remind your legions of the price they must pay if they wish to pursue my colleague Niger's ambitions for him. And with that clarified, I presume that your business with us is done.'

The spymaster nodded, his face impassive.

'As you wish, Tribune.'

He stalked away, and after a pause for the reply to Niger's renewed offer of truce to be digested the eastern legions' horns sounded, and the eastern legions started advancing up the slope again to restart the fight. Dubnus shook his head at the surreal nature of the negotiation.

'Those sounded like the words of a man who was expecting a goat-fuck, with us as the goat, and now finds that the goat has its horns up his arse! And now he's going to report back that we're not surrendering, which will piss off the man who commands all those poor bastards down there!' He nodded to Marcus and Varus. 'So return to your places, gentlemen, and only sound the alarm if the cohorts you're overseeing are at the point of collapse!'

Marcus saluted his friend with a weary grin and turned back to the right flank, waving a hand at Varus as he headed in the opposite direction. Lugos and Lupus fell in behind him, the giant voicing a question in his deep bass rumble.

'They cannot beat us without losing too many of their men. Why do they still fight when the logic of the situation must be that they would be better to allow us to leave?'

'At moments like these I miss Arminius most of all.' The Roman looked out over the battle line at the oncoming enemy, close enough for the mix of abject fear and grim determination on their faces to be all too evident. 'He always had a way to make a joke of such a ridiculous situation. Let's just say that we're playing a game of who blinks first, shall we? Niger's man just invited us to blink, and we declined and proposed another round of kicking each other in the balls to see if one of us gives in.'

Seeing another cohort erupt into action, as the attackers came up the slope with their horns blaring, he walked down the line's rear to where their first spear was watching critically, shouting instructions to his officers that Marcus doubted they could hear. He leaned in close to speak in the veteran officer's ear.

'Where's your tribune?'

The centurion grimaced and pointed at the battle raging in front of them.

'Young Furius? In there. I told him not to be a fool, but he just gave me that "do you know who I am?" look, drew his swords and went in anyway!'

Marcus nodded resignedly, looking for and finding the point in the enemy line where the action seemed most intense, and the easterners most concentrated. Turning to his two escorts he raised a hand.

'You two need to stay out of this, it's no place for men who aren't armoured, and the soldiers can pull my body out if I stop a blade.'

He moved to the back of the line at the spot where he guessed Furius was fighting, shouting the order at each legionary in front of him to rotate until he was in the second rank and could see the tribune, fighting like a madman with two swords and defying the enemy legionaries who were screaming abuse at him. At his feet half a dozen corpses told their own story, but he looked as if he were tiring, the points of his blades starting to slip lower as their weight told on muscles from which the first flood of battle-inspired energy had faded. He nudged the man alongside him, a steady-looking legionary whose composure slipped visibly when he realised that a bronze-armoured tribune was in the line beside him.

'When I give the command, take three paces forward and cover us with your shields. I'm going to get that young idiot out before he gets himself killed.'

'What command, sir?'

The Roman laughed tersely.

'I'll shout the word "now", if you can hear me over the scream-ing. But you'll know the moment when you see it. Tell your comrades and be ready!'

He took a moment to compose himself, and to allow the men around him to prepare themselves, then set his feet ready to move, took a deep breath and went forward in three quick steps. Going side to side with Furius and levelling his swords at the pack of legionaries facing the tiring tribune, he shouted a challenge at the younger man without taking his eyes off the enemy facing them.

'You want to fight, do you?'

The younger man goggled at his unexpected presence.

'I—'

But he had no chance to complete whatever it was he was intend-ing to say before Marcus was into the enemy soldiers, attacking with all the speed he had, killing first one and then another with swift strokes of his blades that cut the first man's throat and put the point of his gladius deep into his second victim's mouth, the blade's point stopping when it exited the back of his neck and hit the inside of his armour. Wrenching the blade free and spinning to his right, he swung his spatha's long blade backhanded to smash another man to the ground with his helmet dented so badly that the skull beneath it had to be broken, roaring a challenge at the shocked easterners that was in reality meant for Furius.

'*You want to kill?*'

The enemy soldiers were shrinking away from him, terrified by such an unexpected onslaught by the blood-soaked monster in bronze who was running amok with apparent impunity.

'*Then have some of this!*'

He switched his focus to the men to his left, hammering the spatha's blade into their shields in long raking cuts that had them ducking into the cover of their boards' protection before scything the sword low to hack into an ankle with horrific results, severing foot from leg. As the stricken soldier toppled over, the Roman stepped back and turned to face the astounded Furius, raising a booted foot and kicking his unsuspecting colleague back into the mass of men behind him, then jumped after him before the cowed enemy could gather the wits to stab him in the back.

'Now!'

The legionaries obeyed his order and stepped forward to protect the two officers with their shields, and Marcus sheathed the spatha, allowing the gladius to dangle from his left hand as he looked down at the shocked Furius.

'Every time I surrendered to the bloodlust, or the lust for glory, or whatever it is that makes young fools like I was and you are do the stupid things we do, it cost the lives of good men. You were a moment away from having a dozen of them come for your head, and your men would have been forced to sell their lives needlessly to save yours. So if you're determined to kill yourself, just take this honoured sword and end your life with it to save us all the trouble!'

He stared down at the stunned tribune for a moment longer, then extended his free hand to the younger man, pulling him back onto his feet.

'Or you might just decide to fulfil the role that your men need you to play. Because you're no use to anyone dead. You choose.'

He stalked away with the two Britons following him, Lupus pushing in front of him and killing an eastern legionary who managed to burst through the Fourth's line with a swift pass of his blade before the enemy soldier could regain his wits. Lugos stared over the line with the advantage of his seven-foot height, rumbling a warning to Marcus.

'The line is weak here. And they are sending more men! I see them gathering at the bottom of the slope!'

The Roman turned to the younger of the two men, as Lupus wiped his blade clean with the dead legionary's tunic.

'Run back to Dubnus and tell him that I need two centuries! He can have whatever's left of them back once we've seen off this latest effort.' He watched the Briton run back towards the command group for a moment, then turned to look for the cohort's first spear, gesturing the giant to follow him.

'This is going to be a long afternoon, Lugos, with plenty of opportunity for you to avenge Arminius!'

'What, they're stopping fighting again? This can only mean one thing.'

Dubnus shook his head in disbelief as the battered ranks of the enemy army drew back from the point of contact with the Fourth's equally depleted battle line, not simply pausing in their attack but pulling back to their start positions in an untidy withdrawal of shattered, shambling men. The Fourth's legionaries leaned exhaustedly on their shields and contemplated the dead and wounded from both armies between the two battle lines, far more easterners than there were defenders, their faces betraying the numbness that had taken over their emotions as a reaction to the battle's seemingly unending horror.

The fight had raged for over four hours, off and on, with the enemy legions surging back and forward from the point of contact with the Fourth, alternately attacking and then pulling back to reorder their line and fill the gaps carved in it by the defenders' spears. With every retreat the legionaries had wondered if the enemy was spent, only to have their hopes dashed by their renewal of the assault once they had taken on water and reordered their ranks, the attacks executed ever more wearily but continuing nonetheless. And if the Fourth had reaped a bloody harvest of each fresh thrust, they had lost men to every attack, and the relentless nature of the easterners' continuous series of assaults had significantly weakened a defence that had initially seemed impregnable.

The dead were two or three corpses deep where they had fallen at the points of maximum effort, where some eastern officer or other had commanded his men forward to earn him glory and only succeeded in getting the majority of them killed. The wounded ranged from those who were effectively already dead to those men on both sides who had been unable to get back to the safety of their own ground, or who had been stranded when the eastern army had fallen back from the point of contact. A wounded legionary struggled out from beneath the bodies of a pair of easterners that had protected him from discovery and death while the enemy line had railed at the defenders, limping up the slope and back into place and picking up a spear and shield to the wry congratulations of his tent-mates, while the opposing line merely stood and watched in silence, looking out bleakly at those of their comrades scattered across the goresoaked battlefield who were begging for the mercy stroke. After a moment Dubnus nodded knowingly at the parting of the enemy ranks he had been expecting.

'Yes, here he comes again, for the third time of asking.'

The Briton pointed out the now familiar figure of Sartorius pushing his way through the exhausted eastern line, the beneficiarius picking his way across the blood-soaked thirty-pace-wide strip between the two legions until he was close enough to shout his latest message across the gap, nothing in his demeanour betraying any loss of certainty in the eastern army's eventual victory.

'The emperor has instructed me to entreat you to surrender one last time, Fabius Cilo! He is filled with pride at the courage and determination displayed by both sides of this unnecessary slaughter. And so he is willing to give you one last chance to do the sensible thing and lay down your arms. He offers you the opportunity to leave the battlefield, with your weapons and with rations provided, and to march back west along the Via Egnatia to rejoin your own army. And in return all he asks is that you swear to take no further part in this campaign. You may of course view such an offer from my mouth as nothing more than a ruse to leave you defenceless in the face of an armed and implacable foe, and so the emperor has decided to leave you under no illusion as to the sincerity of his offer.'

Scaurus stepped forward.

'And he intends coming here to make that offer?'

Sartorius smiled back at him.

'Hardly! It would only take one half-decent archer to achieve what all of the usurper Severus's legions will never manage. Fabius

Cilo is invited to join me in returning to where the emperor awaits, and there to discuss the terms of an honourable surrender.'

'And in my own turn I must point out that were the legatus to accompany you away from the protection of his legion it would hardly be surprising were we not to see him again!'

'So what do you propose?'

Scaurus turned to Cilo.

'Will you meet him in the neutral ground between the two armies? It's the least likely place for either side to attempt any dirty tricks, and every moment that we're not fighting them is another moment in which our men can recover themselves, and another moment closer to dusk.'

The legatus nodded solemnly.

'I will. And since I know Niger to be somewhat verbose, I'll do my best to keep him talking.'

The tribune turned back to the waiting spymaster.

'We propose a meeting in the neutral ground between our two armies, with shield-bearers from both sides to provide safety.'

Sartorius nodded, waving a hand in a gesture that managed to combine gracious acceptance and condescension.

'Very well! In the event of the emperor's agreement I will indicate the appointed spot. A single horn will sound to signal acceptance.'

He walked back into the enemy line and silence fell, punctuated only by the agonised screams of the more seriously wounded on each side as they were brought to the attention of the legions' exhausted capsarii, the bandage-carriers whose only option for most of their patients was to give them the mercy of a swift and relatively painless release from their suffering.

'How many men do you think we have left?'

'Unwounded?' Dubnus rubbed his face wearily. 'A thousand? Perhaps fifteen hundred? And another thousand or so wounded who can fight.' He shook his head and turned away from the sight of the enemy line being packed with fresh troops drawn from further down the line on either side. 'And no, we can't move men to put them in the shop window for this negotiation, because if we do we'll be gifting them an easy win on both flanks.'

'As opposed to a slightly harder win?'

'If they can muster the energy to attack again, perhaps. If you want me to make the backdrop look a bit shinier I can put the last of the reserve in, but that's all we have. One century.'

'Do it. We might as well.'

The mournful note of a horn sounded across the silent battle-field and Scaurus nodded at his new first spear.

'And now we have to go and speak to Pescennius Niger and tell him how he might win, but how that victory will come at a cost that will make his army a pushover once Severus's exercitus Illyricus arrives. Who knows, it might even be the truth.' He looked over the heads of the legionaries and pointed at something he'd spotted behind the enemy line. 'It looks like this is a more formal party than I was expecting.'

The imperial party's presence behind the attacking army was given away by three legion eagle standards progressing along the rear of the cohorts facing them.

'I presume the purpose of this vulgar display of his standards is to reinforce the message that further resistance is useless. But I suppose that military etiquette demands we follow their example?'

Dubnus turned and shouted a command at the knot of legion-aries gathered around the legion's standard-bearer, whose symbol of the legion's pride would be the Fourth's last and most bitterly fought point of resistance.

'Aquilifer! To me!'

The burly centurion strode down the tattered battle line and saluted smartly.

'Gentlemen, how can I serve you?'

Scaurus pointed out at the procession of eagles behind the enemy line.

'We're going out there for a chat with the man who thinks he's the emperor, and he's decided to show off his legion standards, just to make sure we know what we're facing. Make sure you hold ours nice and high, will you?'

Niger's party emerged onto the corpse-strewn ground in front of their battle line, the men of his bodyguard picking a path for him to tread that avoided the worst of the blood-soaked mud that had been stamped into a slurry six inches deep in places where the gore had puddled. The emperor walked forward with great care, picking his footsteps to avoid sinking a boot into any of the ankle-deep pools, which were already buzzing with flies. A pair of men were walking behind him, one of them the spymaster Sartorius, the other an as yet unidentified legatus, and behind them came the chief of his lictors and the three standard-bearers.

'Shall we go and meet the current master of the east? Match the number of his bodyguards please, Dubnus, and we'll do without the usual escort of barbarians on this occasion. Just you and Tribune Aquila should suffice, to match his two companions.'

The legionaries opened their line to allow the party to pass through and into the open space between the armies, and the selected men who were forming Cilo's impromptu bodyguard started forward gingerly much as their praetorian opposite numbers had, only for the legatus to stride forward without any hesitation.

'I'm not going to make myself look a fool by prancing from one scrap of dry ground to the next! This is the blood of Rome's sons, and I shall honour it rather than trying to pretend it hasn't been spilled!'

He splashed through the foamed mud, his face set in hard lines rather than emulate the look of distaste on Niger's face at the pervasive smell of faeces and urine and the coppery stench of blood.

'Kill me!'

A legionary whose sword arm had been amputated at the elbow used his remaining arm to push himself up shakily from the recumbent position that had led the soldiers who had combed the battlefield for survivors to miss him. One of the bodyguards drew his sword and made to deliver the mercy stroke, but Cilo barked an order at him.

'Hold!'

He marched over to the shaking legionary and drew his sword, while Niger watched from where he was waiting with a perplexed expression at the unexpected delay. The soldier stared up at him uncomprehendingly, his face so heavily coated with the dark-red mud that his features were completely indiscernible, while the legatus turned to the enemy army and called out in a clear voice.

'This man might be from the Danubius frontier or from Syria. I will never know which it is, and it does not matter to me either way. Because he is a man of Rome, and his loss is as grievous to the empire no matter what his origin! Go to the underworld, fellow citizen!'

He stabbed down with the sword and killed the wounded man neatly enough that Dubnus nodded approvingly, flicked the blood from the blade and resheathed it, then resumed his progress to the spot where Niger was waiting. The emperor waited for some sign of obeisance from him, and was nonplussed when Cilo simply extended a hand in greeting.

'It is customary even for a man of the senate to offer the emperor the usual gestures of respect and obedience, Legatus Cilo!'

Cilo replied to Sartorius without either taking his gaze off Niger or lowering his hand, his answering tone cordial and yet edged with the dignity of a Roman gentleman.

'And were Pescennius Niger *actually* the emperor, hailed as such by our colleagues in the senate in Rome, then I would be the first to offer him my humble greeting and lifelong loyalty. Indeed I may well have reason to do so, if his army can best that of my master, the emperor Septimius Severus, and march in triumph into Rome as the emperor did only a few weeks ago. For now, however, he is very well aware as a fellow father of Rome that my oath of loyalty to the emperor appointed by the senate compels me to greet him as a much-respected colleague, rather than as the master of the empire. If that is a problem then we will have to resume our hostility, and see how many more good men will have to die today . . . on *both* sides.'

Niger smiled thinly, clearly irritated but apparently unwilling to throw away the negotiation over a point of disputed etiquette.

'I will tolerate your reticence to display any disloyalty to the man who was lucky enough to be the closest of the challengers for the throne to Rome, and who has gathered half of all the legions to him, Fabius Cilo! Although I will not call you colleague, as I am very sure of the dignity and correctness of my reign.' He gestured down at Cilo's gore-spattered legs, the result of splashing through the battlefield's filth, where his own white leggings were only flecked with blood. 'And besides, we both seem to have ruined perfectly good pairs of boots in reaching this spot, which would make it a pointless sacrifice not to at least essay to reaching some sort of agreement, would it not?'

Cilo looked around him at the bodies strewn across the open ground.

'I agree, there have been a great number of more costly sacrifices today. So, what is it that you would like to discuss?'

'Come, Fabius Cilo, you know what the—'

The legatus overrode Sartorius's interruption with all the patrician scorn he could muster.

'You would be wise *not* to speak to a member of the senate in that tone, beneficiarius, or you might find yourself moving from the list of men to be arrested and interrogated when this war is over to the one composed of men to be tortured and executed! I asked your master a question, and I was not aware that he needed you to speak for him.'

Niger turned to Sartorius and dismissed him with a wave of his hand, and the spymaster inclined his head in deliberate respect before turning away. The emperor returned his attention to Cilo, gesturing to the man standing at his shoulder.

'You know my general Asellius Aemilianus, of course. Before we turn our thoughts to how to deal with this matter, I would consider it a courtesy if you could share the latest news from Rome.

Horse couriers might well be faster than your fleet, but who knows how many of the messages sent to me by my supporters actually evaded my opponent's opposite number to that vulgar but useful man. I ask for nothing more than your thoughts as to the situation in the city now that Severus has taken control.'

Cilo nodded with a thoughtful look, as if he were pondering just how much to reveal to Severus's rival, and Marcus knew that by saying anything at all he risked putting his life at risk, should it prove materially useful to the emperor's sworn enemy.

'I will tell you what I can. You obviously know that Didius Julianus was declared an enemy of the city and executed?'

'I heard the word murdered, but if it was done with the approval of the senate then I suppose that would be too strong a term. Some praetorian or other, I heard.'

He fixed his gaze on Scaurus, and held the stare, and after a moment the tribune knew he would have to speak. He bowed, inclining his head just sufficiently for a gesture of respect rather than obeisance.

'Your intelligence from the city must be good, sir.'

'Better than you can imagine, Rutilius Scaurus. I found your appointment to this doomed expedition an interesting happenstance, given the way that our paths have crossed over the years, first in Dacia and then in Gallia. Tell me, where is that magnificent animal of a senior centurion you usually had at your shoulder, the man who won you victory on both occasions?'

'He lies under a tree behind the line of men behind me, gone to meet his ancestors.'

Niger nodded, closing his eyes for a moment.

'How disappointing, and you have my sympathies. This war will take many more good men before it is done, and leave Rome so much the weaker. We can only hope that the empire is not bled so much as to make it vulnerable to its enemies. And my condolences are genuine despite our temporary enmity. His loss must be a bitter one.'

Scaurus nodded dourly.

'Enough to make me minded to fight to the death today. Sir.'

The emperor nodded with a knowing look.

'We can only hope that won't be necessary. But well met, Rutilius Scaurus, and I will pray that this is the last time our paths cross in time of war.'

He turned back to Cilo.

'But tell me, Fabius Cilo, what of my children? I had word that they were being taken to safety, but nothing more.'

This was a decision point for Cilo, Marcus knew, revealing that the source of Niger's information could not be within the emperor's consilium, which had been briefed as to the matter of his enemy's children, and that Severus had clearly chosen not to reveal their capture directly to their father as yet.

'You have both been sentenced to death in absentia, yourself with the potential for mercy if you surrender, your greatly respected colleague Aemilianus without, for the crime of misleading the emperor as to his loyalties for so long before declaring for you. And your own children, and those of Aemilianus, and of every one of your senior commanders and officials in the east, have all been taken into custody by the throne.'

Niger took a moment to absorb the news, closing his eyes again. When he opened them there was a sheen to them not far from the spilling of tears.

'And so I see that I will have to defeat the usurper to have any chance of ever seeing them again. He will use them as a bargaining tool to whatever degree I allow, whether to force his victory or in the hope of reversing a defeat. Which makes it imperative that I triumph today!'

He thought for a moment and then continued, fixing Cilo with a hard stare.

'I am minded to pursue this battle to its bloody end, and to destroy your legion to the last man simply to set an example of what must follow if Severus is unwise enough to advance into Asia. But I recognise the value of being seen to be magnanimous. You can still walk away from here with your eagle, your weapons and your dignity, but with nothing else. Which means that the terms of a potential agreement to end this battle are simple enough, Gaius.' The emperor stepped forward and spoke more quietly. 'As I say, you may walk away, with your arms and your dignity, and with sufficient rations to keep your men alive until you reach Severus's army. All you have to do is accept that you lost this fight and were allowed to withdraw, and swear an oath that none of you will take any further part in this campaign, in reflection of the fact that I hold your lives in the palm of my hand. Is that too much to ask for the survival of your legion? I won't even ask any of you to swear allegiance to me.'

The legatus shrugged.

'Which would mean that you would get a victory to tell your people about, and gain the initial advantage over Severus. And you would take a legion off the game board for the rest of this war. Not a bad result for you. And what do I get? I was named Severus's comes imperatoris before I left Rome, but even that won't save me from the wrath that he will visit on me if I take him back news of a defeat and a legion that's not allowed to fight for him until you're dead. I might as well die in battle here, because he'll have me executed for treason if I accept those terms.'

Niger turned his hands over to display their empty palms.

'I have nothing left to offer you, Fabius Cilo, so you'll just have to decide what your answer is going to be. There are only three hours to sunset, and we both know that with the darkness comes an uncertainty in battle, which I cannot afford to risk. So think quickly . . .'

His statement trailed off as an eagle came into view over the trees behind the Fourth's line, flying slowly with majestic sweeps of its wings. The emperor raised a hand to point at it, raising his voice to be heard by both armies, every word infused with triumph and pride.

'An omen! The gods have chosen to show their favour for my rule! At this, the moment of my victory over the usurper Severus's first attempt to defeat my army, an eagle has chosen to display its power and grace in my favour!'

All present watched as the magnificent bird circled over the two armies, and after a moment it became clear that it was descending in a slow, lazy spiral that seemed to be centred on the two men who were negotiating the fate of Cilo's legion. With one last circle, and now close enough for the detail of its feathers to be visible, it spread its wings wide and extended its talons in readiness to land. As the men on both sides stared in amazement, the bird stooped in and took up a perch on the eagle standard whose aquilifer was standing close behind Cilo.

'Gods below . . .'

The emperor was shaking his head in disbelief at the sight of the bird of prey gripping the standard's right wing, while Cilo waited for some sign as to whether it would fly away. Marcus, standing next to the aquilifer, muttered an instruction intended for the centurion's ears only.

'Don't move a muscle. If the bird stays put we might just walk away from here undefeated.'

The centurion nodded almost imperceptibly at Marcus's instruction, keeping the standard immobile and looking up at the perching raptor with a stupid grin.

'Shall we wait and see if the eagle decides to change its perch, colleague? It is, as you say, a powerful omen!'

Cilo's face was an impassive mask, and his tone was level, but Marcus knew that he would be exultant at the turn of events. The emperor turned to the man standing behind him.

'Have the army make some noise, would you, Aemilianus?'

The general turned to face his men and shouted a command to his officers.

'Salute to the emperor!'

The response was instant: the army of the east erupted into shouts of 'The emperor!' that combined into a rolling wall of sound, the din strengthened by the blare of the three legions' horns. Niger fixed his gaze on the eagle, willing it to fly away, and after a moment added his voice to that of his men.

'Fly, damn you!'

The bird looked out across his army with a bright unblinking stare, and after a moment spread its wings and flapped them vigorously, making all present hold their breaths. But rather than leaving its perch it furled them again, sat for a moment and then defecated across the aquilifer's gleaming helmet and his armoured shoulder. The men of the eastern army fell silent, while from the ranks of men behind the eagle a slow swelling of disbelieving mirth strengthened until every man who could see the eagle was laughing. At length discipline was restored, and as silence returned to the battlefield Cilo turned back to the emperor.

'Well now, colleague, as you say, that's quite a signal from the gods.'

Niger lowered his gaze from the eagle to Cilo, his face red with the anger that clearly had him in its grip.

'This changes nothing!'

Cilo shook his head.

'On the contrary, this changes *everything*. You were the one to declare an omen while the bird was still in the air, and with a choice of four eagles to alight on it chose our lonely standard. And then, when you had your legions do their best to scare it off, the only reaction it made was one of disdain that every man in both our armies will understand all too well. If that's not a sign then I'm not sure what you think would qualify?'

The emperor waved a hand in denial.

'This battle will continue! My legions will overwhelm what's left of yours in no time!'

Aemilianus leaned in close to his master, speaking quietly into his ear. Cilo laughed softly.

'What your inconstantly loyal general is telling you is that the men behind you look like they've just seen the omen of their deaths. Whereas mine are reinvigorated, reassured that their cause is just, and are ready to fight to the death. You might persuade those legions to advance, but whether they'll fight and die to defeat us is another matter completely!'

He shook his head with a mock-rueful expression. 'But if this negotiation is over then I suppose I'll have to go and give them the news, that they will have the chance to reap yet more of the strength you will need when the emperor arrives at the head of ten legions, eager to avenge the loss of this one. If you can put us away before the sun sets, of course.'

Niger turned and walked a short distance away, but before he had taken more than a couple of steps Aemilianus was speaking urgently in his ear.

'What's he saying? My hearing isn't as sharp as it used to be.'

Scaurus shook his head at Cilo's question.

'I can't hear the words either, but look at the man's stance and you know all you need to.'

The enemy general's urgency was obvious, and after a whispered discussion the emperor turned back to face Cilo, his face set in a resigned expression.

'I am persuaded to allow you to leave with your honour intact. It seems that your legion's bravery in the face of overwhelming odds is sufficient to allow me to be magnanimous in victory, and to allow you to depart from here with your armour and weapons.'

'Without any formal admission of defeat, and unbound by any oath not to return? And with the supplies you promised, were we to swear to refuse to fight against you?'

Niger nodded, looking as if he had a bad taste in his mouth.

'The supplies will be provided before darkness falls, in return for your agreeing that this battle is done, and will not be renewed. You will march away to the west tomorrow and you will be shadowed by our cavalry until we deem that you have genuinely given up hope of delivering your master Severus the result he hoped for. Is that agreed?'

'I will need carts to carry the supplies that we'll need for a week's march for three thousand men, and more to carry my wounded that are unable to march.'

Niger stared at him for a moment, perhaps minded to refuse the demand, but whatever it was that he was about to say was forestalled by a high-pitched scream from the eagle, which flapped its wings vigorously for a moment before settling back onto the perch of the Fourth's standard. The emperor turned away, his face a mask of dejection at the inauspicious turn of events, speaking over his shoulder.

'You will be provided with whatever we can spare.'

He walked away, no longer mindful of the state of his boots, and with the hem of his cloak accumulating a bloody edge from the splashes as he trudged through the battlefield's gory puddles. As if on cue, the eagle spread its wings and flew away with one last defiant screech. Cilo turned to Scaurus with a quizzical expression.

'Is that the outcome you hoped for, Tribune?'

The younger man looked back at him for a moment and then nodded.

'In that it spares the remainder of our men, then yes, Legatus, it is. Thanks to your ability to negotiate with a man who considers himself the master of the world.'

'Thanks to the random intervention of such a magnificent bird of prey, more likely. We can be grateful to the gods for sending such an omen, and to Niger himself for calling it for his own while the eagle was still deciding where best to perch, the fool.'

Sartorius re-emerged from behind the enemy line and made his way across the ruined ground to join them. He saluted Cilo with a satirical smile that made clear that his punctilious politeness was an act that he had decided to adopt in order to avoid further conflict, now that the battle had been brought to a close.

'I have been ordered to assist with your withdrawal from Thrace, Legatus. Rations and supply transports will be provided shortly, although we have no spare medical supplies or personnel to assist with the treatment of your wounded. You will be escorted along the Via Egnatia by our legion cavalry for a day, to make sure you intend returning to the west, and the emperor hopes not to see you on a field of battle again, as he will have no qualms with completing your destruction in the event that we cross swords again.'

Scaurus stepped forward, holding his hands away from his sword and dagger but with an expression that made it clear that he was close to violence.

'We will accept the negotiated terms of this settlement, clear in the knowledge that we had the beating of your three legions with our one, because we would have held you off until darkness and then run amok through your dispirited legions, to who knows what end? You can count yourselves lucky that the eagle promised to us by an omen landed on our standard, I'd say.'

The spymaster shrugged.

'And we'll never know the answer to that, will we? Take your defeat, and the honourable departure from the field of battle that might have seen you all dead, and run away with them to your master.'

He turned as if to leave, but stopped in his tracks at the tone in Marcus's voice.

'You are a coward, beneficiarius! You sought to capture, torture and kill me and my friends in a dirty war of back-alley ambushes, never once intending to take any risk yourself. And your bandits killed a good friend of mine, stabbing him in the back without giving him the dignity of a fight. We sent them all to the underworld in revenge for that insult to his memory, but doing so did not satisfy our desire for revenge – far from it! Take that away with *you* and think on it. And while you're doing that, ponder on this.' He took a step forward to go face to face with Niger's man. 'In every battle we fight in this pointless war I am going to be looking for you and the man who gifted you this position. And when I find you there *will* be a reckoning!'

Sartorius shrugged.

'The chance of us ever meeting again is remote, Tribune, so I wouldn't trouble yourself overmuch with that possibility. Better to worry about those left behind in Rome, perhaps?'

Marcus's eyes narrowed.

'Thank your gods you have the protection of our agreement to cease fighting, Sartorius. Because I know for a fact that the next time I see you one of us won't leave the place of our reacquaintance.'

'Your warning is noted.'

The beneficiarius shrugged and walked away, seemingly untroubled by the threat.

'Do you wish to swear an oath to the Lightbringer in this matter?'

Marcus shook his head, staring at the spymaster's back.

'Thank you, but there is no need. The goddess who watches over me has already witnessed my solemn promise to see that one sent to sleep in the mud.

'I suppose we can consider ourselves fortunate.' Cilo leaned in towards the fire and warmed his hands in its glow. 'We have escaped with half a legion's strength, if we count the wounded who will survive, and with our eagle, and most importantly with the dignity of a battle not lost. We can join Severus's army with our heads held up as men who saw off three legions with less than the strength of one, and whose cause was blessed by an omen that could have been sent by Jupiter himself!'

'Of course Niger and Aemilianus will declare the battle to have been a famous victory.'

Having given voice to his cynicism, Scaurus looked about him at the fires lit across the narrow plain where the Fourth had camped the previous evening. The legion had formed up and marched away from the site of the battle to their previous night's camp, leaving their dead for the eastern legions whose first spears had sworn to treat them as their own and add them to the funeral pyre planned for the next day. Having washed themselves in the stream one century at a time, gathered wood and then slumped exhaustedly around their fires to eat the cold food that had been provided to them like starving men, they were for the most part asleep.

Cilo shook his head.

'For now, perhaps, but the history books will correct that fallacy when we come to write them. If I know Severus, there's no way he will allow such a falsehood to dwell for long, once he has had Niger and Aemilianus executed.'

'I thought he had decided to spare Niger?'

'He might have said that, when it was the right thing to say. But this battle will have changed that calculation, and I doubt he ever intended it in any case. The moment that his colleague decided to oppose him with strength of arms he was condemned to death, whether he realises it or not.'

'And his children?'

Cilo shook his head.

'Are probably still alive, but not for long once their father is taken. No emperor will leave even defenceless innocents alive when they might grow up to seek revenge on him in ten or twenty years.'

Marcus and Scaurus exchanged glances, but Cilo was oblivious to just how close to home his statement was to the younger man.

'But for now – well done, gentlemen! You performed as well as your reputations said you would, and I am grateful. Tell me what I can do for you in return, and if it lies within my gift I will be honoured to reward your service.'

Marcus looked behind him at Julius's corpse, wrapped in a cloak secured with dead soldiers' belts. Lugos had carried their dead friend away from the battlefield without a word, placing him on the turf by the fire before joining Ptolemy to discuss the meaning of such a transitory existence. Touched by the gesture, Dubnus had sat with them both for a while to express his gratitude, and if he had come away shaking his head in bafflement at their conversation, he had refrained from ribaldry at their expense as a mark of respect.

'We will bury our friend on that hill tomorrow, and shed tears for his loss. He leaves behind a wife and two children, and cares for my own son too, but has no home other than that which we can rent for them. Would your gratitude stretch to the provision of a roof over their heads?

The patrician nodded with a speed that gratified Marcus.

'Of course. I will send a message to my agent in Rome to find an appropriate dwelling, in a decent area away from stink and slum. The man served his emperor and me to the full extent of what he had to give, and honour demands I recognise his sacrifice in the most practical way I can.' He turned to Scaurus with a questioning look. 'But tell me, Rutilius Scaurus, I heard you swearing to have revenge on both Sartorius and Niger earlier. Do you really mean to kill an emperor?'

'I do. My oldest friend was stabbed in the back on their orders, and I cannot let such an insult pass unavenged. If I have the chance to expunge it by the death of either of them I will do so. I have sworn to the Lightbringer that I will do this in his name.'

Cilo nodded his understanding.

'An oath to kill an emperor, even a usurper who wears the purple in vain, is a weighty thing to carry around. But then you know all about regicide, do you not?'

For a moment Marcus wondered if the senator was aware of his murder of Commodus, but as he continued it became clear that he had a different emperor in mind.

'Your murder of Didius Julianus was achieved in such a manner that you will never be identified as the killer, but this would be very different. You will only be able to get to Niger on the battlefield, and even then you are most unlikely to succeed, as he will be surrounded by a determined bodyguard who see him as their ticket to wealth.'

'I know. And were I to succeed and live I would be infamous, hunted by his followers and quite possibly ostracised by my peers in Rome for such a base crime. And yet I will take that revenge, given the opportunity, in the time I have left before Titus's curse claims me.'

'And I will not swear any such oath, but I will stand with my friend when the time comes.'

Cilo looked at Marcus for a moment, weighing the certainty in his face.

'You too? I suppose I shouldn't be surprised, given your reputation, but I'll give you the same warning: killing an emperor might be more of a weight around your neck than you can imagine.' He stood, stretching wearily. 'I must go and find the young gentlemen who did not die today, and listen to their tales of the battle like the surrogate father I am to them this far from home. Furius Aculeo in particular had the look of a man whose experience today has stripped away the last vestige of his boyhood, and made him the man he will be for the rest of his life. Just heed my warning: to kill a failed usurper under senatorial orders and with the cloak of anonymity granted by a praetorian uniform is one thing, but to deliver this sentence of death to Niger without that protection from his followers would be altogether riskier.'

He stood up stiffly and walked away, leaving the two friends looking at each other.

'He's right, to some degree. Killing an emperor in the manner we have sworn might be an act that a man regrets for the rest of his life.'

Marcus shrugged at Scaurus's statement.

'Perhaps. But the truth of the matter is that neither of us is capable of not seeking revenge for Arminius. And besides' – he took a moment to savour the memory of the moment that he had strangled the emperor whose acts had resulted in the deaths of his family and his wife – 'better to be hunted by those who would seek revenge in their turn than to be haunted by the spirits of those whose memories demand revenge.'

'And after the first time it all seems so much simpler?'

They shared a knowing look.

'And that too. Who knows, we might never get close enough to either Niger or his accomplice to avenge our friend, but the prospect of what might follow either of their deaths troubles me less than the idea that they might escape the consequences of their actions.'

Scaurus held out a hand.

'So, given the choice of fading back into the shadows or seeking vengeance for the murder of a friend, we make the only choice we can.'

Marcus took it, looking into his friend's eyes.

'Vengeance.'

Historical Note

With the publication of *Vengeance* the first of the two story arcs in the Empire series was brought to a tidy close. Book Twelve could have been the end of the series, had the readership been weary of the characters and their doings. With (no spoilers here) that first arc complete, from the start of Marcus Valerius Aquila's new life in Britannia to the conclusion of the book in Rome, I was half expecting to leave the familia bickering with each other in a taverna and walk away to play with another time period. That we've continued even a short way into the second arc is a source of great pleasure to me as the author of the series, and I hope that you will feel the same way when you've read this introduction to the Severan era.

And what an era it is, for anyone with an interest in the ancient world. Septimius Severus ruled from AD 193 to AD 211, and died in York while campaigning against the northern British tribes. In the intervening period he fought two contenders for the throne and mounted several wars against the usual suspects, all of which means that there is a rich seam of military action to be viewed through the eyes of the cast of characters who populate these stories.

So, *Storm of War* and its historical backdrop.

Severus took the throne in AD 193 mainly by dint of being closer to Rome than either of his rivals, Niger (in Syria) or Albinus (in Britannia), and by being better supported militarily than them, with sixteen legions to Niger's six and Albinus's three. He was, as the story implies, very much in the blocks and ready to run when the unfortunate Pertinax, his predecessor as emperor, was murdered by the praetorians and his throne sold to an unwise Didius Julianus. His appointment to command the three Upper Pannonian legions, combined with the support of the governors of Raetia, Noricum, Lower Pannonia, Upper and Lower Moesia, Dacia and Upper and Lower Germania, gave him an unassailable force, legions that he was swift to march south and use to cow Rome into swift submission. And there really was a former frumentarius (secret police officer) Marcus Aquilius Felix, a specialist in the 'murder of senators', assigned to kill him, and Felix really did – wisely - turn his coat to achieve high rank under his new master.

With the capital taken and the hapless Julianus dead, Severus had his boot on the empire's neck, and was determined to convert his military advantage into the removal of any threats from his two rivals. Not that a preponderance of legions was enough to make the resulting civil war a sure thing, but it did give him the advantage in taking the war east to remove Niger from the board, while keeping a somewhat hapless Albinus at arm's length with insincere promises that he would inherit the empire on Severus's death. Bestowing the title of Caesar, traditionally that of the heir apparent, upon his rival seems to have been enough to mollify Albinus's concerns and, crucially, keep his dangerous legions in their barracks.

With a winnable one-front war thereby guaranteed, Severus set out his plans for a campaign against Niger, displaying a habit that was to be a feature of his command, that of keeping his generals off balance by never allowing any of them to become too successful or too comfortable. While the commanders who had led the march south from the Danube might have expected high rank to result from their loyalty, the plum position of leading the exercitus Illyricus (the Pannonian legions) forward as an advance guard for the main force went to an unregarded senator who had been adlected – promoted – out of the equestrian class a decade before, but whose career had thereafter gone nowhere. In appointing a man with practical experience of the eastern theatre of war, and who is likely to have lacked political ambition, Severus was setting a pattern that would be a hallmark of his early years as emperor, dividing and ruling his commanders and avoiding too much power accreting to one man.

And another such appointment was that of Lucius Fabius Cilo, Severus's key man in the senate, to command a force tasked with taking first Perinthus, a few days' march from the strategic target of Byzantium, which was under threat by another Severan army, and then moving to attack the great city in turn. And it is here that I have to admit what might be a significant leap of imagination.

Was a legion shot like an arrow from a bow across the oceans under Cilo's command, to attempt to take Perinthus? Probably not. It is more likely, whether Cilo took a legion with him or simply travelled to take command of local forces, that road transport would have been used, along the Via Egnatia described in the story, a road that ran from the Ionium Sea all the way to Perinthus and Byzantium. But when you consider that a sealift would have been much faster than marching such a great mileage, even given the increased distance involved in the sea voyage, I believe that the author's conceit just about holds water here (and allows me both to have some nautical fun and to bring Titus the naval prefect back into the story with quite some impact).

Cilo and Niger clashed in front of the city, to that much the histories do attest. Niger inflicted heavy casualties on his rival general, and claimed a victory by means of a coin issue, being blessed with the name 'a new Alexander' by his supporters, possibly sycophantically. But in taking the offensive against the Severan force he well and truly cast his dice, and an incensed Severus declared both Niger and his general Aemilianus public enemies. No detail of the engagement itself is known other than the claimed outcome, which provides the leeway for it to be written it as a bloody battle of attrition that neither side could really have claimed as a win.

And did an eagle really take roost on the Severan eagle at the critical moment? It's genuinely possible.

Dio writes that '*When the war broke out, Niger proceeded to Byzantium and from there advanced against Perinthus. But he was disturbed by unfavourable omens that came to his notice; for an eagle perched upon a military standard and remained there until captured in spite of efforts to drive it away, and bees made honeycomb around the military standards and especially around his images. For these reasons he returned to Byzantium.*'

I do expect that the act of an eagle landing on a battle standard on an actual battlefield might have been more celebrated as an omen than was the case, but an author learns never to look a gift eagle in the beak, as it were. I'm happy to admit that the eagle's subsequent act of defecation was all my own work, and based on the description in the distant days of my youth of payday as 'golden eagle day', for reasons you will either know or have to work out for yourself!

I hope you have enjoyed the book, and I can assure you that Scaurus, Marcus and the familia will be back in action very soon on the other side of the Propontis, as Severus's army takes the fight into the enemy homeland. I heartily recommend that anyone who wants to read more about Severus and the era in which he ruled procures a copy of Anthony R. Birley's *Septimius Severus: the African Emperor*, which will provide an excellent account of the emperor's life and the events described herein.

The Roman Army
in AD 182

By the late second century, the point at which the *Empire* series begins, the Imperial Roman Army had long since evolved into a stable organisation with a stable *modus operandi*. Thirty or so legions (there's still some debate about the Ninth Legion's fate), each with an official strength of 5,500 legionaries, formed the army's 165,000-man heavy infantry backbone, while 360 or so auxiliary cohorts (each of them the rough equivalent of a 600-man infantry battalion) provided another 217,000 soldiers for the empire's defence.

Positioned mainly in the empire's border provinces, these forces performed two main tasks. Whilst ostensibly providing a strong means of defence against external attack, their role was just as much about maintaining Roman rule in the most challenging of the empire's subject territories. It was no coincidence that the troublesome provinces of Britannia and Dacia were deemed to require 60 and 44 auxiliary cohorts respectively, almost a quarter of the total available. It should be noted, however, that whilst their overall strategic task was the same, the terms under which the two halves of the army served were quite different.

The legions, the primary Roman military unit for conducting warfare at the operational or theatre level, had been in existence since early in the republic, hundreds of years before. They were composed mainly of close-order heavy infantry, well drilled and highly motivated, recruited on a professional basis and, critically to an understanding of their place in Roman society, manned by soldiers who were Roman citizens. The jobless poor were thus provided with a route to a valuable trade, since service with the legions was as much about construction – fortresses, roads and even major defensive works such as Hadrian's Wall – as destruction. Vitally for the maintenance of the empire's borders, this attractiveness of service made a large standing field army a possibility, and allowed for both the control and defence of the conquered territories.

By this point in Britannia's history three legions were positioned to control the restive peoples both beyond and behind the province's borders. These were the 2nd, based in South Wales, the 20th, watching North Wales, and the 6th, positioned to the east of the Pennine range and ready to respond to any trouble on the northern frontier. Each of these legions was commanded by a legatus, an experienced man of senatorial rank deemed worthy of the responsibility and appointed by the emperor. The command structure beneath the legatus was a delicate balance, combining the requirement for training and advancing Rome's young aristocrats for their future roles with the necessity for the legion to be led into battle by experienced and hardened officers.

Directly beneath the legatus were a half-dozen or so military tribunes, one of them a young man of the senatorial class called the broad stripe tribune after the broad senatorial stripe on his tunic. This relatively inexperienced man – it would have been his first official position – acted as the legion's second-in-command, despite being a relatively tender age when compared with the men around him. The remainder of the military tribunes were narrow stripes, men of the equestrian class who usually already had some command experience under their belts from leading an auxiliary cohort. Intriguingly, since the more experienced narrow-stripe tribunes effectively reported to the broad stripe, such a reversal of the usual military conventions around fitness for command must have made for some interesting man-management situations. The legion's third in command was the camp prefect, an older and more experienced soldier, usually a former centurion deemed worthy of one last role in the legion's service before retirement, usually for one year. He would by necessity have been a steady hand, operating as the voice of experience in advising the legion's senior officers as to the realities of warfare and the management of the legion's soldiers.

Reporting into this command structure were ten cohorts of soldiers, each one composed of a number of eighty-man centuries. Each century was a collection of ten tent parties – eight men who literally shared a tent when out in the field. Nine of the cohorts had six centuries, and an establishment strength of 480 men, whilst the prestigious first cohort, commanded by the legion's senior centurion, was composed of five double-strength centuries and therefore fielded 800 soldiers when fully manned. This organisation provided the legion with its cutting edge: 5,000 or so well-trained heavy infantrymen operating in regiment and company-sized units, and led by battle-hardened officers, the legion's centurions, men whose position was usually achieved by dint of their demonstrated leadership skills.

The rank of centurion was pretty much the peak of achievement for an ambitious soldier, commanding an eighty-man century and paid ten times as much as the men each officer commanded. Whilst the majority of centurions were promoted from the ranks, some were appointed from above as a result of patronage, or as a result of having completed their service in the Praetorian Guard, which had a shorter period of service than the legions. That these externally imposed centurions would have undergone their very own 'sink or swim' moment in dealing with their new colleagues is an unavoidable conclusion, for the role was one that by necessity led from the front, and as a result suffered disproportionate casualties. This makes it highly likely that any such appointee felt unlikely to make the grade in action would have received very short shrift from his brother officers.

A small but necessarily effective team reported to the centurion. The optio, literally 'best' or chosen man, was his second-in-command, and stood behind the century in action with a long brass-knobbed stick, literally pushing the soldiers into the fight should the need arise. This seems to have been a remarkably efficient way of managing a large body of men, given the centurion's place alongside rather than behind his soldiers, and the optio would have been a cool head, paid twice the usual soldier's wage and a candidate for promotion to centurion if he performed well. The century's third-in-command was the tesserarius or watch officer, ostensibly charged with ensuring that sentries were posted and that everyone knew the watch word for the day, but also likely to have been responsible for the profusion of tasks such as checking the soldiers' weapons and equipment, ensuring the maintenance of discipline and so on, that have occupied the lives of junior non-commissioned officers throughout history in delivering a combat-effective unit to their officer. The last member of the centurion's team was the century's signifer, the standard bearer, who both provided a rallying point for the soldiers and helped the centurion by transmitting marching orders to them through movements of his standard. Interestingly, he also functioned as the century's banker, dealing with the soldiers' financial affairs. While a soldier caught in the horror of battle might have thought twice about defending his unit's standard, he might well also have felt a stronger attachment to the man who managed his money for him!

At the shop-floor level were the eight soldiers of the tent party who shared a leather tent and messed together, their tent and cooking gear carried on a mule when the legion was on the march. Each tent party would inevitably have established its own pecking order based upon the time-honoured factors of strength, aggression, intelligence – and the rough humour required to survive in such a harsh world. The men that came to dominate their tent parties would have been the century's unofficial backbone, candidates for promotion to watch officer. They would also have been vital to their tent mates' cohesion under battlefield conditions, when the relatively thin leadership team could not always exert sufficient presence to inspire the individual soldier to stand and fight amid the horrific chaos of combat.

The other element of the legion was a small 120-man detachment of cavalry, used for scouting and the carrying of messages between units. The regular army depended on auxiliary cavalry wings, drawn from those parts of the empire where horsemanship was a way of life, for their mounted combat arm. Which leads us to consider the other side of the army's two-tier system.

The auxiliary cohorts, unlike the legions alongside which they fought, were not Roman citizens, although the completion of a twenty-five-year term of service did grant both the soldier and his children citizenship. The original auxiliary cohorts had often served in their homelands, as a means of controlling the threat of large numbers of freshly conquered barbarian warriors, but this changed after the events of the first century AD. The Batavian revolt in particular – when the 5,000-strong Batavian cohorts rebelled and destroyed two Roman legions after suffering intolerable provocation during a recruiting campaign gone wrong – was the spur for the Flavian policy for these cohorts to be posted away from their home provinces. The last thing any Roman general wanted was to find his legions facing an army equipped and trained to fight in the same way. This is why the reader will find the auxiliary cohorts described in the *Empire* series, true to the historical record, representing a variety of other parts of the empire, including Tungria, which is now part of modern-day Belgium.

Auxiliary infantry was equipped and organised in so close a manner to the legions that the casual observer would have been hard put to spot the differences. Often their armour would be mail, rather than plate, sometimes weapons would have minor differences, but in most respects an auxiliary cohort would be the same proposition to an enemy as a legion cohort. Indeed there are hints from history that the auxiliaries may have presented a greater challenge on the battlefield. At the battle of Mons Graupius in Scotland, Tacitus records that four cohorts of Batavians and two of Tungrians were sent in ahead of the legions and managed to defeat the enemy without requiring any significant assistance. Auxiliary cohorts were also often used on the flanks of the battle line, where reliable and well-drilled troops are essential to handle attempts to outflank the army. And while the legions contained soldiers who were as much tradesmen as fighting men, the auxiliary cohorts were primarily focused on their fighting skills. By the end of the second century there were significantly more auxiliary troops serving the empire than were available from the legions, and it is clear that Hadrian's Wall would have been invalid as a concept without the mass of infantry and mixed infantry/cavalry cohorts that were stationed along its length.

As for horsemen, the importance of the empire's 75,000 or so auxiliary cavalrymen, capable of much faster deployment and manoeuvre than the infantry, and essential for successful scouting, fast communications and the denial of reconnaissance information to the enemy, cannot be overstated. Rome simply did not produce anything like the strength in mounted troops needed to avoid being at a serious disadvantage against those nations which by their nature were cavalry-rich. As a result, as each such nation was conquered their mounted forces were swiftly incorporated into the army until, by the early first century BC, the decision was made to disband what native Roman cavalry as there was altogether, in favour of the auxiliary cavalry wings.

Named for their usual place on the battlefield, on the flanks or 'wings' of the line of battle, the cavalry cohorts were commanded by men of the equestrian class with prior experience as legion military tribunes, and were organised around the basic 32-man turma, or squadron. Each squadron was commanded by a decurion, a position analogous with that of the infantry centurion. This officer was assisted by a pair of junior officers: the duplicarius or double-pay, equivalent to the role of optio, and the sesquiplarius or pay-and-a-half, equal in stature to the infantry watch officer. As befitted the cavalry's more important military role, each of these ranks was paid about 40 per cent more than the infantry equivalent.

Taken together, the legions and their auxiliary support presented a standing army of over 400,000 men by the time of the events described in the *Empire* series. Whilst this was sufficient to both hold down and defend the empire's 6.5 million square kilometres for a long period of history, the strains of defending a 5,000-kilometre-long frontier, beset on all sides by hostile tribes, were also beginning to manifest themselves. The prompt move to raise three new legions undertaken by the new emperor Septimius Severus in AD 197, in readiness for over a decade spent shoring up the empire's crumbling borders, provides clear evidence that there were never enough legions and cohorts for such a monumental task. This is the backdrop for the *Empire* series, which will run from AD 182 well into the early third century, following both the empire's and Marcus Valerius Aquila's travails throughout this fascinatingly brutal period of history.

The Chain of Command
LEGION

LEGATUS ——— LEGION CAVALRY (120 HORSEMEN)

BROAD STRIPE TRIBUNE

5 'MILITARY' NARROW STRIPE TRIBUNES

CAMP PREFECT

SENIOR CENTURION

10 COHORTS
(ONE OF 5 CENTURIES OF 160 MEN EACH)
(NINE OF 6 CENTURIES OF 80 MEN EACH)

CENTURION

CHOSEN MAN

WATCH OFFICER   STANDARD BEARER

10 TENT PARTIES OF
8 MEN APIECE